THIS TIME OF DYING

REINA JAMES lives in Sussex with her husband. This is her first novel.

From the reviews of *This Time of Dying*

'This restrained and unnerving novel gains strength like the virus it describes... As the crisis peaks, class expectations crumble and an unlikely love story develops... James registers the tiny details of suffering and the book ends almost like a fever breaking, showing that such a scourge can randomly take anything in its path, leaving behind misery, but also human dignity.' **Time Out** ****

'James graphically describes a plague that wiped out families and overwhelmed the war-weakened infrastructure. However, the true terrain of the novelist is arguably the response of her characters to their afflictions. Here, James's isolated protagonists prepare the ground admirably for their individual witness and response to the calamity. A finely written and affecting novel.' **Guardian**

'James skilfully conveys the suppressed panic and claustrophobia induced by the sudden and deadly prevalence of the disease. Yet members of the local community still find time to disapprove of [Henry and Allen] for their association. This is a muted but moving novel about the persistence of the ordinary during extraordinary times.' **Financial Times**

'A rich and absorbing story about the 1918 epidemic of Spanish influenza. Henry Speake is a young undertaker, rather cowed by his scary band of sisters. He has coped with mangled bodies sent home from the trenches but is overwhelmed by the dreadful power of the epidemic. In his state of fear and uncertainty he is drawn into a relationship with a schoolteacher who has been recently widowed. A five-star weepie.' **The Times**

'The novel is fascinating, as James uses small, filmic scenes to build an overall picture of the fear and chaos in a London reeling from World War I, where the presence of death in unknown and uncontrollable forms was a terrifying reality.' **Metro**

'Written in deceptively plain and unsentimental prose, the novel is sophisticated in structure. The author manages to dip into many different characters' heads to paint an intimate portrait of how the flu impacts an entire community already decimated by war: from the elderly doctor who cannot live up to the weight of his duties, to Henry's 'masculine' sister, seething in resentment because she believes she could run the family business more ~~competently than her brother~~. A highly compelling and recommen ... r's Choice

'The book portrays a vivid and realistic picture of life as the First World War draws to an end. The poverty, the intractable nature of society, the jealousies that sometimes curse family life and a growing sense of a rapidly changing world are all evident. As for the two damaged survivors, one is left to hope that Henry and Allen will wing through.' *Mslexia*

'Literary rewards can be found in the unlikeliest places. Take, for example, London in the year 1918, where a deeply-repressed undertaker is struggling to cope with a huge increase in his workload. Henry Speake not only has to deal with the grievously injured young soldiers sent home from the front lines to die, but also contend with a deadly outbreak of influenza. Hardly the most uplifting of subjects; but in Reina James's sensitive hands it becomes surprisingly enjoyable... Henry's hesitant friendship with a local widow slowly begins to blossom and as their relationship develops, James leads them and her readers into unexpectedly rewarding territory.' *Yorkshire Evening Post*

'Two of the author's own grandparents died in the [Spanish Flu] epidemic, bringing a personal touch to this tender tale of middle-aged romance.' *Glasgow Herald*

'Unusual and compelling, strangely engrossing... Reina James has researched the period fastidiously but she carries her knowledge lightly. Her style is clean, clear and laconic, yet such is the strength of her characterisation that the protagonists' secret fears and forlorn hopes take possession of the reader's imagination and inhabit it to the exclusion of all else.' *Independent on Sunday*

'Reina James has taken the 1918 flu pandemic as her subject, weaving around it a story of middle-aged romance. Struggling with the aftermath of the war, the shortages, the sheer grimness of life, funeral director Henry Speake has to contend with a growing number of non-military deaths. His experiences are sharpened by the chance find of a doctor's documents and letters. Convinced that the country faces an epidemic, Speake sees no government assurance, help or recognition. James, who lost two grandparents to the flu, builds her story with great skill, and, with the possibility of a new epidemic on the horizon, gives us a well-imagined vision of society facing a terrible calamity. Highly topical and emotionally involving.' *Publishing News*, Book of the Month

'Reina James has written a war book with a difference, capturing vividly scenes of life (and death) in the last days of the Great War, with every detail of her characters' thoughts and feelings meticulously delineated, as is the background to the funeral trade in an age so totally different from ours. As a social documentary it is a fascinating read.' *Funeral Service Journal*

This Time of Dying

Reina James

Portobello
BOOKS

First published by Portobello Books Ltd 2006
This paperback edition published 2007

Portobello Books Ltd
Eardley House
4 Uxbridge St
Notting Hill Gate
London w8 7sy
UK

A CIP catalogue record is available from the British Library

9 8 7 6 5 4 3 2

ISBN 978 1 84627 046 8

www.portobellobooks.com

Designed by Richard Marston
Typeset in Electra by Avon DataSet Ltd, Bidford on Avon, Warwickshire
Printed in the UK by CPI Bookmarque, Croydon, CR0 4TD

In memory of my maternal grandparents, Edric and Christina Williams, who died of influenza in November 1918.

ONE

'The disease simply had its way. It came like a thief in the night and stole treasure.'

Ministry of Health Report on the Pandemic of Influenza 1918–19

Monday, 14 October 1918

Thomas Wey got dressed very slowly, feeling for his buttons and doing them up without looking down at his shirtfront. The trousers were more difficult but he sat on the edge of the bed and pulled them on, squinting slightly as his head was dragged forward by the motion of his arms. He left the waistcoat and tie on the chair and spent several minutes getting into his coat, stopping often to rest. Dressed, he was too hot. The pain was wobbling towards the front of his face and down into his teeth so that every movement was a shock, even though he planned it carefully and did nothing to surprise himself.

His first objective was to reach the table where he'd put the letter. Fixing his eye on the envelope's white rectangle, he put his left hand on his temple and used his right to guide him on a path that allowed him to rest on various pieces of furniture. A cough, excited by movement, halted him but he finally achieved the table and leaned on it for a minute, touching the letter with his forefinger. He thought he would fall but the strength remaining in his arms held him up while his legs swayed and twitched. A sharp pain in his chest was beginning to interfere with his breathing, letting him inhale but only to a certain depth; the cough was producing a rusty-orange phlegm that made him retch.

By the time he reached the front door he was barely conscious, sliding down the railing to the pavement and then flopping on to the gate as he tried to locate himself; he could see the post box, a red fleck in the distance. As he turned to it the space in his lungs diminished further. He was drowning and there was nothing in his field of view but the hard grey stone of the street.

*   *   *

I was working in the window, sanding down a lid, when this little lad came running up and banged on the glass, shouting, 'There's a blue man in the road!' I didn't understand him at first but I could see a crowd beginning to gather so I went out to have a look. When they saw me, they stood away. That often happens wherever the body is; there's a parting and a standing back.

The boy followed me through the crowd. He pointed down at the man who was lying half on the pavement and half in the road. 'Look, he's blue!' And yes, he was. His lips and ears were purple-blue, like a plum, and the skin on his face was mottled and pale but still tinged with blue, as if he'd been wiped with an inky rag. He was thirty-five or thereabouts and wore no shoes or socks. He had no hat that I could see, either on his head or off. His left hand was half under him, with a bit of paper poking out, but the other was lying across his chest, so I took his wrist and felt for a pulse, more for the sake of the crowd than anything; he was obviously dead.

The traffic was building up by then, people honking and shouting, so a couple of us lifted him up and took him into my workshop. I was alone that morning, Walter and Albert having gone off with a coffin for a woman who'd died the night before. We put the man on one of the benches and I sent the boy to get Frank, the local sergeant, then I cleared everybody out and waited; I don't like to touch anything when I'm on my own like that, in case there's money and so forth. I stood away, but I couldn't keep from looking. That was unusual. I never look as a rule; why would I? We must have been there a full five minutes until Frank came in and made a racket, banging the door shut and whistling.

The dead man had dressed all wrong, buttons skew-whiff, no tie, bare

4

feet. The clothes were all good quality, so he had money or he'd had some in the past. His hair was a bit long and his nails were dirty but he seemed clean enough; without undressing him, we couldn't be sure if he'd been sent home wounded from the Front. There was nothing in any of his pockets to help us out, only a few coins and a key in his coat and a bloody handkerchief in his trousers, nothing with a name on or an address.

'I heard a woman in the crowd,' I said to Frank. 'She was saying she'd seen him on the steps of number seventeen. That's more or less where we found him, on the street. She said he was squeezing his head between his hands and swaying about. She thought he was daft.'

Number seventeen's a boarding house and always busy with people passing through.

'I'll pop round there,' Frank said. 'See if they know who he is. You telephone the mortuary.'

When the van had taken the body, I went to finish the coffin I'd been working on and that's when I found the letter. For a moment, I thought the postman might have dropped it on the first delivery but then I remembered that the man had been holding something when I'd gone to him in the road. I hadn't thought anything of it at the time but now it was in front of me, on the floor, I felt nervous. I don't remember ever waiting for an important letter but I imagine that you might be a bit jittery when you see it, in case it's not what you want, or more than you dare hope for. I picked it up and looked at the writing on the envelope.

'Sir Arthur Newsholme, Principal Medical Officer, Local Government Board.' That's all it said. I should have taken it straight round to Frank. It wasn't mine to open. It was government business. But why would anybody doing government business be living at number seventeen? And why was he posting an ordinary letter without a street name? Didn't they use special bags or boxes? Walter and Albert came in then, so I went upstairs to my flat and sat down at the table. And then, I can't tell you why, I opened it.

The letter was written on cheap paper with a mad sort of hand, no two *words the same, some upright, some to the right or left. It was dated for the previous day, which suggested that he'd been too ill to post it straight-away but had forced himself up that morning, thinking he might be about to die.*

Sir Arthur,

I am dismayed to have had no reply to my previous letters and therefore write again in urgency. I repeat: a plague is now among us which may well leave the earth to the animals. You must stop the movement of troops, close our ports and warn others to follow suit. I beg you again not to dismiss this but to visit me at the above address. I am a man of science. I have proof. I cannot write more.

Yours in fear,

Dr Thomas Wey

He must have been a lunatic, was my first thought. And then I felt that I shouldn't have opened the letter at all and that perhaps I should post it on. He might have had a genuine reason to be writing to this man, Newsholme, and I had no right to interfere with that. I didn't know what he'd died of, not then. I didn't post it on. It might never have got to its destination anyway, all crumpled like that and with no proper address, although I could have put it in a new envelope and put another stamp on it.

And this might sound like another strange thing to remember about that day, but when I'd sat down at the piano, which I always do after breakfast, the E flat below middle C had been sticking, swollen with damp. I could never play knowing that a note couldn't be struck, even if I didn't want it. You can't enjoy yourself if you're trying to avoid a note. A piano's not furniture to me. I don't like gewgaws on it: photographs or dried flowers or, worse, real flowers with the danger of the water spilling. It's not a shelf.

I'd sanded down the swollen key before work and I'd been intending to try it out as soon as I could get back upstairs but when I had a moment I walked to Thomas Wey's lodgings instead. I know the landlady there, Mrs White; she said that Frank had already been round to look for anything that might help to get the man buried. Dr Wey had been there for three months or so and he'd never mentioned any relatives or friends to her, except for an uncle, a Mr Wey, who used to send the rent every month because Dr Wey had been sent back from France with what she had always believed was a bad stomach wound, 'or something in that department', as he ate nothing to speak of. I think she was enjoying the fuss because she was only too happy to take me up to his room so that I could see for myself.

The bed was as he must have left it with filthy handkerchiefs dropped here and there on the blankets. There was a pen, ink and some sheets of paper on the table, and a few clothes hanging in the wardrobe, with a hat and a pair of shoes. Ten or twelve books stood in two stacks on the floor, next to the bed.

Mrs White said, 'He went sudden, didn't he? I haven't seen him for a day or two, but he was there at breakfast on Friday, picking away. You'll get paid, don't you worry. The old boy's never late with the rent.'

I went to the table and tried to see what Thomas Wey had written but it was hard to read in the dim light and I didn't want to appear over keen.

Then she asked me if I'd like to take the papers. 'I don't want the bother of sending them off, do I? Do you want anything else?' She indicated the wardrobe with her thumb.

'I'll just take these,' I said. 'In case.' Now I had, so to speak, stolen his letter and his other writings. There have been opportunities all my life to take from the deceased and it had never occurred to me to do so. The papers compounded my dishonesty and I have no excuse for it. I asked Mrs White if she knew what he did with his time but of course she had no idea; he was in and out at all hours, that was all she could say. She gave me the old man's address for billing and I went home with the papers held between my hands.

Lunch was laid out for me but I pushed the plate aside and prepared to *read, seeing the words* 'Particular Circumstances' *underlined at the top of the first page and a list of dates, each with its own description of weather. That's when my sister Nora came for me. She always starts to shout when she's halfway up the stairs – 'Henry! Henry! Coo-ee, it's Nora!' – she can never wait until she's in the room. She'd had a letter from her son to say that he was being let out of the military hospital and expected home by two o'clock. I was wanted for the welcoming committee.*

*   *   *

Sarah was standing at the window, staring out. She waved at him through the lace curtain.

Nora opened the front door. 'You took your time; we've had tea set for hours. I don't know why Samuel wants to do it on his own, it's two trams and a walk.' She helped him off with his coat. 'You're later than you said. What kept you? I'm in a right state. He's probably in trouble somewhere. You keeping your hat on or what? Sarah's here.'

Henry gave her his hat and called through the door to Sarah. 'No sign, then?'

'What does it look like?' She turned away from the window as he came in. 'You told Nora you'd follow her back.'

'I've been busy.' He was the senior to four sisters but Sarah, the sergeant-major, had bullied him into early acquiescence, then Nora and Elsie had followed on, the group gathering in strength as they aged. Rose, the youngest, had walked into the workshop as soon as she was steady on her feet and stayed close to him thereafter. She was gone now, not dead but as well as, right across the world to where he couldn't follow.

'You haven't missed anything,' Sarah said. She picked up her knitting and sat by the empty fireplace, her mannish voice incongruous with the pink wool on the needles. 'We haven't had tea yet and she won't let me light the fire till the boy's home. Not that he ought to be coming back at all, not in that state.'

'We don't know what state he's in,' Nora said. 'Don't go on.'

'We can guess, can't we?' Sarah peered at the pattern and pulled a length of wool from the ball. 'It's getting a bit dark in here, isn't it? I can hardly see the needles. Don't you fancy a lamp on?'

Nora went to the window and pulled the lace to one side. 'Poor Samuel, he'll be worn out – two trams and a walk, I don't know. Be tiring for anybody, that would.'

Henry sat on the piano stool, looking out into the room. He had nothing to say. Nora was too busy prattling to have a conversation and Sarah was digging away at the knitting with her mouth tight shut. 'He'll get help if he needs it, there's always someone willing,' he said, finally. 'I'll play a bit, shall I?'

'No, don't,' Sarah said. 'This waiting's enough, without you giving us the benefit. Anyway, he might not remember where he lives. We've got to keep an ear open. Why don't you go and have a look round? He's ever so late and we'll have to draw the curtains in a minute if we want the lamps on. Go on, quick march.'

Henry got up.

'As if he'd forget where he lives,' Nora said. 'What a thing to say!' She followed Henry out to the hall and watched while he put his coat on. 'Suppose they thought Sam wasn't up to it? They'd tell us, wouldn't they? If they'd kept him in?'

'He'd have found a way. I'll have a walk about.'

He left the front door on the latch and looked up and down the road. It had been a dismal, grey day, and now it was nearly dark at half past four. He felt cheated, as he always did, that the sun was setting without having shown itself. A sound, not footsteps, was coming from the far corner; a man on crutches came into view. Henry waited. It was almost certainly his nephew, even though a great deal of the face was squeezed together, obliterating an eye. The man waved from the elbow, his hand as limp as a rag. As Henry walked towards him, Samuel – he could see now that it was Samuel – staggered, nearly losing control of the crutches.

By the time they got to the house, Henry was supporting him altogether, leaving the crutches to fall over the step. As he hoicked him up to the door, he caught sight of Nora, immobile at the window, and then Sarah was there, helping him to get the boy inside.

'Over here! Over here!' Nora was turfing the cushions out of a chair and calling Henry to it, but before they could get him down Samuel's nose started to bleed, great gushes of hot red blood, spouting on to their clothes and across them, down to the carpet.

With a shout, Nora ran to get cloths and water. She had had no time to adjust to Samuel's missing parts, or to the parts that were left; the blood obscured the detail of his face. All she had seen was the eye socket, crudely darned.

'Be careful, Henry!' she shouted from the kitchen. 'Don't touch him.' She ran back into the room with the bowl and dropped it roughly next to Henry, spilling water on his knee.

Henry wrung out the flannel. 'Undo his collar, give the boy a bit of air. And somebody light the lamps.'

'Ma?'

Nora knelt by the chair and fiddled with the buttons; the blood was caking on them, making it hard to get a grip.

'There, Sammy, there. You're all right,' she said. When he saw her, right up near his face, he smiled with his lop-sided mouth and tried to speak but the effort made him cough. His eyelid was drooping now, as if he were struggling to stay awake. 'Don't you worry, Sam, my Sam.' She was so close that she could see every pucker and pleat in his reddening skin. Most of his ear had gone, and his cheekbone, but she only needed a patch of face to see that it was her boy. A little more blood fell from his nose and landed on her wrist.

'Hea'sore,' Samuel said. 'Wanna lie down.'

'He needs to get to bed.' Henry rinsed the cloth out in the bowl. The water was too bloody to use now. 'I'll carry him up.'

'This can't be right. Why did the hospital let him go?' Sarah said. She spoke normally, in her deep, cracked voice, and they realized they'd been whispering.

Samuel's eye was closed now. 'Lie dow',' he said, slumping back into the chair.

Henry looked at Nora. 'He's got a touch of influenza, I'd say. And he's worn out. See how he is tomorrow.' He took the sweating Samuel in his arms and led the procession upstairs, leaving the women to undress him and settle him down. They washed the rest of the blood away, rubbed camphorated oil into his chest for the cough and folded the right leg of his pyjamas neatly, putting it flat on the mattress.

Samuel shivered and felt for the bedclothes, trying to pull them up to his face. 'Col',' he said.

When the others had gone home, Nora wrapped herself in a blanket and took up her position by the bed. During the night, the tip of Samuel's nose turned purple, then his face, the scar-lines accentuated by the darkness of his skin. He died while she was running to the doctor.

*　　*　　*

Tuesday, 15 October

Sarah told me that Samuel was dead. She helped Nora to lay him out and I got a coffin ready and carted it over that afternoon. When I'd lifted him the night before he hadn't weighed more than a boy, which was bad enough, and he'd been out of balance in my arms, like all the amputees – but him being that purplish-blue, like Thomas Wey, that really took me aback.

For the best part of the night, I'd tried to make sense of what Wey had written. There were words scribbled so loosely that I couldn't read them, columns of initials, pages filled with dates and figures, and then other pages with more numbers, possibly temperatures. But on one page were several legible sentences, many of them repeated, and that was the one I fixed on – it could well have been a page of notes for his letters to Sir Arthur Newsholme.

He'd written: 'The world's body can hardly draw breath; it is sick and brought to its bed. Its wounds are open. The young spill out. There are no circumstances, save peace and universal quarantine, that can afford even the slightest hope. Death is crossing every sea.'

And near the bottom of the page: 'This pestilence will not be confined. I have examined the dead in France and I have seen the first young die in London. I fear we are lost.'

There was a great deal of flowery language here, more like poetry than science, but I have to admit that I was caught by it. I understood him to mean that we were all to die of some pestilence or other because the world had been made sick by young men – the life-blood, you might say – dying in such numbers. But what form had he believed this pestilence would take?

Samuel's colouration was the same as Thomas Wey's. You could say that any deceased is greyish veering to blue, and some are blue altogether if the circulation's defective, but this particular shade was as if you'd mixed some red in it to make it more purple. When they got round to calling it something, they gave it a pretty word, a flower name: heliotrope. My mother always grew it near the back door – she called it 'cherry-pie' – and the smell was lovely, as sweet as any cake. If I'd had a say in it, I wouldn't have called it that; it was quite the wrong comparison.

Dr Tite had written broncho-pneumonia on the certificate but I had my doubts, even then. We put Samuel in the front room on two chairs, and Nora asked me to put the lid on straightaway so she didn't have to see his face, which I think she might have done even if it hadn't changed colour. In Samuel's first letter home he'd said not to be too upset about his leg. He hadn't mentioned his face and the eye; she'd been glad enough that he was coming back at all. When the lid was on, she said what I'd heard from others so many times before: that she wished he could have been sent off whole, not leaving bits of himself in France with no Christian burial. She was seeing the lost leg like a lonely thing that wanted comfort.

It took a bit of getting used to, the men coming back with bits shot off and their faces looking like God knows what. I've had no shortage of grim sights but some of these have turned my stomach. If a man falls into machinery in London he probably started the day with a good breakfast, not up to his knees in mud, frightened out of his bloody wits. My first wounded man, he'd lost his lower jaw. And he had no right arm from the elbow down and a long scar down his back. I don't know how he'd lasted. How did he eat? When he got back home he was on his own; his wife disappeared the day she saw him. Then he'd swung at himself with an axe, made a terrible mess of his shoulder, and when that didn't work he tried to stab himself. In the end he jumped from a high window with nothing on but a vest. On the Front they often had to leave the bodies out there, out on the land. They were left to rot, that's what I'm told. Why should they risk another life to bring back the dead?

I told Nora I'd sit with her but she said Sarah was coming later so I went home and finished another coffin I had to have ready.

*   *   *

'I'm sorry to bother you. Is Mr Speake here?' Allen waited by the shop door, holding it open and leaning in without crossing the threshold.

Walter was filing accounts. 'I'm afraid he's busy at the moment. May I help you?' he said, raising his neck and tilting his head, a birdlike posture that he always adopted for his first meeting with the newly bereaved. The effect was compounded by a sharp wave of white hair and turned-out feet.

'It's a personal matter, thank you. Perhaps you could say that I called? It's Mrs Thompson. From St Matthew's school.'

She was well-spoken, handsome in a skinny way with a bit too much between the ears; that was his summation and it changed only insofar as his professional detachment towards a potential customer became curiosity at her being an acquaintance of Henry's. 'If it's a personal matter then I could go and see if he's free to come out.'

'Could you?'

'I could.' He put the papers he was holding on to the desk and waved her to a chair.

Henry was at the back of the workshop, talking to Albert and planing down a lid. 'There's a lady here,' Walter said, when he was close enough to talk quietly. 'A Mrs Thompson. She says it's personal. Do you want to come through or shall I ask her to leave?'

'I'll come out.' Henry took off his apron and swapped it for a jacket that was hanging from a hook behind the door. 'Are you going home?'

'No rush.'

As Henry came in, Allen walked towards him and held out her hand. 'Mr Speake. I've just heard about your nephew. I wanted to say how sorry I am.'

'That's very kind of you, Mrs Thompson. To bother to come in, that's very kind.'

'I believe he was only recently out of hospital?'

'Yesterday.'

'Oh dear, I'm so sorry.'

There was a pause then Henry said, 'Are we still rehearsing tomorrow?'

'We wouldn't dream of asking you—'

'I'll be there. Half past five. That's right, isn't it? Half past?'

'It is. But we won't expect you.' She was solemn, even though Henry was smiling. Was there a lack of feeling for the boy? Perhaps they were estranged, or perhaps the business of undertaking separated you from the experience of loss? She adjusted to his response and said, 'But of course we'd be grateful if you came.'

'I'll be there.'

When Allen had gone and they were closing up, Walter said, 'What're you up to, then, rehearsing what?'

'I'm helping out with a bit of piano-playing, that's all.'

'They must be desperate.'

'Very funny.' Henry turned off the light and took the keys from his pocket. 'Two to do tomorrow, we'll need to be off sharp.'

*　*　*

'It's not as if I can get it myself, is it?' Mrs Lily Bird was holding up the corner of a tablecloth and pointing it at Allen as evidence. 'I've been waiting since six o'clock. You did promise you'd be back. I suppose you think it doesn't matter if the daisies are pink or blue or *brown*.'

Allen went to the top drawer of the sideboard and chose a skein of yellow embroidery silk. 'Perhaps we should put these on a tray, next to your chair. That would be easier, wouldn't it? Then you wouldn't have to wait for me.'

Her sister was already cutting a length of silk. 'Don't be ridiculous,' she said, separating the strands. 'They'd get dirty. They do perfectly well in the drawer. I usually know what I'll need, it's just a question of you being here when you say you will.'

'Where's Ada?'

'I've no idea. Where should she be?' The threading of the needle was taking a long time.

'Didn't you ask her to fetch your silk?'

'I don't like her in the drawers.' Lily found the eye of the uncompleted daisy. 'I know you trust the girl—'

'Implicitly.'

'—but for all you know she's keeping a man in the basement and feeding him on our rations.'

'We always have enough. She ekes it out very well.'

15

The fire was still burning. Allen sat in the chair opposite and watched as Lily finished the flower, turned the linen, knotted the thread and cut it with small, elaborate silver scissors. She undid the frame. 'Fold this for me. It's finished. It can be ironed and put away.' Tomorrow the table-cloth would be placed on the accumulating linen in the chest at the foot of her bed; Lily's sewing was her triumph, the proof of her endurance. 'Where have you been?'

'I was talking to Mr Speake, the undertaker. One of his nephews has just died…' As she was saying this, she knew that Lily would ignore her but she carried on, partly out of respect for the dead boy and partly out of the malicious pleasure that she took from driving Lily into a blunt, disapproving silence. 'He was injured in France but he died here, at home.' She pressed the last fold against her hip and put the neat square on the table. 'He was just a boy.'

'I don't want any dinner. I'm going to bed now,' Lily said. 'Ring for Ada.'

Allen rang the bell and helped her sister to her feet. The dining room, adjacent to the room they were in, was now a bedroom, saving Lily the effort of having to manage the stairs. By the time they reached the door, Ada had appeared and was sent off again to fetch warm milk and a biscuit.

* * *

Vi stirred Walter's tea. 'She just came in? Not invited or anything? She should have written. That was too bold by half. And was he pleased to see her?'

'Pleased enough. They were nodding away like a couple of Chinamen.'

'He's an old fool if he thinks he can make himself welcome with her sort. And she can't be that bright if she's chasing after Henry.'

Holding her cup with one hand, she picked up the frying pan and slid its contents on to a plate. Their kitchen had no spare spaces. Whenever a space might crop up, because something had been eaten or broken or given away, it was filled immediately with whatever might fit. Walter occupied one end of the small table and Vi the other.

'Is she after him, then? I'll have that mustard when you've finished.'

'She'll have her work cut out. I'm for him, you know that, but it's not right, is it? Living alone, playing that bloody piano. A man can't live like that.'

'Wouldn't suit you. Can I have that mustard?'

Walter passed her the pot and caught her hand. 'Wouldn't suit me.'

'Stupid old bugger.'

*   *   *

Wednesday, 16 October

Henry raised himself from the piano seat to watch the teachers gathering on stage for the Tableau: a group of wounded prisoners being harried by their German guards. Many of the staff had come down with influenza and the stand-ins were being shown their positions with a great deal of finger-poking and laughter. When everyone was still, Allen looked across at Henry; he sat down again and played, a composition of his own with the jazz in it smoothed out and replaced by simple rhythms.

There were five more Tableaux interspersed with songs and poems and a grand finale of the ensemble singing 'Till the Boys Come Home'. Afterwards, as Henry was pushing the piano back to the wall, Allen and her friend Ruth came to thank him.

'It's coming on,' Allen said. 'We're grateful to you, really. It makes all the difference.'

She introduced Ruth, who said, 'All the difference,' then put her hand on Allen's shoulder. 'You should hear how rotten it usually sounds.'

'I'm pleased to be useful.'

They walked together to the main door where Ruth said her goodbyes and ran off to a waiting motor-car leaving Henry and Allen by themselves on the step.

He said, 'I could see you home. If you'd like.'

'Why not? I hate these dark evenings.'

The street was very cold. They walked for a while without speaking.

'Your nephew,' Allen said eventually. 'Did you have much to do with him?'

'Not really.'

'Is it rude of me to ask?'

'No. It's just that I didn't know him, not that well. We're inclined to keep ourselves to ourselves. I'm not in and out of my sisters' houses, not really.'

'How many?' She looked at him.

'Sisters?' he said, without turning. 'Four. Sarah, Nora, Elsie and Rose.' Another silence. 'Rose, she's the youngest. She went to live in New Zealand. That's a house I *would* be in and out of.'

'Why did she go?'

'She met a man.'

'Do you write to each other?'

'Her more than me. How many in your family?'

'I've got one sister.' She rarely said unkind things about Lily Bird and then only to Ruth, but there was something oddly anonymous about this conversation being carried on in the dark; he could be baring his teeth, she could cross her eyes and stick her tongue out. The temptation to specify Lily's wrongdoings was such that she had to put her hand to her mouth and hold it closed.

Two women passed them and acknowledged Henry. When they were out of earshot he said, 'Both lost family this month.'

Lily was instantly forgotten. Allen wanted to tell Henry Speake that she was able to discuss his job without revulsion. 'Loss is your business, isn't it?' she said. Did that sound as if she were uniting death with financial gain? 'I mean, it's the very nature of your business. Loss and grief.'

'Not always. You'd be surprised, Mrs Thompson. Death brings out the best and the worst in people, men and women alike.'

'Some deaths might be cause for rejoicing.'

'Most certainly, they might.'

'After suffering, do you mean?'

'Not always.'

'No, of course not.' They were turning towards each other now, with small movements of the head. 'One could imagine all sorts of stories.'

'And you'd be right,' he said.

'There are children in the school whose fathers won't be seen. They hide indoors; they can't work. They're all but dead. What are we to look forward to?'

'I don't think we'll know for a year or two. Not really. I'm hoping the organist comes back to church with both legs.' He said it without meaning to be funny but Allen laughed. 'It's the truth. There're too many pedals on the thing. I get by without them; I just use my hands.' He broke step with her and looked down. 'I've got stupid feet.' They were in her road.

'The next rehearsal's on Monday. We'd appreciate it if you could be there.'

'I'll do my best.'

✻   ✻   ✻

It's not as if we were strangers to influenza. It came every year, some worse than others. My father died of it in the spring of 1891, when I was twenty-three. We called that the Russian 'flu. It was probably the worst bout that I can remember; five of us went down with it and we had to let the business go elsewhere for over a week – we lost a good dozen funerals. We got ill one by one, each man working till he couldn't stand, until there was only my father left, and when he couldn't even pick up a nail he fell into bed, and that was his last day. And there I was, out of bed days before I should have been, twenty-three years old and running the business with three sisters still at home and me not really sure that I wanted to be in the trade at all. I can still remember dragging myself about with the consequences of it, right through to the autumn.

Walter offered to lay my father out for me, but it didn't seem right. There was something about me having to do it. My father wouldn't have wanted Walter to see his private places either. When he was in order, I shaved him and combed his hair, half expecting him to push me off. I remember doing it as if he were alive, as gently as that. Then I put him in his suit. He was shorter than I'd expected. I can usually measure a man by eye and get it right to the quarter-inch, but my father was a full inch and a half shorter than I'd thought. I put him in oak with a lead lining, as he would have wished.

I'd started to enquire about the embalming side by then, before he died, just out of curiosity. Dad wouldn't have allowed it. He thought of it as an American invention, and that meant newfangled, a circus trick knocked up to make money. Of course, he knew about the one or two who'd tried it here, but what my father stood for, what you might call his key, was the continuance of family traditions. If you found a new way, a better way – if you took those traditions and shook them about a bit – then you were insulting all the things he cared for. It's not American, I'd say to him, preservation, it's as old as old Egypt, but he wouldn't countenance it. Before the war I did a marvellous course with Nodes, over in Walthamstow, and after that I used it whenever I could, which turned out to be once in a blue moon. There weren't many that could afford it, and I didn't have anywhere on the premises where I could do the work, no preparation room or anything like it, so I'd attend to the body wherever it was resting. Of course, a lot of people did think it was like mutilation, interfering with the deceased. I could only do my best to explain. It's always interesting to me, the people who choose to take up with a new idea and the people who fold their arms against it.

I could have embalmed my father, to make life easier for us more than anything – there was a bit of a wait for my uncle to come down from Manchester – but in the end, out of respect, I left him to his own devices.

My mother died three years before him. She was standing at the kitchen table, rolling pastry and singing with me – a song from Iolanthe: *'Every journey has an end,/ When at the worst affairs will mend' – and I had my back to her, washing my hands at the sink. She fell over like a tree, straight on to the floor behind me. I thought she'd dropped the bag of flour and I turned round, still singing, but she wasn't where I'd left her, she was flat out, with her arms bent round the chair legs. I remember looking at her and thinking: where's it gone? That bit of her that had been laughing and singing and rolling out the pastry?*

I did mention it to my father, a few months later, when he was filling in the ledger. I asked him if he'd ever thought about where a person is, in the body. He didn't even look up. 'I'd get on with your work, if I were you,' he said. And that's where we left it. But I still think there's a lot to find out. Say a good man comes back with a head wound. He might have been the best husband, the best father, then suddenly he's smashing out at them all, cursing and kicking. Is the damage to his head taking over his soul? Has the good man disappeared or is he cornered somewhere else, inside himself? And will God judge him on who he really is or on who he became because of a piece of shrapnel?

*　　*　　*

Thursday, 17 October

Too old now to bend easily over the bed, Dr Lionel Tite dropped his long, thin body into a chair and looked at Nora over his spectacles. 'Touch of influenza?' His drawl – a soft, cynical insult, originally adopted to weed out the fraudulent – had long since become part of his general demeanour. Patients and their relatives made him tired.

'I'm feeling ever so slightly worse,' Nora said. While she was talking, her eyes closed as she drifted in and out of sleep. 'Ever so slightly…'

'Plenty of fluids, Mrs Butcher, barley water…' Nora wasn't listening; her legs jerked suddenly, lifting the bedclothes. Tite wanted to stay in the chair and read the newspaper, drink a cup of tea and smoke for a while. He got up, levering himself with the chair arms, and said, 'Oh, God,' so quietly that it sounded like an exhalation.

Sarah came in and approached the doctor with her fingers folded round a shilling's worth of coins. He opened his hand and she placed them in his palm without comment. Although they met occasionally at the bedside during a birth or after a death, no intimacy was possible between them; none the less, she believed herself to be his equal and had only called him in at Nora's insistence. The giving of the shilling irked and embarrassed her.

'Aspirin, fifteen grains, say, or twenty.' He walked to the door. 'Too many to see. I won't call again unless she worsens.' Outside, he turned left and walked to a house a few yards away. The list in his bag was very long.

*　　*　　*

'And if every apple weighs four ounces, then how many apples must the man sell to make up a pound and a half?'

The children were scattered, their number reduced by a quarter. Very little light was coming through the tall windows of the classroom and Allen had to squint to make out what was happening in the back row. Two girls seemed to be whispering, their heads close together.

'Quiet there! Come on now. How many apples?' She turned to the blackboard and held up the chalk. 'Here's the first.' She drew a circle and wrote *four ounces* below it. A frowning girl put her hand up.

'Please miss, it's six,' said Connie wearily. She was a ten-year-old crone, always fussing at the world, never easy with herself or anyone else.

'That's right. Very good, Connie.' There was more noise at the back. 'What's happening here?'

As Allen walked down the centre aisle, the children turned in formation to watch her progress, their heads swivelling as she passed. The girls who had been speaking were leaning on each other, their faces hot and red. By the time she reached them, one of them had collapsed on to the desk and the other, losing her support, had fallen back into the chair.

'Bessie!' Allen put her arm out and touched the child to her right without taking her eyes off the girls. 'Get Miss Bartholomew, quickly!'

The children around them began to get up and move away.

'Are they dying, miss?'

'Don't be silly. Sit down, everybody. *Sit down!*' She brought the second girl forward and tried to lean her on the desk. Neither was fully conscious, and both were breathing strangely, making little grunts and sighs. The sudden nature of their prostration was exactly as the other teachers had reported; she could feel the light uplift of fear in her throat as she stood with a hand on each child's head, waiting for help. The hair under her hands was hot and damp. The other children were sitting now, some of them crying, all looking at her, waiting. Two women came into the room, trying not to run but walking so fast that they bumped into the desks and chairs.

'It's Liza and Ettie,' Allen said. 'They're not very well.' Between them, they lifted the girls out of their chairs, half carrying, half walking them to the door. One of the women turned to look at Allen and mouthed, *how many more?* Allen shook her head and looked away, the children were watching.

She went back to the front of the class. 'Liza and Ettie are just a little feverish. They'll be back with us in a few days, we can be sure.' She picked up the chalk, wanting to divert them. 'We still haven't finished our work with weights and measures. Who remembers how many pounds there are in a stone?' The old woman-child put her hand up. 'Yes, Connie?'

'Please, miss. I've got a terrible sore throat.'

*　　*　　*

I put the papers and the letter by my bed and looked at them night and morning, wishing that I'd thought to examine the books piled on Thomas Wey's floor. It occurred to me to ask Mrs White if she'd disposed of them but there was no excuse for such a question. I even thought of writing to his uncle to ask for an appointment. But on what grounds? I couldn't divulge that I'd kept the letter and there was no likelihood of Thomas and I having been friends. Once, in the dark, I imagined him at my side but that stopped as soon as I lit the lamp.

Do the dead come back? I hear stories all the time. There was a woman, years ago, that I came to know. Her husband was a rough man, always prone to hitting out. He was mending a roof and swearing at the man below for being slow with his bucket. The man below pissed in it, in full view, and sent it up steaming at which the husband went berserk, lost his footing and broke his neck. She wanted the body lying in the bedroom so that's where I set the coffin up, on two chairs. Every night, when she was asleep, she saw him leaning over the bed with his fists up and every morning she'd wake up bruised, that's what she told me. I saw the bruises, but I couldn't say if they were caused by a dead man. After all those years of him being rough with her, she wasn't surprised; he'd expected her to follow on, that's what she said. To his way of thinking, she should have killed herself and carried on looking after him wherever he'd gone. I think she felt bad that she hadn't. But the night before I went to collect him for the funeral, she'd hammered three-inch nails into his feet to stop him walking home. If he comes back, she said, I'll hear those nails tapping on the floorboards.

And the battlefields, the dead all crammed together. When that many

24

die, how is it dealt with? Are there spirit armies, on the lookout for grace and deliverance? I've had it said to me, and I believe it to be true, that a soul has to come to some accommodation about its earthly life before it can progress, but how does a man accommodate the sight of his friends turning black out there in the open? And the fear of his own mutilation? We see the dead here, but it hardly bears comparison; it'll always be between us, those who saw and those who didn't. And for the dead, perhaps it's the same, perhaps it takes them that bit longer to settle what they know compared to the other souls.

So, Thomas Wey's letter. It preyed on my mind from that very first day. What 'proof' did he have? Was it in his head, the proof, or hidden somewhere in a vault or a strongbox? I presumed him to be a doctor of medicine; did he have first-hand evidence? Did I have the theory at my bedside, scrawled on those sheets of paper? I'd never heard of Arthur Newsholme either, but then I'd hardly know the name of every man serving in government. Why had he not written directly to Lloyd George?

As more people fell ill I debated with myself: should I pass the letter on or should I assume it to be the ravings of a man in the last stages of fever? I felt very alone in this, being sure that Walter would dismiss me without ceremony and that Allen would have little sympathy with my having stolen the letter at all; the divulging of confidences would have required a closer friendship in any case. There was no point whatever in talking to my sisters. In the end I put on a record – 'Indian Rag' – and tried to work out how Dave Comer plays the left hand part.

*　　*　　*

'What's he up to?' A small boy, the one who had alerted Henry to the blue man, was leaning on the shop window. Walter banged on the glass. 'Oi!' he shouted. 'Get off there!' The boy slid to his knees, lowered his head and rested his hands, palms up, on his thighs. It was a strange position for a young child. Tutting with irritation, Walter went outside. 'All right, all right. Let's get you up. Come on, on your feet.' As the boy stood up, he lifted his face momentarily and revealed an expression of such misery that Walter put his hand out and clasped him by the shoulder.

'Are you hurt?' he said. 'Let's hear it. What's the matter?'

'My m-m-mmum…' The boy put his hand over his mouth and stared at Walter.

'Your mum, what?'

'My m-mum's…' He toppled into Walter's stomach, crying miserably.

Henry appeared through the door and raised his eyebrows.

'I don't know,' Walter said. 'Something to do with his mum. You got a handkerchief on you?'

They went into the shop and sat the boy down. When he was able to speak, he told them that his mother was dead. In their bed, in the night. He hadn't been able to wake her and he knew what that meant, so in the end he'd come here because that was what you did. She'd been ill for a bit. Made him rub Russian tallow on her, back and front. His name was Peter, his father was in the navy and the woman downstairs looked after him when his mother was at work but there'd been no answer when he knocked.

Margaret, Henry's housekeeper, made the boy some breakfast and then Walter took him home and told him to wait downstairs while he went up to the room with the neighbour. The mother was certainly dead, still flaccid and lying on a soiled blanket. Walter straightened her legs and measured her, leaving the neighbour to lay her out, then he went round to the doctor's house and left a message with the maid.

When he got back to the shop, Henry was writing in the ledger. He looked round and said, 'How's the lad?'

'The woman downstairs'll have him. Mother's dead right enough. I've told Doctor Tite.'

'What was it?'

'Not sure.'

'Might it be influenza?'

'It might.'

'Was she young?'

'She was young.'

'Was she discoloured at all?'

'Not to remark on. Why?'

Henry shook his head and shut the book. There was ink on his middle finger; he wiped the excess on the blotter and rubbed the rest away with the handkerchief he'd given Walter to use for the boy. 'I was curious, that's all.'

'Well, she was a nice greyish-white, poor girl. Do you fancy a pot of tea?'

*   *   *

Allen took off her jacket and lay on her side of the big bed. School had finished badly that afternoon, with a diminishing and bewildered staff trying to reassure their dwindling classes. Many of the children had gone home to sick families and would return the following day, ripe with infection. There was escalating anxiety in the staff room. The concert had been cancelled; she would call in on Mr Speake the next day and apologize.

Turning on her side, she pulled her dead husband's pillow towards her and rested her face on it, crushing the pillow into her cheek. Edward's smell still pervaded the linen, or else she imagined it and willed it to return, resurrecting him through a hundred launderings; it had saved her to hold the pillow and use it as a totem. On the worst days she had worn his clothes, holding herself in his shirt and jacket with his hat over her eyes.

The room was dark and cold; there was some comfort in that. As she moved her foot she became aware that her shoe was still buckled on it and thought momentarily that she was doing a bad thing, making the counterpane dirty, but then she remembered Liza and Ettie and forgot the shoe. Her thoughts were scattered: she re-lived the girls' collapse, felt a pulse in her own head and a momentary fear of infection, considered her disappointment at the cancellation of the concert, the disruption of the timetable and how she would have to give extra tutelage to the sick when they came back. Outside her door, Edward's tuneless long-case clock began to clang out the signal for dinner. She held the pillow closer for a long minute then she rolled over and got up.

After Edward's death, the already widowed, ailing Lily had pressed to be offered care and accommodation, and Allen, despite her misgivings, had not been able to think of any sound excuse to refuse her. The ground floor was re-arranged to suit her needs and one of her first requests had been that the clock, which then stood in the main hall, should be sold or given away. After negotiation the thing had been moved to the first floor, outside Allen's bedroom, where it was still faintly audible to Lily but less likely to keep her awake. Allen saw the clock as an ally and sometimes sang out with it in feeble, private protest.

Dinner inevitably followed the seven o'clock chimes. She would eat at a small table while Lily had her food on a tray. Allen ate whatever Ada chose to present her with, but Lily's food was usually pale and soft with the exception of beef tea, the brownest nourishment she would take.

Lily had no gift for conversation, punctuating silences with outbursts of ill-considered opinion; she feared the Belgian refugees, loathed the Suffragettes, was appalled at the rise of the working classes and described Allen's work as 'unnecessary do-gooding'. If she chose not to listen when Allen was speaking she would examine the silver or stare into space. Sometimes she would cut in and shout for Ada, then remember to cough with the effort it had caused her. Allen periodically invented appointments that might relieve her of the dinner hour, then caved in at the last minute, dreading the repercussions.

With the light on, she could see that her blouse and skirt were badly creased. She took them both off, put on a dress and looked at herself in the mirror; her eyes were sinking into their sockets and she was as pasty as a convalescent. Was she to tell Lily about this growing wave of illness? To stay silent was in some way dishonourable, a slur on the sick. To discuss it was to excite panic. During the time it took her to brush out her hair, curl it back on to her head and pin it into place, Allen had chosen to avoid the conversation altogether and go out.

Could she tell Lily that she had a headache and needed fresh air? That was limp and might simply result in dinner being delayed. She could say that she had been sent a note concerning an emergency meeting, something to do with the concert. If there were repercussions, it was too bad. She would drop in on Mr Speake to tell him that the concert had been cancelled.

*   *   *

'I'm stopping now, Mrs Thompson. Perhaps you'll come upstairs and have a cup of tea? Margaret's drying out the leaves, I'm sure of it. Every potful's greyer than the last.'

Allen was aware that the situation was unusual. Was there a danger of impropriety? They were middle-aged and she was widowed, which gave the encounter some decorum, but it could equally be said that a teacher with an eye to keeping her job should do nothing that could possibly be misrepresented. If Lily knew, she'd be furious.

Allen nodded and said, 'Yes, I'd like that.'

Henry locked the shop door and turned out the lights. There was a moment's confusion at the foot of the stairs as to who should take the lead, then Henry stood back and held out the flat of his hand, giving Allen priority. When they got to the landing, he offered to hang up her coat and stood away while she took it off. The rack was in the shadows but she could see that it was overcrowded. 'In here,' he said. They were in the place that Henry called the piano room, although he said it served him equally for eating and reading. The gas lamps were already on, electricity being supplied only downstairs; a small fire provided extra light.

'Make yourself comfortable,' he said. 'I'll tell Margaret we'll need another cup.'

Allen sat on the threadbare sofa and took off her hat. She knew him to be single and assumed that he must be referring to the maid. From the sloppy state of the room she understood that Henry took no notice of his surroundings and that this Margaret woman took advantage of his indifference. In fact, Margaret had realized early on in her employment that Henry cared less about his living conditions than he did about the workshop. She took care of the piano and the gramophone, both of which had to be scrupulously dusted every morning, and once a week she wiped down the piano keys with a cloth wrung out in vinegar water. Whatever else she approached was done with limited interest. Henry took no notice of her at all, other than to thank her for his meals and give her money for shopping.

He came back, still in his working jacket, and went straight to the fire-place to poke at the burning coals. 'That's a lot of work to have done on the music,' he said. 'I hope it won't be wasted.' This was said peevishly, as if the work had been his alone.

'The concert's bound to be on before the end of term. I hope you don't feel that we've taken advantage of your time, Mr Speake?'

'There's less of it than I'd like, that's all.' He leaned forward, amenable again. 'Plenty of grey tea, that's my prescription.'

Margaret knocked and came in with the tray. She made a point of looking down, not wanting to acknowledge Allen. Having been brought up to believe that a man and woman should meet alone and in private only if they were married, Margaret was as unnerved to be in their presence as if they had been rolling naked by the fire.

Allen waited until Margaret had gone out and shut the door. 'Are you very busy?'

'More than usual.' Henry poured the tea and gave Allen her cup. 'Quite a lot more.' He put his hand in his breast pocket and left it there for a moment. She assumed him to be checking on an order or a bill.

'This is usually a busy time but there's no doubt about it. We're very busy. I shall be up early in the morning.'

'Two more children collapsed in class today. They just fell.'

'In the old days they used to call influenza the knock-me-down fever. And we've had Russian and now it's Spanish. You don't hear of Welsh 'flu, do you? Or American?' They drank tea. 'Is your husband in France?'

'He died at Mons.'

'I'm sorry, Mrs Thompson.' The answer had clearly disconcerted him. 'I don't know what I was thinking, asking you such a thing. Please forgive me.'

'It's perfectly all right. I've got quite used to saying it.'

'That doesn't mean I should have asked you.' She thought he was about to say more but he lowered his head and looked at his hands, spreading them out like a woman examining a manicure.

'You're very accomplished on the piano,' she said. 'Did you teach yourself?'

'I had a few lessons, nothing much. I could always pick things up.'

'What do you play when you're by yourself, here in this room?'

'Modern things. I like jazz, American music.'

'Is that altogether different? I mean, the playing of it.'

'The separation of the left hand, that's the real bugbear. You think you've got them swinging along and then you lose it. It's like trying to speak two languages at once. I learn things from the gramophone but you can't hear the piano properly on records, that's the shame of it, not through the band. I'd like a record of the piano on its own, to work out the notes.'

'Will you play something to me?'

'Now?'

'Why not?'

'I don't play it to other people.'

'I'd be very interested.'

He hesitated. Any embarrassment that either of them might be feeling was being dissipated by the – to Allen – neutral and – to Henry – tremendous, topic of music. He went to the piano and sat down. 'This won't sound like the real thing.'

Fully involved with the novel nature of the moment, she watched him as he stretched along the keyboard and lifted his foot on and off the pedal, moving his head in time to the steady rhythm set by his left hand. The simple remedy of new experience was invigorating her. A new room, however shabby, and a new sort of conversation, even a new sort of music; all this was exactly what she needed and the last thing she would have known how to define had she been asked an hour ago. He played the last notes and bent his head to signal the end of the piece. She applauded while he got up and shut the lid.

'I enjoyed that very much,' she said.

'I usually just play jazz for myself.' He was awkward again. 'I'm not used to having an audience.'

*　*　*

Friday, 18 October

I wrote to Sir Arthur Newsholme, waking early before Margaret had stirred. In order to explain my coming across Thomas Wey's letter, I pretended that I had found it in some papers that his landlady had given me to deal with and that those same papers had described some 'research' which I felt Sir Arthur might be interested in. Thomas's other letters had clearly not been replied to, hence his 'I write again', so I didn't mention them at all. I wrote and re-wrote several times, with each version becoming more raggedly written until in the end I tore everything up and set fire to it in the grate. People were coming down with influenza, that much I was sure of, and nearly all the dying were young, but to suggest that we might shut the ports was bordering on the insane.

The burning of the letters didn't help at all. Thomas Wey and I had become companions and my nursing of his papers was a poor way of showing my regard. Write to Sir Arthur, he would have said. A last wish for a dead man: write to Sir Arthur and give me peace.

I also found it awkward to be keeping certain events to myself when my habit was to discuss most things with Walter. I've known him since I was seven years old. My grandfather had died and my father needed another pair of hands. Walter was sixteen, small for his age he tells me, and a good carpenter, even then. When he came into the shop to ask if he might be considered, he brought this little cupboard with him; he'd made it for his mother to keep precious things in. He told me later that she'd never used it, 'in case she broke it'. That was what she'd said. The truth was she had nothing to keep, except the cupboard, which, of course, she couldn't put into itself.

My father took him on straightaway. Walter's sixty-one now but he can still help me to lift a big man down the stairs when we have to. I'd describe him as compact. There's never any waste with Walter, not in his work and not in his body; you feel that you couldn't pinch an inch of his skin, that everything fits tight. He's got a proud chest, a neat walk and a way of talking that puts things as they are, rather than as you might want them to be. We work together like left hand and right, and if you were watching you wouldn't know who was leading who. Vi, his wife, she's been very good to me, kinder than my sisters, I'd say. She's from Ireland, from Kerry, in the west.

He never liked Allen. Apart from, as he put it, me getting ideas above my station, he was wary of her as a woman. 'She's like a bloke,' he said. If Walter were to run the world, he'd say that women should provide the comfort. Vi isn't slow to tell him off but she loves him like a mother duck and he says she's given him the two things he always wanted in a wife: good food and a soft body. I never wanted a wife at all. I got all the comfort I needed from sitting at the piano. That's not to say I didn't like the idea of a warm back to lie against, but then I'd have had to put up with all the other business that went with the front half: talking when you *wanted to be quiet and giving up your time when you needed it for your-self. Like any man, I'd had sex when I could get it, but if I could have married the piano, I would have.*

Walter can fit two pieces of wood together by eye, so that they slip into each other like putting your finger into a custard, and he's proud of it, but he'll always pop his chest out when he's talking to people he thinks of as properly schooled, just to let them know he won't be cowed. He's more like my father than I am in some respects, which is why I couldn't show him the letter: neither man would succumb to imagination.

As for old Albert, I couldn't tell you what he's thinking about and I'm sure he wouldn't be interested in me either. He started here three years ago, when young Horace joined up and I needed an extra pair of hands. Horace was useful to me: a good carpenter. He died at Passchendaele.

There wasn't an exact moment when I really began to think that Thomas Wey was on to something but the end of that week was of some consequence.

*　　*　　*

'Ada tells me there's some awful sickness going about. Why didn't you warn me?' Lily Bird was in bed. The room was lit by a thin crack of grey sky between the heavy velvet curtains but Allen needed only the minimum of light to see the expression on her sister's face. It was always offended, as if something disgusting had been pinned under her nose at birth. 'And where were you last night? You know I can't digest my dinner properly if I have to eat alone.'

'I had to go to school. The concert's been called off until everyone's well again.'

'You see!'

'There's nothing to worry about, Lily. You're perfectly safe here.' Allen stood at the end of the bed, balancing her briefcase on the bedstead. 'And if I don't leave now I shall miss assembly.'

34

'Tell Ada she's to wear a mask.'

'I can't possibly do that.'

'And I don't think you should go to school.'

'I'll be careful. It's autumn and we're all a bit low,' Allen said. 'There's nothing to worry about. And Ada's perfectly well, really she is. I'll be home at about five o'clock.'

Lily closed her eyes and pulled up the embroidered sheet. 'Tell her to wear a mask.'

'I can't do that.'

'Then go away.'

*   *   *

'We were getting worried, Mrs Thompson.' Mr Morris greeted Allen at the staff room door and made a mark on some kind of register, concocted to deal with the emergency. 'You're rather late. Please look at the board for your revised duties.'

The room had many empty chairs; the usual complement of teachers was reduced by at least a quarter. Those who had come in were talking quietly in small groups and some greeted her with relief. She went straight to Ruth and sat beside her at the table where she was marking books.

'Good morning to you. Not that it looks terribly good in here.'

'There'll be some doubling up today. Carthorse has just put a note on the board.'

'I know. Are you working or can we talk?'

'I can stop.' Ruth put the cap on her pen. 'But you're in competition with half a blotty page on wool production. Have you got news about anyone?'

'No. Have you?' Allen pulled her chair closer and pinned a loose strand of hair back into place.

'No. I thought I might make a few visits later, just to see how they're getting on.'

'I'll come with you if you like.'

'You wanted to talk. What monstrous doings have you done?'

'Here's the thing: I absconded last night. Ran away.'

'You—'

An elderly teacher interrupted her by dumping a pile of books on the table. He leaned on them with his fists and said, 'My class with yours. Arithmetic. Ten o'clock. I'm geography. Mrs Peal's off and these are marked.' He lifted both fists and brought them back down on the books. 'Subtraction.' As Ruth thanked him, he turned with a wave and walked slowly to the door.

'Poor old Wallace,' she said. 'We should be wheeling him up and down the corridor.'

The bell rang.

'We'll think about who we should visit,' Allen said. She was grateful for the interruption; was she as selfish as Lily, that she should talk about herself when the school was in such disarray? 'Assembly, then. I'll see you at break.'

*   *   *

'Nora's on the mend. She'll be up and about next week, I'd say.' Sarah had joined Henry, Walter and Albert for an early cup of tea in the workshop. They sat between the planks and benches, surrounded by the paraphernalia of the trade, their feet embedded in the sawdust carpet.

'Your Margaret's a shocking cook,' Sarah said, tapping her biscuit on a length of elm. 'That's disgusting. Could be one of your off-cuts.'

'Bring your own next time,' Henry said.

'I will.'

'You been busy, then?' Walter said. 'Mind you, silly question. If we have, you have.'

'I have. I've done a good half-dozen this week. Henry, what's this I hear about you playing for a school concert?'

'I'm not. It's been postponed. Too many sick.'

'That's as maybe. But why ask you in the first place?'

'Our Henry is a cut above, that's why.' Walter winked at Sarah.

'He's available more like,' she said. 'They must be running low on piano players.'

'I like a bit of music.' They all turned to look at Albert, forgotten in the corner. 'A sing-song an' that. Nothing like it.'

Henry got up. 'One of the teachers, she heard me play at church and she asked me, that's all. Don't make anything of it. This influenza, it's nothing like it was in the summer, is it?'

'No. They're going down quicker and staying down longer. There's more of them dying. And the colouring up – you can't say we've seen a lot of that before, can you?'

'And they're young.' Henry said. 'More than you'd expect.'

Sarah nodded. 'That's true. I'd say we're in for a busy few weeks.' She put the last bit of biscuit back on the plate. 'And you tell that girl of yours to give up cooking. I don't know how you put up with it, eating her rubbish.'

Walter picked up a hammer and brought it down to within an inch of Henry's arm. 'He wouldn't notice if she fed him bad-egg pie.'

'Just leave it, will you!' Henry shouted, swiping the hammer away.

'Oi, oi, watch it,' Sarah said to Walter. 'You're dealing with a maniac.' She put on her coat and adjusted her hat. 'I'll be off, then. Say hello to Vi and tell her I'll pop in next time I'm round there. 'Bye, Henry. Watch what you're doing with that hammer.'

He lifted a hand in dismissal.

*   *   *

'Should we get permission from Carthorse?'

The childish tampering with Miss Carter's name was one of the more obvious signs that Ruth was Allen's junior. Her exuberance could be trying, as could her tales about her nine-day courtship and precipitate engagement to Jack, a soldier who'd been posted to France the day after the celebration party. For her part, Ruth was continually exasperated by the tales of Lily Bird's behaviour and was always encouraging Allen to resist. What's the point of suffrage, she would say, if we oppress each other?

'I think we'll have to get Miss Carter to agree,' Allen said. 'We can't just barge in. We're teachers, we'll be representing the school. What are you actually thinking of doing? I mean, is this a mercy call? Are we being cheerful and offering prayers or is it soup and damp flannels?'

'That's rather horrible. I'll go on my own if you'd rather.'

There was shouting in the playground and then silence. They ran to the window, expecting to see another child falling in delirium, but the teacher on duty was reprimanding a sheepish boy. The two women touched each other briefly on the arm and went back to their chairs.

'I'm sorry I was flippant,' Allen said. 'I'm probably just trying to ward it off. What exactly did you want to do?'

'Just turn up, I suppose. Ask how the children are and if there's any way we can help.'

'We might be seen as interfering.'

'Then we'll leave. Come on, break's over.'

'And suppose we catch it?' Allen said.

'Then we'll look after each other.'

'You're a dreary heroine in a cheap novel.'

'I'm a kind teacher with crusading zeal and you're a cruel cynic. And what was it you were going to tell me this morning?' They were on the stairs, whispering. 'You were absconding or something. Have you left the hideous Lily?'

'Not now.'

'Not what now?'

'I don't want to talk about it now. Later, at lunch.'

* * *

'Mr Speake?' The woman was properly dressed but had forgotten her hat. Intimidated by Henry's height and bearing, she put her hand on top of her head and looked up. 'It's my Catherine.'

Catherine was her daughter, nineteen years old and seven months pregnant. She'd been working on the Monday morning, then come down with the 'flu between lunch and tea. Quinine, suggested by the chemist, had been of no use. The girl had died in the night and now the woman's husband was feverish and two of the younger children couldn't get out of bed. Her neighbour had told her to fetch Sarah for laying out and Sarah had told her to come here, to Speake & Son.

Henry knew that he would have to deal with the arrangements later. The story had used the woman up; she was hardly present. 'I'll visit you between five and six o'clock,' he said. 'You get back there now and I'll be along shortly.'

'You'll be along shortly,' the woman repeated. 'I'll get back there now. Thank you, Mr Speake.' She left the shop, with her hand still fixed to her head.

*　　*　　*

I'd dealt with two funerals on that Friday morning. I don't know if either of them had died of influenza but they were both young. I'd put them in their coffins on the Saturday before I'd met Thomas Wey and started to take more careful note of the bodies I was picking up, particularly the discolouration. Two or three funerals a week would usually be my average, except in epidemics, like the Russian 'flu. The summer bout had certainly made a lot of people poorly and there had been a few more deaths than expected for the season; now it was one a day or more. Walter and I took stock of the wood we had available, which was a poor supply, the whole business of getting timber being extremely difficult in any case what with permits and rationing and the different-coloured forms that you had to fill in and present to the timber controller. If we'd been making furniture, I could have seen the point, but the public had no desire to be buried in shrouds. What did they think we were to do? In the end we were forced to buy some ready-made but they lasted no time at all.

On the Friday afternoon, I went to measure up for a woman who'd lost her daughter. The woman had been a bit fuddled when she'd come in the shop at midday – she was so like a rabbit that I'd had to speak quietly for fear of her bolting – but when she answered the door to me at six o'clock she'd quite forgotten who I was or why I was there. When I told her, she stood looking at me as if I'd fallen out of the sky; then she let me in, still not speaking, and lit a candle to guide us upstairs. She went up first, with me following.

There were two rooms at the top, one on each side of the staircase. The door on the left was open and I took the candle from her and went inside, expecting to see the deceased. Two children lay in the bed, both feverish. I turned to say something to her but she was leaning against the door with that same absent look. I don't know who else might see it – doctors, I suppose – but it's a look that says, 'I'm off and you can't follow.'

'Have you called the doctor in?' I asked her but of course she wasn't up to talking so I tried the room opposite to see if that's where the body was. The bed in here was bigger and the side of it where Sarah had laid the daughter out was tidy. Next to her, with his arm across her chest, lay a dead man who I thought must be the woman's husband. The light from the candle was poor but I could see that they were both terribly cyanosed. The woman, I think her name was Mrs Crook, came up behind me and put her hand on mine, frightened the life out of me actually. So we both stood there for a while, with me thinking about Thomas Wey and her thinking God knows what. I can remember feeling an unpleasant sort of excitement that Thomas was turning out to be right and that this pestilence was taking hold. We were disturbed by a boy running up the stairs and coming into the room to find Mrs Crook, which set them both crying, her being released by seeing one of her children in good health. I measured up and sent the boy to get Sarah and the doctor back again.

We spent that evening working in the shop and Vi brought us in some food. Sarah showed herself again as well. Samuel was to be buried the next day and although she never said as much, she seemed to want a bit of company.

*　　*　　*

Saturday, 19 October

'Lily Bird's having rather a bad morning. Can you wait a little? I'll ask Ada to bring you some coffee.'

'What does bad mean?' Ruth said.

'She's sure Ada's infectious. She wants her to wear a mask and she doesn't want her touching the food and now she's insisting that we seal all the windows.'

'Couldn't you just lock her away?'

Ada knocked at the open door of the drawing room. 'Please, ma'am, Mrs Bird's shouting for you.'

'Thank you, Ada.' Allen looked at the far wall, took a breath and then looked back at Ruth. 'Just a minute or two. Do you mind?'

'Of course I don't.'

'She'll be furious that you're even in the house.'

'I bring bacteria.'

'You bring fortitude. I'll stand firm.'

Ruth took a newspaper from her bag and started to sit down, then changed her mind and went to the door where she stood, listening. From her own upbringing in an open-minded, benevolent family, she had absorbed the idea that all intimidation was tyranny, whatever the circumstance. Even though they had never met she knew for a fact that Lily was a wily, pious despot whom Allen was sheltering less through kindness than as a buffer against widowhood. Ruth was brazen in her dislike and Allen tolerated it – there were even times when she felt bold enough to join in – but she always came back to the same unshakeable position: her sister must stay.

The sound of raised voices, one shrieking and the other steady, came from Lily's room. Then both voices went quiet and eventually Ruth heard Allen in the corridor saying, 'Be brave, Lily. We've dealt with far worse.' There was a muffled reply, then Allen said, 'I'll make sure. You sleep now.' Ruth heard a door close and footsteps heading away, presumably down to the kitchen. She arranged herself in the chair and opened the newspaper. Deep in her body, indignation was rolling itself into a sizeable ball; she was rigid on the cushions. Had she been able, at that moment, she would have thrown Lily on to the streets to beg, or better, transported her to the trenches.

Allen came in and closed the door. 'I think she's asleep. Shall we go now?'

'If you like.'

'I'm sorry I've kept you waiting.'

'Please don't worry.' Ruth tried to fold the newspaper, tearing it as she forced the crease into place. She spoke a little more loudly than she needed to. 'Are you sure you want to do this? I can visit them quite well on my own.'

'Of course I do. Are you angry? I was as quick as I could be.' Allen looked at the table. 'Ada forgot your coffee. Do you want some before we go?'

'She didn't forget, you didn't ask her. And no, thank you. I don't want anything.'

'I think I've persuaded Lily that Ada isn't the angel of death.'

'Jolly good. Shall we go?'

'What's upset you?'

'We're late, that's all.'

'Please don't be cross.'

'I'm not.'

'You are.'

Ruth walked to the door and turned to face Allen with her right hand raised and the palm directed out. Allen knew the gesture well: Ruth used it often with the children. 'Look here,' Ruth said, emphasizing the words with a forward thrust of the raised hand, 'I want us to visit these families. And I'm annoyed with Lily because she's wasting your time and being unreasonable.' Ruth's fingers were so rigidly splayed that Allen could see shiny pink and cream patches on the stretched skin. 'And you seem quite unperturbed by her behaviour.'

'I'm used to it.'

'You were going to stand firm.'

'I did.'

'How?'

'Ada's still here. Please keep your voice down. I don't want to wake Lily up if she's asleep.'

The hand closed into a fist. Ruth lowered it slowly to her side. 'You always compromise.'

'I do what I think to be right.'

'I think you do what you know will cause the least fuss.'

'Not always. Please stop now.'

As they stood together at the door, Allen appeared to Ruth to be – in this moment – a foolish, ageing woman with a weak, offended face. Her lips merged unpleasantly into the skin surrounding them; her cheeks were dragged flat by failing muscle. There was too much eyelid and too little eyebrow. There was even a suggestion of fluff above the mouth, of the type that would inevitably grow into a moustache.

Ruth appeared to Allen – in the same moment – as a belligerent, ugly child squaring up in the playground. There was no history of dilemma in her face. She would set herself against obstruction and walk, bright-eyed, over the wounded. Allen might have opened the door then and Ruth might have left and they might always have thought of each other as the martyr and the zealot but Allen sneezed instead and Ruth found a clean handkerchief in her pocket.

43

'Do you still want to visit the children?' she said.

'Of course I do.'

'What about Lily?'

'I've made Ada a mask.'

*   *   *

'She wouldn't have gone in any case, even if she'd been well.' Sarah stood by Samuel's coffin with her hand on the lid. Elsie, her sister, was on the other side of the trestle; the smell was not surprising to them and they made no allusion to it. 'All that earth!' Sarah said, mimicking Nora. 'That horrible earth!'

'Don't!' Elsie looked at the wall as if she expected to see Nora through the brick. 'Shall we see if the poor love wants to get up and say a proper goodbye?'

'I'd leave her be.' Sarah looked at the table. It was bare except for a plate of sliced onions, left there to deodorize the room. 'What about afterwards? We can't just walk off. They'll want a glass or two to warm them up.'

'They can come to me,' Elsie said. 'I'll find them something.' There was a knock at the front door. 'I'd better sit with Nora while Henry takes him out.' She kissed her fingers and touched the coffin.

'Quick march, then!' Sarah said. 'Let's not keep Henry hanging about. You know it makes him tetchy.'

*   *   *

If Connie Allday's face was an early sketch of features worn down by anxiety, her mother's was the completed work. As Allen and Ruth introduced themselves she tapped her foot loudly on the step and scowled at them, pulling her eyes further out of shape. 'Are you trying to say she ought to be at school? Only she can't get up.'

'No, no,' Ruth said. 'We just wanted to enquire after her.'

'Well, she's bad. Is that all?'

Ruth leaned forward. 'Is there anything we can do?'

'Do? What d'you mean?'

Allen was leaving this to Ruth, not being sure herself, just yet, about the exact extent of their benevolence. She had no wish to march into anybody's house and assume command; she had no knowledge of nursing and had never had a child of her own. The implication of their interference, that they could cope where others were failing, was a fantasy not yet put to any kind of test. The one thing that they had agreed not to volunteer was the one thing that the majority of these families were most in need of: money.

Ruth had come to the decision, supported by Miss Carter, that they would do whatever was required so long as it placed them in no jeopardy; Miss Carter had included the risk of infection here until Ruth had argued, successfully, that they were as likely to catch influenza at school or on the street.

'Is there anything we can do to help you, Mrs Allday?' Ruth was asking again. 'Does Connie need anything?' This being the first time in her life that anyone had volunteered to do something on her behalf, Ivy Allday had no ready answer. She shook her head and closed the door in their faces, leaving a trace of eucalyptus on the air.

Ruth was embarrassed; a red flush worked its way up from her neck to her cheeks. She glanced briefly at Allen who said, 'We must have seemed quite mad to her, don't you think?'

'Why?'

'She thought we were condescending.'

'We wanted to help.' Ruth pulled the list of addresses from her bag and unfolded the paper.

'Poor Connie,' Allen said. 'That poor child.'

They walked towards the junction in silence while Ruth consulted the list. 'I think we should have something to offer when we knock,' she said when they reached the main road. 'I'm going to buy some books or some crayons. Something for the children to do while they're in bed. You're still not sure, are you? I'll go by myself, if you like, really I will. There's a shop there that might have something. If you don't want to come I'll be perfectly all right.'

'Of course I'll come, but Mrs Allday wasn't in the least bit keen. Weren't we implying that she couldn't manage?'

'I don't think so. If we're to be useful then we've got to make the effort and not mind if some people turn us away. I knew it might be difficult. Are you going home?'

'No.' Allen lifted her collar against the cold. 'I'll stay with you.'

* * *

Thomas Wey's uncle didn't come to the funeral; he was bed-bound. He told me to deal with things as I saw fit and that I would be paid accordingly. When I collected the body from the morgue, I took Thomas's letter, intending to bury it with him, but it stayed in my pocket. I think that by that time, I'd started to see the letter as mine, my inheritance from the man.

The events in that woman's house the afternoon before had put me in a very anxious state. Having spent the best part of the night awake, reading the newspapers that I'd bought for the purpose and finding no mention of influenza, I knew that I would be ridiculed if I chose to write to any member of parliament; but a man who lives near the foundations and sees a crack in them has to tell his master if he doesn't want the house to fall down. That's a bit flowery but I hope the sense is there. How was anyone to know that I was seeing the first deaths of a promised pestilence if I failed to report on it?

We were burying Samuel and Thomas on the same day and I chose to marry the services up, partly to save time but also to allow Thomas some attendance at the church. What sort of life had the man had? I assumed that his parents were dead, hence the uncle's interest, but he had refused my suggestion of a notice in the newspaper and had led me to understand, without saying it in so many words, that Thomas was a solitary soul and would have been indifferent to the service, however it was conducted.

I'd spoken to the mortuary about his stomach wound; his injuries were such that he could barely have eaten enough to stay alive. He was a doctor; he must have realized the state that he was in and been driven to pursue his research before he starved to death. Why else would he have chosen to live in London with a landlady like Mrs White when he could have stayed in Surrey with the uncle and been properly cared for?

I hired in an extra four men so that there would be no time lost in the carrying-out. Quite a few turned up for Sam: Sarah, Elsie, Sam's uncle George and some of his friends from the army, all of them wounded men whom I imagine had made friends with him in hospital. That was a fair number. The bereaved often stay away but he did have quite a turn-out. Reverend Sucerne did a decent address for him but nothing was said about Thomas, except that I recited the letter to myself and prayed he should be remembered for his life's work. Then we took both coffins up to the graves and put Thomas on a trestle whilst Sam was committed.

Afterwards, the men and I left them all there and went a little way along to Thomas's plot. It was colder than it had been and I can't tell you why, but I felt it. You get used to standing in all weathers, and that particular cemetery seems to attract the wind like no other, but I had difficulty controlling my teeth, they were chattering so much. When the men lowered him in and I pulled away the batons, I had the sensation that a hand was pulling from the other side, trying to stop me. I know that was my own mind making up nonsense but even so I clung to what the Reverend was saying. There was some confusion in my mind at that point as to whether I was present as Thomas's undertaker or his companion.

While we were finishing there, the others started to walk back – or limp, I should say, most of the soldiers being on crutches. As soon as the Reverend had come to the end of the final prayer, I should have followed *them, but I found it difficult to come away and sent my men off without accompanying them to the carriages. In the end, Sarah came for me and I had to explain that I owed this deceased a particular amount of attention thanks to the generous payment that had been made by his relative. She may not have believed me but nothing more was said.*

I went back there later, by the light of the full moon, just to make sure that everything had been properly taken care of. I was better prepared this time, with a thick woollen vest under my shirt, but even so the night air was very sharp.

*   *   *

Sunday, 20 October

There were several poorly filled pews for the morning service. Henry faltered over the verses of the first hymn, leaving out some notes and then hitting two at a time with uncertain fingers; later, he neglected to play an introduction and had to be prompted. Allen kept watch over him, alert for any sign of illness, but the only movement he made was during the reading from the book of Habakkuk when he shook his head slowly at the mention of pestilence. Afterwards, she was last in line at the porch, having stopped to pick up a fallen pile of prayer books. The vicar, Richard Sucerne, was eager to talk, keeping her hand in his for longer than necessary as he asked her about the effects of the influenza outbreak on the school.

'You're struggling rather, I believe?'

'A great many teachers have fallen ill. And too many children.'

Releasing her hand but still holding her with an unblinking stare, he nodded his head very slowly. The effect was hypnotic and underscored by air whistling into his nose. 'So brave of you. To work on in such circumstances.'

'Mrs Thompson?' Henry was in the porch. 'And Mr Sucerne – I'm sorry, I didn't hear you announce that hymn.'

'There's nothing to apologize for, Mr Speake. As I was saying to Mrs Thompson, we're all living in rather trying circumstances. I know how busy you are. How busy we both are.' He looked at Allen. 'How busy we *all* are.'

'I must get back to my sister,' Allen said.

'I'm coming your way,' Henry said. 'I've got a job in the next street.' His foot was already on the path. They said goodbye to the vicar and walked in silence until they were round the corner.

'Thank you for rescuing me,' Allen said.

'From what?'

'Our shepherd. He has an unusually persistent handshake.'

'Ah.'

The indifference with which he met the information made Allen blush. She had no idea why she should have said anything so intimate; she had embarrassed them both and there was nothing she could add without complicating things further. The vicar's hand still hung in the air; she would have to introduce a new, safe topic. 'You're visiting someone?'

'Mr Bateman. He died last night.'

Allen stopped walking. 'But I teach his boy!'

Henry said, 'I think it was influenza,' and walked on for several steps until he noticed that she was no longer next to him. Rather than walking back, he spoke to her from where he was.

'I think it was influenza,' he said again.

'Do you?'

'His wife thinks so.'

'That poor family. They've only just lost Daisy.'

'I know.'

'That was measles.'

'I know.'

'Of course you do.'

She caught up with him and they resumed their walk. Yet another passer-by acknowledged him, several had greeted her, most looked surprised to see them together. Now she must arrange a visit to the Batemans' house; it was unlikely that Mr Bateman would be the only victim and his son had been complaining of a headache on Friday afternoon. As for Mr Speake, he was clearly not wanting to talk and there was still a good five minutes to the road where he would turn off. Why had he wanted to accompany her? Should she mention that she understood him to be exhausted? She decided to keep up her end of the conversation; influenza seemed to be the only topic.

'Ruth – Miss Bell – and I, we visited some of the sick families from our school yesterday.'

'Did you? And what did you discover?'

'Discover?'

'I mean, about the illness. Was there a pattern? Age, for example, or the incidence of cyanosis?'

'I don't understand.'

'The sick turning blue. Purply-blue.' They stopped again; this time under his direction. He leaned forward. 'Did you see any of that?'

'No. I've heard of it, but I can't say that I've seen it.' Was this professional interest? Perhaps he was trying to plan ahead; age would be relevant to coffin size and so forth. Or was he simply being morbid, wanting to know about colour? 'Why? Have you? Have you seen it?'

'Yes, I have. It seems to happen when the person can't pull back. They discolour and succumb.'

'That's horrible.'

'It is. Look here, Mrs Thompson, I've got to get to the Batemans' house. I don't suppose you'll be taking a walk this afternoon?'

'After lunch. I always walk to the river and back.'

'I could meet you there, by the bridge.'

'Two o'clock?'

'Two o'clock.'

❋ ❋ ❋

'I don't feel much like lying in,' Walter said. 'I can't get back to sleep.'

Vi was dressed and had a cup of tea in her hand to give him.

'Well, you might have told me before I bothered to bring this up.'

'You get the breakfast on. I won't be a minute.'

'A bit of bacon?'

'Just the job.'

Vi allowed Walter a certain amount of time in bed on a Sunday morning; then, after church, if he were up to it, he might do a bit of gardening or make a toy for a grandchild, otherwise he was excused all duties until one o'clock. After dinner, Vi held sway for the afternoon: Walter would read out loud from the newspaper while she did a jigsaw puzzle, or they would go for a walk and a cup of tea out. If Walter was getting up early, then he was troubled. He came down straightaway, dressed loosely in a shirt with the collar open. She put marge on his bread and stirred a little sugar into his tea.

'You kept me awake,' she said.

'And how did I do that?'

'Dancing round the bed.'

'Sorry, love.'

He cut a piece of bacon and lifted the fork to his mouth. She picked up her cup and went to drink. They looked at each other in a way that people who have been married for forty years or more are not inclined to look; they searched each other's eyes, without smiling, until the principal issue had been conveyed.

'So what's he up to?' Vi sipped at her tea.

'Hard to say.' Walter ate the bacon and fiddled with a thread of gristle caught in his upper front teeth. 'We've never seen him with a girl for more than a week, have we? But this Mrs Thompson, he's keen. I'm sure of it.' The gristle came away. Vi held out an empty plate to receive it. 'So that's one thing,' Walter said. 'The lady friend.'

'Is he talking about her?'

'No. But he doesn't like it if anybody else does.'

'I saw her going in there.'

Walter stopped chewing. 'When?'

'Thursday night. When I took that pie round to Hilda.'

'That was late.'

'Half past seven.'

'Why didn't you say?'

'I don't know. Didn't want to stir the water. Anyway, it might have been business. Was it?'

'No.' Walter held up his cup to be re-filled.

She picked up the teapot. 'I just can't believe that woman would have taken a shine to him. I mean, he's a good man in his own way but he's not for the likes of a teacher. And he's settled like he is. He wouldn't want to cause the upset, would he? All the talk... Perhaps it's Samuel dying that's put him out of sorts.'

'Not a chance.'

'Well, he shouldn't be seen with her. It'll do neither of them any good. Is that what's kept you awake? Him and her? What's the other thing?'

'I can't nail it down.'

'You want to have a word. Tell him to act his age.'

*   *   *

While I was playing for the morning service I had the idea of talking to Allen and letting her in on Thomas Wey, just to get her opinion, but then, when it came to it, I changed my mind. I changed it again several times – tell her, don't tell her – but in the end I kept it to myself. She does go straight to the heart of a thing, not getting alarmed in the normal way, but I thought she might in this case and I didn't want her flapping and causing a fuss. There was also the strong possibility that she would believe Thomas to be mad.

We talked for quite some time, mostly about influenza from a general point of view. I explained about cyanosis so as to alert her, if it should happen in any of her families. For my part the conversation was a struggle about whether to speak or stay silent and I remember now that I was disappointed, because I still had the entire burden of the letter on my shoulders. From Thomas Wey's point of view, the conversation was ridiculous. And the end of the war was certain: there would be no men left to fight it.

TWO

'We have studied, particularly, the report of the Medical Officer of the Local Government Board. We conclude, after mouthing such plaguey syllables as "meningococcic" and "saprophylic" – oh, that doctors had never heard of Greek! – that there is no cure, no remedy, small hope and little help.'

Daily Mirror, 24 October 1918

Monday, 21 October

As Henry came into the room, Dr Lionel Tite made a half-hearted attempt to stand then sank back into his chair. 'I'm off out,' he said, 'so state your business.'

Henry was dressed for a funeral; he held his top hat and gloves in front of his groin. 'I'm sorry to bother you so early in the morning, Doctor Tite, but I thought I should ask for your opinion on this epidemic.'

'I haven't got an *opinion*, Speake. I'm too busy. Have you got an *opinion*?' The doctor's chin jutted forward as he spoke, but the rest of his body was still. His eyes were bloodshot and he looked like a man who might fall asleep where he sat.

'I don't have an opinion, no. And I know they're not all dying—'

'No, they're not.'

'—but so many of the young ones are. And I wondered if you might be having thoughts on the matter.'

'The "matter", as you call it, is to get round the sick and back in time for bed.'

'But the cyanosis—'

'Oh, go home, Speake.' Dr Tite went to the desk and opened his bag to put away the stethoscope. 'If I can't help them,' he said, snapping the bag shut, 'then they're yours.' He rang for the maid. ' And do keep well.'

* * *

'We'll go to hell! We'll pay for this!' A man was walking up and down outside Speake & Son in the morning fog, shouting and banging a snare drum that hung from a belt round his waist. 'We'll go to hell! We'll pay for this!'

Walter had moved the man on several times but he was back again and banging more loudly every time he passed the window. 'I'll have to get Frank,' Walter said, his voice getting louder as the drummer approached. 'Not that locking the poor sod up'll help. I mean, you never know, do you? He might be right. Have you seen the state of him?'

'No, I haven't. I'm going out the back.' The drumming crescendo came to a climax. Henry shouted, 'And shut him up, will you?'

'I told you, I've tried. I'll get Frank.'

'We'll go to hell! We'll go to hell!' The drummer was standing outside their window, yelling and staring at them through the glass.

Henry ran to the door and opened it so quickly that the man was still looking at Walter when Henry grabbed at him and tried to pull the drum away. There was resistance and a tangle of arms and drumsticks; after a few seconds the belt had broken and the drum was off. The man hit Henry on the cheek and was hit back with such force that he fell to the pavement and lay there with his arms over his head and his legs curled up like a baby.

Walter had been too late to stop the punch but now he held on to Henry's arm. 'That's enough!' he said. 'You stop that!'

People watching from the windows of neighbouring shops came straggling out. Some pedestrians gathered, not too close, oohing and aahing. Henry and Walter helped the man to his feet. The crowd waited, expecting further drama, and then went on their way, disappointed; a boy stopped to stamp on the drum skin and got scattered applause when his foot went through.

'What are you doing that for?' Henry said, staring at the drummer's burned and blasted face. 'Driving us bloody mad.'

The man picked up what was left of the drum and then found the sticks. He banged the rim and looked at Henry. 'Got to do it, chum. Got to do it.'

Walter took charge. 'Then why don't you do it in the park, on the bandstand?' he said. 'If you've got to do it, then that's the place.'

'Got no drum now.' The man banged the rim again. 'He told me to come to you and now you're telling me to go to the park and then he'll tell me to come to you and I'll be here and there and that'll take all day. So I might as well stay here and get on with it.'

He lifted the stick but Henry stopped his arm. 'Who told you?'

'The man in the park.'

'There's no man in the park who could have sent you here. If you don't bugger off, I'm getting the law in and then you'll be locked up. Make your choice.'

The man pulled his arm away and banged the rim of the drum again, loudly enough to make the two men wince, then he moved off, talking to himself.

'You can't help feeling sorry for him,' Walter said. 'Burnt like that. What got into you?'

'He was making too much noise.'

'That's no reason for you to clout him.'

Frank, the policeman, joined them as they went into the shop. 'I hear there's been a bit of trouble. Something about a fight?'

Walter said, 'We had a barmy drummer. And Henry here decided to give him a pasting.'

'He shouldn't have done that,' Frank said. 'That's bad, that is, Henry. Where is he now anyway, this drummer?'

'I don't know,' Walter shrugged. 'I told him to go and play on the bandstand, but he's as likely to be anywhere.' They were inside now, walking towards the workshop door. Henry stopped with his fingers on the handle and stood still, looking down at his feet. Walter changed course and walked towards the desk. 'You got anyone ill in the family, Frank?'

'Not in the family. Neighbours, that sort of thing. We've got quite a few men off at the station. I've been picking up all sorts, falling in the street. We had one go under a car this morning. I thought he was a goner but he only broke his leg. You got anyone?'

'No. We've been lucky.'

'I'll have a look for the drummer, then, shall I?' When he was outside the shop Frank knocked on the glass to attract Walter's attention and put his fists up like a boxer.

'We'd better get on.' Henry opened the door to the workshop and reached up to the hook for his apron.

'You'll have to live this down,' Walter said. 'There'll be talk.'

'It'll be forgotten. There's more important things.'

Albert, deaf to the world outside, was pouring melted paraffin wax into a coffin and then tilting the box this way and that to perfect the seal. He looked up as they came in and nodded. Four other coffins stood on trestles, all at various stages of construction and finishing. Walter and Henry put on their aprons and took a coffin each.

'Vi said she saw that Mrs Thompson popping in here,' Walter said after a while. 'Good company, is she?'

'I like talking to her, if that's what you mean.'

'Right, I can see that. Only I'd have thought she was a bit above your station. If you don't mind my saying.'

Henry picked up a sack of sawdust and poured it into the coffin he was working on. As he smoothed it flat, he looked up and lifted his eyebrows.

'Well, she is,' Walter said.

'I've finished.' Albert was at his elbow. 'What's next to do?'

'You can line this one.' Henry cut a length of calico from the bale and gave it to Albert. 'I'll go and ask Margaret to bring us down a bit of lunch.'

Nothing was said about Allen during the meal. Walter did his best to explain about the drummer to Albert, then there was a long silence before they washed and got dressed for the afternoon's funerals.

'I don't want to see you make a fool of yourself,' Walter said at the door as he was putting on his gloves. 'And I've known you long enough to say what your father'd say if he were here. I'm looking out for you, that's how it is.'

'There's no question of stations coming into it. We just like talking. You tell Vi not to get herself in a stew.'

'And what about that drummer? What do you think your father would have had to say about that?'

'He might have done the same.'

'Not in the street, not in public.'

'Are we doing these funerals? Because the men are all here and we're late.'

'I'm only looking out for you.'

'I'm grateful.'

'I should hope so.'

＊　　＊　　＊

Lily Bird was too weak to get up. Her legs had given way as she'd attempted to rise for breakfast and, as usual on such mornings, she had retired to the empire of her bed to continue her needlework. Refusing Ada's attentions, she had insisted that Allen should wash her and plait her hair before leaving for school, only calling her back once to request a thicker shawl. The gas fire, as Lily had pointed out many times, may once have been adequate to heat the room for dining purposes but it barely kept the ice off her drinking water and was unequal to the task of warming an invalid, even now that the windows had been sealed.

She took the antimacassar from her work basket and laid it over her lap. The satin stitch on several of the leaves was poorly executed, the result of sewing in bad light, and would have to be unpicked and re-sewn. She sighed, vexed at the chore but pleased at her willingness to remain obedient to the task. From her position in the bed, she was able to reach everything that Allen had laid out for her: the sewing frame, the work basket with its complement of tools, the tray of silks and a painted tin bowl in which to deposit discarded thread.

Choosing a small pair of scissors, Lily snipped down the middle of one of the soft green mats and pulled at the strands with her nails, thinking as she did so that not being able to walk about and settle one's own affairs was very trying and made all the more so by Allen's insistence on employing Ada. She was a truculent, dirty girl, utterly unfit for domestic work. She spoke before she was spoken to! A thieves' den would have suited her better, or a travelling circus… Here Lily's imagination was stirred. She knew very little about circuses but a juggler came into her mind and then a lion tamer. What would Ada do in such a place? Several shoeless, surly children took the place of the lion tamer and ran into a caravan… but there was nothing in Lily's education to complete the picture. How did one furnish a caravan? She sprawled Ada over a table, adding several empty bottles – to indicate chronic drunkenness – and a man, possibly a foreigner, slouching at her side.

The man, even though he was clearly a fiend, led her thoughts to marriage and to her dear, departed Godfrey; and from there to his views on domestic recruitment, which she had repeated and memorized over the years. 'A servant, having no responsibilities other than the discharge of the master's will, has therefore the simplest task of all: to provide faultless execution of all that is requested, nothing more. A task,' Godfrey would add, 'aided by the administration of punishment and praise in equal measure from a master devoted to the servant's care.' He had been a dear, fair man. Her eyes welled with tears. She turned to reach under the pillow for her handkerchief and as she did so the scissors slid from her thigh across the counterpane and disappeared, she assumed, in the direction of the floor, although there was no sound to suggest a landing.

Her tears dried. If she were to unpick the second and final leaf, she would inevitably need the scissors long before Ada brought cocoa at eleven o'clock. She sat up as best she could and searched around her, even though she had seen them travel beyond her reach to the edge of the bed. There was another pair in the basket, a bigger pair; she would have to make do. That she should live in fear of a servant! If Godfrey had thought for a minute that she would end her life in this awful house, he would have made provision for her to be properly cared for by nuns.

The last thread from the first leaf was proving to be awkward and Lily hurt the bed of her thumbnail with the nail on her middle finger as she picked it free. She sucked at the wound, blaming Allen – a response well-established since childhood, initiated by envy and now made firm by obligation. The last home they had shared under Allen's direction had been a wooden doll's house. Allen had insisted that the kitchen be used as a classroom and that the maid be given privileges entirely out of keeping with her circumstances. It was a prophetic toy. She should have produced the doll's house as evidence. How can you ask me to live with you? That's what she should have said to Allen. *It would be like living with the dragoon guard.* Yes, that was good. She should have said exactly that. It would be like living with the dragoon guard. Was the doll's house here? She had no idea where half the old things had gone – it really was too bad.

*   *   *

On the Monday morning I'd visited Dr Tite. I'd worked out that if the doctors knew anything, they were probably keeping it from the rest of us. The old sod was no different than he's always been, although he likes to pretend that the war's brought him down. Even so, I got the feeling that he was as much in the dark as anyone. Not that I was in the dark, not really. Thomas Wey had told me something very particular. There were so many people sick and, as I said to Dr Tite, it wasn't that they were all dying, not at all, but those that were *dying were unusually young. And that's what he must have known and what he'd never condescend to talk to me about.*

Of course, I could have written to the doctors that I'd struck up some kind of relationship with, the ones that had gone to the war, to ask if they knew anything about a Dr Wey, but I didn't think I had a good enough grasp of the language to put my points across and besides, what power did these men have to alert anyone? It might come across to you that I was stupid in those first days, not being able to come to a decision about what to do. I'm not defending myself, but I think it was too big a responsibility for an ordinary man; although, having said that, my recurring thought was that no man, however extraordinary, had the means available to do as Thomas had begged. The very idea that the ports could be closed! And would we leave our armies where they stood? Or bring them home and surrender to the Germans? As I say, it was too big a responsibility for any man, ordinary or extraordinary.

All of which left me stranded. I'd had the notion that I might write to the newspapers, but then I imagined such a letter arriving at a desk in a busy office. It would be sure to end up in the wastepaper basket. And if it were taken up by the wrong person, it would only be used as a means of causing panic, not of changing the outcome.

Did I want Thomas to be wrong? There was something in this that gave me pleasure: the idea that we might be on the way out. There were times when I imagined myself alone, the only man left on earth. And I wondered if I might feel that I had to bury the dead – at least, the dead in my vicinity. Then I thought of starting up somewhere in the wild, away from the bodies; and I even considered, if I did survive, how I might get a piano away to such a place. That led me to thinking about New Zealand and then, because I'd had a letter from Rose that morning, I thought of writing back and telling her everything, but to what end? I missed Rose a great deal. If she'd stayed here – and there's no explaining why I should think this – then I doubt that I should still be in the shop. I do think I might have taken up the piano in a proper way and tried to make a go of it. So I did write, but only a short letter to tell her about Samuel, which I should have done sooner. The letter would take six weeks to reach her – an age. We might all be dead by then. There was a mad man outside that day, telling us we'd all go to hell. I hadn't considered that part of it at all. If there was nobody here, then millions of souls would have to be housed, above or below, and how would that change the order of things? Would the other place be bottom-heavy, with hell having the advantage? Walter thought I'd made a fool of myself but he had no idea what the man was suggesting.

*   *   *

Lily was trying to unpick the second leaf when she heard muted conversation and laughter coming from somewhere on the ground floor. Ada must be saying goodbye to her secret lover; they'd crept up from the basement, assuming that Lily was too ill to notice. He was probably planning to sneak back later in his army boots – his stolen army boots – and ransack the house. Ada would help him, keeping watch as he went from room to room, taking everything of value. And what about the food? How could she be sure that her meals had not been picked over? Ada's secret lover, rummaging through the larder, eating what he pleased…

The blade of the scissors was too thick to slip below the silk. In future she would be sure to have several spare scissors, but what was she to do now? Godfrey would say that a plan must be devised. What were her options? She could start something new without finishing the anti-macassar – but that would be so unprincipled she might as well give the thing to the Germans. She could call Ada – if the girl answered! – and get her to retrieve the scissors. She could also try to find them for herself. The idea was dangerous: she might be able to get up, but would she be able to get back, unaided?

If Allen were to find out that she'd fallen out of bed, she would be angry with Ada, and Ada's truculence at being accused might then result in her dismissal – a point in favour. But if Ada were to find her on the floor, she would have to be picked up, which would mean a great deal of intimate contact – a point against. Ada's portmanteau of disease was unlikely to be limited to influenza.

Excited by the possibility of independent action, she decided to make the attempt. She would leave the bed. With great care, Lily moved the basket, the frame, the tray and the bowl to one side and leaned them in on one another to counteract the movement of the mattress. It would be very silly to retrieve the scissors and lose something else! Taking a deep breath, she pushed back a triangle of bedding and bared herself to the room. It was colder than she'd expected, without the covering. She would have to be quick or risk catching a chill. Turning on to her side, she swung herself forward so that her legs fell over the side of the bed; then she twisted her body and brought it upright, sliding down in an attitude of prayer.

The scissors were not immediately visible but, clinging to the bedclothes, she leaned to the right and left, looking round for some glint of silver. Despite the hard floor and her precarious position, she was happy. She had chosen to leave the bed and she had left the bed and now she was looking for her scissors and when she had found them she would return to her sewing. It was an adventure and she had planned and executed every step herself. Then she moved her leg slightly to the right and put her knee on a pair of cold, hard ornamental handles. Crying out with pain, she moved too quickly and lost her grip, falling headlong to the floor.

Ada, who was outside with the cocoa, heard a cry. Without quickening her step, she came in, put down the cocoa and knelt at Lily's side.

Lily opened her eyes, saw Ada's masked face and turned her head away. 'Don't you touch me,' she shouted.

'But I'll have to, ma'am. I can hardly leave you here, can I?' Ada got her hands under Lily's armpits and hoisted her on to the bed, ignoring the complaints and threats.

'I was ringing and ringing. Where were you? What were you doing? I was coming to find you. I thought you'd been taken ill.'

'I didn't hear you, ma'am. I didn't hear the bell at all and I've been listening out, like I always do.'

'You weren't listening. I shall tell my sister as soon as she comes home. Now go away and stop bringing germs into my room.'

'Your cocoa's by the bed, ma'am.'

'Ada?'

'Yes, ma'am.'

'I believe I dropped some scissors. They're on the floor by the bed. Pick them up and give them to me.'

Ada nodded, understanding. 'Yes, ma'am. And I'll listen out for that bell again, like I always do.'

*   *   *

'Go straight upstairs.' Ruth waved the maid away and pushed Allen gently in the small of the back. 'Mother and Father are out visiting.' One end of the second floor was her private territory: a bedroom and a small sitting room furnished to allow her independence with her friends. The sitting room had been made ready, with a fire burning and tea set out on the table. When her coat was off, Ruth lit the Primus stove under the kettle and spooned tea into the pot. 'I keep forgetting to ask you about whatever it was you did the other day.'

'What I did?'

'You said you'd run away. Absconded, that was the word. What from and where to? Or can I guess?'

'There's nothing to guess about.'

'Well, I'm going to try. I'm sure you absconded from the Lily Bird. At a gallop. As to your destination—'

'Stop it, Ruth. You're making up stories.'

Allen's feelings about Henry – she had stopped thinking of him as Mr Speake – were not altogether clear but she regretted what she now thought of as her girlish attempt to confide in Ruth. The evening at his house and then the walk after church on Sunday had developed, in retrospect, into cordial and interesting conversations, beneficial to both. And yes, she had left Lily to dine alone but it had been essential to warn him of the cancelled concert.

'I didn't spend the evening with Lily,' she said. 'That's all it was, my running away. So tell me about Jack.' She looked at the photograph on Ruth's table and saw the letter propped up against it. 'You've got news.'

'It's the undertaker, isn't it? Did you abscond with the und—'

'Stop it. Tell me about Jack. Is that a new letter?'

'This morning.'

'And?'

'He says he's all right, except for the grub. He's sick of tinned stuff and he wants us to live on a farm and grow fruit.'

'Wasn't it pigs last time?'

Ruth joined Allen on the sofa. 'I think it's whatever he's hungry for. If women went to war, Mother says, there'd be decent food. She says it about everything: "If women went to war…" What I said to her this morning was that if women went to war, they'd see what they were doing and come straight home.'

'Do you really believe that? What about nurses?'

'They're not there to kill each other.'

'But they're making it easier for the men by patching them up. I think some women would be perfectly happy to fight.'

'What about you?'

'Not me,' Allen said. 'I'm coming to the idea that fighting isn't useful, whoever does it. Isn't four years enough? There won't be a man left to pick up a gun.'

'But then some things have to be fought for. You fight for what you believe in, don't you?'

'Not with artillery.' She looked down at the rug. 'I don't know what I'd fight for. Edward died with a gun in his hand. Nothing changes, does it?'

After a pause, Ruth said, 'Did he used to write about the things he was looking forward to?'

'He wanted to be by the sea.'

'Did he? Was there a special place?'

'Not that I know of. We never went before the war. It was probably the most peaceful thing he could imagine.'

'Every time I get a letter, I think it's the last.'

'I used to think that, too.'

'And when it *was* the last, was it any different? I mean, did you get a premonition?'

'No. Nothing at all.'

'I shouldn't have asked you that.'

'Of course you should.'

The Primus hissed and the fire crackled. They were alone in the world; alone in the safe, warm, red room. This place, for Allen, had something about it that reminded her of Henry Speake's flat. Why was her only refuge a cold dark bedroom? Why could she not make herself a room that hissed and crackled?

Ruth got up and brought a plate of bread and margarine to the small table by the sofa. 'I'm not sure I like you being friends with Mr Speake, you know. It's inviting bad luck, that's what I think sometimes. Don't you mind? When you think about what he does?'

'He does what we ask him to do.' Allen took a piece of bread and folded it neatly in half so that it cracked open at the seam. 'Would you sooner have to do it yourself?' she said, eating quickly and then sitting back with her arms folded.

'Of course not! It's just that I never thought I'd actually know one.'

'You make him sound a freak, like a baby with two heads.'

'The Misses Wheeler and Martin were talking about you this morning. I heard them.'

'And what did they say?'

'They said that you were seen.'

'By whom, doing what?'

'Out walking, with the undertaker. Bringing the school into disrepute.' The kettle came to the boil. Ruth made the tea and then stood holding the lid of the pot, forgetting to put it in place.

'Did you say anything?'

'They didn't know I was listening.'

'Is it because he's an undertaker? Is that really what's upsetting you?'

'I'm not upset.'

'You don't like it.'

'The others, they're offended because he's *not your sort*. And they think you're being a very bad girl, walking out with a common fellow.'

'I'm not walking out with anybody.'

'You know I'm Mr Speake's very own standard-bearer when it comes to him being a working man. I'd be all for it if you wanted to… you know. It's not who he is; that doesn't matter so long as he's decent. It's what he *does*. I don't like being too close to that sort of thing. I almost feel I might catch it. Don't you understand?'

'But you are close to it! We're all close to it.'

'I know. But it's not my *job*.' While she was talking, Ruth had brought the pot to the table. She put it down and said, 'Are you really friends with him?'

'We don't argue,' Allen said. 'Which is more than I can say for you. Is there anything I do that meets with your approval?'

'Not much. I've got the list here.' She took a piece of paper from her skirt pocket. 'After tea, shall we have another try at Mrs Allday?'

* * *

As soon as Ada heard Allen on the step, she came to the door with her mask hanging round her neck. 'Mrs Bird wants to see you straightaway,' she said, taking Allen's bag and putting it on the hall table. 'It's been an awkward sort of a day, ma'am. Mrs Bird's quite upset.'

'What's she upset about?'

'I'm so sorry, ma'am. She fell out of bed,' Ada said. They were both talking very quietly. 'Says she was coming to find me because I didn't hear her ring. Well, of course I would have, if she had. But she didn't and I know it. I think she was getting out of bed herself and I don't know why she'd do anything so silly but I found her on the floor.'

'Where is she now?'

'Still in bed, ma'am. Won't let me near her.'

'Thank you, Ada. I'm sorry about this.'

'It's all right, ma'am, really it is. But I do listen out for her and I swear she didn't ring when she says she did.'

'I'll deal with this, Ada. Please lay out the supper, if you would. I'll take Mrs Bird through myself.'

As soon as she heard Allen opening the bedroom door, Lily began to shout. 'What's she been telling you? Did she tell you that she refused to answer the bell? Did she tell you that I thought I'd been left alone?'

'Why isn't the gas fire on?'

'Because I told Ada to turn it off!'

'It's very cold in here. She told me that you'd fallen out of bed.' Allen turned on the light. 'Have you hurt yourself?'

'Of course I've hurt myself! I want the doctor.'

'I'll telephone him shortly. Let me help you get up. Then we can sit together and be warm.' This was exactly the tone of voice that Allen used in school, cajoling and kindly.

'I can't walk.'

'Your chair's outside.'

In the time that it took to get Lily dressed, they found that she could stand if she leaned on the bedstead but that unsupported, she simply toppled over; this 'weakness' was an everyday matter and gave Allen no concern. The only apparent injury that Lily had sustained from the fall was a small bump on the head which hurt if pressed but was otherwise inert. The chair was brought in from the corridor and they made

71

their way to the drawing room and the supper laid out on the table by the fire.

'Ada's made you some nice soup,' Allen said.

'I won't eat it.'

'Why on earth not?'

'I've told you, she's dirty and she's carrying disease into this house. I won't eat until you get rid of her.'

'Lily, you really must stop this ridiculous story-making about Ada. She's been with me for years. She's good at her work, she's clean and decent, and I've never had the least reason to criticize her. She does her best for you, she really does.' Still the school voice, but sterner now: ethical and fair.

'I'm not eating until you get rid of her.' The refusal of food had initially been an improvisation but now Allen saw that it was policy. 'I'm not eating anything she might have touched.' Ah! They both saw the loophole. 'Not even if *you* prepare it. I won't eat until she leaves.'

'I can't dismiss a perfectly good servant because you've got it into your head that she's dirty.'

'She's not just dirty. She brings her soldier here—'

'Soldier?'

'—when you're at school. They're going to ransack the house. I've heard them talking.'

'That's nonsense.' A few months before, Allen had come across Ada kissing the woman who delivered the milk. The kiss had been shared with such passion that Allen had chosen to ignore the occasional overnight stay, affecting surprise when she found them together in the kitchen.

'You don't know anything about her,' Lily said. 'You're never here. I'm left alone all day and expected to defend myself. *I want you to get rid of her.*'

'I can't.'

'Then I won't eat.'

All the years of Lilyness had been a preparation for this moment. The battle was joined. 'I have a solution,' Allen said, to test the strength of the front line. 'Why not have a servant of your own, chosen by you and paid for by you?'

'Why should I? I'm a guest in your house.'

'Because I'm not going to ask Ada to leave.'

'Then I shall starve myself to death. I'm going back to my room now. Please put me to bed.'

Later, Allen wrote a list: Lily must be seen by the doctor; Ada must stay; Henry must be visited.

She slept soundly with Edward's pillow held close to her body.

*　　*　　*

Tuesday, 22 October

Sarah noticed it before I did, the way people weren't shaking hands. She'd come in with payment from a woman who was too ill to get to the shop; I'd buried her daughter the week before. 'They're all doing it,' Sarah said. 'Standing there like guards on parade.' There wasn't a street without its sick, she said, and in some streets it was every house. We'd had three call-outs on the Monday and when I came down to the shop on the Tuesday there was already a note through the door and somebody else waiting for me to open up.

It was during one of the call-outs that two events occurred. The first was coming across Herbert Winter as he stood looking into a butcher's window. He'd been working for Woodbridge but the business had closed some months before and that had left Herbert with no employment and a house full of grandchildren, two sons having died recently. I took him on then and there, in the street, and he came back with me to the shop. He wasn't a stranger to Walter, of course, living nearby, and I knew his work must be of good quality or Woodbridge wouldn't have used him for thirty years or more. I put him straight on to the finishing, having first explained that we were to be a little less particular; not with the sealing, of course, there was no point in neglecting that, but certainly with the sanding and polishing and so forth. The important thing, to my mind, was the need to get the bodies buried and out of the way of the living, not to produce a perfect coffin. I doubted that anyone would notice a slip in standards and if they did, I would have an answer ready.

Herbert was always a strange man. He was very red in the cheeks, with yellowing horse-teeth and he had the habit of holding his hand over his mouth when he laughed, the laughter itself being of the braying kind. He liked a joke and found his own, of which he told too many, the funniest of all so that you were always hoping for him to be serious. He had reason enough to keep a straight face with one son lost in the war and another under a train. And I think I always understood that he laughed in a nervous way; he certainly had no sense of humour. At that time we were better served by having him there than not, so we all made the best of the braying and did our best to keep up with the demand while we still had supplies.

It didn't strike me as odd then, how I kept going. You'd think, looking back, that I might have given up. Every day, as the evidence in support of Thomas Wey's claim contrived to bring home the truth to me, I grew more certain that we were approaching the end; and every day I took up the tools of my trade and behaved like an ordinary man. The nights were very difficult. In that second week, when the sick and the dead were mounting up and disturbing the general running of things, I would sit in my chair till three or four in the morning, holding Thomas's letter, with my thoughts running in all directions. I could have played the piano except for the noise and did try with the soft pedal down but it was so unsatisfactory as to be useless.

I sometimes thought of Allen in those early hours. With the concert cancelled there was no reason for us to meet, but on the morning that I bumped into Herbert I'd written her a short note, asking if she might like

74

to visit. It was impertinent, I know, but she was the only person I could conceive of telling about Thomas Wey and although I had no immediate intention of saying anything, there was a comfort in thinking that I might, should the occasion arise. I posted the letter in the box that Thomas had been trying to reach on the day he died.

*　*　*

'Now, look here, you,' Sarah said to Harry. 'You keep away from your mum, just for now. All right?'

'The girls are wanting their tea.'

'You can knock up a bit of bread for them, can't you? Go on, you keep the others away, like a good boy. I'll look after your mum. Go on.' Sarah shut the door and turned back to her niece. 'So there you are. All taken care of.'

There was very little light coming into the room. The window was big enough but the day was dark and the bed, tucked into a corner, was in extra shadow from a looming double wardrobe. Sarah manoeuvred herself into position and lifted the tented sheet away from Jen's bent legs.

'You're almost there,' she said, feeling for the baby. 'Come on now. Do what I say, love. You'll be all right.' Jen started to cough but another contraction caught her breath and she almost choked, torn between the need to expel air and the need to take it in. Sarah kept her hands on Jen's knees and waited, saying, 'That's it, you're all right,' until her breathing had returned to what passed for normal, with an inhalation every second and the air only lifting the upper part of her chest.

There was a noise on the stairs, a child calling for Jen, and then Harry's voice ordering the offender back into the kitchen. Jen looked up at Sarah and closed her eyes. 'Hurts.' She lifted the hand on her chest and let it fall again, twice. 'S'all raw.'

'Is it, love? What, when you're coughing?'

'Mmgh—' The word disappeared into another contraction. This would be Jen's sixth child, the first and second delivered by Sarah and the last three born so fast that if Jen hadn't got to the bed they would have fallen on the floor. She was in the third stage of labour now, but her face was blue and Sarah had no hope for her at all. Sick mothers, dying mothers, dying babies, dead babies; there was never a month without its share. In her experience, birth and death rolled themselves to an end and however you interfered, even if you called the doctor, you'd only be allowed to save the souls that were meant to stay. She'd seen a baby no bigger than the palm of your hand, fed with a dropper and kept warm, who'd grown up to be a mother herself, and a baby – the week before – who'd come out looking like a wrestler and had died in his sleep without a sound.

Jen lay still, too weak to cough or speak. 'Now then, let's see how you're doing,' Sarah said. 'Open your legs and let me have a squint.'

To Sarah, still a virgin at forty-eight, the female organs were a billet for pain. The few times in her early life that she'd been curious and touched herself had been no incentive to marriage and the more births she'd attended the more divided her body had become. She barely noted herself below the waist unless she had a problem with elimination; she lived in her upper half, accompanied by her hands – her two king-pins – and the pleasure of having a mouth and ears. 'Marry?' she'd said in her twenties, when asked why she wasn't courting. 'What could I need that's worth the risk?'

When the baby came, Jen was too weak to finish pushing him out and Sarah had to pull him free. His skin was purple. Sarah cut the cord and cleaned him up, then she wrapped him loosely and put him next to Jen so that their heads were close on the pillow. 'He'll need a bit of looking after,' she said. 'But you have a hold of him for a minute while I sort you out.'

Jen lifted a hand and put it on the baby's body but she kept her head flat on the pillow and her eyes closed. Sarah went to the door and shouted for Harry. He came running with one of his sisters and tried to see through the gap but Sarah blocked his view and told him to find out why the doctor hadn't come and then to get Elsie, his gran. He was back in twenty minutes. The doctor had been out for hours and nobody knew when he'd be back, and Gran was at work but he'd told the man at the door that she should run home fast. Sarah followed him downstairs and boiled up some water for the baby.

The children were all sitting at the table. Harry had made them stay in until there was news.

'She's not that well,' Sarah said, when they asked her. 'And you've got a little brother, but he's not that well either.' Two of the girls started to cry. 'It won't help if she's got to worry about you lot. So you all behave and do what Harry tells you. Your gran'll be here soon and we don't want her worrying, do we? Bring her some tea, Harry, when she gets here. And don't make a racket coming up the stairs.'

By the time Elsie arrived, Jen was delirious.

'I've tried to call Tite out but he's obviously up to his eyes. I've given her quinine,' Sarah said. 'And the baby's taken a few drops of water. Look here.'

She led her sister to the cot where the baby was lying naked: boils were starting to form on the purple skin of his trunk and legs. He kicked out, crying and moving his fists. 'She's given him the 'flu. That's all I can think. And he's got something poisoning his blood. I'm trying to cool him down a bit.'

'Poisoning his blood? What is? What d'you mean?'

'He's got something poisoning his blood, that's what I mean.'

'Why didn't you get me? You should have called me when she started. And I didn't even know she was ill. Why didn't you tell me?'

'I didn't know myself. I've called you now. And you couldn't have done anything anyway.'

Elsie went to the bed. 'Jen? Jen love? You're all right, sweetheart. You've got a lovely little boy, my darling. Look.' Jen turned her head and said something that neither of them could understand. The baby began to cry again. 'He's not going to last his first day, is he? Why have you always got to take over?'

'Keep your voice down, Else. It won't help.'

'You should have called the doctor straightaway.'

'I did. I told you, he's not there.'

'Well, another doctor, then.'

'There aren't any other doctors. You know there aren't.'

Elsie began to cry. 'Get someone else, a real nurse or something. Look at her,' she said. Jen's head was lying back on the pillow. Her face was lavender-blue and her lips, nose and ears purple; her eyes were partly open, the whites just visible under the blue lids. 'She doesn't even know I'm here!'

'Doctor Tite'll come when he can.' Sarah took Elsie by the arm. 'Come on, love. It's horrible this. You don't want to be on your own, do you?'

'No. No, I don't.'

'Then we'll wait here together. I'll tell Harry to get the girls to bed. You think of a name for the boy.'

*   *   *

Sarah's message was quite far down on Lionel Tite's long list of visits. The morning surgery was lengthy; he had turned the least sickly away. Walking to and from his car at the house-calls had allowed for more interruptions from passers-by and often, by the time he got to a patient, there were others in the house developing symptoms and needing his attention. By nature deliberate, and even in his youth he had moved slowly, if the time he had allotted to an activity was insufficient then the activity would be curtailed rather than the time stretched. At one o'clock the list was barely halved.

He had a good lunch of stewed rabbit and strong coffee and then started his afternoon round with a visit to John Drummond, an elderly friend with cancer of the pancreas. The doctor had few friends left, losing some to old age, a few to the war and the rest to his disposition – cynicism and melancholia were high walls to jump. Those who made the attempt were rewarded with his sincere, if unexpressed, affection. John was lying propped up on the sofa, half asleep, with a newspaper open on his chest and a straw boater tipped forward on his head.

'Lionel,' he said. 'Good of you.' He dropped the paper on the floor and straightened his hat. 'Have you lunched?'

'I have. Was it a better night?'

'Not the best.'

'Pain?'

'Yes.'

'Let me give you morphine.'

'No.'

'Then go to bed.'

'Can't, you know that. Bed's too bloody final. Get yourself a drink so I can smell it.'

There was decent whisky on the sideboard. Lionel poured himself a measure and held the glass under John's nose. 'I can't stay long.'

'Still busy?' John waved the glass away.

'Very. Have you eaten anything?'

'Not much.'

'Not much what?'

'A little soup.'

'Did it stay down?'

'No. And don't ask me any more questions. The answer's piss, shit and vomit. Piss and shit and vomit.'

'Who's been in to see you?'

'No one. Amy is coming up soon. Is it only here, do you think? The influenza? There was nothing in the paper.'

'I think it's getting about.'

'Are you worried?'

'Not particularly.' Lionel raised his glass. 'To your liver.' He drank the last mouthful of whisky, looked in his bag and put a small box on the table. 'Tell the nurse to give you these. They should help a little. If you need me I can come after evening surgery.'

John raised his hat. 'Bring a sirloin with a bottle of claret.'

*   *   *

Wednesday, 23 October

'I'll take them all in. They're not to be split up,' Elsie said to Sarah. 'It's bad enough them losing Jen like that without them losing each other. I've got two rooms so Harry and the little ones can sleep in the back and I'll have the two eldest and the baby in with me. We'll all muddle in together – Harry's ever so good with them. And we'll all chip in a bit, won't we, to cover food and clothes and so on, till their dad gets back from France.'

'And who's going to pay the rent?'

'The rent?'

'The rent,' Sarah said, rolling the 'r' and landing heavily on the 't'. 'Who's going to pay for this place while it's lying empty?'

'I hadn't thought of that.'

'I didn't think you had. They'll stop Jen's money—'

'It was a pittance.'

'It paid the rent. You'll have to find out how much it is. The book'll be somewhere. Have you written to Stan yet?'

'I was going to do it today. I thought I'd wait a bit and see how this little one gets on. I didn't want to have to write twice. What do you think I ought to say, then? It's funny, him getting a letter from here with bad news – you'd think it'd be the other way round. Not that I'm saying it should have been but it's funny all the same.'

The small kitchen was warm and smelled of mutton stew. Naked in the cradle and too weak to cry, the baby was making thin, cat-like sounds. Elsie squeezed a clothful of tepid water over him and mopped up the floor with a towel under her foot. 'He likes that,' she said. 'He's a dear little one, our Reggie, aren't you, my sweet? It was Harry's idea,' she said, 'calling him Reginald. And we think it's very smart, don't we? Yes, we do.'

'You shouldn't get too fond of him. He's not got much of a chance.'

'He'll get whatever he needs while he's here. And I'm not going to cry, so don't look so worried. I've done all my crying for now, where nobody else could see me.' Elsie's face was soft and full of folds. 'I've put a note through the doctor's door. When he comes for Jen's certificate, he can look at Reggie and tell me what he thinks.'

The lid of the pan started to lift and rattle. 'When Nora first had the 'flu,' Sarah said, getting up and choosing a spoon to stir with, 'she got me to ask him in. He told her to take some aspirin. I ask you! I had to give him a bob for that. As if I hadn't dosed her up already! And there wasn't anything he could have done for Jen, she was too sick. Believe me, Else, she'd have died whatever we did. It wasn't your fault or my fault or anybody's bloody fault. She died. That's the way of it. And this poor little soul's going to have to make his mind up. He'll stay or he'll go and we're doing all we can for him. You're only storing up more misery if you get too close.' She put the lid back on the pan, licked the spoon and put it on a plate. 'That's very nice.'

'You've not had children,' Elsie said. ' So how can you know? I should have done more for Jen. I should have. You can't know, that's the truth. Not till it's happened to you.'

'We've all lost people we love.'

'But it's not the same as a child, is it?'

'If you say so.'

Near to tears, Elsie started to set the table. Sarah got the plates from the rack and put them by the range, then she put her arms round Elsie and held her closely. 'Watch that fork,' she said, when the moment had passed. 'You'll have me in hospital.'

'They'll be back from school now. Aren't you staying for a bit of stew?'

'I'd better not, I've got calls to make. I'll pop back to see how the baby's getting on.' Sarah looked round the kitchen. 'This place isn't much. What about letting it go altogether? We should have a talk, all of us, and see what's best. Have a word with Henry, when you see him later.'

'Mind you don't catch anything.'

'I could do with the rest.'

* * *

We were eating an early lunch in the workshop and Walter was looking at a copy of The Times *that somebody had left in the office the day before. 'Here,' he said. 'Listen to this. They're saying it's worldwide.'*

'What is?' Herbert asked him, but there was no need. The pestilence was off out to the four corners, like a pall. That was how I saw it then, when Walter was reading: the cloth being pulled up and over us. When he started to tell Herbert some of the other things in the newspaper, I slipped upstairs to sit with Thomas's letter for a few minutes. Walter and Herbert had seen the upsurge in trade. They thought that we were in for a bad lot of influenza and they probably assumed that 'the world' meant the odd outbreak here and there, nothing more. Even if they had thought that the world was coming to an end, I doubt that either man, or Albert for that matter, would have wished to be in any other trade. So long as we were able to work, we had no choice but to carry on.

And then I thought about my sister, Rose. There was no logic to it, but I'd persuaded myself that New Zealand might be a haven, like a ship set far out to sea. That was my wish, pure and simple, and it made no sense. Rose was no safer than a man on a crowded underground train.

If The Times *or any other newspaper had been given permission to print the facts then the Cabinet, I assumed, must believe themselves confident of controlling the outbreak. Otherwise, why risk causing panic? Of* course, if they'd been fully informed, by Thomas or anyone else with his line of reasoning, then quarantine would have been enforced, but it was hardly up to me to write to a minister when the truth had been made available to anyone having the good sense to interpret the news. The peace of mind that this brought me lasted for several days. It was no longer my responsibility to deliver Thomas's letter: the facts were out and those in power could make what they wanted of it.

We were due to leave the shop at one o'clock. I was outside talking to the carriage-master when Elsie came up the street, hand in hand with Harry. They walked with a dull sort of step and it turned out that Jen had died of influenza after giving birth to a boy and that he was as sick as he could be. Sarah was doing her best to keep him going. I told them that I'd get there as soon as I could and Harry shook my hand like a man and thanked me. I wasn't close to Jen but she was Elsie's daughter and my niece, so what with her dying and Samuel and now the baby knocking at death's door, our family was setting out to meet this pestilence with open arms.

There were three deceased that afternoon, two with influenza – although the families had been told different – and a drayman who'd fallen into a cellar and broken his neck. I think the newspapers had been widely read because there was a look we were getting as we passed by – not just hats-off-and-I'm-spared-again but more of a don't-remind-me. And I remember a sparrow that travelled with us for part of the journey; it perched itself right on the corner of the cart, looking at me, its little eyes fixed. We were out for a long time and delayed further on the journey home by a fire at the butcher's shop which jammed the main road with fire engines and people looking on. The smell was attracting crowds; I imagine they were hoping for some free cooked meat when the fire was put out.

Allen had written. She welcomed my invitation, she said, and would Thursday evening suit me? Even though she was coming at my suggestion, it did strike me as odd to be bothering with the social niceties, not that I saw us talking together as a social thing. The time was coming when I

83

would have to tell her about Thomas Wey and all the talking previous to that would be a setting for it. I wrote a short note in return and then Walter and I finished a stock coffin, the last one, for Jen, and started another order that had been measured for. By the time I'd had my supper it was getting late and I should have gone straight out, but I put a record on the gramophone and played along with it for a few minutes, just to settle myself.

It was nearly nine by the time I got to Jen's. The baby was in a shocking state but they were all so concerned with him that Elsie said it was a blessing as it had knocked Jen's death into the second division.

Harry helped me with the carrying in and then he asked me if I'd have him as an apprentice; in ordinary circumstances I'd have been pleased to train up such a good, serious boy and I told him so, but I also told him that we'd have to wait and see, what with the war and everything. He seemed satisfied with that and then I asked him to help me carry Jen down and put her in the coffin. He showed no particular feelings for his mother but there were no other men left in the family, apart from me and his dad in France, so I imagine that he was getting on with his new position. I felt a certain sympathy for him, a boy with sisters.

When the body was ready I called the others and they all came in, Elsie and the girls. Elsie had cut a piece of hair from the baby – you couldn't call it a lock, there was so little of it – and she put it in Jen's hand. Then she stood back and said, 'He never did turn up, the doctor. Sarah sent I don't know how many messages but he never came.'

'He's worked off his feet,' I said. 'Has he not given you a certificate?'

'I haven't seen him.'

He should have come but I wasn't surprised, not after that conversation I'd had with him. He'd looked no better than a standing corpse. Then I asked Elsie what she wanted to do with the coffin and she asked me to cover it, so they all said their goodbyes and I put the lid on in a temporary way so that Dr Tite could always see the body if he needed to.

Of course, the big question for Elsie was what to do with the children.

She insisted that they stay together but that added up to Harry, four girls and the baby, if he lived.

'What about you and Nora, then?' I said to her when the children had been sent up to bed. 'You could sort it out between you.' The way I saw it, the children wouldn't be split up if they lived with family, even if it was in different houses. Otherwise, I could see Elsie taking it all on, in her soft way.

'She's still getting over the 'flu. I won't ask her for a bit. And Harry wants to learn the trade, Henry love. How would that suit? He'd be out of mischief and I wouldn't have to worry about him getting a job. And he'd be set up for the future to look after the little ones.'

'It's not a good idea, not at the moment.' That was all I could think to say. And of course she asked me what I meant, not at the moment. I said we were having a bit of a time and had she forgotten the war, but of course she came back with how much we'd be needing the young to take over as soon as they could. I couldn't argue with that so I had to say the 'flu was causing us a few problems with supplies. Harry and I, well, we could have a proper talk in a few months or so. Anyway, the lad had to stay at school till he was fourteen, which she said would be in January, so that put an end to it.

We spent another half an hour writing a letter to Stan, telling him about Jen and the baby, and then I went home. What did it matter about the children? A note was waiting for me on the mat asking me to call at a house with three dead the following day. All my thoughts were coloured now – the future was very close by, whatever intentions we might have.

*   *   *

'Quite. Dreadful.' Dr Tite stood at the foot of Lily's bed. It was generously provided with pillows and looked particularly soft and yielding. A plate of food – a slice of tart and some stewed apple, left by Allen before she went to work – lay untouched on the bedside table.

Lily had spent the previous day in anticipation of a visit, but the doctor had even denied her the courtesy of a message to explain his absence. Now that he was in the room, she was unable to challenge him and had become peevish instead, accusing Allen of delaying the initial telephone call. 'And I could have broken my neck,' Lily said. 'I could have been lying there all day with my neck broken, do you see? Nobody cares if I live or die in this freezing room.'

'Shall we?' He waved his hand to indicate that she should pull away the bedclothes. Although there had been no deliberate decision to conserve energy, his already slight repertoire of gestures had diminished further with the multiplication of the sick. The more houses he visited, the more slowly he climbed the stairs and the less he was inclined to do when he reached the upper floors. At least Mrs Bird had had the decency to house herself near the front door.

Her embroidery was in the way; he was forced to help her while she piled everything on the other side of the bed, fussing about creases and lost needles. Between them they cleared a space; she revealed her slight body. He pointed at her nightdress and she lifted the skirt slightly, allowing him to inspect her calf and ankle. There was no sign of any injury. With another wave to indicate that the bedclothes could be pulled up again, he took out his prescription pad. 'For the pain,' he said.

'And what about my head?'

'Head?'

'I fell on my head!' She offered her scalp and pointed at the site of the injury. He left her there for a second or two, then he took her head in his hands and bent to examine it more closely. There was nothing to be seen other than pale skin showing through thin, pale hair.

'Hmmm.'

'Well?'

'Out of danger,' he said, releasing her head with a little squeeze. 'Look here. Why aren't you eating?'

The day before, when Lily had been waiting for the doctor and

86

refusing to eat any food brought to the bedroom, she had come to define her situation in what she perceived to be political terms. 'I'm on hunger-strike.'

'*What?*' Dr Tite found an unexpected cache of energy. Had they not been given the vote? He was sure they'd got the vote now…

'I won't swallow food until my demands are met. I will have water,' she said, indicating the covered jugs on her bedside table, 'but only if it's brought to me by my sister.' In all her life, she had never taken a stand. Despite her position, prone in the bed, she pulled back her shoulders and lifted her chin. 'You understand, don't you? I'm in danger. I must be protected.'

'Danger from what?' His mouth hung open; his eyebrows were pulled low.

'Ada!'

'Ada?'

'Germs. And her murdering soldier. She's trying to kill me!'

Dr Tite assumed Ada to be a servant. He never took any notice of servants unless he was actually called upon to treat them and even then he didn't pay attention; they were simply a disease or an accident. He tried to call up an image of the woman who'd let him in. Old? Young? He couldn't have described a single defining feature. 'She seems adequate to me,' he said. 'You're overwrought. I shall prescribe you a different tonic.' His next call was to a second-floor flat. He would have to ask this Ada woman for some coffee to set him up.

'I won't take it!'

'Try this tonic for—'

'*No!*'

'I'll see what I can do.' This was a useful and long-established ploy, said with a pat to the hand and settling to all parties. 'The tonic. Four times a day.'

'Not until she goes.'

'Yes. I'll see what I can do.'

Ada brought him his coffee in the drawing room and he made the effort to examine her face: it was rather handsome for a servant, if a little too knowing about the eyes.

*   *   *

Thursday, 24 October

Lily sewed. Despite turning from side to side, sitting up and lying flat, she had found no position for reading that allowed enough light on to the pages without causing her discomfort and pain in the joints: a book was too heavy to bear and magazines and newspapers were too unwieldy. The words were dull in any case. Lily sewed inaccurately through the day and then, when it was too dark to see, she slept until Allen came in and turned on the light, which allowed for several more hours at the needle, wearing mittens. Although Ada had been banished from Lily's immediate vicinity, she was still in the house, going about her business, creaking and thumping. Allen would inevitably come to her senses – Lily saw herself, skeletally thin but exultant, as Ada was pushed out on to the street – but in the meantime, alert to every noise, Lily was poised for intrusion; had she been a dog, she would have barked.

Her appetite, negligible to start with, had entirely run down, and two small jugs of water, replenished night and morning, were enough to satisfy her thirst. The issue of her sanitary arrangements had been resolved after a great deal of discussion and the outcome, as it stood, was that she would achieve the commode if her legs allowed it and make use of the bedpan if they didn't. With the aid of her stick and a handle – a strong piece of cloth tied to the bedstead – she forced herself to get to the commode whenever possible, the bedpan being unstable on the mattress and having to lie by her after use until Allen came to empty it.

By this third day, a general routine had been established. Before attending to herself, Allen came to Lily and helped her to the commode; silence was maintained. After breakfast, Allen prepared for school and then helped her sister to wash, provided her with a clean nightdress and set out the sewing things, all of this done to the refrain of Allen pleading with Lily to reconsider her decision and Lily refusing to reconsider until Ada was dismissed. Being deprived of the fire had made no difference, neither had the possibility that sheets and nightdresses would eventually run out, Lily's assumption being that Allen would do the laundry.

'And have many more fallen ill? ' Lily said to Allen while her hair was being brushed and plaited.

'I don't know. Was Doctor Tite helpful?'

'I've decided not to see him again.'

'Why on earth not?'

'Because he'll carry the germs in here and drop them all over my bed. I don't know what you're doing but it feels as if you're trying to pull my hair out by the roots.'

'I'm sorry.' It had never occurred to Allen that a doctor could take infection from house to house. Why had she never thought of it? Lily might well have a point. 'But you can't be without a doctor.'

'I don't need a doctor now. You can look after me.'

'Then you must let me bring you food.'

'No.'

'How can I look after you if you won't eat?'

'I will eat.'

'I'm glad to hear it.'

'If you get rid of Ada.'

'I really don't understand' – Allen had said this many times – 'what it is about Ada that upsets you so. This fancy, that she's malignant – why should she be more infectious than I am?' She put the last pin in Lily's hair and stood back.

'I might decide that I don't want to see you either.'

'Then who would look after you?'

'I might choose,' Lily said with dignity, 'not to be cared for at all.'

'Don't be so foolish.'

'It's in your hands, isn't it?'

'I won't take the blame for this. Shall I help you back to bed?'

'I can hardly get there by myself.'

Before Allen left for work, she brought Lily fresh water. 'I shan't bring you anything to eat today. We can't afford to waste more food. Do you have what you need?'

'I do.'

'Are you resolved?'

'I am.'

'I should be home at five o'clock. Ada's here if you need anything urgently.'

'I won't.'

* * *

'It's very philanthropic,' Miss Douglas said to Ruth. 'But just because I teach them doesn't mean I want to wipe their noses. Isn't that right, Miss Cooper? I said, we don't want to wipe their noses.'

Miss Cooper said, 'I think it's very kind of you' – she directed her words at Ruth – 'to be walking into the pit, so to speak.'

'It's no more dangerous than coming into school or being on the street.'

'I always put this over my nose.' Miss Cooper pulled out a heavily camphorated handkerchief. 'I don't think you can do better.' She looked at the empty chairs surrounding them. 'We're so very few today. One does get nervous. I mean, not everyone gets well, do they? It's really rather awful, the way it's creeping up on us.'

Allen sat back in her chair, watching Ruth and Miss Cooper. She was so often excluded from staff room intimacies that she had decided to present the more pensive, insular part of herself as if the choice to be alone was hers; in reality, it was as disagreeable to be here as it was to be at home. Allen made a sudden association between Lily's mad campaign and their father's gangrenous foot; he had resisted any medical intervention, even when their mother had threatened to kill herself. They had gathered round the stinking bed, the three of them – he must have been in intolerable pain – to hear him make the announcement: he was to die on his own terms and anyone who loved him would let him be. If his wife were to commit suicide, he'd said, she would be with him all the sooner and she would appreciate him having both feet, which he would not have if the surgeon took one off.

Lily was seeing herself as she must have seen their father: a hero, standing firm. How long did it take to die from starvation? Was she, Allen, being as obdurate as Lily? Could she, *should* she, employ a new maid and ask Ada to leave? Perhaps Lily was expecting her to cave in – to leave work and become the devoted sister in a house sealed against infection. Was she actually prepared to let Lily die? Would she be judged responsible for her death?

'I'm afraid we're making ourselves more susceptible.' Mr Morris had come into the staff room and positioned himself at the noticeboard. 'Germs thrive in dirt. Miss Carter has asked me to say that we must do the best we can with our own classrooms. The children can help. I shall assemble mops, disinfectant and dusters in the hall for collection after assembly.'

'What about the cleaners?' Allen said. 'We shouldn't be usurping them, surely?'

'Mrs Thompson, there is one cleaner in today. One.' He held up his index finger and raised his eyebrows. 'And she, try as she might, is unlikely to get round the whole school. As I say, dirt is a great harbour for infection. I believe that those of us who are still manning the ship should do all we can to stay afloat. I shall certainly be expecting the children in my class to take responsibility for their circumstances.' Mr

Morris pointed at the noticeboard. 'And Miss Carter has asked me to bring this to your attention. Anyone who is taken ill today should try to anticipate collapse and make their own way to the sickroom. Will you be sure to alert your classes?' He looked at his watch. 'Assembly in five minutes. Thank you.'

When the door was closed Allen said, 'I really can't ask the children to clean.' She expected some support, if only because Mr Morris was generally thought of as a bore, but even Ruth agreed with him.

'My room's quite dirty. I think it's a good idea. We could have it done by the first break.'

'I'll join you,' Miss Cooper said. 'Why not?'

'Why not?' Miss Wheeler looked at Allen and looked away again but not too quickly. 'We must think of the school. It's for the common good.'

The other teachers mumbled and nodded in agreement. They were all standing up now, preparing for assembly. Allen said nothing more. Her solitary protest had not been thought out; cleaning would be a perfectly sensible thing to do.

Mr Fisher, friend to Mr Morris, cleared his throat and spoke, a little too loudly. 'Your class has had an unfortunately high proportion of absentees, Mrs Thompson. May I suggest that it would be to the general behoof of the school were you to insist on the application of disinfectant to all four corners of your room?' The words were obviously unkind, that much Allen was sure of, but by the time she had made sense of the rebuke, Mr Fisher had left the room with the other teachers.

Ruth stayed behind. 'That's what I was trying to tell you,' she said, coming closer but not offering herself for comfort.

'What were you trying to tell me?'

'It's not about the state of your room.'

'I know.'

'There's concern. Some people think you're being rather stupid.'

Allen took a breath to speak and then closed her mouth. The cold-shouldering had been general, not dramatic but wearing, like a chronic ache. Mr Fisher's attack was a new development and she had to give herself time to consider her response. 'I can't talk about it now,' she said. 'But aren't they concerned about your friendship with me? I'm compromising you, surely.'

'Nobody's said that. They know I'm—'

'They know you agree with them. We're late for assembly.' They left the room and walked down the tiled corridor. 'We mustn't oppress each other. Isn't that your credo?'

'I don't want to oppress you.' The sound of the morning hymn, thinly sung, began on the floor below. 'Please come home with me this afternoon. We can talk.'

'I can't. I've got to deal with Lily.'

'Afterwards?'

'I'm going out.' They were downstairs now, outside the assembly hall. 'I'm visiting Mr Speake.' Allen opened the door a crack and slipped in before Ruth could think of anything to say in reply.

*   *   *

After that talk with Harry about him wanting to be an apprentice, I began to think more clearly about Thomas's forecast and realized, with some sense of being a traitor, that he had been at odds with his own theory. In his letter, he'd said that the plague would leave the animals in charge of the earth, but in the papers I'd taken from his room he had described the young – no other – as 'spilling out'. Were the rest of us – the ageing and the infant – therefore not included in his calculations?

Two babies, a boy and a girl, would suffice to start a new world. That two children should survive alone was unlikely and unwelcome, the offspring having to marry each other, but if two could survive then why not two hundred or two thousand? The elderly would die out in their own time but could be put to good use for their last years in the instruction of the young. All that being so, was Thomas stretching the truth to make his

93

point? Of the cases I'd come into contact with, no age had been spared the infection but the greater mortality did seem to settle on those in their twenties and thirties, leaving the rest to recover. Was there some other pestilence following on from this? Or some lasting and terrible consequence that we had yet to encounter?

I delayed going to bed until one or thereabouts, but had yet another difficult night. Either Thomas was right and, for reasons yet unknown to me, we were condemned, or else he was exaggerating and there would be survivors; enough to save the human race. I never entertained the idea that he might have been mistaken altogether.

By six o'clock I was up again. I had several members of one family to measure up for early in the morning and then two funerals before midday, so I prepared what I could and left things ready for Herbert when he came in. I did my best to avoid taking him out; he was inclined to find a joke where none existed and to make a show of himself in public. I found it difficult to understand how Woodbridge had put up with him and could only assume that Herbert had developed the habit since the loss of his sons, as I had no memory of being disturbed by this behaviour when I'd come across him in the past.

One of my usual bearers had fallen sick. When his wife came in to tell me, she offered to take his place and said she could lift as well as any man. I declined. Women do work in the trade now but not bearing – you couldn't allow it. If we were all to die of influenza then the balance of men and women being askew was unimportant, but I'd been telling Walter for years that we'd never get back to normal with women doing the majority of men's jobs. Men were dying out of all proportion. Apart from the war, we had the men who were coming home to die of their injuries and then the men who were dying of everyday illness, heart failure, enteritis, that sort of thing. Murder and suicide never stopped and then, when the epidemic started, some were probably dying with whatever they had in the first place and influenza on top of it, like a grand finale. Women were dying, too, I'm not saying they weren't, but the balance was in their favour.

94

The note that had been put through my door the night before had only given me the address and the name of the sender, John Lorymer, and informed me of three deaths. I was at the house not long after dawn but they were already up: John Lorymer himself, the children and some other people in the family. He was a big man but when he told me that his wife was one of the deceased, I have to say my heart sank; we were going to need the wood for two coffins to accommodate her.

She'd been confined to bed for some time, I knew that. It was a wonder that the legs on the bed hadn't parted ways with the frame. She was so out of the ordinary that I did actually measure her – I'll normally gauge by eye – and while I was doing it, he stood there with his head bowed, holding her hand. I was taken by that, the idea that he might feel love for this woman who could hardly have been able to sit up without a pulley. John and I agreed that she shouldn't be left on the bed for any length of time so I hired three extra men and went back on the Friday morning, delaying some of the other work to deal with it. The three men and Walter brought her downstairs in the belt and web, with me conducting, and we put her in the coffin on the dining-room floor as I had no faith in any support. There was no indication of influenza. The cause of death, according to Dr Tite, was an apoplexy, but the other two deceased, the wife's young sister and brother-in-law, were both heliotrope from ear to ear.

The sister and her husband were set on trestles next to Mrs Lorymer. We'd nearly got them tidy when this child came in, a sallow girl of six or seven with a dirty pinafore and her hair hanging loose. Walter couldn't see her from where he was standing and I should have shooed her out, I suppose, but there was something about her manner that caught me. She said nothing, only stared at me and then at the coffins. Walter saw her then and he was so surprised that he shouted at her, something like, 'What are you doing here!' but she didn't cry or even look at him. Then she pointed at the coffins on the trestles and took this doll from behind her and shoved it towards me. 'Please put her in the bed with Mother,' she said. She'd painted the doll's face a bright sky-blue.

That shut Walter up. I presumed the girl's mother to be Mrs Lorymer's sister – I was right – so I thanked her and put the doll in the coffin, right down where it wouldn't be seen. When we got outside Walter told me what he thought, but I saw no harm in it. If some of the children were to be allowed to live then it would do them no harm to know the truth about what was happening to their parents.

*   *   *

Allen found the mopping of the floor to be quite restful; there was no dirt to speak of and the smell of disinfectant, although she had no faith in its power to parry influenza, was comfortingly pungent. The children who were in cleaned their own desks and then the empty ones nearby, making a competition of it and asking her to choose the winner. Then they wiped the skirtings and the chairs together, companionably like quiet friends. After lunch one child in her class had a gushing nosebleed and was sent home which made the others edgy and intractable. She tried to calm them with a game of question and answer, ending the day with a prayer for the school, the staff and the children, well and unwell.

When she was collecting her coat from the staff room, Ruth asked her if she might change her mind and accept the offer of tea. 'Please come,' she said. 'We can talk about Lily and what you're going to do.'

'I'd rather not. Aren't you going visiting? There must be plenty of children you can help.'

'I'd like to help you.'

'Goodbye, Miss Bell,' Miss Cooper said, her camphorated handkerchief at the ready. 'I do hope I'll see you tomorrow. One simply never knows, does one?'

Before Ruth could answer, Allen said, 'And goodbye to you, Miss Cooper.'

Miss Cooper turned her eyes to Allen without moving her body, like a statue horribly brought to life. 'Of course,' she said. *'You'll* know exactly how many of us are succumbing to this dreadful thing.' The eyes swivelled back. She took her hat and coat from the stand and put them on with some difficulty, not wishing to relinquish her hold on the handkerchief. Ruth offered no assistance. They watched her leave the room.

'Please come,' Ruth said. 'I hate this, us not being friends.'

'I'm not sure you understand what I want from a friend.'

'Then please come and tell me.'

'Not tonight.'

'Because of Lily?'

'And Mr Speake.' Allen looked at Ruth, waiting for judgement.

'Tomorrow?' Ruth said, after a pause.

'Perhaps.'

When Allen got home, Lily was lying in the dark, asleep. The noise of her door being opened woke her instantly. 'Allen? Is that you?'

'It is. Do you want the light on?'

'Of course I do.'

Allen came to the bed. The shawl that Lily was embroidering lay folded at her side, the fringes perfectly spread on the counterpane. The frame, the work basket, the trimmings bowl and the tray of silks were in formation, balanced away from the edge of the bed. Lily was on her back, ordered and in line, staring at the ceiling. Her hair, plaited on top of her head, was pushed forward slightly by the pillow, making her look raffish, like a man at the races with a tilted hat. She brought her right hand into view, skimming it across her body under the bedclothes, barely disturbing them. Her fingers came to rest on the bridge of her nose.

She looked at Allen who said, 'Shall I get you some tea?'

'No.' A pause. 'Thank you.'

'Do you have a headache?'

'No.'

'Shall I get you something for it? Perhaps it would help if you were to eat something.'

'Water, that's all. And empty the commode.'

Allen picked up the jugs, one empty, the other full. 'Are you still intending to pursue this – *campaign*? Even if it makes you ill?'

'I am ill.'

'Iller, then.'

'Ada.'

'No.'

Lily shut her eyes and returned her hand to its place alongside her body. Allen was dismissed.

*   *   *

Walter was looking for something on a low shelf. For a moment he affected not to have heard Allen's question, then he stood up and turned to face her. 'Mr Speake's out the back, Mrs Thompson. Come in, if you choose.' He bent back to the shelf with the precision of a clockwork toy. 'Through there,' he said, lifting his arm behind him and pointing to the workshop.

'Thank you, Mr Stephens. Perhaps I should wait here?'

'Then you'd be waiting rather a long time, I'm afraid. He's busy, you see.' Walter had no intention of straightening up again in order to run messages. She could brazen it out for herself. 'Through there, that's where you'll find him.'

The door was panelled oak. Allen touched the round brass handle and hesitated, unable to decide on the appropriate means of entry. She could knock but the loud grating of a saw coming from inside the workshop would cover the sound and she would be left standing – good entertainment for Walter, who clearly disapproved of her visit. She could wait until there was a break in the sawing but then Henry might start again, just as she knocked, and the sound would go unnoticed and Walter would prevail. There was no option but to open the door and step inside.

Henry had his back to her. A lightbulb hung from the ceiling directly over him, pinpointing his hunched shoulders. He was working on an enormous coffin, shortening a plank of pinky-white wood and talking to himself. The words were indistinguishable but there was the upward lilt of a question, followed by the downward lilt of a reply. He was engrossed in the argument, oblivious to her gaze. Around and behind him in the room were coffins in every stage of production, from the cut shapes to the polished, lined and complete. She was surprised by the coloured bales of cloth and the soft things – shrouds? – folded on the shelves and the mixture of smells, always present on him but here in full potency: sawdust, varnish, paraffin and turpentine. The saw cut through the last shreds of the plank. Henry ran his hand over the edge of the wood and turned, sensing that the door was open.

Allen took a step into the room. 'I'm rather late. I'm so sorry to have disturbed you,' she said, speaking over him as he greeted her. 'Perhaps I should call back tomorrow?'

'No, please. I'll finish this later.' Henry hung the saw on the wall and undid his apron. 'Did Walter show you in?'

'He told me where to find you. I didn't expect it to look quite so like a draper's.'

'Those are the linings and so forth, the domette and calico. That sort of thing.'

'Has it been difficult to get the cloth?'

'Occasionally.' They scrutinized the area of the room occupied by the bales, as if noting the quantity of stock.

Walter knocked and entered simultaneously, opening the door to its fullest extent. 'I'm popping home for a bit of supper,' he said, 'or Vi's going to be round here wanting to know why not. I won't be closing this, if you don't mind. I'll see you later, Henry. In an hour or so. Good evening, Mrs Thompson.' He looked at them both, lifted his chin and walked out.

Until then, Walter had found a way to be impertinent that was almost laughable – like a grudging child in class – but this was an open rebuke. If Walter was in Henry's confidence then he must be aware of the irreproachable nature of his friendship with her. This blatant rudeness, uncorrected by Henry, was even more distressing than Miss Cooper's volley in the staff room. She was awkwardly close to tears.

'We've been working late,' Henry said after a pause. 'He's not been home much.' He put on his jacket. 'Neither have I, come to that.'

At that moment, Allen had the choice: to go home, with every proper excuse, or to stay and defy Walter. She turned to the shelf behind her and picked up a brass nameplate, examining it closely. Henry started to say something about the particulars of coffin furniture and she nodded without listening. He was in a difficult position; this she understood. It would be difficult for him to chastise an employee in his present predicament – how was he to manage without staff? Walter, on the other hand, was behaving shamefully, humiliating her and insulting Henry. She put the nameplate back on the shelf and looked at him with the flat, impassive face she reserved for unruly children.

'Walter seems to disapprove of my being here.'

'He has very particular ideas. He sees himself as a bit of a father to me, that's all. You must take no notice.'

'You allow it, then.' What was she doing? If she persisted, she would prove herself to be Walter's boorish equal. 'I mean, you choose not to correct him.'

'He has a point of view, Mrs Thompson. He says that we should hold to our given stations and not presume on anyone else's. He may be right, but I've told him that I disagree. He'll put across what he believes and I'll do what I think's best.' He smiled at her, displaying teeth below his dark moustache. It was a rare smile and a good one, so that she saw his face differently; he was less dour than she thought, less severe. He seemed to be not in the least bothered by her bluntness. 'I have to stop now, for a bite to eat. Will you join me? I told Margaret you might.'

The choice was made. 'Yes, thank you.' She spoke if she stood in a hotel lobby, not positioned between empty coffins on a floor thick with sawdust. She looked down at her shoes: they were embedded. Her precious stockings were in danger; minute slivers of wood clung to the bottom of her skirt.

He followed her eyeline and said, 'I hope your shoes aren't spoiled. I haven't had time to sweep.'

'It'll brush off, won't it?'

'Of course it will.'

'Then no harm's done.'

When they were at the top of the stairs, she took off her coat without being asked and handed it to him. The room was as she remembered it, except for the table, which had been laid for two.

'I'll just go and wash my hands,' Henry said. 'I won't be a minute. And I'll tell Margaret we'd like to eat, shall I?'

'By all means.' Nothing had been done to smarten things up for her, a fact that was entirely comforting. Artifice – and it would be artifice for Henry to insist that his room be cleaned – was a flimsy foundation for friendship. He was being true to himself and therefore to her and she liked him for it.

She heard him calling to Margaret and then the indistinct but clearly irritable reply. He shouted, 'I'm sure there'll be ample,' and came back into the room.

'The food should be ready in a minute,' he said, sitting in his chair by the small fire.

'I hope my being here hasn't caused Margaret any problems?'

'I should hope not.'

'That coffin you're making – it's unusually large.'

'It's for a woman who died this morning. A big woman.'

'Was it influenza?'

'An apoplexy. And two others in the same house with influenza.'

'Are they all as big?'

'You could put them both in hers and have room to spare for a third. And how's the visiting? Are there many more sick at your school?'

'Many. We're barely getting through the day.'

She thought that Henry was about to reply but he cleared his throat and got up. 'Why don't we sit at the table? If we're lucky we might have some food put in front of us.'

*　　*　　*

Elsie held the dead baby in her arms. 'It must have been in that half-hour,' she said to Sarah. 'Only I had to go home and collect a few clothes and when I got back he was gone and Harry was beside himself, poor boy, thinking it was his fault for not looking every other minute. As if he could have done anything.' She looked down at Reggie's purple face and stroked his cheek. 'Poor little soul, sweet little darling soul.'

'I'll take him off you, then,' Sarah said. 'If you've done your goodbyes. I take it you've registered everything?'

'No. No, I haven't.'

'You should have done it by now, you know that well enough. You've only got a few days left.'

'Well, I haven't. And I know what I'm meant to do but I've got no certificate.'

They could hear Harry shouting at the other children to be quiet. A car drove past outside and tooted twice.

Sarah spread the fingers of her left hand across her face and tapped her nose. 'You'll have to go and wait in the surgery till he sees you. Get a certificate for Jen and we'll put the baby in with her afterwards and no questions asked. Do you want him wearing that?'

'It'd be nice, wouldn't it?' With one movement, Elsie straightened the skirt of the gown and stroked the body. 'Your mum'll be pleased to see you, Reggie sweetheart, that's the truth.'

'He's not baptised.'

'Course he isn't. Sick like that. Why? Are you saying he won't get to see his mum?'

'I'm just saying.'

'As if God's going to say no to this little soul. It was hardly his fault, was it? He'll be there with Jen. I know what God's going to do – he's going to put them back together like they would be now.'

'Give him to me, then, Else, there's a good girl. I'll tidy him up.'

'Do we tell Henry?'

'When we see him. Now come on, I've got someone else to lay out before I can get to my bed.'

*   *   *

Allen and Henry arranged themselves at the table just as a blushing and indignant Margaret arrived with the food: rissoles, potatoes and gravy. She laid it all out without speaking, left the room and came back with a cake and tea things, her gaze always directed to the tabletop. Henry dismissed her without a thank you and pushed the dish of potatoes towards Allen. 'I won't be able to stay up here for long,' he said. 'Walter'll be back soon.'

'Are you working every night?'

'That's how it's turning out.'

He speared potato and rissole neatly on his fork, then used his knife to gather salt from the side of the plate and pat it on the food; Allen cut a slice from the rissole and tried to determine its provenance without lowering her face to the table. It was certainly brown and appeared to have onion in it. She ate; it was adequate.

'How many of your children have succumbed?' Henry said, between mouthfuls.

'I'm not exactly sure. At least half the teachers are away.'

'And deaths?'

'Not so far. Not that I've been told. You'd know before me, surely?'

'Not necessarily. There's more men in the vicinity.'

'This must be the busiest time for you, the winter months…' As if he sold mufflers! How easy it was to sound foolish in conversation with an undertaker. 'I mean, with bronchitis and pneumonia and so on.'

'It is. You're right. But not like this.'

'Do you think this is out of the ordinary?'

'Most certainly. And there are low supplies of wood and not enough men to dig the graves. We'll be wrapping the bodies in shrouds and burying them in pits. We won't be able to leave them, not for weeks on end.' He spooned more potatoes on to his plate and pushed the bowl towards her again. She ignored it.

'You're talking as if we were in the middle of a plague.'

'That's what it is.'

'But most people are getting better. They get ill and then they get better. That's not a plague.'

'Have you read a newspaper?'

'Not this week, no.' The newspapers were piling up, unread, in Lily's room. 'But I know that people are dying, if that's what you're trying to say. Of course they are. But most people are getting better. Really they are.'

While she was talking he was clearing his plate of the last scraps of fritter and pouring milk into the cups. This conversation was disagreeable. She had come hoping for solace of some kind – perhaps the possibility of a sympathetic ear with regard to Lily, even some advice. And the music. She had so enjoyed the music. The teapot handle was on her side of the table. He was saying something; he gestured that she should pour.

'The thing that marks this out' – he was still talking about influenza – 'is that the old are surviving and the young are not. It came to me the other day that we might even be reduced to the kernel of life, a new Adam and Eve. Not as adults, you understand, but as small children. I can certainly say that I've never seen an epidemic like it.' His voice trailed away and he sat back with his hands folded on the table. 'So you see, when you say that this plague is *not* a plague, you're wrong.'

Allen had missed – or misheard? – the main thread of his argument. 'Are you saying that you've read this in a newspaper? That it's a plague?'

'The facts are there. They wouldn't print that word, though, would they? Not unless they wanted to cause panic.'

There was nothing she could say. She was creating gossip and eating bad food in order to be frightened by a man who had nothing to talk about but a looming pestilence. She drank her tea and put the cup back in the saucer. 'I'd better go. You'll be needed downstairs. Thank you for supper.'

'Walter's not here yet. He always calls up.'

'I've got to get back to my sister.'

'If you're sure.'

'Quite sure.'

*　　*　　*

'What's the matter with her, then?' Gladys stroked Ada's hair away from her forehead and leaned in closer. 'You've got a hair there on your top lip, a black one. It's a proper moustache.'

'Shove off. You can't see a hair in this light – you're making it up. She's crack-brained. Been like that since she got here only now it's worse.'

'So she won't have you anywhere near her?'

'Not likely. If she had her way I'd be on the street.'

'And Mrs Thompson, what does she say?'

'She doesn't say much but I can see what she's thinking. She'd have Mrs Bird out before she'd have me out.' Ada turned over and snuggled her nose into the space under Gladys's chin. Her skin smelled milky and comforting. 'I could always come and live with you.'

'My mum'd love that.'

'She might.'

'She wouldn't. Anyway, you wouldn't want to leave, would you? You're in a bloody palace.' The first time that Gladys had seen Ada's room she had refused to enter, thinking that Ada must be trespassing. 'Does Her Nibs know you live in here?'

'How would I know?'

'She might have said something. Tried to get Mrs T to push you back to the top floor.'

'If she did, I never heard her.'

They lay in silence and then fell asleep until they were disturbed by the thump and rattle of the water pipes.

'She's late back. You staying?' Ada said.

'I could. Are you sure it's all right? With her, I mean?'

'Seems to be. I'll have to be up at six.'

'You're always up at six.'

'You tired?'

'Not really.'

'Is it putting you off?'

'What?'

'The moustache?'

'What d'you think?'

'Give us a kiss, then.'

* * *

Allen heard their voices as she tiptoed to her room from the lavatory; she paused momentarily to listen. The milkwoman, briefly seen, had struck her as a friendly, endearing sort, but that she should be physically attractive to Ada – indeed, physically attractive to anyone – was a surprise. Who was to say what it might be in one person that excited lust in another? Pinned there in the dark, Allen felt that her whole body was swelling to meet them; the surface of her skin was so alert that she merely had to touch her own forearm to feel aroused. Impossibly, she wanted to find Edward in her room, sitting up in bed, bare-chested, his signal to her. She waited a little while longer, holding her hand to her breast, then she went to bed and lay awake until Ada knocked on the door at half past six.

*　*　*

Friday, 25 October

I found it more difficult than I'd imagined, trying to get even a small part of the truth across to Allen. It all started badly with Walter buggering about. I told him what I thought: that he'd gone out of his way to make her feel like a German with a bomb but he had nothing to say to that except to ask if I'd taken her upstairs. We didn't speak for a while but you can't work in that sort of atmosphere so in the end we found a way of getting on, although he took every opportunity he could to mention my father and how he might do this or that. It was all very unsatisfactory. I knew that I'd have to write to Allen and arrange another time, making sure that Walter wasn't anywhere near.

When we got back from the Lorymers on the Friday morning, I went straight round to Thomas Wey's lodgings. I was still preoccupied with the idea that he might just have been exaggerating to demonstrate his theory. And the conversation with Allen – not that it was a conversation, with her arguing the opposite – was all I needed to tip me into going. I could think of no acceptable reason to be bothering Mrs White and had tossed and turned the previous night trying to think of some story or other that would account for me turning up. So far as leaving the shop was concerned, I told the men that I was visiting Vasey, the carriage-master, with a query about the availability of horses. We'd soon need a further supply for the extra funerals and I could easily call in on Mrs White's house as I passed. I could have said that I was going out to get a paper but the visit seemed to warrant a more substantial excuse.

Mrs White answered the door herself as the maid had influenza, and I was more or less told that the girl had come down with it deliberately to get out of the dusting. In the end, having come up with no decent strategy, I made enough conversation to complete the niceties and then asked straight out: 'Those books by Thomas Wey's bed. Are they still here?' She'd thought to sell them, that was what she said, but in the end, after looking through them and finding them to be full of difficulty, she'd given them to a ragman in exchange for a small pair of chintz curtains for the back bedroom.

'And I don't suppose you remember what any of them were called?' I said, but of course she didn't, not a word from a single title. And she didn't show any surprise that I should be asking either. Nothing out of the ordinary held significance for her unless it bore relation to her domestic life, like the business of the sick maid. Had I told her that the maid was an insignificant speck and that we were all to be brought down, her first thought would have been to fear for her supplies of potted fish.

I was going down the steps when she called me back. A journal had arrived that morning, addressed to Dr Wey, and she'd been unsure about what to do with it. Perhaps I wouldn't mind cancelling the subscription? She didn't want anybody banging on her door, asking for money, and as I'd already dealt with Dr Wey's papers… Mrs White had taken the journal from its envelope. I looked at it briefly without seeing its title.

'Certainly I'll do that for you,' I said, but I had no intention of cancelling anything. I would write to the editors that evening and inform them that I, Thomas Wey, had changed my address. And I told her that anything else that might come through the door, she was welcome to bring it down the road to me. We parted the best of friends. I wonder now if she could read at all. It would certainly account for her reluctance to deal with anything of a printed nature.

I put the journal under my coat, seeing the title on the cover as I did so: the Friends' Quarterly Examiner. I went back to the shop with my hand held securely on it. There would be no opportunity for me to read alone *that day but I did manage a few minutes upstairs on some pretext and used it to look briefly at the contents. Was Thomas a Quaker? My first feeling was one of disappointment. How could that be of any use? Of course, as I realized later when I'd made sense of my thoughts, if he was a Quaker then I'd been given a useful insight into the man's way of thinking.*

I hid the journal in my bed and read it that night, every single word of it. Nothing stuck out – except a poem – although I must say that I approved of a great many things that were said, such as war being a 'monstrous and inhuman evil'. Of course, if he had been a pacifist, the threat of pestilence might have been his way of trying to frighten the politicians into a truce, but then why wait all these years? These doubts came to me and went away as quickly. If I needed any confirmation of what I saw daily with my own eyes I had only to look at the newspapers: the whole world was afflicted. That was when I began to think again about sending the letter. There was nothing being said about closing the ports or stopping the soldiers. There was nothing being said about a calamity being upon us. Was it too late? Why was the government not taking a hand to it?

The poem affected me greatly.

> *I am in deep woods,*
> *Between the two twilights.*
> *Whatever I am and may be,*
> *Write it down to the Light in me;*
> *I am I, and it is my deed;*
> *For I know that the paths are dark*
> *Between the two twilights.*

Those were the first few lines. I read them over and over and then got up – it was three in the morning or thereabouts – to find some melody I could put to it on the piano. There were very few rhymes but the rhythmic pattern was clear enough; it was a waltz. The tune wrote itself quite quickly. I was falling asleep on the stool by this point but it was too late to go back to bed so I put it all down on manuscript paper, hid the page inside some sheet music and napped in the chair until Margaret laid the table for breakfast. She asked me if I'd enjoyed playing the piano, which meant I'd woken her up.

✳   ✳   ✳

'I haven't got over it at all,' Nora said. She was dressed but not carefully, lying on the bed with her blouse undone at the neck and a stain on her skirt. Her voice, never pleasing, was caught between two notes; she scratched away at them both without ever coming to rest. She turned away from Sarah. 'Mind you, it's only just over a week and I was ever so poorly. I must have caught it off Sam. I'm sure I did… you don't know till you've had it. You can't imagine. You just…' She lifted her hands, held them in the air and then dropped them. 'Pfoof. Like that.' She stopped talking for a few seconds, remembering the moment of collapse. 'And now I'm all washed out. If I walk about I go light in the head and I get so *hot* and I've been wanting to give Elsie a hand but I can't, I really can't.' She closed her eyes and blew the air out of her mouth, flapping her lips and making a soft blubbery noise.

Sarah sat silently through the recital, her back straight on the hard chair. When she was sure that Nora had finished, she said, 'Do you want anything doing while I'm here?'

'Well… I wouldn't say no if you offered to take a bit of washing, only I've used up the sheets. Would that be an awful bother? Only I know what it's like, a bit of extra washing on top of what you've got already and I expect you're—'

'Just tell me where they are.'

'In the kitchen, on the big chair.' The words triggered a paroxysm of coughing and for several minutes she fought for breath, retching into a handkerchief and hitting at her thigh with her free hand.

Sarah tied up the washing and put it by the door, then she sat down again and waited, looking away. When Nora was quiet, she said, 'Henry thinks it'll be best all round if you and Elsie look after the children, two girls each and Harry in between. Keep them together till Stan gets back. Not that he will, necessarily.'

'Don't say that. You mustn't say that. I'm surprised at you, Sarah.'

'It's the truth.'

'It's bad luck, that's what it is. I can't believe you're saying such a terrible thing.' She coughed. 'You'll start me off again.'

'Will you take them in?'

'I don't know. I'm not sure if I'll be up to it. It might take me weeks before I'm over this.'

'Nobody's asking you to do it this very minute.'

'And why can't Elsie manage on her own? Harry's practically a man now. I'm sure they won't need anyone else interfering. And I couldn't possibly look after a baby.'

'The baby died. Last night.'

'It didn't. Did it? What a shame.' She tutted and pulled herself up a little on the bed. 'Well, you could say it's one less to worry about, that's the truth.'

'So is that your last word? You won't be helping out?'

'What about you? Why can't you do it?'

'I'm working all hours.'

'And I've lost my Samuel, haven't I? And I'm ill.' Nora's voice was fading; there was sweat on her face. 'Get me some water, won't you? I can't talk any more.'

Sarah got up and put on her coat. 'You'll find a way, I'm sure.'

*   *   *

'We've been given the order to close,' Miss Carter said, rattling the papers in her hand so loudly that they sounded like flags caught in a wind. The few remaining teachers stood in her office, each in a pool of space. 'This is inevitable news, an awful thing to have to do, but so many of us are ill that we simply can't continue.' She rattled the papers again and stopped.

'Thank goodness,' one of the teachers said. Then they all joined in with 'at last' and 'there aren't enough of us' and 'we couldn't have gone on'. The big window was wide open and the room was as cold as the street. Allen had placed herself at the back. She put her hands in her pockets and drew her elbows in.

'I shall inform the parents by letter that we'll be closed from tomorrow until the illness abates… the children will be told at assembly this morning. I should also tell you that Miss Barron…' Miss Carter covered her mouth with her hand and stood blinking as tears filled her eyes. Some of the teachers began to cry. One of the men coughed loudly. '… Miss *Barron* and Mrs Peal have both passed away, as have Liza Turner and Bessie Johnson. The school will be sending flowers and letters of condolence… but you may wish to… commiserate with their families individually. Their addresses are on the noticeboard.' Some of this was said so falteringly that she had to repeat it. Without realizing it, the teachers moved closer together; some of the women held each other by the arm. 'And I beg you all to think twice before conversing with any of the children, or each other, at too intimate a distance. We none of us know who might harbour this disease. Please try to reassure the children as best you can and give out whatever work you think they should be doing in the interim. I shall write to you all as soon as I have any information about re-opening.' She wiped her eyes and nodded her head once to signal that she'd finished. As they left the room she remembered to say, 'You'll find a box of surgical masks in the corridor. Please take care of yourselves…'

Allen's classroom was empty; the children who were at school would be congregating in the hall for assembly, an arm's width apart. Bessie's small chair was tucked in under the desk and Allen pulled it free and sat down, looking ahead of her at the empty blackboard with the mask in her hand. The children would need to pray for Bessie and Liza. Perhaps they could sing a hymn in class before they started their lessons. Allen went to the blackboard and wrote: *'For two dear teachers, Miss Barron and Mrs Peal, and two beloved children, Bessie Johnson and Liza Turner. We mourn their passing. "Safely, safely, gather'd in".'*

'Are you all right?'

Allen jumped and dropped the chalk.

'Sorry.' It was Ruth. 'I didn't mean to startle you. I can't think what to say to them. Have you thought?'

Allen picked up the chalk and wiped her fingers on the duster. 'No. I don't suppose I have.'

'We don't want to frighten them.'

'They're frightened anyway.'

'I'd like to talk to you. Shall we go somewhere after school?'

'Where?'

'I don't know. I don't think I want to go home, though, not straight-away.'

'We should be in assembly.' Allen pushed Bessie's chair under the desk. 'Come on. We'll talk later.'

By the time the last bell was rung, three teachers and four children, in various stages of debility, had been collected or taken home. As those remaining met in the hall to close the day, Miss Carter repeated her earlier warnings about intimacy, added some advice about cleanliness and the covering of the nose and mouth, and reminded them that any work they'd been set to do at home had to be properly completed. 'There will be a brighter tomorrow,' she said. 'Do let us all pray for that.'

Ruth and Allen stood by the gates with some of the other teachers and said goodbye to the children. A girl approached Ruth with a card in her hand.

113

'I've been making this for you,' she said, holding it out, 'and Miss Wheeler said I could finish it today. Is it all right for you to have it if I've touched it?' Ruth took the card. It was decorated with dried violets and a white ribbon sewn under the words 'Kind Thoughts': Inside, the girl had written 'Hoping You Stay Well, love Dora'. Without thinking, Ruth leaned forward and hugged her; some of the other teachers shouted at them to separate. Ruth and Dora tightened their grip briefly and pulled apart.

'Thank you,' Ruth said. 'I'm very touched.' Before Dora could say anything in reply, her mother appeared, pulled her round, checked her forehead for fever and bustled her out to the street.

'She must be very fond of you,' Allen said.

Ruth nodded. The last children were being taken away; the playground was empty.

* * *

On the Friday evening I was called to a house in a street I rarely visited, it being right on the edge of my normal area. The woman who answered the door was dressed in quite ordinary clothes; in fact, there was nothing unusual about her at all, not even in her manner, which was pleasant and peaceful and gave no suggestion of having just lost a husband. We went to the bedroom where the man lay and then, to my complete confusion, she began a conversation with the body while she dealt with me. It gave me the jumps.

'He wants elm,' she said. 'All right dear?' Like that, to me and then to him: 'Elm with a violet lining and not to worry about a shroud? Are you sure, dear? No, that's right.' And this to me: 'He wants his brown suit and his best hat. And make sure to give him violet lining.'

I asked her if she truly believed that he could hear her – although it's most unusual for me to ask anything so personal – and she said that of course he could, and that she could hear him, too. She must have seen something in my face because she offered me a cup of tea and we had a chat, with me not giving anything anyway – so far as I was aware – and then she said, 'There's someone you want me to get through to, isn't that right, Mr Speake?'

I was so taken aback that I said yes, there was someone. The next thing I knew she was drawing the curtains shut and sitting in front of me with her eyes closed and her hands folded in her lap. I was reluctant to speak in case I spoiled things but she opened her eyes just as I was about to ask her what was happening. 'I can't get a thing,' she said. 'Not from the one you want to talk to. Has he recently passed over?' I said yes, that it was a matter of days and she said, 'No wonder, then. You have to give them time.'

And that was all there was to it. I suppose I could have asked her if she'd have a word with my mother – I couldn't imagine that my father would have any dealings with this kind of thing – but I'd been hoping for Thomas Wey and that was all I could think of. The other thing I should have asked, of course, was whether she had any prophecy to make about the pestilence. Looking back on it, I missed an opportunity. But then, if I'd been really keen I would have asked her more and I didn't. I think I might have wished her to see me as level-headed. And what did Thomas need time for? I had no history for him but if he were a Quaker you could at least assume that he believed in good behaviour. Wouldn't that hurry things along?

*   *   *

Allen and Ruth walked for several miles in the gathering twilight, self-consciously wearing their masks. Most of the teachers had tried to make the final moments at school as matter-of-fact as possible, treating it as they might an end of term, but there had never been an ending like it – without a handclasp or an embrace – and for the first part of the walk they could speak of nothing but the awful strangeness of the day, that and the deaths.

The evidence was more shocking in unfamiliar territory. When they left the streets that they knew, Allen fell silent. Was this acceleration in the number of victims a sudden thing or had she been so inattentive that she'd missed the true significance of the signs, believing them to be symptomatic of a typical bout of influenza? Could she have missed all these pillow-cases and shirts flapping out of windows? The locked, deserted shops, each with its hand-written notice? What sense of alarm would lead you to announce your illness to the street? Henry had been agitated and she had dismissed him. And now the school was closed!

'You do wonder how much a child understands,' Ruth said. 'They looked for all the world like orphans this afternoon, lined up with no hope. I didn't catch anyone behaving badly all day.' The masks were too thin to mute their voices but the effect was to make them shout a little.

'They've understood as much as any of us, I expect. I was talking to Mr Speake last night…' Allen waited for a moment, expecting Ruth to butt in. 'He seems to think we're on the brink of some kind of plague.'

'Does he?'

'He does. I can't tell you any more, because I wasn't really listening, but I certainly heard him say that word. He said it several times.'

'Why weren't you listening? Did he mean *plague*?'

Allen interrupted her. 'Look at that. Just look.'

They stopped in front of a greengrocer's window. There was very little on display, but what there was had begun to shrivel and discolour; a cat lay asleep by the till, which was empty and had been left open to deter burglars. Facing them, at the front of the window, was a box with the message 'Closed: All Sick!' pinned to it on a roughly torn piece of paper.

Ruth said, 'Mr Speake couldn't have meant the real plague – I mean, nobody's had the symptoms, have they? Not boils or whatever it was?'

'I don't suppose he did. I think he meant some dreadful illness.' She moved away from the window. 'And I think I should get home.'

'Is Lily behaving?'

'No. She won't eat.'

'She won't eat?'

'Not a thing.'

'Is she ill? I mean, more ill than she was?'

'No. She's more mad than she was, that's all.'

'What are you going to do?'

'I don't know. I can't do anything.'

'But she'll die!'

Allen put her arm through Ruth's. The intimacy of the touch was soothing and Ruth made no attempt to pull away. 'I doubt it very much. When she starts to feel really queer, she'll stop. It's a ploy to make me sack Ada in case she brings in the 'flu – you know, all that business with the mask.'

'But you wouldn't, would you?'

'Of course I wouldn't.'

'It's ridiculous. I mean, for heaven's sake!'

'I've told you, she'll stop soon.'

A man appeared at the junction ahead. He held a woman in his outstretched arms; she was unconscious, lying loosely across him. There was traffic, but he ignored it and stepped out into the road without looking, narrowly missing several bicycles and a motor-car that had to swerve to avoid them. His objective was a house on the opposite side of the road, a terraced house with a flight of steps leading to the front door. As he reached the bottom of the steps, the door opened and a group of children, none older than eleven, came rushing out to meet him. He shouted at them to make way and carried the woman into the house, slamming the door with his foot.

'We could knock,' Ruth said when everything was quiet. 'Ask him if he needs anything.'

'I don't—'

The door opened again and the man came down the steps with three of the smaller children at his heels. He swore at them and ran off; the children followed him, half running, clinging to each other and calling out. When Allen and Ruth saw that the children had been left to make their own way – to follow him or to go home – they crossed the road and walked behind them, instinctively keeping guard. The man went into a chemist's shop; by the time they'd caught up he was on the pavement again, with a bottle held tightly to his chest. The oldest child held out her hand for him to take but he barely broke step, calling over his shoulder for them to follow.

'We've been watching them for you,' Ruth shouted, running with them. 'Can we help you?'

The children clambered up the steps; the man was already in the house.

'Please?' Ruth was at the railing.

Two of the children disappeared into the dark hallway. The youngest stayed on the top step and looked back at Allen and Ruth, considering them; her expression was apathetic, as if she'd given up all hope of ever attaching herself to her father. In the instant that they stepped forward, she put her thumb in her mouth and went inside, closing the door behind her.

*　　*　　*

Lionel Tite was looking for a doctor to share his house calls. Letters had been dispatched during the week but the few men who had bothered to reply had been dismissive, even rude – did he really think that the epidemic was confined to his part of London? In the end, to save time, he'd resorted to the telephone but had been thwarted constantly by the apparent dearth of operators at the exchange and the wretched people who answered when he did get through, not one of whom was able to grasp the urgency of his need. There were no doctors to spare, that was the sum of it.

A cupful of coffee was left in the pot. He drank it black with several cubes of sugar, spoke briefly to his wife and let himself in to the surgery through the conservatory door. The nurse was waiting with his list. Most of the patients had been through the prostrate phase of influenza and had come looking for relief from coughs and debility. Lionel dealt with them all quickly – he knew it to be inevitable that he would eventually misinterpret symptoms – and went out to his car.

The morning progress through the calls was exhausting but a system had emerged: while waiting for admittance he would take his pad from his pocket, fill out the prescription and sign it; once in the house he would position himself in the sickroom doorway, look briefly at the bed, tear off the prescription and give a condensed address about the value of whisky and open windows and the idiocy of getting up too soon. He saw no point in investigating further – the survivors would pull through and the doomed would not.

His last call was to John Drummond. The maid showed Lionel into the drawing room but neglected to tell him that John was no longer on the sofa. There was no bedding folded in preparation, no tray of medicine. Although he could see that John was no longer there, he continued to examine the sofa, like a half-wit.

'Gramp's in bed, Uncle Lionel.' Amy, John's granddaughter, had come into the room without noise and was now standing behind him with her hand on his sleeve; she was not his niece but he had been 'uncle' to her from her second year. 'Will you come up?'

'How is he?'

'Very low.'

'When?'

'This morning. He said he was bored with the sofa and preferred to stay in bed.'

'Is he conscious?'

'Utterly.' They were on the landing, a few feet from his door. Amy whispered, 'I'm being jolly. That's what he wants.'

Lionel nodded. He had no children and Amy, in her brusque, effective way, contained all the qualities he knew he would have funnelled into his descendants. She had been encouraged to think for herself and was intending to train as a doctor. 'We'll be jolly,' he said.

Although the room was south-facing, a large cedar obscured much of the light and gave what there was a greenish watery tinge, an effect made more marked by the predominantly green wallpaper. John Drummond lay awake, his head turned to the door in anticipation of his visitor.

'Good of you to come,' he said, his voice more than ever like a badly blown flute. 'I was going to come down. I'm only here because Amy is a bully.'

For the last few months, John had been carried to the sofa every morning and returned to bed for the night; he knew that Lionel understood the gravity of the change and Lionel, in turn, knew that he must not allude to it. 'Why don't you get rid of that tree?' he said, pulling a chair up to the bed without lifting it an inch from the carpet. 'The view's not so bad. Let a bit of light in. I told you not to put it so close to the house.'

'I like it.'

'Been better off with wisteria.'

'Wisteria's for women.'

A nurse knocked on the open door and came in far enough to speak to Amy who listened closely and shook her head. As she steered the nurse out of the room she said, 'Will you drink something, Uncle Lionel? Or have something to eat?'

'Whisky, thank you,' he said.

'Make it two.' John raised his forearm and put out a finger. 'One for me.' When Amy had left the room Lionel drew back the bedclothes and revealed John's distended abdomen. 'May I?' he said.

'You may. But I'm not the slightest bit interested so keep your findings to yourself.'

Lionel made his assessment quickly. 'Pain?' he said.

'Yes.'

'Pills not working?'

'No.'

'Morphine?'

'Not yet.'

'I'll give you something else. Anything you want to report?'

'I'm off to the races. And taking Nurse.'

Every one of John's children had been born in this bed, into Lionel's grasp. He had been present in this room at the passing of John's parents and the passing of John's wife, and in between and in every circumstance he had seen people close to death, but not one of them, until now, had been his friend. He replaced the bedclothes and said, 'We'll all go to the bloody races.'

Amy came in with a tray, knocking first and waiting for Lionel to answer. She poured the whisky, served Lionel and put her grandfather's glass on the bedside table. 'If you're very good and get better soon you can have the whole bottle.'

'Darling girl.' John made no move to touch it. 'If this doesn't cap the lot, me lying here when you've come all this way for a few days.'

'We'll have you downstairs by tomorrow.' Amy sat on the window seat. 'When you've had a rest. And I'll play the piano for you and you'll wish you were back up here.'

'How are the sick?' John turned his head to Lionel and then, realizing the incongruity of his question, he laughed. They laughed with him and he said it again, adding, 'the paying sick, that is.'

'Proliferating. Thank God I've retired.' This was Lionel's joke, his retirement having coincided with the beginning of the war and therefore being suspended for the duration of it. 'I'm telling them all to drink whisky and stay in bed till they feel better.'

'Let's not talk about influenza. It's too dreary,' Amy said. She found some other topics, anything that would entertain, until her grandfather eventually went to sleep. They sat with him for several minutes more, watching the bed and listening, then Lionel got up and indicated that they should leave.

When they were out of earshot, Amy said, 'The nurse tells me that Cook and a maid have collapsed. Should you see them?'

'Nothing I can do. Get someone to give them aspirin and open the windows. Don't go near them, that's my best advice.'

'I won't go home, not now. Will you be back soon?'

'Tomorrow. Telephone if you need to. Good girl.'

* * *

Saturday, 26 October

After breakfast, Allen sat on her bed and wrote to Henry Speake, telling him that the school was now shut. If he intended to play for the Sunday morning service, assuming that it was still to be held, perhaps it would be possible for them to meet afterwards to discuss the epidemic? When the letter was finished she sat with it in her lap and read it through several times, playing with the corner until a crease developed in the paper. Her friendship – was it a friendship? – with this man had caused her to be ostracized. The present crisis in the school had overshadowed her behaviour but there would inevitably come a point where she had to defend herself. And that dinner had been most unfortunate. She was no longer sure that she even liked him that well; even so, she was apparently intent on continuing their conversation...

The conflicting thoughts piled up, one upon the other, until her judgement was obscured and the corner of the letter was almost hanging off. To be true to oneself, was that not the imperative? Another meeting would determine whether the friendship was important to her. She took a fresh piece of paper, wrote the letter out again and prepared it for the post. If Walter had triumphed then she might not get a reply in any case.

The plan for the day was to go out with Ruth. Since their walk the day before, she was more determined than ever to visit ailing families and

Allen had eventually yielded. She had no desire to stay in the house and be encumbered with Lily. The visits were to continue until the epidemic was over – 'or until we catch it,' as Ruth had said, 'which would be most unfair if we're doing good works.'

Lily's ablutions had been dealt with before breakfast. She was even more wild-eyed and determined than the day before, demanding that Allen obtain a fresh batch of plain napkins to embroider and a selection of silks to replenish the basket. If Allen had been recently introduced to her, without being told anything of her history or her present state, she would have assumed her to be exhilarated, almost euphoric about some recent circumstance. Despite – or because of? – her fast, Lily was holding vigorously to her aim and suffering no apparent ill-health, allowing Allen to stand against her to the finish.

She went downstairs to tell Ada that she wouldn't be home for lunch.

'I was just coming up, ma'am. To see if you needed anything.'

'I'm waiting for Miss Bell. I wanted to tell you that I won't be home till four or so.' There was a tray on the kitchen table, set with a cup and saucer and an enamel jug topped with a folded cloth. The kitchen smelled of camphor and menthol. 'That's not for Mrs Bird, is it?' Allen said. 'Because she won't want—'

'I know, ma'am. I know.' They looked at the tray. 'It's for me, ma'am. If that's all right.' 'Of course it is. Are you not feeling well?' It was a ridiculous question; she was obviously flourishing.

'Yes, I am. I mean, I'm feeling very well, ma'am. It's just that I've got a lot of mending to do and I thought I'd take up a cup of tea.' She remembered the jug. 'And I've got a bit of catarrh. I thought I'd have an inhalation. That's what the jug's for.'

The lie was transparent; had it been an excuse about ink spilt on a copybook or one child accusing another to save her own skin then Allen would have said, *Come on now, tell the truth. You'll feel all the better for it.* Instead she said, 'I'll be home by four o'clock. Perhaps you'll be good enough to keep an ear open for Mrs Bird.'

'Yes, ma'am. And if she calls for you, ma'am?'

'I'm afraid she'll have to wait. You're not ill, Ada, are you sure of that?'

'I'm sure, ma'am. Like I said, it's catarrh, that's all.'

Ruth came shortly after Allen had left the kitchen. They hardly spoke in the hall; keeping significant conversation away from Lily's room had become the habit now. Allen merely put on her mask and pointed at the front door. Halfway down the street, still thinking about Ada and the jug, she posted the letter to Henry. If Ada was well… Ah! Taking Ruth by the arm, she turned back to the house. 'It's Gladys,' she said. 'I think Gladys has influenza.'

'Who's Gladys?'

'Ada's… friend.'

'And you think she's in your house? With influenza?'

'I don't know. She might be.'

They went to the kitchen first but Ada had left, taking the tray. Her apron was hanging over the back of the small armchair, not folded but carelessly thrown.

'I'm going upstairs,' Allen said, taking off her coat and hat and lowering her mask. 'This is wrong.'

'You can't just accuse her, she might have been telling the truth. You don't know, do you?'

'She wasn't.'

'This Gladys might have a cold. That might be all it is.'

'And what do I do if she's ill? I mean really ill?' Allen closed the door to muffle their voices.

'What do you mean, what do you *do*?' Ruth realized that her mask was still on; she pulled it down to her chin. 'God, I hate this thing.'

'She can't stay here, can she?'

'Why not?'

'Because—'

'You're not thinking of putting her out?'

'I'd never do that, you know I'd never do that. But I could send her home in a cab. We could wrap her up and send her home.'

'And you could let her stay and Ada could nurse her.'

'That's impossible. I'm going upstairs. I've got to find out.'

'I'll come with you. I'll wait on the landing.' Ruth had started to climb the stairs to the second floor when she saw that Allen was waiting below. 'Aren't you coming up?' she whispered.

'Ada sleeps here.' Allen pointed behind her.

'What! Why?'

'Shh! The attic was damp.' The excuse was lame. 'Not now,' she said, before Ruth could ask any more. With a finger raised to indicate that she was about to eavesdrop, she leaned against the door; a small noise, possibly the opening or closing of a window, was followed by a voice – and then another! She lifted her hand to knock, faltered and lowered it again.

To find Gladys in the room at all was going to be embarrassing enough; to find her ill in Ada's bed would be absolutely appalling. And what if she really did have influenza? Visiting the sick was one thing; to discover the sick in one's own house was beyond anything that she'd had to deal with since Edward's death. Lily's idiocy hardly compared. But Lily would crow, oh, how she would crow!

'Can you hear anything?'

Before Allen could answer, Ada opened the door. She stood back with her head lowered, allowing Allen a proper view of the room, and said, 'I'm sorry, ma'am. I'm ever so sorry.'

Gladys, or a woman that Allen took to be Gladys, was on the bed and clearly in a very bad way.

'Ada!' That was all that Allen could think of to say. The enormity of the invasion had robbed her of coherent speech.

Ruth appeared at her side. 'Do pull your mask up,' she said. 'What's the matter with your friend, Ada?'

'I think it's the 'flu, ma'am. She's fainted away on the floor and I got her on to the bed and now she's… I'm so sorry, ma'am. I'm so sorry. I didn't know what to do, really I didn't.'

The sound of a bell, wildly rung, came up the stairs. Lily wanted attention.

＊　　＊　　＊

I had four funerals on the Saturday morning, all sharing an early service; there were very few mourners. Another of my bearers had sent a message to say he'd taken to his bed and several of the gravediggers were down which meant that there'd been uncertainty about the funerals taking place at all. In the end I found a willing man: a visitor from Wales, sharing a room in the same house as my sick bearer and having had some experience in his home town. The sexton got extra help from the men he had available but they refused absolutely to work after twelve on any future Saturday. As I'd had the same chorus from the bearers – the funeral workers were banding together – I remember thinking that if we had no graves open at least it would spare me the problem of getting the coffins to the cemetery.

Walter, Albert and Herbert had all come in without complaint to do whatever was needed but the four of us were on the point of being overwhelmed, however many hours we worked. There was no hope of finding someone with experience; the young ones were at the Front and the older ones already attached or working for themselves, so if I wanted an extra pair of hands it would have to be a boy, and if I wanted a boy then the boy I wanted was Harry. Elsie had said that he was still at school but the schools were closing now, I was sure of that, and in the meantime he could come to me in the evening and make himself useful with sealing and putting on handles and so forth. I could take him out as well, like my father used to take me, and get him used to the measuring and lifting, for as long as we were able to work.

I was seven when I first went out with my father. I don't remember if my mother said anything against it but I would imagine not. The body was in a factory of some sort – there was so much noise I had to cover my ears – and my father made me run my hand up the arm. See how it feels, *he said*, so you won't think twice about it next time. Take his hand. Go on, shake it. I touched that man as if he were going to come to life and hit me, and as for holding his hand, if a choir had started up, you'd have heard them singing C and C sharp at the same time. I must have looked a funny sight because my father laughed – we were alone with the body or he wouldn't have made me do it. After that, I was expected to do anything without complaint. For the most part, I was put to sanding. In those days we made a lot of furniture; you had that trade and that's how you made a living. The coffin-making was in addition to it, particularly in the winter months. My father gradually dropped the carpentry and took up more of the funeral business and I was expected to follow on, which of course I did.

Harry might well be dead before he'd learned to cut a straight edge but he was willing to work and therefore useful to me. I told Walter what I proposed to do and he was happy enough, so I went round in the afternoon to see if the boy was free to start.

Elsie and the children were clearing out the place. She'd decided to move them all back to her house so that she didn't have to go back and forth every day. I'd just missed Harry, he'd gone off somewhere. I told her what I was thinking but I might as well have been talking to myself.

She said, 'The baby's dead. We've put him in with Jen. I had to go down to the doctor's in the end and he gave me a certificate without seeing her or anything. So I've registered Jen, but because I hadn't said about the baby we've just put him in with her. Nicely dressed, of course. That'll be all right, won't it, Henry love?'

What was the point of standing by the law? 'I didn't hear a word of that,' I said. 'Of course it'll be all right. And did you hear what I said about Harry?'

'What was that?'

'I need another pair of hands and he's a sensible boy. I'll pay him a bit and that'll help you out as well.'

She began to cry but I told her to stop. It turned out that Nora was still bad from the 'flu and she didn't want anything to do with the children. Elsie was going to have to raise them on her own till Stan got back. I told her to send Harry down as soon as she liked.

*   *   *

Napier
Hawke's Bay,
26 October 1918

Dear Henry,

How are you, dear? Thank you for your nice letter. So far away but always in my thoughts. I expect you're getting busy now with winter on the way. We're having some nice sunshine and looking forward to long summer evenings – what a funny thing it is, I always think, you having the shivers while I'm outside in a frock. Don't be cross about it, dear. You've just had a summer of your own after all, even if you never will take a day to yourself to enjoy it.

The news that I know you'll want to hear is this: Flora is taking her first steps!! Such pretty little feet and I wish you could see her hobbling round the room, falling – and no tears! – and then standing again and all the while we're shouting her on like a Derby horse. Grace is ever so superior, of course, and stands on one leg just to show what a real girl can do when she tries. They are both beautiful and I shall have photographs made so you can see your lovely nieces and kiss them.

Archie's still stuck at the military camp at Trentham and we don't see him. I shouldn't complain or I'll be cursed. At least he's not over there with you, although it might come to that. And I'd travel with him on the troop ship and surprise you! Every day, especially when I'm out with the girls, I think of you, Henry dear, and miss you so and our sing-songs with the pee-an-o.

So what other news? I've made a good friend called Peggy. Her little girl is friends with Grace and we get on so well that it's quite bucked me up. And! Her dad was an undertaker! In Scotland, where they came from, and then he gave it up and came to Auckland to farm. So we have a lot in common. Her husband is over there in France but she says he has a guardian angel who knocks away the bullets and sends them back to the Germans!

Well, that's all for today. They say the post is getting there. Give my best to the big sisters – I never write to them (and I never said much either!). You've always been my special brother and you always will be! There's been a bit of sickness about and I'm looking after some children for a neighbour who's poorly. They're little b—'s – nothing like my angels!

Give my love to Walter and Vi.

With my very best love to you always,

Rose xxx

*   *   *

The Reverend Sucerne had spent the first part of the morning officiating at a funeral for four and it was still early enough – barely eleven – for him to take on some pastoral work before lunch, visiting the stricken. The most needy had been noted by his wife, Muriel, but she always left him to plan the route that would allow him to cut the simplest path on his bicycle; it was most annoying to double back on oneself and pass the very street that one had been in an hour before. The list was by his chair, with a street map and a glass of sherry. He would plan and she would take dictation, writing the addresses in their proper order, the whole business taking no more than ten minutes and saving twenty.

Speculating about the epidemic in his sermons, he had taken the public position that God, in his providence, might well be offering man an antidote to the cruelties of war. 'Matthew tells us,' he exhorted, 'that Jesus Christ healed "divers diseases and torments" and we, in His name, have been given work to do. Let us show charity to any who ask and have faith that Christ will work through us to aid the sick.'

Tacitly, he believed that the epidemic was a punishment; degenerate behaviour was apparent wherever one looked, even in the church grounds. On one occasion he had entered the church itself and found a couple on a pew, in full sight of the altar, and one only had to read the newspapers to see that the decline was universal. Punishment, deplorably, was not reserved for the guilty but generally dispensed so that the good, as ever, were paying heavily for the bad. This disparity between Richard Sucerne's public and private views was an example of his reluctance to engage in open disagreement, a prospect more distressing to him than any amount of loneliness brought about by having secret opinions. That he was disagreeing with God – by holding to his belief that retribution should be more fairly meted out – had not occurred to him. As he prepared to leave the house, he was called to speak to Mrs Thompson on the telephone. She was apologetic about disturbing him but her sister, Mrs Bird, was in some distress.

'I'm very sorry to hear that.' Mr Sucerne looked sympathetically at the wallpaper. 'Is it influenza?'

'No, no. Goodness me, no.'

'Not that I wouldn't visit if it *were*. In fact, I'm just on my way out—'

'It isn't that at all. The only thing I can say is that my sister is in a state of some… agitation. I think it best if you see her for yourself. There's nothing I can say that would adequately explain her state of mind. If you have a moment, at any time… She's adamant that you're the only person… she's adamant that it's you she must see.'

'I'm leaving now.'

Mr Sucerne told Muriel that he would be home for lunch at half past one, shrugged on his coat and put the list of calls in his pocket. She pushed his hands away from the buttons and did them up herself, then smoothed his hair and caressed his cheek. 'You know I don't approve,' she said, handing him his hat. 'You're not as strong as you seem to think. And what happens if you catch it?'

'I shall go forth in a cloud of holy disinfectant.'

'You can say that as often as you like, it's still ridiculous. Why should you be safer than anyone else?' Muriel opened the front door and leaned on it, watching him as he adjusted his hat in the hall mirror. 'And don't forget to put on your mask. Have you got it with you?'

'In my pocket.'

'Show me.' He pulled out the first inches of the mask. 'Good. Half past one, then.'

When the door was shut he looked at his itinerary. The Thompson house was a street away from the last name on the list; he would have to double back.

*   *   *

'I heard you, that's how I knew you were here. You were shouting.' Lily's voice was hoarse. 'And don't come in here with your mask down.'

'I wasn't shouting,' Allen said. 'I was calling out.'

'I knew it was you. I know your voice. It doesn't matter, anyway. Have you telephoned for Mr Sucerne?'

'You asked me to. Of course I have.'

'You don't usually do as I ask. Is he coming?'

'He said he would. He was on his way out anyway so he's going to drop in when he passes. Shall I tidy you up and put the fire on?'

'No. I want him to see the state you keep me in.'

In the few hours since Allen had last seen her, Lily had deteriorated. Her eyes, normally as sharp as a barn owl's, were sunken and cloudy, and the true state of her face, made alert and mobile by elation, had begun to reveal itself. She was grey and papery – dehydrated, starving and not a little mad. A napkin lay on top of the basket, its corner pierced through with an unthreaded needle. Was Lily not sewing? The morning was overcast but Lily had told her to turn off the light.

'Shall I leave you, then?'

'Go away.'

Allen went back upstairs to Ada's room. Now that the secret was out, she had become the competent nurse and, with Ruth's help, had put Gladys to bed. The window was open, a strategy initiated by Ruth and insisted on whenever they visited an ailing family. The room was cold.

'You must have a fire, Ada,' Allen said. 'Light one when you want. How is she? Is it influenza?'

Ruth said, 'Of course it is. She's got a fever and a terrible headache and her period's so heavy she's soaked her skirt. She'll have to stay.'

'Would that be all right, ma'am?' Ada had tears in her eyes. 'I'll look after her in my time and you won't even notice that she's here, really you won't.'

'Is there anyone that needs to know?' Allen said. 'A relative of some sort?'

'She's on her own, ma'am. But I'll tell the dairy. I'll pop out later, when I've finished.' Ada leaned over the bed and put her hand on Gladys's forehead with a movement so full of grace and affection that Allen felt her throat tighten. It was somehow indiscreet to remain in the room and she gestured to Ruth that they should leave.

'Come down when you're ready, Ada,' she said. 'And please ask me for anything you need.'

As soon as the door was closed, Ruth started to speak but Allen stopped her and led them both down to the basement. When they were in the kitchen, she said, 'Lily's got some mad notion – I've no idea what it is – and I've had to telephone the vicar because he's the only person she'll talk to. She looks terribly unwell.'

'How long is it since she's eaten?'

'I think today's the fifth day. She seemed to be enjoying it. I know that sounds absurd but if you'd heard her you'd know exactly what I mean. And we could all go without food for a few days, I'm sure. I don't know what to do for the best, I really don't.' Allen picked up Ada's apron, folded it and sat down with it on her lap. 'How long *can* you do without food? And still be well?'

'I have no idea. Shouldn't you tell Doctor Tite? He'd be more useful than the vicar, surely.'

'And what are we going to do about Gladys? To have influenza here, actually here, in the house. It's different, isn't it? You'd think we'd be used to it by now, but I feel absolutely unprepared.'

'Ada's capable. You won't have to do any nurs—'

'If Lily thought we had influenza here and a *stranger*…'

'I thought Gladys was Ada's friend?'

'You know what I mean. She's a stranger to me.'

'Why did you give Ada that room?'

'I don't know.' Allen picked the apron up from her lap, held it in the air and then crushed it between her hands. 'I found the nights quite alarming. Without Edward here. Anyway, her old room was rather damp – there's a leak somewhere in the roof.' She had to repeat the excuse she'd used upstairs; even Ruth would be appalled to think of a servant being housed like a guest. Ada herself had utterly resisted it.

'Does Lily know?'

'No. No, of course she doesn't. Look, it's not important now. So you think we ought to ask Doctor Tite to look at Gladys?' Allen was interrupted by the doorbell. She got up. 'I'll let Mr Sucerne in. I expect Ada's still upstairs. Anyway, she's not dressed to open the door. Will you wait till he's gone?'

'Of course I will.'

*   *   *

Henry wrote the remaining details in his book and put away his pen. The widow opposite him was a young woman, less than half the age of the deceased. Her attitude throughout his visit had been crisp and discourteous. He cleared his throat. 'I think that's everything,' he said. 'I'm afraid it may be ten days or so before the funeral can take place but we'll bring the coffin tomorrow afternoon.'

'Ten days? I want the funeral in a week, Mr Speake.'

'I can't guarantee it, I'm afraid. I'll be able to give you the exact date tomorrow.'

'Why can't you guarantee it?'

'We're unable to keep pace. There aren't enough gravediggers to do the work.'

'Why not?'

'Because there are so many deaths from influenza.'

'But my husband died of a fractured skull! Surely you must have time set aside for people who've died properly? And what if I were to enquire elsewhere?'

'I'm afraid that's unlikely to be—'

'In other words, I'm paying for a service that you can't provide.' She rang for the maid. Henry stood up. 'I can hardly say I'm pleased, Mr Speake. I hope you have better news for me tomorrow.' There was no response to the bell.

'I'll see myself out.' He walked towards the door.

The woman rang again and then pushed past him and looked out into the corridor. She called but there was no answering voice. Henry started down the stairs. The maid was lying face down in front of him, her feet spread wide on the hall floor and the rest of her rising at an angle on the steps.

'She's collapsed,' Henry shouted. 'Where shall I take her?' He bent to pick the girl up. She was small and light and he cradled her, waiting for instructions.

'Get her out of here!'

'Where does she live? Doesn't she live here?'

'I don't want her. Just get her out!'

The girl was bewildered, looking at him with blind eyes and then focusing on his face. He left the house and stood on the step with her in his arms, asking her questions until she answered him. She was called Louisa. Her mother was a few miles away but she could go there; she would be looked after. A cab came up the street. He stopped it and spent some time arguing with the driver but at the presentation of the fare, the girl was eventually put on the back seat and taken home.

When he got back to the shop, Harry had arrived and been put to sweeping. 'We'd better have a bloody good story cooked up,' Walter was saying to Herbert Winter. 'I can't see me telling a customer that there's no coffins.'

'Put two in together,' Herbert said. 'That'll do the trick. Squeeze 'em up nice and cosy.'

The second post had come late, the postman telling Walter that they were lucky to have a delivery at all as he was doing the work of two other men. There was a letter from Allen. Henry took it upstairs and sat on his bed to read it. Her school was shut – he'd heard about that already. She would be at the service on Sunday. He went to his desk and wrote a brief reply suggesting that they meet afterwards for a talk and asking if there was anywhere she could think of where they might not be disturbed. Then he posted the letter and went back to work.

Walter was still complaining. He'd spent the best part of the morning trying to buy wood or coffin sets or even ready-made coffins, but with little success.

'… and what were they thinking of, sending skilled men over there!' he said to Herbert. 'Even sending off the gravediggers! And then the buggers that are left won't do any bloody overtime! And as for the bloody timber, you'd find it by the ton if you knew how to get round the regulations. You won't see many politicians being buried in shrouds.'

Herbert Winter said, 'Plague pits it is, then,' and laughed till he was dark red about the face.

* * *

'Mr Sucerne's here to see you,' Allen said. 'Shall I put on the light?' She'd tried to warn him about Lily's declining state at the front door, but she knew that Lily would be suspicious if they took more than a minute to reach her. He would have to make the best of it.

'No light. Is he wearing a mask?'

'He is.' Allen put out her hand to suggest that Mr Sucerne might like to enter the room before her but he demurred and, after a slight hesitation, she took the lead.

'Mrs Bird,' he said, as soon as he saw Lily. 'I believe you asked to see me.'

'I did.' Lily was sitting up. She'd tried to arrange her hair with her hands and had missed several lengths, which were hanging oddly from different parts of her head.

Mr Sucerne was used, when visiting even the most seriously unwell, to the invalid being properly presented; Mrs Bird was unkempt. His last meeting with her, a communion service some weeks before, had been so uneventful that he'd barely noted it. Except for the small disturbance of her bath-chair advancing on the altar, she could be described as the ideal parishioner, attending regularly and demanding nothing. She appeared to have suffered considerably in the interim. Were there problems in the family? Was Mrs Thompson in distress? The room was cold enough to use as a larder.

'Well, here I am,' he said. 'At your service.'

There was a chair near the bed and another some distance away. Allen chose the further chair and sat down. 'I hope this hasn't inconvenienced you,' she said. 'We're very grateful.'

'I'm here to serve my fl—'

'Go away,' Lily said to Allen. 'I want to see Mr Sucerne by myself.'

'Really, I—' He stood up, fractionally later than Allen.

'Would you mind very much?' she said to him. 'I shall wait in the hall.'

'You'll do no such thing.' Lily was outraged. 'I want you to leave us *alone*.'

Mr Sucerne looked from one woman to another. 'I'll be happy to talk to your sister, Mrs Thompson.'

'Then please call me if you need anything. I'll be in the drawing room. Is that agreeable to you, Lily?'

'Yes. Go away.'

When the door was closed Lily waited for a full minute before speaking, her head cocked in an exaggerated display of wariness. When she was sure that Allen was no longer outside she said, 'Do we speak in confidence?'

He could smell her breath from where he sat; it was an unusual and rather unpleasant odour.

'Of course.' The question always preceded a declaration about misdemeanours. He relaxed; this was an ageing, infirm woman who needed to clear her conscience. 'Whatever it is that's troubling you, Mrs Bird, do please be reassured that it will go no further,' he prodded himself, 'than this.'

'My soul…' Lily was unable to continue. Tears reddened her eyes and spilled over on to her cheeks. She found a handkerchief somewhere in the bed and blew her nose. Mr Sucerne sat quietly, patting his knee in sympathy. With the handkerchief held to her face, Lily said, 'How does one become a holy martyr?'

Too difficult! He took so long to reply that Lily spoke again. 'Will God hear me? Will He hear me?'

'In answer to your first question, I believe that one becomes a martyr by bearing witness to one's faith, even if it means losing one's life.' Was he to be engaged in theological debate? 'As for God hearing you, Mrs Bird, God hears us if we whisper. God hears our thoughts. God hears us always.'

'Then I'm a martyr, do you see? But I fear that God may not understand me. I fear that my sacrifice may not be understood.' She lowered her voice and moved in the bed, leaning towards his chair with one arm stretched straight on the mattress in support. 'I believe that Ada is a murderer.' She paused for emphasis. 'And I would sooner die than surrender to the enemy.'

'Ada?'

'The maid! Ada is the maid and she's German, do you understand? She's German. She lets soldiers into the house. I fear for my life. But my soul, Mr Sucerne, my soul!'

He recovered his poise. She was mad. 'Your soul is safe,' he said.

'But if I die by my own hand? Will God know me to be a martyr?'

'Are you intending to kill yourself?'

'I've refused to eat.'

Dear God! 'Is that wise?'

'I must take my stand against the enemy.'

'Then we must pray together for a fitting resolve.'

When Mr Sucerne left the bedroom he found Allen waiting silently in the hall. Echoing her sister, she held up her hand for silence and gestured that he should follow her to the drawing room.

'Whatever Mrs Bird may have told you,' Allen said, 'I must let you know that she's refused to have a fire, insists on staying in her room and has eaten nothing for five days.'

'Your sister spoke to me in confidence, but I would suggest that a doctor might be called.'

'He was. He came on Wednesday.'

'I see. Perhaps he should be called again.' He longed to say more but it was out of the question. 'And the school, Mrs Thompson. How dreadful for you all. We must pray for deliverance. There'll be two services tomorrow, even if I'm the only man in church. Might you come?'

'I'll do my best.'

He shook her hand at the door and held it for several seconds longer than necessary. 'I do think she should see the doctor.'

'I'll see if I can persuade her. Thank you.'

'Tomorrow, then.'

'Possibly.'

＊　＊　＊

Sunday, 27 October

Henry's absence in the organ loft was referred to by Mr Sucerne, who pointed out that the inconvenience to the congregation was as nothing compared to the endeavours being made by Mr Speake and others of his profession in the current crisis. The few worshippers present attempted to sing without accompaniment but it was a dismal sound; their voices were scattered about the church and unable to settle on a communal key.

'Has the doctor attended Mrs Bird?' Mr Sucerne asked Allen on her way out.

'Not yet,' she said. 'I've left a message.'

'Please let me know if I can help in any way.'

'Of course.'

'Reverend?' An elderly woman grabbed at Mr Sucerne's sleeve. 'Reverend?' Her nose and mouth were covered with a silk scarf which had been tied at the back with a large bow; a low-brimmed hat obscured her forehead and left nothing but a thin slit through which Allen could see only shadow. 'Would it be possible for you to—'

Allen said, 'Thank you,' to Mr Sucerne and left, glad of the interruption.

Henry was waiting for her at the church gate, dressed in his visiting clothes. In her memory he was usually in an apron or an ordinary jacket; she was a little daunted by his formality. 'I didn't expect to see you,' she said. 'I thought you were too busy.'

'I told you I'd be here.'

'We missed you at the service.' She took off her mask.

'I've had two families to visit.'

'Who?'

'Susan Matthews and Horace Towler.'

She shook her head. 'I don't know them. You must be working round the clock.'

'Almost.'

'May I offer you coffee? If you have a few minutes?'

The conversation during the walk was general and slightly awkward. At the door, Allen said, 'We have to go in quietly. I'll explain when we're in the kitchen.' The words were out before she realized her error: he would assume that she was taking him to the basement because he was a tradesman and not fit for the house. And didn't one always see the undertaker in the drawing room? He would be doubly insulted. In her confusion, she almost closed the door on him. 'I'll explain,' she whispered. 'Just follow me.'

Ada, with permission, was spending the morning in her room with Gladys. The kitchen was warm and dark; Allen had left a tray set with the things she would need to make coffee.

'Please sit down, Mr Speake,' she said, putting on the light. 'Would you like something to eat?'

'No, thank you.'

She put her coat on the back of a chair and filled the kettle. 'We're down here because my sister's ill. I didn't want to disturb her.'

'Influenza?'

'No.' He was an odd figure at the table; the blackness of his clothes sucked the light out of the air. She was compelled to look at him. 'She's starving herself to death.'

'Good God!'

'She says that the maid's intent on giving her influenza and if I don't dismiss her she simply won't eat. Of course, I wouldn't *think* of dismissing her.'

'Couldn't you pretend to do as your sister asks?'

'And who would she think was looking after the house?'

'Why not you?'

This was an obvious solution and one that she had batted away as unworkable in the first days. What had started as an explanation of Lily's madness was now a defence against her own stupidity. She sounded like a murderer! With the school shut, she could easily do the housework and cook for herself. 'You're right, I've got time now,' Allen said. 'That's what I'll tell her. I'll say Ada's gone.'

'Why not?'

'I had no intention of telling you about my sister. I wanted to apologize for being so nonchalant the other night.' She leaned against the dresser. 'You were right, of course. Will it get worse?'

'It will.'

'Why are you so sure?'

'I've been told.'

'By whom?'

'I found a letter from this man, a Doctor Thomas Wey. He was trying to warn the government. I didn't post the letter on but there's no need now. They must know what he was trying to tell them.'

'What was he trying to tell them? How did you find the letter?'

'He died of influenza on the street near me. I brought him into the workshop and the letter ended up on my floor.'

Allen came to the table and sat down. 'But what did he know? Why was he trying to warn them?'

'Because he had to.'

'What did it say, in the letter?'

'That we should stop moving the troops and close the ports.' Henry was looking at the tabletop and moving his fingers one by one, left to right and then back again. 'And he said that the earth would be left to the animals.'

'To the *animals*? Does he mean that we're all going to die?'

Henry looked up. 'That's what he's saying.'

'Have you told any one else?'

'I'm telling you.'

'Do you believe him?'

'He might have been exaggerating to make his point. Or it might be that we don't understand the consequences.'

'Of what?'

'Of this visitation.'

Allen thought of Gladys bringing the end of the world into the house. It was impossible to take all this in. Why was he telling her? This Thomas person was probably a conscientious objector out to make a point. The world had survived the real plague in primitive conditions, without the advantages of medical science.

'I'm sure the government must have some plan in mind if things get worse,' she said. 'Don't you think?'

'I'm waiting to see what they might do. Perhaps I should have posted on the letter?'

'It would never have reached a minister. They must get strange letters all the time. May I talk about this to anyone?'

'I don't think so.' He stood up and took his hat from the nearby chair.

'It's between us, then.'

'I wanted you to know what I know. You probably think it was wrong of me to read the letter—'

'Not at all.'

'—but having read it, I have some responsibility in the matter.'

'I'm sure they'll be doing everything they can.'

They were at the door. Henry opened it for himself and said, 'I think it's important that we talk again.'

'About the letter?'

'And what may come of it.'

He held out his hand and she shook it, briskly.

THREE

'No one has a good word for the latest scourge, the "Spanish 'flu". Women go about handkerchief to nose and reeking of antiseptic. The two pet pastimes are sneezing and skipping – the first not caused by 'flu, but by the use of Kruschen Salts to prevent it by getting rid of the germs, the second by way of keeping warm in the healthiest way. An impromptu sneezing party proved rather a frolic; the guests passed round the salts, sniffed and sneezed into properly disinfected hand-kies in a disinfected room. There may be developments with competitions, the best sneezer to get a prize; or, if members of the minority sex are present, bets might enliven the proceedings, which would certainly often become hilarious.'

Ladies Section, Illustrated London News, 2 *November* 1918

Monday, 28 October

'I'm sorry, sir. You might think badly of me for the rest of time but I can't stop in this house. I hope you can manage, sir, but that's that and I'm off.' Eric Bevens's maid, who was also the cook, curtsied and turned on her heel.

'Annie! Stop, girl! You can't just *leave!*'

But she was gone, clattering down the stairs to the kitchen. There was silence and then a door slamming and more clattering as she ran up from the basement to the street.

His mother and his wife were confined with influenza; could they be left alone while he went to work? What if his mother were to fall from her bed? What if his wife heard the noise and fell from *her* bed in the attempt to reach his mother? He took off his hat and put down his brief-case. The general opinion would be that his negligence had caused the injuries – impossible to take the risk! Hiring a nurse would be prohibitively expensive; none of his acquaintances in the vicinity was well enough, or reliable enough, to call on, and by the time any of his children had made the journey, if indeed any were capable of it, he would be home from work in any case. There was no alternative; he would have to take the day off.

After writing a note to his office he visited the two sickrooms and reassured the patients that another maid would be found by nightfall. Neither appeared to care; both were overcome with fever and too ill to talk. He left them to sleep. The priority now was to obtain the services of a maid who could cook. His mother had always taken charge of the employment of servants. He had never enquired as to her technique but common sense suggested that one might start with an agency. Would they advertise? He went out to post the letter and get himself a newspaper.

On the way home, Eric Bevens reflected on his present duties. Cleaning was entirely unfitting and unnecessary – how much dirt could accumulate in the course of a day? Nursing was a question of surveillance and medication, nothing more. He had no need to cook, except for himself, which was fortunate as he'd never seen a raw egg or cut a slice of bread; he had never actually entered the kitchen – *terra incognita* in his own house!

It was now nine o'clock, two hours since breakfast, and he needed something hot to drink. He would make himself tea and look through the advertisements for a reputable firm. With his hat and coat hung up and the newspaper under his arm, he approached the basement door. It was his very own kitchen, it belonged to him and contained items, also his, that were simple enough for a woman to use; none the less, the threshold to it, this common door, had assumed a new significance and he opened it cautiously.

Just inside there was a small landing, no bigger than a double step. The smell was familiar – the ghost of it had seeped through the floorboards into the lower rooms and hung strongly about the maid. Undiluted, it was dank. The staircase was dark and uncarpeted; he turned back to find and light a lamp and then resumed his descent. At the bottom were several closed doors to either side of the passage and an open door leading into the kitchen. The day was overcast and the poor light that came through the basement window would never have allowed him to read his paper. There was an unlit lamp on the table; he put his own next to it then looked around him and took note of the shelves and cupboards.

The stove, which Annie had thankfully lit before her decision to leave, made the room perfectly warm; warmer, in fact, that any of the rooms upstairs. The kettle was next to the hob; he filled it and put it on to boil, then made a tour of the cupboards, noting their contents and taking some of them out for his day's rations: bread, butter, a tin of spaghetti, a tin of tomato soup, a tin of apricots and a small pot of damson jam. Tea – not much of it – was in a caddy by the stove. The milk eluded him for a full minute but he eventually located it in a cooler on the dresser; there was half a bottle, which would be enough. The sugar was not to be found. Annie had probably taken it with her.

He put tea in the pot – too much? too little? – and filled it to the brim with boiling water. This he knew to be correct. The location of the tray remained a mystery but the kitchen was comfortable and it would be silly to carry everything upstairs. He opened the paper, lying it flat on the table and standing the lamp at its corner. The news first, he thought, and then the maid. Before he could pour the tea, it would have to brew; this he also knew to be correct. He lined up the tins and the pot of jam, and poured a little milk into his cup. His first foray into the kitchen had proved to be a singular success.

*   *   *

'I don't know when I'll be back,' Walter said to Vi. 'You'll have to keep supper warm.'

Vi finished making the bed and brought up the quilt, leaning in to straighten the pillows. 'I suppose Henry's doing his fair share?'

'And what do you mean by that?'

'He walked away from church with her yesterday. I don't know where they were going but it seems they were close. Did she turn up at the shop?'

'She wouldn't, not after what I said to her.' Walter's hair was sparse but he liked to part what there was and then smooth it flat with his hand.

He looked into the mirror from various angles and spoke to Vi's reflection. 'If you must know, I'm running things. You're as likely to find him gaping at the wall.'

'Have you told him what you think?'

'What about?'

'Any of it. All of it. His name's at stake. Doesn't he care?'

'I've said a few things. We're doing our best – there's no shame in running out of supplies. It's not as if we've got secret timber for the rich.'

Vi shut the window. 'Don't get your shirt out, I was only asking.'

'I don't know if it's that woman or not, but I'm having to keep too much of an eye on things and there we are. I've told you now. Are you happy?'

'Of course I'm not happy. Not if you're not happy.'

'You're a silly woman.' He pulled up his braces and put on his waistcoat. 'You tell Hilda to look after herself. And she's not to take that baby out where there's people.'

'Or?'

'Or I'll have to put her over my knee.'

'I'll fetch your lunch. It's packed up.'

'I don't like you going on that bus.'

'If I'm going to get 'flu, I'll get 'flu.' Vi tied a scarf round her neck and pulled on her hat. 'And if I'm not, I'm not.'

'Did you work that out on your own?'

'I did. Aren't I clever?'

*   *   *

On the Sunday morning, I'd waited for Allen outside the church. She suggested that we go to her house as it would allow us to talk in private. While we walked I asked her, purely for conversation, where she'd lived before her marriage. When she told me, I was taken aback. I'd helped to put her father in his coffin. I can't have been more than eighteen or nine-

teen at the time and because of her married name being different there had been no reason to make the connection.

The man had only been dead for an hour or two but his leg was rotten and he had smelled bad. There was a black leather belt lying on the pillow next to him. The wife – that was Allen's mother, of course – tried to snatch it away before we reached the bed but it was too late, I'd seen it and it was ragged at both ends. She told us that her husband had refused all treatment and I took the belt to be the thing he'd used to chew on.

My father and I went back with another man to put him in the coffin and get him down the stairs. We were on the landing when a young girl came from behind us and took the lead. She just led us down and stood there in the hall, like a solemn old man. When we got to the bottom, my father told her to go and play with her dolls or whatever and she stalked off. She's different now, that goes without saying, but as soon as I remembered, I could see that face and how it had adjusted. Under the circumstances, I decided to keep my recollections to myself. People don't always like to be reminded.

As soon as we got to Allen's house she started to make a fuss about being quiet, so we sat in the kitchen. It turned out that her sister was starving herself because of the maid. All Allen had to do was to pretend that the maid had been sent packing. Why hadn't she already done so? I made the suggestion and she thanked me.

Then I said that I was keen to confide in her about something. She was quite collected about it and showed no ridicule at Thomas Wey's predictions. In fact, she was curious about the whole business. She didn't even comment on my opening a letter that wasn't intended for me. Even so, and I have no understanding of this, I felt no relief at having unveiled myself. In fact, I felt a great need to get away and had the strange experience of seeing her looming in on me, although we were a full table's width apart.

Walter had been in the workshop since nine o'clock. There was no need for me to say where I'd been – I was simply out on business. We worked right through to the evening, interrupted by people knocking for us and three visits out with coffin deliveries, one to the woman who'd sent her servant into the street and another two for a house where the mother had died along with one of her children. The woman with the sick servant had tried to get what she called 'a proper service' elsewhere and had been unlucky but she was no less impolite; I wish now that I'd taken the coffin to a more deserving customer.

A strategy would be needed when we were quite unable to provide coffins and it occurred to me to ask at the mortuary; they might well agree to take the overflow. If the dead outgrew the living until burial was only possible in pits – who would dig them? – then we would need something like the old plague carts. The numbers were increasing daily but there was no plan that I knew of to provide for the situation.

On the Monday, I was up before Margaret had set the breakfast, glad to be out of bed after a night spent shifting from side to side. There were things that I'd meant to tell Allen: my being given the Quaker journal, for instance, and the subsequent discovery of the poem. If I could have carried on the conversation with her then I certainly would have, but the urge to leave had been too strong for me. It doesn't matter what I'm doing, when that feeling starts then I have to get out. That's the phrase I get in my mind: I have to get out. I'd been surprised by its appearance in Allen's kitchen but that's the way it happens, out of the blue. She knew I had to get to work so I doubt that she made anything of it, but I was annoyed with myself none the less.

As soon as I was dressed, I went to the piano and played through the song I'd made of the poem. The melody was fair, although it required a greater talent than mine to do justice to the words. My singing was hardly up to it either and I wanted very much to hear a good voice take charge and perform it with some accomplishment. I had the thought that Allen might sing well and made a start at notating the piece for her.

The prospect of another day spent visiting and measuring was enough to make me want to run off. When I got down to the shop, a man was already knocking at the door; as soon as I let him in, he grabbed my hand

and held it firm, not letting me pull away. He'd woken up to find his wife dead in the bed next to him and their baby dead in its cot. There was nothing I could say, but I sat him down in my office and let him cry until he was able to give me his particulars. The child was small enough to be buried with the mother and for that I had to be grateful as it saved wood. The men and Harry were all in by eight o'clock. I expected one or more of us to drop at any time so the full complement was a relief. We were starting to watch for it; if anybody so much as sat down you'd be thinking the worst and you could see people keeping themselves to themselves, even in families. The man who'd grabbed my hand was the first living soul to touch it for some days. It didn't bother me. If I'd become faint-hearted about what I put my hands on, I would have had to retire.

When the men had been allotted their work I went down to the mortuary and made enquiries as to future housing of the dead. They'd been given no word from the authorities and the man I spoke to refused to consider that there might be a need for it. I could have said more but he would find out for himself, and I have to say I took a certain satisfaction in that.

*   *   *

Allen had asked Ada to wake her at the usual time even though the school was closed. She heard the knock and called out her thanks. Then she remembered Gladys. 'Ada? Come in, if you would?'

'Yes, ma'am.' Ada was in her uniform but without an apron. Her head was bare and her collar undone. 'I've not dressed yet, ma'am. I didn't think you'd ask to see me.'

Allen got out of bed and came to the door in her nightdress. 'You look exhausted. Have you been up all night?'

'Yes, ma'am. Gladys isn't doing very well. I didn't like to sleep and leave her to herself. Not all night through.'

'Do you think the doctor should see her?'

'I don't like to put you to the trouble, ma'am. But I do.'

'I'll ask him. Have you had any breakfast?'

'No, ma'am. I was going to wait till you were having yours and then I was going to give her a bit of a wash. I've done everything I should, ma'am. In the house, I mean.'

'I'm sure you have. You go and help Gladys. I'll be along shortly.' She dressed quickly, taking the first dark skirt and subdued blouse that came to hand. Her agenda had been decided: she would telephone Dr Tite, tell Lily that Ada was no longer in the house, see what could be done for Gladys and make some arrangement to meet Henry Speake. Their conversation had ended too abruptly; his description of that strange letter had been animated but his despondency was plain and she needed to know more. There was also planning to be done with Ruth. Allen's interest in the children was sporadic; not for the first time, she wondered at the ease with which she had walked away from the school. Ruth appeared to keep them in her care, even at a distance. Faced with the class, Allen gave of her best but in their absence she was happy to forget them.

She ate in the kitchen: bread and marmalade with tea. A change had taken place in her; she was aware of it but not altogether sure of its nature. It had been brought on by the atmosphere of crisis – had a bomb gone off in the street she could not have felt more disorientated by events. There was significance in the state of her hair; how could she have left it to hang loosely about her face? Her elbows were on the table. She had cut the bread badly and then taken the knife from the butter and used it to get marmalade from the jar. Her drab clothes had a part in it, too, as if she were preparing for dirty work and had lost all delicacy of manner. A more robust personality had entered her day and it was encouraging her to behave like a rough, rather boorish child. In its favour, she knew that it was also summoning a vitality too long suppressed and diverted.

She was glad that there was controversy; her spirit was on the move.

Plaiting her hair roughly at the nape of her neck, she went upstairs to the telephone and prepared herself for the ever-increasing wait before an operator became available.

Dr Tite's wife had to be petitioned in the most dramatic terms before she agreed to pass on any message to her husband. He was exhausted. He was stretched beyond endurance. And had Mrs Thompson not been so well regarded by them both she would have allowed the maid to take the call without coming personally to the telephone. She was terribly sorry but he was quite unable to visit another patient that day. The list was ridiculously long and no one could be added to the top of it without having to drop someone off the bottom. She would ask Dr Tite to visit when he could. If he could. In the meantime, he was suggesting fresh air in the bedroom, aspirin for headache, plenty of fluids and light food only, if tolerated.

In order to explain herself without alerting Lily, Allen had taken the telephone receiver into the drawing room, pulling the wire so taut that it threatened to leave the wall. 'It's my sister,' she said, when Mrs Tite stopped talking. 'Mrs Lily Bird. She doesn't have influenza.' Was she speaking too loudly? 'She's starving herself to death and I'm extremely concerned for her.'

Mrs Tite made no sense of Allen's news and replied that loss of appetite was usual with fever. She would put Mrs Bird on the list for the following day; that was the best she could do. The call was over and Gladys hadn't even been mentioned. Allen put the telephone back in place and went to see Lily.

She was asleep, lying on her back with her mouth open. The embroidery clutter had been put away the night before – 'If nobody appreciates what I'm doing then why am I blinding myself in this gloom?' – and the bed was tidy. Allen stood watching her, undecided as to the best course of action. Should she wake her and deliver the lie? Or wait to be summoned by that exasperating bell? The difference in their ages was a mere four years, but in the present situation Allen saw her sister as she might have seen an ageing vexatious parent, with shared experience as the only bond. Lily could wait. Gladys was next on the list.

The window in Ada's bedroom was open and the fire lit, as Allen had suggested. Although Ada was trying to give the appearance of being competent, standing by the bed like a soldier on report, she was clearly distressed, squeezing her hands together and glancing at Gladys every few seconds. 'I've washed her and changed her and tried to give her water when I can and I've rubbed her back and her chest with grease. What else I can do?'

Gladys's hair was ratty with sweat; she was breathing quickly but appeared not to be struggling for air. Hearing voices, she opened her eyes.

'It's all right, love. I'm here.' Ada leaned towards the bed with her hand in the air and then pulled herself upright, remembering Allen. Gladys closed her eyes again and said something that neither of them understood.

Allen wanted to say, *please hold her, comfort her,* but instead she said, 'Doctor Tite probably won't be able to come until tomorrow. Do you think we can manage till then? I don't suppose there's much he can do, in any case.'

'It's not up to you, ma'am, you don't have to do anything. It's up to me. It's kind enough of you to let her stay.'

'Don't be silly. Do you want to go and have some breakfast? I'll sit with her.'

'I don't want to, ma'am. Really I don't.'

'I'll have to bring you something on a tray.'

'You mustn't!'

'Then go and eat something. I'll be perfectly all right. And Ada, you must be very quiet in the house.'

'Ma'am?'

'We've got to pretend that you're not here.'

'Why?'

'Mrs Bird made you wear that mask, didn't she? And then she didn't want you in her room.' Allen had slipped into her teacher voice. 'Now she's saying she won't eat if you're in the house. It's making her very ill so the best thing we can do is to pretend that you're not here. Do you see?'

'Are you getting another maid in, ma'am?'

'No! Of course I'm not. I'm going to pretend that I'm looking after things on my own.'

Gladys was murmuring in her sleep. They waited to see if she would wake up; she wiped her mouth with the back of her hand and fell silent again.

'So I've got to keep quiet?'

'I'm sorry, Ada. I'm sorry that Mrs Bird has been so – *rude* to you. She's not well. Do you understand?'

'Yes, ma'am. I most certainly do.' She smoothed Gladys's hair. 'When am I going?'

'You've gone.'

'I'd better keep my shoes off, then. We don't want her thinking there's two people in the house, do we, ma'am?'

When Allen was alone, she sat by the bed, examining Gladys's face for any sign of cyanosis. Where did it start? On the cheeks? The mouth? She would write to Henry as soon as she had told Lily her lie.

*   *   *

Eric Bevens was regretting his decision not to have a telephone installed. In order to find a maid quickly he would need to consult various agencies that day. Letters could be written but even if they replied by return it was unlikely that a suitable girl would be in place by the following morning. He had three options: he could take another day's leave; he could abandon the ailing women for half an hour while he visited an acquaintance who had a telephone; he could abandon them for an hour or more and take a bus to the street where several of the agencies were situated.

The cost of the calls – he would, of course, reimburse the acquaintance – would be more than the cost of stamps and greatly more than the cost of bus fare but he would gain in peace of mind by having to leave the house for a shorter time; the writing of letters would mean only a single minute's walk to the post box and was therefore the best option in terms of risk but his work would pile up for another day and he was loath to put himself in bad odour when so many staff were already off with influenza.

If his wife and mother were asleep, then he would choose the telephone. His mother made no response when he entered her room but his wife was awake, lying with her arm extended across the bed and her face turned to the door. She had come through the worst of it but she was thinner than before, with sunken eyes and matted hair.

'How are you, dear?' he said. 'Can I do anything for you?'

'A clean nightdress. Tell Annie.'

'She's not here, dear.' He had hoped to announce the news about Annie's departure in conjunction with the arrival of the new maid. 'Could you wait a little while?'

'Where is she?'

'I'm afraid she's… she's gone.'

'*Gone!*' Had she not been bedridden, Mrs Bevens would have run to her mother-in-law, shrieking.

'I have the matter in hand. I shall find us a new maid today.'

'You?' The word was a croak.

'Today. I promise.'

'Priddy & Cole. Agency.' It was all she could manage. She closed her eyes and turned her face into the pillow.

'I'll see to it,' he said. 'And please stay where you are. You're not to get out of bed while I'm out of the house.'

His acquaintance was willing to let him use the telephone – 'although they've asked us not to, you know; hardly any operators' – and Priddy & Cole were glad to send a maid, although they were keen to stress that staff were almost unobtainable and that had his family not been such loyal clients he would have been disappointed.

By noon the maid, an apparently fearless woman, had arrived and been given the barest tour of the house – 'Mrs Bevens will have to advise you as to your duties when she's well. In the meantime, I expect you to use your common sense. If something can't be found, you'll have to do without it. I shall want dinner at seven o'clock.'

There was no longer any need for him to stay in. He asked the maid to prepare him a ham sandwich, ate it quickly – where had she found the tray? – and went to work.

The note justifying his absence had yet to arrive. He explained the nature of the crisis to his immediate superior, then settled himself at his desk. Many other desks were empty; a colleague had fallen off his chair that very hour and been taken away in an ambulance. The chief clerk approached him to say that Mr Nelms had been away since Friday; his share of incoming mail was to be apportioned between Mr Bevens and Mr Capabelli and the backlog cleared as soon as possible. Mr Bevens had long harboured the thought that Nelms was a slacker: an hour at the man's desk confirmed the opinion. The correspondence was in a shambles; some of it was dated as far back as the previous month. He replied to six queries and complaints of a general kind and was then delayed by a letter so unusual as to make him read it a few times over. The writer, a Dr Wey, was describing an imminent plague and asking for the ports to be closed – this written four weeks previously and addressed to Sir Arthur Newsholme. The symptomology was accurate enough but one could hardly describe a winter influenza epidemic as a plague. Should he show it to the chief clerk? After a moment's deliberation, Eric Bevens wrote a general reply, put the day's date and his initials at the top of the page and set the letter aside to be filed.

*   *   *

When Allen went back to Lily's room, she found her awake, still lying on her back.

'I've got some news for you,' she said, putting on her mask. 'And I'm sure you'll be delighted. Ada's gone.'

'When? Come closer – that's enough! I can't see you properly. Put the light on.'

The light was on. Was Lily going blind? 'Last night. She left after supper. I helped her to carry down her bags.'

'I didn't hear anything.'

'Why would you?'

'Are you sure? Has she really gone? She might be hiding!'

'She's gone, Lily. She left last night. I saw her go myself.'

Lily snorted. 'And you didn't see her come back.'

Allen's intention, to be generous in defeat, had pre-supposed that Lily might be moderately gracious in triumph. Lily!

'Shall I wash you now?'

'No.'

'Would you like some water?'

'No.'

'Will you eat something?'

'No.'

'Why not?'

'I prefer not to.' Whatever Allen might say, Ada was still there; Lily knew it. Her tentacles, her antennae, they were searching the house and finding traces of Ada on every floor. 'I prefer to die by my own hand.'

'Lily!'

Her expression changed so quickly from the haughty woman to the terrified child that she might have dropped one mask and revealed another. 'Or will you let her murder me?' She began to cry, tearlessly, with an open mouth.

'No one's going to murder you! Ada's gone. You and I are here by ourselves and I'm going to look after you. We'll sit in the drawing room and eat together by the fire. I'll read to you while you're sewing. Those napkins aren't finished. You'll want to finish those and put them in the chest.' Allen came closer to the bed but Lily recoiled and she moved away again. 'Let me make you some soup. Shall I?'

'I can't.'

'You can't what?'

'I can't leave this room.'

'Not with me?'

'Not at all.'

'I'm going to bring you some soup, Lily. You've starved yourself. Once you start eating again, you'll be well.'

'And you can tell Ada that I know she's here.'

'She's not here.'

'She is.'

'Why won't you believe me?'

'Why should I?'

'Because I'm your sister.'

Allen's limited sympathy had been exhausted. Of course she was telling the truth! How dare Lily assume otherwise?

'I'm going to bring you some soup and, whether you choose to eat it or not, it will stay by your bed for the entire—'

'Why aren't you at school? Isn't this a Monday?'

What could she say? 'Yes, it's a Monday. The school's closed.'

'Why?'

'Because of influenza. And that means I can take over Ada's duties, do you see?'

'They've put it through the pipes. The Germans are putting it through the gas pipes!'

'Lily, stop it.'

'God have mercy on us.' She pulled the bedclothes up to her chin and peered over her knuckles at the room.

'I'll get your soup,' Allen said. 'And then I have to do the washing.'

The people waiting outside the surgery door had distributed themselves into an oddly formed queue, with some patients so separate from the rest that the gap could have accommodated a further three. Inside, Lionel Tite took his seat and aligned the diary with the prescription pad. There were more dead to certify, more visits to the sick with their wretched staircases, more exchanges to be endured with the barely convalescent mob outside – was there no end to it? A long period of silence, that was his wish; to be quiet in the silent dark. If one sat quite still, then eventually one lost all feeling in one's fingers and toes; with time, would that spread over the body? He closed his eyes and relaxed into the chair. He could still hear the traffic on the street, the telephone bell and then his wife's voice. He knew what she would be saying; the doctor was inundated, a visit was unlikely at present, she could only suggest... the voice broke off. His wife was at the door.

'It's John Drummond's maid,' she said. 'Amy has influenza. What do you want to do?'

'I'll be there in an hour. And tell Nurse to let them in.'

He was developing a system that allowed him to greet, diagnose and prescribe in under a minute. By ten o'clock he was parking the car outside John's house.

Amy was sitting up, bleeding heavily from her nose into a large towel. She caught sight of Lionel and pointed a finger in greeting, her eyes wide with fear. The blood continued to flow, splashing on to the sheet and hitting the nurse's apron. In an attempt to reposition herself, the better to support Amy, the nurse moved a step to the right and lost her hold altogether. Amy slipped down, gushing blood over the bed and choking on the blood in her throat.

The nurse recovered herself and tried to sit Amy up again. Lionel, careless of his suit, took the other side. When she was stable, with a towel held to her upturned face, Lionel said, 'I'll keep her steady. You clean her up.' Amy tried to speak but he silenced her and told her to be a good girl while the nurse fetched water and fresh linen.

The bleed slowed to a trickle and then stopped. He helped her to lie down and waited with her, watching while she fell asleep. 'Does Mr Drummond know?' he whispered to the nurse.

'No, Doctor.'

'Temperature?'

'Only a hundred, Doctor.'

'Window open.'

'I know, Doctor.'

'I'll tell Drummond. I'll be back this afternoon.'

'Very good, Doctor.'

'Change that uniform, will you?'

He went to the bathroom first and looked at the blood on his clothes. The jacket would need to be properly sponged but he was able to clean his hands and face. He would have to write to Amy's mother and tell her that Amy wouldn't be home for at least two weeks.

John Drummond was wide awake, lying on his side. 'Why are you here so early?' he said as soon as Lionel opened the door. 'Am I dying? And where's Amy? She hasn't been in to see me.'

Lionel said, 'Good morning,' and pulled his usual chair up to the bed. 'Amy's got influenza. I've just left her.'

'Poor darling. Is she all right?'

'She's not in any danger. I'll drop Phyllis a line.'

'Thanks. What's that all over your jacket?'

'Blood. Patient with a nosebleed. It'll scrub off.'

'What can you do for Amy?'

'I'll keep an eye on her. And you?'

'In the pink.' John was barely audible now, his dry lips clacking on the words.

'So I see.'

'Bugger off. Look after my darling girl.'

'I'll see you both later.'

'I hope so.'

* * *

Tuesday, 29 October

Henry picked up the hammer and positioned himself with the first nail.

'Wait a minute, love,' Elsie said. 'I want to give Reggie this.' She held out a sweet biscuit. 'Can I put it in his hand?'

He lifted the coffin lid. The baby was a patchwork of awful colours. Elsie kissed the biscuit and pushed it into his fingers, then she stroked Jen's forehead and touched her cheeks. 'God must hate me. I'm being punished and I don't know what I've done.'

'You've done nothing,' Henry said. 'They died of influenza, not to punish you. Can I put this lid on now?'

'Go on, then. Close it.' Elsie stood back. 'I can't help feeling guilty, can I? I should have got the doctor in, I really do think that's what I should have done.'

'The doctor wouldn't have—'

'By the time I saw her she was half dead. Sarah should have told me, really she—'

'Are you saying it's my fault?' Sarah interrupted her. She stood in the doorway in her hat and coat with her bag held low in both hands.

Henry began to close the coffin. Sarah came in, standing near Elsie to make herself heard above the noise of the hammer. 'Are you saying a doctor would have saved her?'

'He might have!'

'Why didn't you ask him, then?'

'Because you said there wasn't anything he could do.'

'And I meant it.'

'And they died!'

'And they died.'

Elsie began to cry into her handkerchief. 'I'm sorry, Sarah.'

'You can't help looking for a reason. The doctor couldn't have saved them, I promise you that.'

'I've finished.' Henry stood by the trestle. 'If you're ready I'll get the men to take her out.'

Elsie nodded and put her hand out to Sarah. 'I'm sorry, love. You did your best. I know you did your best.'

The service – for five deceased, two of which were Henry's concern – was taken by a retired vicar, pressed back into service. When he found that no prayer book had been placed for him on the lectern, he went in search of one, creeping down the aisle and then back again with the book held high by way of explanation. He faltered over the names of the dead and ignored the mourners, concentrating his attention on the text, which he clung to throughout the service.

The younger children had been left with a neighbour but Elsie had agreed that Harry should travel with his mother's body on the hearse. Still too small to be a bearer, he stood at the back of the chapel with the men and then followed the coffins out in Henry's shadow, keeping himself apart from his grandmother and the other mourners. At the point of committal, Elsie tried to draw him to her but he resisted, standing in imitation of Henry with his cap in his hands and his head bowed.

'That's a wrong thing you've done, bringing Harry,' Sarah said to Henry when they were walking back to the carriage. 'What were you thinking of?'

'He's with the firm now. He's got as much right as any of us.'

'He's still a boy.'

'I'd say he behaved himself impeccably.'

'What would Dad have said to it? He didn't allow you out till you could carry.'

'I was out before I could write.'

'Delivering.'

'Things are different now.'

'Some things don't change. There are standards. Not that you'd be interested.'

'If you want the job, Sarah, you just say.'

'Tch.'

*   *   *

Mrs White looked through the first post, holding the envelopes like a pack of cards and dealing them out into piles. Four of her six tenants were too ill to open letters and the house, as she was fond of saying, had become nothing less than a hospital; she looked in on the sick at least once a day and there were many landladies – she could name names – who would have thrown the poor souls out on to the street. Bills and circulars intended for her perusal were put behind the clock on the mantelpiece and the rest of the mail left on the hall table to be collected by the recipients or taken up to the bedridden. One item remained: an official-looking envelope addressed to Dr Wey. Having established the custom of giving Dr Wey's affairs over to Mr Speake, she put the letter straight into her bag for him to deal with. Why would a busy woman want to open a dead man's post?

*   *   *

'Mrs Dassett? Are you there?' Ruth knocked again and shouted through the letterbox.

Joan Dassett heard a voice and half opened her eyes. Some of the children stirred, disturbed by the noise. A foot – Dora's? – was on her stomach. It was hot and heavy; she lifted it as gently as she could and found a space between them to put it down. The voice again, more loudly this time: '*Mrs Dassett. Let us in!*' Had she shut the door? If the door was shut, then somebody was trying to get in. She must get to the door. The door, the door. Her fingers were enormous, like fat trees; her lips were as big as her fingers. The door, she had to open the door or the soup would spoil and the soup was good soup and if she boiled the good soup… There was no possibility of standing up so she crawled, banging into a chair and catching her hand on a shoe, and then having to stop, nearly spilling over into a faint. At the junction with the passage she adjusted her body to turn it to the left, to the door, and then looked up – ah, the pain behind her eyes! Scraping her knees on the boards, she forced herself to the door then climbed, clinging, until she could grasp the knob and turn it. 'Here!' she said and then fell back to the floor, remembering not to push the door shut with her hand on the way down.

Allen and Ruth were still on the step but turning away, one to the left and one to the right, in the hope of finding a compliant neighbour and gaining access through the back of the house. As soon as they heard Mrs Dassett fall they ran back; the gap available to them was narrow but they squeezed in, trying not to push her.

'She's fainted.' Allen bent down and put her hands under Mrs Dassett's shoulders. 'Let's get her back to bed.'

The room stank of stale urine. Of the five children lying top to toe, one, the youngest, was blue about the lips; he was conscious and staring at them. The others were asleep or delirious with fever. There was room for Mrs Dassett at the edge of the mattress and they put her there, facing out, away from the children.

'He's blue,' Allen whispered.

'Yes. Yes, I know. Look, we'll wash them on the bed. The sheets'll have to stay put. And why hasn't anybody come down from upstairs?'

Allen looked up, as if the ceiling might have information written on it. 'They could be sick. I'll go and investigate.'

'I'll boil up some water.'

The stove had gone out. To light it and wait for the water to heat would take too long. Ruth filled a bowl with cold water and found a clean bit of cloth. There was soup in a saucepan and a loaf of reasonably fresh bread on the table; if any of the children was well enough to eat there would be sustenance until their mother was well again. She went back to the bedroom and started to wash Dora.

The two rooms on the ground floor were occupied by Mrs Dassett and her children; both her parents and three of her grandparents lived upstairs. The kitchen, shared by all, was in her part of the house and it was often left to her to cook for both floors. Her husband was at the Front and her brothers also, their various families scattered out of reach.

Allen found Mrs Dassett's parents in the first stages of influenza: the man on his back with his mouth wide open, the woman on her side with her hand raised in acknowledgement of their presence by the bed. They needed nothing, she said, except perhaps some water. Were the children all right? Allen told them that Mrs Dassett was ill, chose to lie about the child with cyanosis and said that she would bring water in a few minutes. There was a full chamber pot by the bed with faeces floating in it; it was more than likely that the stained floor around it was due to the overflow – the smell was dreadful.

Allen knew that she should empty the pot. If she left it as it was, they would have no choice but to get themselves downstairs or soil the room. The whole dilemma of her visits to the sick was being distilled in her reluctance to perform this act. This was calling for an extreme, an *utmost* generosity in her. The regular emptying of Lily's commode had exhausted her selflessness. There was a difference – too great a difference – between the concept of charity and the reality of defecation and disease. She closed the door and walked past the other bedroom, the room with the ailing grandparents. Ruth would have to deal with upstairs.

The visit ended badly. Ruth was angry and reproachful – 'If you haven't got the stomach for it, then why didn't you say so! I could have found someone else!' She had used her time industriously: the children were washed, food given where needed, medicine administered and the elderly made decent. Allen had cleaned the kitchen and carried out a fruitless tour of the neighbours to see if any might keep an eye on the family.

They stood by Mrs Dassett's bed to say goodbye. The child with cyanosis was still conscious, smiling up at them with a blue mouth. The other children were asleep again, their hot bodies as separate as space would allow.

'I'll come back in a few hours,' Ruth said to Mrs Dassett. 'Just to see if you need anything. And I'll take your key this time.' The slightest of movements. 'Is that all right?' Another movement. 'Till later, then.'

Outside, Allen said, 'That boy's in danger.'

'I know.'

'Are you really going to come back?'

'We can't just leave them.'

'Do you want me with you?'

'I think I can manage. I'm sure you'd rather not bother.' Ruth put on her gloves. 'Why don't you go home?'

'Why don't I? I'll call in on Tite and leave a message about the boy.'

*   *   *

I spent the morning conducting funerals, Jen's among them, leaving Herbert Winter to man the shop. He was told to take simple details from callers and to get on with various jobs; the one thing that could be said in his favour was that he had no need of supervision. Several new orders had come in but the important news concerned a letter that had been delivered from Mrs White for my attention. She'd given Herbert the impression that we had an understanding about some secret business and he seemed to find it smutty, laughing in that way of his, with one hand held over his mouth. It made us all uneasy and embarrassed but it wasn't something you could mention, like a dirty habit or impertinence; even so, I was finding it more difficult to bear and had to turn away as soon as he started.

The letter was from the Local Government Board and addressed to Dr Wey. They wished to apologize for the long delay in replying – staff shortages had overtaken them – but wished to assure him that his comments had been noted and would be looked into. Signed, E Bevens. My immediate thought was that I should write back, in Mrs White's name, saying that Dr Wey was dead and that there was no need for further correspondence.

Then I found myself thinking that this man had no intention of looking into anything; he'd admitted quite freely that they were overwhelmed. I could adjust the date on the second letter – I now thought of it as my letter – put it in a new envelope with handwriting as near to Thomas's as I could manage and address it to Mr E. Bevens in the hope that a renewed entreaty might pass to someone of a higher rank. And what then? If they wanted to meet Thomas they would go to Mrs White's, and the trail that led from there to here and back again might as well have been painted in phosphorus and I would be up to my neck in fraud.

If I'd heard of any arrangements being made to help us out – and by 'us' I mean the public, not just the trade – I would have had no reason to be considering any further action but as it stood there were only two explanations for the government staying quiet: they were uninformed or they'd decided to abandon ship, as it were, leaving us all to die.

Herbert had put the ordinary post on my desk. A note from Allen lay at the bottom, which was a welcome find. She wanted us to meet and made the suggestion that I should come to the basement door that evening and have supper with her in the kitchen. She would expect me at eight unless I wrote to the contrary. I decided to take the letters with me and let her read the evidence for herself. It took me a while to think of a story that would satisfy Walter as to why I was leaving the shop, but I came up with the idea of a late visit to Mr Sucerne; he might well have had some useful information passed to him by Dr Tite, and a brief conversation about the shortage of funeral materials and gravediggers would suit us both. I telephoned, making sure that Walter could hear me, and made the arrangements with Mrs Sucerne; her husband would see me but I wasn't to keep him talking. She spoke to me as if I were selling ribbons. Did she think the dead would bury themselves?

We had a funeral for three after lunch and then I took Harry out to do a delivery and some measuring; it was useful to have him for the light bodies, leaving Walter in charge at the shop. We were standing by the cart at the end of the calls when we heard a dog howling – I guessed it to be waiting by its master's body. We tracked it down, walking in a zigzag way until we found ourselves in an alley with a row of hovels running down one side. They were open to the world with rubbish piled in the doorways and the roofs caving in. We went down the row until we found the place with the dog. It was a brown and white mongrel, so thin you could see all the bones along its back. As soon as it saw us, it began to whimper; it wasn't interested in fighting us off, it just wanted us to know that its master was dead.

We couldn't see very well by this time but the man, if it was a man, was bloated and coming away from himself. He'd been spared a nibbling by rats but it was impossible to say how he'd died. He must have been there for a month or more, with the dog at his side. It was the first time that Harry had seen anything like it and he was sick on the floor in front of me – the smell was bad enough, I have to say. We couldn't do anything. There was nothing on the cart that we could carry him in and in any case he would certainly have ruptured as we picked him up. Harry wanted to take the dog but I made him come away. The creature had made itself comfortable, lying with its head on its master's leg, and you could see it only had a few days left in it. We went back to the shop and I told Frank, the police sergeant. What he did about the man I never found out, but Harry referred to the smell and the dog for some days until I had to tell him to be quiet.

* * *

Lionel Tite was going through his list of afternoon calls. Some of the names were foreign to him, some known and tolerable, some beyond help, some he would prefer not to see under any circumstances. He put the pen down. 'Charlotte!'

'What?' His wife was watering the ferns in the waiting room. The nurse had failed to arrive and Charlotte, as ever in the circumstances, had taken over during morning surgery. She came in, holding the jug. 'What, dear?'

'Why is Mrs Bird on my list?'

'She's not eating, Lionel. I did tell her sister that nobody eats with influenza but she was adamant.'

'She's on hunger-strike.'

'Good heavens!'

'It's a waste of my time.'

'Of course it is. Isn't it a matter for the police?'

'Good luck to them.' He was going through the list again, striking out the malingerers.

'Mrs Thompson's bound to telephone again.' She pressed a finger into the soil of the consulting room fern and found it to be adequately moist. 'What do you want me to say?'

'Whatever you like. Tell her to use force if she has to.' Lionel put the abbreviated list in his pocket and stood up. 'I'll end up at the Drummonds. Can't say when I'll be home but it'll be in time for evening surgery.'

'Your flask's been put in the car.' There was a knock at the front door – a heavy knock, repeated several times. 'And I'll see who that is. Do they think we're deaf?'

His bag was packed. All he needed was his coat and scarf. As he approached the hall, he saw his wife in the porch, having a heated conversation with a woman. The maid had been given the watering jug to hold and was standing to the side; his wife turned to her for a moment and revealed the visitor to be Mrs Thompson. Without breaking step, Lionel changed direction and retreated into the drawing room.

'Doctor Tite?' Allen called over Charlotte's head. 'Doctor Tite? I'd appreciate a word with you. About a very sick child.'

'The doctor's on his way out, Mrs Thompson.' As small as she was, Charlotte was managing to block the entrance, holding her arms out on either side of the doorway. 'He really can't stop to chat with you now.'

'I don't want to chat, Mrs Tite. I've just been visiting a house where the entire family's down with influenza and one of the children is turning blue. So far as I understand it, that's a very dangerous state. Please let me see the doctor. I can't just leave this boy to die.'

'Is he one of the doctor's patients?'

'I have no idea.'

'The doctor's on his way out. I'll give him your message. That's the best I can do.' The sister's hunger-strike appeared to have been supplanted by this child. Charlotte softened. 'There are too many patients wanting his care, Mrs Thompson. He's working alone; you know that. He can't possibly visit every one.'

Allen stared into the house. 'I feel so helpless,' she said.

In the drawing room, Lionel was standing, bag in hand, waiting for a signal from his wife. The murmur of conversation carried on. He was wasting time, precious, precious time; whatever technique Charlotte was employing to discourage Mrs Thompson, it was clearly having no effect. He would walk past them, brazenly, and drive away. He opened the door and went into the hall, stopping to pick up his coat and hat from the stand. Allen saw him and leaned forward, lifting her arm and opening her mouth to speak. Charlotte and the maid turned to see what had attracted her attention and, at that moment, Allen decided to walk between them and enter the house.

Lionel lowered his head and kept walking towards the front door.

Allen said, 'Doctor Tite, I beg you. Please would you take a moment to visit a child with cyanosis? I have the address here.' She held out a piece of paper.

Few things irritated Lionel more than patients using medical terminology. He shook his head and ploughed on as Charlotte took Allen by the arm and held her firmly on the spot. 'Please leave the doctor alone, Mrs Thompson. I've told you. He has a full list for the afternoon and many of the patients on it will be just as ill as this child. You really must go home and look after your sister.'

'My sister?'

Charlotte pushed gently to start Allen's progress towards the door. 'I thought you said your sister wasn't eating very well – when we spoke on the telephone? I'm so sorry that Doctor Tite hasn't been able to visit her' – Allen was moving now and nearly out of the house – 'but as I've been saying—'

'My sister's not at all important. It's the child that concerns me.'

'Hospital!' Charlotte gesticulated with her finger to emphasize the word. 'Why didn't I think of it before? Take the child to hospital.'

'I could—'

'You must.'

Lionel was in the car now; he turned the key and pressed the starter pedal. As the engine came to life, Allen looked round.

Charlotte, poised to restrain her, said, 'I hope you're able to help that child, Mrs Thompson. I really must go in now.'

The car moved away. Allen gave Charlotte the piece of paper with the Dassetts' address. 'If the hospital won't take him in,' she said, 'perhaps Doctor Tite could visit tomorrow.'

* * *

Sarah pushed a sack of sawdust away so that she could gain access to the chair. 'You want to tidy this place up. Isn't that your job, Harry?' The boy looked at her. His cap was sloped over one eye and he was still pale from vomiting.

'Just seen a bad body,' Walter said. 'A stinker.'

'Put your cap on straight.' Sarah beckoned to Harry. 'And come here so I can have a word with you.' He turned to Walter for consent and then made his way through the disorder, trying to control his face. She pulled him down so that he was kneeling on the floor at her side. 'You shouldn't have been there this morning,' she said, close to his ear. 'But your mum would have been proud. And there's no shame in feeling queasy. You ask Walter.' Her hand was resting on his shoulder; she patted him briskly and said, 'Off you go now. Quick march. Sort this muddle out.'

'I don't want to go home,' Harry said.

'Who said you had to go home?'

'Wal– Mr Stephens. He said I could if I wanted to be with Gran.'

'Did he say you had to?'

'No.'

'Well, then. You get this floor clean. You can see your gran soon enough.' Sarah got up. 'Is Henry about, Walter?'

'If he's not outside, he's upstairs.'

'I'll go and have a look.' The yard was empty. She opened the door to the flat and heard the piano. With all that going on down in the workshop! He'd driven them all mad from the first day he'd lifted the lid, when he was four years old and she was barely two. She made as much noise as possible going up the stairs and into the room but he showed no sign of having sensed her arrival and only stopped playing when she put her hand in front of his nose as he looked at the upper end of the keyboard.

'Good afternoon,' she said. 'I'm glad to see you've got a bit of free time. And don't you want a lamp on? It's like a cellar in here.'

He peered up at her. 'What is it?'

'I want to talk to you.'

'I've got to get back to work,' he said, banging the lid shut. 'I haven't got time for one of your homilies so you might as well not start.'

'You've got time to play that ruddy piano. And why are you being so rude to me? I thought your new friend might have taught you a few decent manners.' Sarah hadn't intended to refer to the new friend – she had expressly decided to stick to the point – but now that the subject was raised she pursued it. 'It's not your style, is it? Courting?'

He bent to tighten his shoelaces. 'We'll leave my friends out of this, thank you. If you've got problems with the girls you'll have to sort them out yourself. There's no end to this' – he straightened up – 'and nothing I can do except what I have to do. I've taken Harry on. That'll help Elsie.'

'You took him on because you needed him. And no end to *what*?'

'To this… circumstance. As to Harry, I could have had any one of twenty boys.'

'Aren't you the big man?'

After a long pause, Henry said, 'What's the matter, then?'

'What *isn't*, more like.'

'I told you. Harry—'

'It's not just Harry. It's the way you're running things. That funeral looked as if it'd been put together by a mob.'

'I'm doing what I can.'

'You've cut corners.' The room was nearly dark now, their faces bobbed over their black work clothes. Sarah looked at Henry's tight mouth and thought that this was how it had been from the beginning; he would always get angry if you made a comment, believing you were out to do him harm. 'I know you're having to struggle to keep up but we've got standards.'

'*We've* got sta—'

'If we'd been of a mind, we could have taken over from Dad and left you out altogether. It would have been Speake and *Daughters*.'

'Don't make me laugh.'

'There are women doing this job and you know it. *And* they've had to learn to do it just as well as their husbands or whatever. From the state of things downstairs you might be glad of someone to bring a bit of order in. It's a midden, your workshop.'

'I told you this morning – you can have it all whenever you like. You can knit yourself some coffins and dig the holes to put them in. You get your money every month. You all get your money.'

'Why are you so rude and sour?'

They said no more to each other, each going their own way at the bottom of the stairs. When Sarah got to the shop door she was faced with a man on the other side, making his way in. She opened the door and stood back.

'Please take a seat,' she said. 'Mr Speake will be with you in a moment.'

* * *

Amy was lying down, the pillow behind her in bright contrast to the heliotrope of her face and neck. She appeared to be in no distress although, when questioned by Lionel, admitted to a sore throat, a headache, a 'slight' soreness in the chest and pain in her joints if she moved at all.

Lionel lifted her hand from the bed and kissed it. 'Don't you want more pillows?'

'Flat's better,' she said. 'How's Gramp?'

Despite the nurse's warning, the shock of seeing Amy in this state had allowed his feelings to outwit him. He kept the hand in his for a moment, on the pretext of taking a pulse.

'I'm seeing you first.'

'Write to Mother?'

'I did it last night.'

'Thanks.'

'I'm told you slept well.'

'Mmmm.'

'Can you read?'

'Eyes are too sore.'

'Could somebody read to you?'

'Will you?'

'If you want. Of course I will.'

'I'll be up soon.'

'You stay where you are. I've got spies.' Did she have no idea of the severity of her illness? Or was she being courageous for his benefit? He pulled a chair to the bedside. 'Are you in the middle of anything?'

'... *Thirty-Nine Steps*.'

The book was on the bedside table. She followed carefully for the first few pages but soon she was deeply asleep, breathing quickly but with no apparent effort. He closed the book and sat looking at her with his hands resting on the cover. There was nothing, in his experience, that was in the least degree successful in the treatment of these pneumonic complications, however bright the patient. She would die within the week.

Except for the clacking sound of his breath, John Drummond might have been a dead man; he was absolutely still in the bed with his arms stretched out beside him on the covers. Lionel had asked the maid for whisky; he poured two glasses now and sat beside him drinking. 'It's Lionel,' he said, when John woke up. 'You've been asleep.'

'You been here all day?'

'Never left the chair.'

John's face was so emaciated that his expression was hard to read. 'Funny. How's Amy?'

'Doing well.'

'Is she in bed?'

'At least a week more.'

'And Phyllis?'

'I wrote to her.' The letter had been a most difficult one to write, urging Phyllis to come down as soon as she was able. 'And how are you? There's a whisky here, if you'd like it.'

'Show me.' Lionel held the glass near John's nose. 'Marvellous.' He closed his eyes and let his head sink back into the pillow. 'Pain's bad today. Anything you can do?'

'Morphine?'

'Yes.'

Lionel bared John's emaciated arm and filled the syringe. 'I'll tell the nurse to give you more when you need it. You should have had this days ago.'

'I hate injections.'

'I don't think you'll mind this one.'

'Will you stay while I'm awake?'

'Of course.'

'I want company.'

'I'm here.'

When John was asleep, Lionel stayed in the chair and looked about the room, hoarding it in his memory for the time when he would want to be here and have no reason for it. With her father dead, Phyllis would certainly sell the house; Amy's brothers had either been killed in the war or were still fighting it and the money from the sale would be a boon to any survivors. Sympathy for the grandfather and granddaughter who'd died in adjacent rooms would turn to indifference soon enough and the story suppressed for nervous buyers. And then the cedar would be cut down to let more light in to the front of the house and he would drive past and look at the newly visible windows and see only cold, vacant glass. These two beloved people would vanish from the earth. There was no reunion, of that he was certain: one could only look forward to extinction. Did one look forward to it? The place where he would have made tears was active. He finished both glasses of whisky and went back to Amy's room to say goodbye.

*   *   *

My visit to Mr Sucerne was brief. The people seem to put up with him but he's a bit of a toady and I couldn't imagine a queue forming if his wife died. She hovered about, fiddling with a long chain she had round her neck and murmuring every time I spoke. He ignored her noise, which only confirmed my view of him. I told him how things were for the trade, he told me what to expect from the gravediggers, and we parted with relief, on my side at least.

I was knocking on Allen's basement door at exactly eight o'clock, with all the things I wanted to show her stowed away in my pockets. It was unusually difficult to start the evening off. There seemed to be no opportunity for a proper exchange during the meal; she was more on edge than I was used to and even general conversation died out several times with her not taking up the subjects I volunteered. When she was clearing away I asked her about her sister and the lie, and mentioned my own difficulties with Sarah. After that we had no problem at all.

Her situation was poor, with the sister starving herself and the maid's friend ill upstairs. When she asked me about the progress of the influenza from my point of view, I took that to be the perfect starting place. I put out Thomas's letter, his papers, the letter from Mr Bevens and the Quaker journal, laying them in front of her on the table with a bit of explanation and then sitting back while she examined them all. She read each one with care, looking up at me before she laid it down and picked up the next. When it came to the journal, the last item, she opened it at the page with the poem – I'd marked it with a slip of paper – and read it through; then she looked briefly at the other writings, stopping occasionally at one page or another before returning to the poem and reading it out loud. Not to me, more as if she were telling it to herself.

'I've made a song of it,' I said when she'd finished, and told her that I thought her voice might suit the melody.

She said that I'd never heard her sing and I replied that you could tell *a good voice by the speaking tunes. Neither of us knew what to deal with first after that, so we sat and looked at the table until I picked up Thomas's letter and held it between us; there was a tear beginning in the fold and I thought that I should glue it on to a clean sheet of paper to lengthen its life. She put her forefinger out to the letter and touched it without trying to take it out of my hand.*

'Do you believe him?' she said. 'Do you really think it might be the end of the world?'

'Not the end,' I said. 'I think there'll be enough children left to start us off again.'

It frightened her, the way I was describing things. Was I really saying that any attempts we might make to ward off the influenza were a waste of time? She asked me, given that the public was never made privy to government plans, how I could be sure that nothing was being done. I couldn't be sure, I said, but so far as I knew, the ports were open and troops were moving across the world. The free passage of men would guarantee calamity.

She said, 'But they can't just keep the troops idle. And if it's true that we're close to armistice, then are you saying that the men have to stay where they are? Not come home? That's absurd.' She was like a child, wanting me to say that the dead bird on the grass was sleeping. She must have seen some impatience in my face because she changed tack and told me that I was in a disagreeable position if Bevens ever decided to find out more about Thomas Wey.

In my opinion, I said, there was little likelihood of further correspondence from Mr Bevens and then I said – and I saw it for the truth – that there was no likelihood of any letter I might write being opened by someone of significance. The experience of declaring myself to her was very different to the experience of chewing things over in private; as I spoke, my indecision fell away.

'There's no point to any of this,' I said in the end. 'There's nothing I can do and no reason to be telling you any of it. The more I explain, the more

I can see that there's no point at all. I should never have disturbed you in the first place.'

'Then why did you?' she said.

I told her that I'd wanted her opinion and she asked me if I still did and I said yes, why not, if she was willing. Then she said – after some hesitation – that she believed my views to be extreme and that my work must have given me a particular inclination to see death wherever I looked. I replied that death was now the only spectacle for any of us and that we would soon have to look no further than an arm's length to see it.

We said goodnight soon after that. As I put the papers back in my pockets, she said that we should meet again and I agreed.

I was back at the shop before I realized that I'd had no urgent need to leave her kitchen, no feelings of having to get out. By submitting to the facts and abandoning my roundabout thoughts, I had arrived at a state of mind that I can honestly describe as peaceful.

*   *   *

Wednesday, 30 October

Ruth had spent the first part of the morning in her parents' company and then an hour writing to Jack, always the most difficult thing. How did one keep up morale without deception? She had seen no shows – always good to describe – and called on no one but Allen and the sick. If she were honest about her difficulties with Allen he would tell her to find another friend; if she were honest about the epidemic and the school closure he would be frightened for her. And what if he were experiencing Spanish 'flu in the trenches? It was more than likely; the newspapers were saying it was worldwide now.

After a few false starts she wrote about the children who were recovering well and a paragraph about her parents and their kindness, then she began to tell the story of Allen and the undertaker, trying to make a joke of it. As she developed the narrative she realized that she was more sympathetic than she'd intended to be, enjoying Allen's adventure and relating it as a burgeoning affair despite the fact that nothing of the kind had ever been suggested. She closed the letter in her usual way, quoting from a poem that she'd written for their engagement, the night before his embarkation:

> I will still love you,
> Always I'll love you,
> When the flowers you gave me,
> Have died in my hair.

The lines had come to her in a dream and their significance had been immediately apparent: they were a charm for him to carry to the Front. She wanted him to know her as the embodiment of patience, holding her post at the lookout, her face turned to France.

There were some cuttings to enclose with the letter – articles about the war and a review of a new play. She folded everything into an envelope and weighed it in her hand; it was too heavy for a normal stamp. If she tidied herself up now and left quickly she would have time to go to the post office on her way to Allen's.

While she was writing she had begun to feel a weakness in her neck and shoulders, the result, she assumed, of an unsettled night. As she stood up a headache assaulted her, then she was hot in the face. The surface of her skin, particularly the soft skin on the inside of her arms, became too sensitive to bear the touch of her blouse. She sat back in the chair with the letter in her hand. Her only experience of illness had been an early, mild bout of chicken pox and she had no gauge against which her symptoms could be measured. Was this nothing more than a chill brought on by walking in damp air? To be ill now would mean that her parents would have to care for her; if this was influenza, she would be caged in her room – and worse, in her bed – for a week at least.

A noise on the landing made her turn round but the pain behind her eyes arrested the movement. Her arms and legs were quivering. She stood and then fell into the desk at the moment that her mother opened the door.

*   *   *

Allen had risen early, dressed and then spent some time lying on her bed with paper and pencil, trying to write a good list for the day. Her sleep had been interrupted with dreams, none of which she remembered clearly, although the predominant image had been a simple one of large machines whirring and sparking. She was in no doubt of her bond with the machinery but had, as yet, no idea of whether she was to restrain the potential explosion or surrender to it. Was it in her power to decide? Henry's insistence that there was 'no point at all' had infected her. Were they all to die? If he were right, then her attempts at charity were futile; her last days or weeks would be better spent in reflection on her own life.

Edward had left for France expecting to be home within months. Their goodbye had been painful because of the separation, not because either of them had expected him to die. Was that for the best? Did one always believe that the bullet would pass over one's head?

And if she did come down with influenza, there was no reason why she shouldn't survive – she'd heard of many people who had been terribly ill and were convalescing now. Henry had no answer to that. *Many* people. They might be low in spirits but they were on their feet. Henry was preoccupied; she had told him so and it was the truth. He saw death wherever he looked. He would see death in an April meadow!

Allen put the pencil in her mouth and picked up the list: wash Lily (a determined item this, not written without repugnance); see if Ada needs help with Gladys; collect Ruth; take the Dassett child to hospital; shop for food. She looked up at the grey dawn filling the window between the open curtains. The room was cold but she had no wish to leave it – unless it was to find Lily unconscious and in the last stages of her fast. To admit that, even to herself, was an awful glimpse into the treacherous whirring machinery. Was she really hoping that Lily would die? The long-case clock struck seven. Allen folded the list and tore it in half; there was nothing on it that she could forget to do. The contrast between her benevolent and murderous selves was a continuing revelation. She put on her shoes and went downstairs to fetch a bowl of warm water.

Lily was lying against a wall of pillows, the only arrangement that suited her for both waking and sleeping. The skin on her face was changing every day, becoming a little darker as it dried out. The rims of her eyes were so red that she might have burnt them; the eyes themselves were withdrawing into their sockets. If she moves too quickly, Allen thought, they'll rattle like marbles in a cup.

'Would you like a wash?' she said. 'And I've got clean sheets.'

Lily shook her head.

'A drink?'

She nodded.

Allen poured a small amount into a glass and held it to her mouth. 'Is it painful for you to talk?' A sip and another nod. 'You'll have to drink more.' Lily sighed and closed her eyes.

'Lily?'

'Mm?'

'You really are making yourself very ill. There's no one here but you and me; no Germans, no Ada. You must believe me – and you must start to eat and drink or you'll make yourself so weak that you won't be able to swallow.'

No sound, no movement.

Allen folded back the bedclothes, alarming Lily so much that she bared her teeth. 'I have to,' Allen said. 'You can't lie here. Help me to get you out of bed.'

'Leave me.'

The temptation to walk away was considerable; Allen had to resist it by locking her knees. 'You smell rather bad. I think you have to have a wash and the sheets have to be changed. I'm going to do it now, because I have to clean the house and go shopping and I don't want to leave you in this state.'

Lily set her jaw and stared at the foot of the bed.

'Well?'

'Leave.'

'No.' Allen reached down and put her arms under Lily. She was rigid, tensing against Allen's attempt to lift her to the chair. 'I shall simply drop you,' Allen said, and let Lily fall awkwardly on to the cushions, her legs sticking out in front of her like sticks. She said nothing while Allen made the bed, watching with her head tilted.

'I'm going to wash you now.' Another struggle, a more difficult one, in which Allen's hands were badly scratched as she tried to wipe Lily's sore red buttocks. From the knees to the ankles, her legs were swollen, in terrible contrast to the jutting bones on her hips and shoulders. It was all very well to walk away from an overflowing chamber pot at the Dassetts'; she could hardly neglect her own sister's ugly, failing body. As gently as she could, she dried the inflamed patches of skin, dressed Lily in a clean nightgown and put her back to bed, on her side this time, to spare her buttocks.

'Now,' she said, 'I'm going to try and get the doctor to you.'

'But the enemy—'

'What enemy?'

Lily shook her head and closed her eyes.

'I can't make you eat, Lily but if you insist on behaving like this I shall have to take you to hospital. You wouldn't like that, would you? Being taken to hospital?'

Lily appeared to be asleep.

'I have to go out now. You'll have time to think.'

186

Hospital! How had she come to *that*! She picked up the bowl and left the room, angry with herself for not having thought of it sooner and equally angry with herself for having thought of it at all.

* * *

The national incidence of mortality, as Eric Bevens could see from the reports on his desk, was rising at a rate previously unheard of by the Local Government Board. The peculiar characteristic of the age distribution was singular in itself: young adults making up the majority of the dead. Sir Arthur Newsholme had sent no communication that pertained to the figures and the few clerks remaining would normally be required to note and file, not to pass judgement. No clerk here was senior to Eric Bevens; no duties had been laid out for him. To accept the bald facts without investigation might appear to be an oversight. He would show initiative. He would make enquiries.

Dr Wey's letter, as yet unfiled, lay on top of the out-tray. Eric Bevens got to his feet, intending to gather post from other desks, and saw the words '*imminent plague*'. He picked up the letter and read it through again. No other correspondence of this nature had been received and although it might have been written in a less inflated style, it certainly described something of the present predicament. Was this man anticipating the epidemic? Did he have information that had not been made available to the government? Was he describing influenza or some other sickness that mimicked it, initiated by an enemy agent injecting poison into the reservoirs? To visit Dr Wey would mean a short detour on his journey home; he would arrive unannounced and endeavour to determine the man's means of prophecy.

* * *

Rose and I wrote to each other every month or so, her more regularly than me, but if she'd been in England I doubt that I would have said a word to Allen, Rose being all I needed by way of an ear. I always put down whatever was on my mind, but with this latest letter, I was very aware of the six weeks that it would take for the letter to reach New Zealand. In that time, who could say what we might have come to? If the letter reached her at all.

I usually said a few words about the family – she didn't feel herself to be part of them any more than I did but she liked to keep up. The main gist of the letter, and I only thought of it as I was telling her my fears about the accumulation of bodies, was that I'd come up with a solution: mass cremation. The absence of pine shells would mean that the deceased would have to be well wrapped and disposed of quickly but it only takes little more than an hour to reduce a man to ashes; with continuous burning you might have been able to deal with twenty or more bodies in a day. I even thought that they could put several in at once, if there was space.

In the years since cremation became available, I hadn't been able to persuade a single customer. The cost restricted many but you could see that the old ideas stood in the way; people saw it as a godless end with nothing left of you to be collected at the Judgement. Faced with having a body in residence for several weeks, would they begin to see the value of it? And with such numbers the costs could be lowered to match the cheapest burial. In fact, as I pointed out to Rose, it would benefit the country if mass cremation were paid for by the local boards.

When I came back from the embalming classes I was always full of what I'd learned and it was only Rose that I could tell in my letters. The recipe for the fluid – alcohol, formalin and glycerine, even syrup would do! – had amused her. The others got the wind up, copying my father. They said I was unnatural. 'You're playing with the dead. Have some respect.' That's the sort of thing Sarah would say every time she caught me looking at my text-book. I'd argue my case and encourage her to read the foreword but she wouldn't even open the cover in case she was corrupted. I reminded Rose about all that and I was feeling quite hearty, imagining her with her wide eyes, when I realized that my wonderful idea was senseless. With the three London crematoria and Woking all going at full pelt, you'd only manage 240 bodies a day, or thereabouts – and that was only if you could pack three into the incinerator. And if you had healthy men to stoke the fires. So even then, after believing that I'd come to a more peaceful state of mind, I was still trying to dispose of the mountains of dead. Does every undertaker feel accountable? My conversations within the trade, and I've chosen to have as few as possible, have never come close to discussing any mutual beliefs.

I went back to the letter and said some of this to Rose, telling her that if you gave me a dead body to bury and a piano to play and asked me to choose, I'd be pulled from both sides with a hand on each. Then I mentioned the song I'd made of the poem and that led on to Allen, which was where I finished, describing how useful she'd been in the matter of Thomas Wey. Not to be able to see my Rose, that was difficult for me. Six weeks makes for a long gap in a conversation. You say, 'How are you?' and she says, 'I'm this or I'm that,' and by the time you read her answer everything's different to how it was when she wrote it. No letter can make up for the sight of a face, when everything that passes between you is understood without a word spoken. I know I could have joined her, she said that often enough. I ask myself why I didn't and the answer's always the same. However much I loved Rose, I feared the world more.

No funeral took me further than the horses could travel; I liked the edge of things to be within sight, not in the far distance. New Zealand might as well have been in fairyland. I was never going to get on a boat and set sail for a place I couldn't find on my own.

*   *   *

There were two dead in the house. 'Don't you want to come in, Doctor?' the woman said to Lionel. 'They're upstairs, my girls.'

The previous visit, to a second-floor flat, had been the finish of him; his back was aching and his legs were so weary that he could barely keep them from buckling. He wrote the death certificates, not even stepping over the threshold into the hall, despite the woman's pleas. The urge to lie down was so overpowering that the smallest push would have sent him sliding down the door-frame. He handed over the certificates and went back to the car, easing himself gratefully into the seat and closing his eyes. This influenza was virulent and it had no cure; he was ultimately impotent. Not much hope for the young, none for the cyanosed, more hope – extraordinary this – for the elderly, but even their prognosis depended as much, or more, on the care they received as on anything that he could offer.

The visiting list was on the dashboard. He opened his eyes, cupped his chin in his hand and looked down the names; not one of them was worth the fight it would take him to get in and out of the car. In a rare eager moment, he picked up the list and tore it into small pieces, stuffing them into the front pocket of his bag. The morning was free. He would go to the Drummonds.

Although he had instructed the nurse to send a telegram in the event of John or Amy dying, there was no certainty that a telegram would arrive – the shortage of operators was making the telephone unusable, so why not every other service? – and for all he knew, the nurse herself had collapsed, leaving her charges to die in the hands of a housemaid. He started the car and drove the short distance to the house; he arrived in fifteen minutes and was relieved to find the nurse there, opening Amy's door. She closed it again and stood, waiting for him.

'How is she?' he said, taking off his coat and hat and handing them to her.

'Miss Drummond had another nosebleed this morning but her pulse is steady. Respiration forty to the minute but only slight chest pain. Cyanosis slightly worse but quite alert.'

'Is she distressed?'

'Occasionally.' The nurse looked at the door. 'Rather badly after the nosebleed.'

'And Mr Drummond?'

'No change from yesterday, Doctor.'

Amy was still lying flat in the bed. She smiled at Lionel and said, 'G'morning,' in a near whisper. There was certainly a deterioration; even a passing stranger would have described the girl in the bed as having a slight hold on life.

'I've decided to be a credit to my profession. How are you feeling?'

'Fluey. Bad smell. How's Gramp?'

'I'm going to see him in a minute. I'll come back and report.' He took her hand; the fingers were blue. 'Would you like me to read to you?'

'Please.'

Despite her love of medicine, she had asked him nothing; she was confiding in the nurse and protecting him. He read to her, looking up from the book every so often to watch her face; she made no comments as she had the day before. By the end of the first page, her eyes were closed.

'I'll come back when I've seen Mr Drummond,' he said to the nurse. 'Call me if you have to.'

As always now, John was asleep. Lionel sat in the chair for a while, fighting his own tiredness but waking with a start every few minutes to find his head lolling on his chest. The bed was large and John was very small in it, taking up no more than a quarter of the space. The mattress was soft; it spoke to him, it summoned him. A rest would give him the strength to continue. His legs ached. He was old, he needed to lie down… Lionel got on to the bed, arranging himself carefully so as not to pull on the sheet. When the nurse came to tell him that Amy was unconscious she found the two men close together; Dr Tite asleep, in his suit and shoes, and John Drummond, newly dead, his hand on his friend's right shoulder.

Despite the cold, Ada's window was wide open. She had given up any attempt to wear uniform, being excused all duties except those which would benefit Gladys, and was wearing her ordinary clothes with a coat over the top. The fire was unequal to the weather and only warmed the air within a foot of the flame.

'How is she?' Allen gave Ada the coffee she'd made for her and went to the foot of the bed. The robust, red-faced Gladys had purple tints in her ears and on her lips; her eyelids were drooping and her attention directed entirely inward.

'She's had a bad night, ma'am. Very hot and not answering to her name.' Ada was shivering, despite the coat.

Was Allen to be honest? There was nothing she could say about Gladys's state without lying or causing more alarm, not that Ada couldn't see the danger for herself. She cleared her throat and said, 'You'd better shut the window just a little or you'll catch a chill. And drink that coffee, it'll warm you up.'

Allen's arrival with food and drink had become, since Gladys's collapse, commonplace. Even so, Ada was reluctant to accept, never taking anything from Allen without saying something about the situation being topsy-turvy. This time, she drained the mug without comment and put it on the bedside table. 'I don't like her going that colour,' she said. 'I've heard that's the worst thing, when that happens.'

'It's not good. I think that's true,' Allen said. Oh God! Gladys might die and Ada and Lily and any number of Dassetts; there was nervous laughter in her throat at the high drama, the *piles* of bodies, the bus that she would have to hire to get them all to the cemetery…

She put her arms round Ada, who accepted the embrace without question, holding her cheek to Allen's and closing her eyes. The consolation eased them both and they stood in silence until Gladys tried, unsuccessfully, to cough, which turned Ada's attention to the bed.

'I've got to go out now,' Allen said. 'I'll come up as soon as I get back.'

After making a short list of necessary shopping, she put on her coat and hat and stood in the hall. There was no sound from Lily's room, and no sound from upstairs. A stranger might have imagined that the house was at peace! Allen had no doubt that taking the Dassett boy to hospital would atone for her lack of 'stomach'. It was still early; she would arrive at Ruth's house in time to forestall any other outing she might have planned.

To Allen's surprise, the maid directed her into the drawing room where Ruth's father, a man she rarely saw, informed her that his daughter was in bed with what they assumed to be influenza, brought on by her determination to visit the sick. He understood that their motives were entirely altruistic – and he applauded unselfish behaviour without reservation! – but thought, nevertheless, that as the older – he paused here – that as the *older* friend, she should perhaps have had the prudence to withdraw from the exercise in order to save the young person *in her charge* from harm, particularly as he and Mrs Bell had rarely been at home in recent weeks. Would she have allowed her own daughter to immerse herself in these infected swamps?

In response, she asked only if Ruth could have visitors. He said no, not for several days. They were probably the same age, Allen and this man – old enough to speak to each other with courtesy and common sympathy – but he had chosen to deny her access to his house and to his daughter. She tried once more, requesting a few minutes in which to reassure Ruth of her love and prayers. She was again refused. Would he pass on a message? He would say that she'd called. If she held out her hand to shake his in farewell, she knew that he would hesitate and the consequent humiliation would make it impossible for her to leave the house with any composure. She thanked him for seeing her and left the room. The hall was empty. Could she run up to Ruth? She went to the bottom of the stairs and looked up; if she were caught there would be a scene and all future visits would be barred.

Mr Bell came out into the hall. She knew that she must look as startled as a thief ambushed in bright electric light. Darting for the front door, she let herself out before he could rebuke her again. Would Ruth have done the same? Would Ruth have allowed a man – even her father – to intimidate her? She would go to the Dassetts and retrieve the morning's momentum.

But Ruth had the key. Mrs Dassett had let her take it so that she could let herself in on Tuesday evening. Had she kept it? There was clearly no possibility that Mr Bell would allow her to go through his daughter's bag. If the Dassetts' door were locked, she would have to ask a neighbour to help her over the back fence. Ruth would want her to do that; Ruth would expect her to carry the flag.

The streets were quiet, except for the increasing number of hearses. People passed her with their heads lowered and their hands in their pockets, compact, masked, warding off infection by shutting down the entry points, raising their faces to pay respects to the passing dead and then lowering them quickly, as soon as the hearse had gone. When she got to the house, she found the door open and an old man in the kitchen. He introduced himself as Mrs Dassett's uncle and said that he'd seen young Miss Bell the night before and that she'd left him with the key and told him to expect her back that morning.

He was visiting his brother – the old man upstairs? – and was most upset to find them all in this state. In fact, he'd had to sleep in here on account of the lack of a bed. Not being a nurse and therefore of no use to anybody, he was thinking that he'd go home rather than spend another night sitting bolt upright on a hard chair.

Allen explained that she'd come to take the boy to hospital. Had he seen him? He had, and a terrible sight it was. They went together to the bedroom. Mrs Dassett opened her eyes and peered at them both. There was no point asking her for permission to take her son; she could barely see.

The boy's whole face was blue. He was unconscious. Allen got him out of bed, disentangling him from the other children, who rearranged themselves into the gap without waking. He was no more than two years old, wet and smeared with faeces. He would have to be washed before she could take him to hospital. The old man led the way back to the kitchen, swearing at them all for wasting his time and money and not telling him to stay at home; there was hot water, he said, if she wanted it, left over from making his tea.

She found a tablecloth and laid the boy on it, washing him as well as she could with a rag torn in two to give her a flannel and a towel. For the second time that day, her disgust had been overthrown – by what? Virtue? Did a mother wash her baby out of charity? Faced with this sick family she felt no kindness, only an urgent need to *do*.

Telling the old man to watch the boy, she ran back to the bedroom and searched the chest of drawers for some clean item of clothing that she could wrap him in to take him to the hospital – why hadn't she thought about this before she left the house? She could have brought linen and shawls, blankets, everything… There was a girl's dress in a drawer and a coat hanging on a hook. She put the coat round him and asked the old man to stay until she came back. How long would she be? She had no idea. All day? She hoped not. He agreed to stay until two o'clock.

There were no taxi-cabs in these streets. She had at least had the sense to investigate the whereabouts of the nearest hospital and if she walked quickly and held him to her, he should be able to stand the cold for the twenty minutes or so that it would take to walk there. He was heavy but she found a tolerable way of carrying him, with the coat-sleeves as a kind of muffler for his throat.

The hospital turned her away. They had no spare beds; there were very few nurses left standing; they were dreadfully sorry but there were so many desperate people…

Allen carried the boy home and laid him next to his mother. The old man was ready to leave. He held the key out, for the undertaker, he said.

He'd just come from upstairs and his sister-in-law was stone dead; he'd left his address on the kitchen table, if somebody would be kind enough to inform him about the funeral.

*   *   *

Telling the few remaining junior clerks that he was on an errand for Sir Arthur, Eric Bevens left work a little earlier than usual. The Tube was erratic now so extra time had to be allowed, and although there were no crowds in the present crisis, he preferred to sit in the emptiest possible carriage. An appointment made with Dr Wey might have saved him an unnecessary journey but Eric Bevens had forsworn deliberation; he was in the mood for enterprise. He found the address without difficulty and saw immediately that it was a lodging-house. Dr Wey was not a wealthy man.

In order to make an impression on the landlady – she might have thought it politic to protect the tenants of her house by denying their existence – the official nature of the visit was emphasized but to Eric Bevens's disappointment, his quarry had passed away. 'Spanish 'flu,' she said, pointing. 'Right there, on the street.'

'Do you happen to know any more about him? The nature of his employment perhaps?'

'I'm afraid I don't know anything at all, sir. But I did give his papers to Mr Speake, the undertaker. He was going to deal with everything for me. It's very difficult in these situations, being left with belongings. I certainly wouldn't want anyone to think I'd taken what wasn't mine to give, but when you're left with belongings, what choice have you?'

He missed the opportunity to reassure Mrs White. There were other, potentially important, questions. 'Did he have any relatives that you know of?'

'An uncle, sir. So far as I know, he's the only one. Mr Speake can tell you more. He's had correspondence with him, I'm sure. Payment and so forth.' Her fear of scrutiny was transparent. 'Why don't you go and have a word with him, sir? He's only down the street. Look,' she pointed again, 'you can see the sign from here. Speake & Son. It's Henry you want, the old man's dead.'

His experience of the undertaking trade – the *dismal* trade, as it was known to him – was confined to the normal run of funerals that any man might have encountered by the age of fifty or so. He had never considered the general undertaker's existence beyond admitting to the unfortunate need of one in relation to a deceased relative. He approached the shop, therefore, expecting to meet a dreary, avaricious man of dull intelligence, quick only to take advantage. Would Mr Speake expect to be paid for Wey's papers? Would he have had the wit not to burn them in the grate?

The man who came forward to greet him bore no likeness to this mental portrait; he resembled the head of a government department.

'Good afternoon,' the man said. 'How may I help you?'

'I was hoping to see Mr Henry Speake.'

'I'm Henry Speake. May I help you?'

'I've been informed that you're in possession of certain papers belonging to the late Doctor Thomas Wey. Am I correct?' Now that he was sure of his ground, Eric Bevens was as blunt with Henry Speake as he would have been with any social inferior. 'Do you have them?'

There was a slight delay, then Henry said, 'May I ask who I'm addressing?'

'Bevens. My name is Bevens. Do you have these papers on the premises?'

'What particular interest do you have in these papers, Mr Bevens?' Speake was interrogating him!

'I'm making enquiries on behalf of Sir Arthur Newsholme at the Local Government Board.'

'The Local Government Board.'

There! Put in his proper place! 'Is it your *practice* to take personal papers from the deceased?'

'No. Most certainly not.'

'The landlady says that she gave you his papers.'

'I must ask what you're hoping to find.'

'Must you? Doctor Wey has an uncle, I believe. Do you have his address?'

'I do.' Henry opened the ledger and turned back the pages. He found the address and wrote it down. 'May I ask you again, Mr Bevens? What do you expect to find?'

'It's government business. Nothing to do with you.' He couldn't look the man in the face in case there was no trace of subservience; unable to settle on any particular object, Eric Bevens's eyes darted from wall to wall and desk to floor, as if he were watching flies.

'Suppose I do have the papers,' Henry said. 'And that I've read them. Does that not make them my business?'

'You've read them?' In the normal course of a year, Eric Bevens might meet opposition in the form of a less than accommodating ticket clerk; this was open contest. The man was belligerent. 'You admit that you've stolen papers from a dead man and read them? And now you're refusing to hand them over to a government board?'

'I've admitted nothing.'

'I shall take the matter further.' He pointed at Henry. 'We may prosecute!'

'Are these papers so important?'

'I won't know until I see them!' Eric Bevens was so angry that he felt hot. Having chosen to pursue this course of action, he was unable to withdraw. He didn't even care about the dammed papers! This wasn't even a plague! The weather was cold. There was an epidemic of seasonal influenza. Next week's figures would show a decline and the whole thing would be over. Still looking anywhere but at Henry's face, he said, 'Good afternoon, Mr Speake. You'll be hearing from me. And from Doctor Wey's uncle, I have no doubt.'

'Good afternoon, Mr Bevens.'

With no more than a brief nod of the head, Eric Bevens stepped into the street. His opinion of undertakers had been revised; they might be avaricious but they were not dull; they were entirely indifferent to moral law and lacking in deference. When the war was over, he would do everything in his power to make the trade accountable.

*　　*　　*

I was visited by Mr Bevens from the Local Government Board, a man without civility. I've been ill-mannered in my life, but not so ill-mannered that I've damaged the business. Any rudeness on my part has always had good cause. I've been severe with some late-payers, for instance, people who refuse to clear their bills. Don't they consider the cost to me? I imagine they see the funeral as their right; I'm the means, nothing more. Sometimes they confuse me with the cause of death; by not paying me, they're reproaching me for their loss. That's another thought I've had many times. If they don't pay then you have to use your judgement but I can be severe, I admit to that.

So far as my meeting with Mr Bevens goes, I was ill-mannered. There was no reason for it, except that I was thrown off balance and unable to think straight. If he'd been more civil, I might have obliged him on the spot. The simple story I could have told, the simple lie – that I had no idea what the papers were about, that I'd taken them to do Mrs White a favour and that I hadn't looked at them from that day to this – would have fixed it. Here are your papers, sir. Please take them away. Or I could have told him that I'd burnt the bloody papers or buried them or sent them to the uncle and they'd got lost in the post.

Would they be of use to the country now or was it too late? If Mr Bevens did read them, would he understand a word? Would I be prosecuted for taking them? Sarah was already accusing me of bringing down our good name. I might very well be taken to court for stealing from the deceased. After he'd gone, I couldn't put my mind to anything; I had to tell Allen.

I was trying to think of an excuse to leave the shop – and this was curi- ous – when she came to find me. One of the families that she'd been visit- ing had lost an old woman and a child. She hadn't laid them out so I told her where she might find Sarah and we made an arrangement to meet at the deceased's house in an hour. We told each other nothing else, nothing that Walter might have misunderstood.

What would Thomas Wey have said if he'd been face to face with Mr Bevens? When Allen had gone I went upstairs to look at the papers again. The stable door, so to speak, was now wide open. I saw him, in despair, refusing to say a word on his own behalf. To soothe us both, I played the piano until Walter shouted up at me to stop and come back to work.

✻   ✻   ✻

Sarah Speake wasn't at home. A woman from the basement flat heard Allen knocking and came up the outside stairs; if Allen wanted Sarah, she'd find her round the corner, at her sister's house, the only one in the row with a red door. The woman apologized for her forgetfulness over the house number but her recent attack of influenza had meddled with her memory. Did she want Sarah for a birth or a laying-out? When Allen said the latter, the woman began to cry. Her husband had died of Spanish 'flu just two weeks ago after being blinded and losing his hands at Ypres. He'd pulled through that and come home. Why would God save a man and then kill him? And she'd had the 'flu that badly herself, he'd died next to her in the bed, turning as blue as you like and her not being able to lift a finger.

Allen murmured her sympathy through the mask. As sorry as she was, the story was more than she could bear. Poised for flight, with her weight on her left foot and her body turned in the direction of the road, she waited until the woman was blowing her nose, then wished her well for the future and walked away, saying something over her shoulder about having to find Sarah before it was too late. Although she was exhausted and her feet hurt, the pleasure of being alone again lifted her step; other people's misery flung a sort of net over her. Did they have to unburden themselves? The sun was setting, another comfort; she never failed to find pleasure in cool, dark air.

Henry had hinted at a rift with his sisters but said nothing to explain it. No two members of a family were alike – think of her and Lily! – but there was a common set of laws in every household. Had he tried to escape? Or was it a law for the Speakes to stay rooted? If there was a rift, then perhaps they disapproved of him; in her eyes, his only fault was a certain single-mindedness and in other, kinder circumstances, he might be less so.

The house was poor but the step was clean and the knocker well-polished. A stocky woman with handsome features answered the door; she had such a likeness to Henry that Allen was confident enough to introduce herself. The woman said yes, she was Sarah Speake.

Allen explained a little of the story: '... and Mr Speake said that you might be able to lay them out. I could go there with you now.'

She was left to wait in the tiny hall. Children were playing upstairs; there was a burst of laughter, then a rhyme she didn't recognize. She could hear Sarah talking to someone in the back room; the walls were thin enough for her voice to carry through. She was describing Allen as 'that woman Henry's been seeing'. The reply was inaudible but Sarah said, 'I'd better go. Don't want to keep her ladyship standing about, do we?'

They knew about her! They said that she was *seeing* Henry! She felt suddenly exposed. She was a contemptible, sordid old woman, terribly misjudged. She was Henry's friend; she was barely that. These women were thinking of her as Henry's – what? Lover? Sweetheart? Sarah came out, pulling on a black hat. Behind her in the doorway, a pretty, curly-haired woman said, 'I'm sorry for your loss.'

Allen said, 'Thank you,' in her school voice. There were probably stains on her coat from carrying the boy; her face was haggard. Had she been asked to paint a self-portrait there would have been nothing to distinguish her from an elderly maid-of-all-work. She pulled her mask up over her nose and waited for Sarah to open the door.

''Bye, Elsie, love. I'll be back later.'

''Bye, Sarah. Goodbye, Mrs Thompson.'

They barely spoke for the quarter of an hour that it took them to get to the Dassetts' house, except to comment briefly on the epidemic and the amount of work that Sarah was having to do. Allen had never been in what might be described as social circumstances with such a woman; her relationship with Ada – her first breach of etiquette before meeting Henry – had never included the niceties of conversation.

As they neared the house, Allen said, 'Mr Speake should be along presently. I'll let you in, then I'm afraid I have to go home.' Sarah would not see them together!

'Will you be arranging the funerals, Mrs Thompson?'

Would she? Sarah had to be paid. And Henry. There would be cards to send and flowers… And somebody would have to write to the father.

'There's an uncle,' she said. 'I'll inform Mr Speake.' They were at the door. She opened it and stood aside. 'You'll find the boy on the ground floor and an elderly person in one of the rooms upstairs. The whole family's got influenza but there are only two… deceased. Or there were when I left.' Allen handed her the key. 'Would you give this to Mr Speake when you've finished?'

'What about the family? We can't just lock them in and leave them to get on with it, can we?'

'I can't do it, Miss Speake. Not on my own.' The woman was accusing her of negligence! 'Do you know anyone who's willing?'

'I'm not saying I do, Mrs Thompson, but they can't be left. Not if they're as you describe.'

'You'll find the uncle's address on the kitchen table—'

'I've been asked to lay out two bodies, nothing more.'

'Please get me the address and I'll deal with it.'

Sarah went into the house and came back holding a scrap of paper. 'Is this what you want?'

'Thank you.'

'I'll get on, then.' Smiling politely, Sarah closed the door in Allen's face.

This time she took no pleasure in the night air. Leaving the Dassetts to fend for themselves had been contemptible but with Lily and Gladys to care for, what time did she have to nurse an entire family? In fact, she couldn't possibly continue to visit any of the people on the list, not when the entire burden fell on her shoulders. And of course, she did recognize that her inadequacy – her *reluctance* – had a part to play in the decision. She was quite honest with herself about that. There must be so many families in the same position as the Dassetts. There were families on her own list who were almost entirely brought to bed. People just had to fend for themselves and survive. Was she to nurse her whole community?

She had hoped to see Henry and he had been expecting to meet her. Sarah's depiction of her would be insulting and Henry would be persuaded that she was too awkward an intrusion into an already fragile family alliance. Had the Dassetts unwittingly destroyed their friendship? And then there was Ruth…

By the time Allen had reached her own house she wanted to dissolve into the paving stones, smoothly, quickly, until the only thing that was left of her was her hat.

*   *   *

Thursday, 31 October

'But are you ill?' Charlotte Tite, up and dressed since seven o'clock, was standing by the heavy wooden bedstead with a thermometer in her hand. 'I don't know what I'm to say to the patients. Shall I say you're ill?

Perhaps that's the thing to do. Are you quite, quite sure that you don't have influenza? If you'd just let me take your temperature?'

'No.'

Lionel had made an attempt to dress but the whole business of getting his feet into trousers and doing up buttons had been so taxing that he'd dropped everything on the floor and gone back to bed. Even prostration was exhausting – one used muscles by simply *being*.

'If I say you're ill then you'll have to stay in. You won't be able to put a foot outside the door. Are you sure that's what you want me to say? That you're ill?'

'Yes, you must.'

'All right, dear. I'll put up a notice.' She sat on the bed, taking care not to position herself too closely to her husband. Their marriage was efficient; in the fifty years since they'd first met, there had been few tendernesses and no impromptu expressions of affection. If she came too close, he retreated; when he'd attempted intimacy – and he had only rarely done this – between the appointed days, she had lain like a stone until the thing was done. His love for John and Amy Drummond was unique and undeclared. Not secret – there was nothing in the least surreptitious about his visits to the house – but simply unspoken. Without understanding the love, Charlotte could have no conception of the grief. Lionel's enervation, in her opinion, was the consequence of overwork. How had an old doctor – and an old doctor's wife – managed to stand in for two or more younger men? If the war were to end soon her first cheer would be for the liberation of the elderly.

'When Phyllis…' he said, trailing off.

'I'll tell you as soon as I hear from her. Will she come down for the funerals?'

'I expect so.'

'You're not using Speake, I hope.'

'Kenyons.'

'Good. I can't abide that man.'

'Let me be. Shut the curtains.'

'Yes, dear.'

By the time Charlotte had hung up his clothes, Lionel was snoring. Whether he was out on his rounds or at home in bed, she still had to occupy herself for the day; making the notice was a diversion and she looked forward to it. After a few false starts she wrote *'Doctor Unwell. Please Do Not Disturb For as Long as This Remains in Place'*, and drew a double line beneath the words in thick black ink before pinning it to the surgery door. Some patients read the notice and then turned away, assuming the doctor to have influenza; others knocked in the hope that the doctor would leave his bed; the more insistent knocked and shouted.

Charlotte stayed upstairs, coming down only to collect the meagre post. She put one letter aside to show Lionel when he woke up. The writer was beseeching the doctor to defy the law. His wife had been dead for five days and although he had begged the nurse and Mrs Tite to pass on the message, Dr Tite had not shown up. He would pay anything the doctor asked if the death certificate could be signed to allow burial. Was his wife to stay in the house for all eternity? Charlotte read the letter several times. Many people had been asking for death certificates by telephone or at the surgery door; she had assumed that Lionel was dealing with the requests. How many dead were uncertified? If he were too depleted to get out of bed, then who would sign them in his place? No man should be asked to spend weeks on end with a dead body. The law would have to yield to the circumstances. In the unlikely event of Lionel unwittingly assisting a murderer, the jury would be bound to exonerate him. How closely had he examined any of the dead during these last weeks? Any one of them might have died of poisoning or suffocation – was he supposed to do a policeman's work as well as his own?

The telephone rang, the first call of the day; a shortage of operators brought its own blessing. She would have disconnected the wires but if it were Phyllis trying to get through, Lionel would be cross.

Straightening her bent back as far as it would allow, she composed herself and picked up the receiver.

* * *

On Allen's return from the Dassetts' house she had neglected to visit Lily or Gladys, getting into bed without washing or turning on the light. She was woken by a knock at the door. The day was immediately before her, a dark presence fastened by weights at her throat.

Gladys was dead. Ada whispered it. They went back to her room together and looked down at the body.

Ada said, 'I'm sorry, ma'am.'

'Don't be foolish.'

'I'll get her taken away as soon as I can. It's difficult, ma'am. This is difficult for me.'

'I'm sure it is, Ada. You don't have to arrange anything if you don't want to. I'll tell Mr Speake, shall I? Unless there's somebody you'd rather…?'

'I'd be very grateful, ma'am.'

Alone in her room, Allen leaned on the wardrobe doors and cried; the tears were unsatisfactory and self-pitying, more to do with a dread of the coming exchanges with Lily and Mr Speake than the death of Gladys or anyone else. After the first uncontrolled sobs she began to snivel, a sound that she detested in the children and had no patience with in herself. Unless she was prepared to affect an attack of influenza, she would have to face up to things. She wrote to the Dassetts' uncle, informing him that his name and address would be passed to the undertaker; then she washed quickly in cold water, dressed and made the bed. Ada would be excused duties for a day or two more.

Wanting to get out, Allen put on her coat and hat before she opened Lily's bedroom door. The smell was dreadful but Allen had no intention of repeating the previous morning's battle; it was Lily's wish to die in her own filth. She was still breathing, although the breaths had to be watched for. Allen would have been ashamed to say it, but she was disappointed. Lily had chosen a first-rate time to crown a life of small, self-centred acts. Why could she not have been traded for Gladys? Why was love not victorious over spite?

When Allen was halfway to Henry's, a young woman came out of a turning ahead of her, walking unsteadily and holding her hands to her cheeks. In the few seconds that it took Allen to draw level, the woman slowed to a stop then drifted across her path and veered towards the gutter; before Allen could catch any part of her, she coiled, snake-like, down to the pavement. The public swooning of pedestrians was no longer a matter of surprise but Allen had never been so close that she needed to be involved in any subsequent first aid. Should she ring on a doorbell? Shout for help? As she knelt down to remove the woman's hat from her face, Allen saw blood gushing from her nose. There was a great deal of blood, on her coat and on the pavement.

The woman said, 'George? George?'

Allen didn't want to find George. She said, 'Where is he?' but she wanted to leave the woman where she was and let the next passer-by deal with the whole affair. Before the woman could answer, a man on a bicycle pulled up beside them. He jumped off and thanked Allen extravagantly before berating the woman for leaving home when she was feeling ill. It was George! Allen was released.

Henry was talking to a customer. As Allen came in, they looked round, the man for a second only, Henry for longer. Her immediate impression was that he scrutinized her face but he might as easily have been adjusting his eyes to the middle distance. He nodded to her and turned back; she waited by the door, watching him deal with the bereaved man. This new vantage point was instructive. Henry was orderly but not consoling, not *comforting*. He hadn't even taken the man into his private office, but allowed him to display his plight in the main body of the shop. When the business was done, they shook hands and walked together towards the door. Allen hovered, holding her position until she was forced to step aside.

As soon as the door was closed, Henry said, 'I'm sorry I missed you yesterday. Sarah told me you had to leave in a hurry.'

'I did, I'm sorry.'

'I was thinking of putting a note through your door but you've saved me the trouble. I've had an unusual visitor. Do you have any time today?'

He was exactly as he'd been in the kitchen on Tuesday night; if Sarah had said anything, he'd chosen to ignore it. Did *he* know that his sisters were making assumptions about the friendship? She flushed, thinking of it. 'I'm actually here because there's been a death in my house.'

'Your sister?'

'No. My maid's friend. Influenza.'

'There'll be a delay, I'm afraid, until we can proceed with the funeral. There are delays all round. Have you registered the death?'

'Not yet.'

'You must.'

'I understand.'

'Will the deceased be staying in your house?'

'She will.'

He hesitated. 'There's going to be a certain amount of – unpleasantness. I could embalm her, if you like.'

'I don't think so. No, I really don't think so.'

'If you're sure. I could be with you at three o'clock. Perhaps we could…?'

'Talk?'

'Yes.'

'I'll wait for you in the kitchen.'

She was in the street before she realized that no mention had been made of the Dassetts. He would think her cold-hearted; she would remedy the situation that afternoon.

Everything in Ada's room was back in order. She was properly dressed in her working clothes and sitting with some mending by the gas fire. When Allen came in she stood up and made an attempt at a curtsy, bobbing and then standing awkwardly with the mending held to her chest. There was a deferential air about her, a sort of meekness that had been absent since her first months of employment. She said nothing, another oddity! Ada, uniquely among servants, was permitted to initiate conversation – only with Allen, of course. When Edward was alive Allen had used two voices to address her, one in his presence and one away from it. This new reticence must be ascribed to grief.

Gladys had been laid out, her dark face neatly framed by two long chestnut pigtails.

'I think we should put the body in another room, Ada, don't you? When Mr Speake comes, I'll ask him to carry her out. And the death must be registered. I'll do my best to take care of that today.'

'Yes, ma'am.'

'Is there any more that I can do?'

'No, ma'am.'

'Please don't think of working today. Mr Speake will be here at three o'clock.'

'Yes, ma'am.'

There was nothing more to say. Only the day before, they had held each other and been at peace; now they were mistress and servant. She nodded her goodbye and left Ada standing by the bed. The thought of going in to see Lily was intolerable. Allen went down to the kitchen instead and made herself an early lunch. Would Henry be expecting something to eat? She found some biscuits and put the tin on the table with a plate beside it, ready for his visit.

* * *

Napier
Hawke's Bay,
31 October 1918

Dear Henry,

How are you, dear? I really mean that this time, thinking of this Spanish 'flu that seems to have got itself well and truly all over the place.

I know I'm writing to you a bit sooner than usual but do you remember me telling you about my friend, Peggy? Well, her father, he's asked Peggy to go up to his station with her children because of the 'flu and the pet has asked me if I'd like to take Grace and Flora and wait it all out with her. If Archie had the slimmest chance of getting out of camp then I wouldn't do it but we won't see him for weeks so I thought we might as well. They say we'll be better off.

Not that I want to throw up the sponge but I have to think of the girls, don't you think? The house was coming on all right when Archie went to Trentham but Peggy says her dad's place is a proper palace. I'll be expecting the best when I get back! Poor old Archie.

I don't know how long it takes for a letter to get away from there so I thought I'd better let you know. I wish you could be with us as I'm guessing that you're very busy.

You know that I love you and if the girls had the chance to meet their Uncle Henry they'd give you a great big kiss as I do now,

All my love to you,

Your loving Rose xxxxx

PS Next time you're sitting at the pee-an-o, play something for me.

*   *   *

I was surprised to find that Allen hadn't waited for me at the Dassetts' house. Sarah had a few words to say on the subject of 'that woman' but I decided to get on with the measuring and let the bait dangle. There was no possibility of getting the bodies buried within ten days so we put the two elderly deceased – one more than Allen had said – into one room upstairs and the other two – the sick ones – in bed together in the adjacent room. As ill as they were, they argued it out but we took no notice. I believe they were related somehow. The dead child was downstairs; his mother was very weak but she refused to let go of the body, and held it to her breast as if it needed feeding. Sarah knelt by the bed and spoke to her. She can be kind when she needs to be, I'll give her that; she went out of her way to do what she could for the other sick children. Anyway, the woman finally let her take the boy and we put him upstairs with the other two bodies. He was very small. I said I'd make him a coffin of his own.

Before we left, Sarah asked me point-blank if I was thinking about Allen – she called her Mrs Thompson, of course – in a courting way. I told her to mind her own business. She said it might be the thin end of the wedge for the shop, if the public saw me behaving like a mad man. I said that my personal affairs had no effect on the way I conducted a funeral. As soon as I'd left her, I realized that by arguing, I'd given her twenty rounds of ammunition. My final retort, the one I kept in my kit bag, so to speak, would have been to tell her that we might as well do as we pleased with the time we had left. As it was, I let her have the last word. 'Her ladyship doesn't like getting her hands dirty,' she said. 'Won't be much good to you, will she?'

I didn't go to Allen's after that. I could have done – I'd left Walter busy in the workshop – but I thought it better to write to her. I had the note ready in my pocket the next morning but she called in before I could put it through her door. We arranged a visit there and then. I'd be lying if I said that Sarah's words hadn't affected me; until I actually saw Allen's face again I was feeling very awkward but there was nothing in her expression to indicate that she might have misunderstood our friendship.

When I got to the house – it was the usual story about going to the basement – she told me to take my shoes off! I wasn't happy about it, never having been asked the like before and not being too pleased about the state of my socks, but I did as she asked and we crept upstairs to the maid's room. That really took the cake. The maid's room was on the same floor as Allen's. Two doors along, in fact. Allen asked me to move the body to a spare room at the end of the corridor, which I did with Ada's help. It was one of the worst cases of cyanosis that I'd seen, so deep a colour that a quick glance might have fooled you into thinking the corpse was a negro. Ada had laid her friend out nicely; I had a coffin ready for someone else that would do very well for her and I promised to bring it round later that evening. The body it was meant for could wait perfectly well for another day.

There was some problem between the two of them that boiled up when Allen told Ada to strip the bed and replace everything with new linen and blankets. From what I understood, Ada was trying to get herself back where she belonged, in the servant's room upstairs. Allen clearly didn't want this to be discussed in front of me, telling Ada that she could do what she liked so long as she was comfortable. I couldn't understand why she'd been brought down in the first place. When I asked Allen about it in the kitchen, she said that her husband's death had changed her feelings about the house. She was frightened in it, especially at night. Having Ada nearby had allowed her to sleep. I'd never heard of such a thing. Would a companion not have been more fitting? She said she couldn't have abided a stranger in the house.

While I was getting my shoes back on I asked her about her sister – was I always going to have to tiptoe about the place? The situation was very poor. Mrs Bird had been told that Ada had gone but she was allowing herself to die of hunger nevertheless. That I had heard of, but only in the severely mad.

Allen listened to my account of Mr Bevens's visit. She shook her head a few times but made no comment while I was speaking. Did she think, I asked her at the end, that there would be repercussions?

'I don't understand why you chose to take him on,' she said. 'Why didn't you pretend that you'd buried the papers with Doctor Wey? You've invited this man to fight you, Henry, that's how it seems to me.'

'I didn't like his manner,' I said.

'But he's from the government! You behaved like a ruffian.'

She was hardly the person to be giving me a lecture on etiquette and I said so, reminding her that servants don't hang their clothes – what clothes they have – in mahogany wardrobes; and neither do they sleep in good linen. When it suited her, she was prepared to do as she liked; why should I be different? I said that I'd taken exception to this man and he might have been Lloyd George himself but I still wouldn't kowtow to him.

She said, 'Then you'll have to deal with the repercussions. If he comes back with an order demanding to see the papers, what will you do then?'

'I could say that I threw them away. Why should I keep another man's scribble?'

'But why didn't you say that at the time?'

'Because I didn't want to.'

She made a face – do as you please – and got up from the table. 'I have to attend to Lily,' she said.

I wanted Sarah to see it, this so-called courtship! From my point of view, we were barely friends. Allen appeared to have no understanding of my character or of the situation I found myself in. I told her I'd return in one hour with the coffin and that she'd better arrange a place for it on the ground floor, as I'd no hope of getting it round the bend in the stairs. I left her clearing the table; she didn't even look up to wish me goodbye. At some point on the journey home, thinking about what had been said, I realized that she'd been calling me by my Christian name without either of us mentioning the fact. I knew her to be Allen, of course, but it had never entered my mind to call her that in her presence. Her name was curious; when I eventually learned the significance of it I found it to be even more so. Originally Ellen, she had survived a boy twin called Alan, born with some malformation of the brain. Her father had combined the two names and brought her up as a boy until her third year when the mother had stepped in and insisted that the child be allowed to grow her hair and wear girls' clothing.

∗　　∗　　∗

Herbert Winter's queer laugh had developed a disturbing addition; he was punctuating the usual braying with a sob and then a crack to the forehead with the heel of his hand. The look of it had so disturbed Walter that he'd tried to intervene by shouting Herbert's name but the interruption had been slight; Herbert had laughed again and hit himself more brutishly. In the afternoon, while Henry was out and Harry and Albert were occupied, Walter sat by him and said, 'Things all right, are they?'

'Never been better.'

'You've had a bit of a time of it, what with this and that.'

'I'm all odd and ends. Nothing to worry about. They made me out of leftovers, didn't they?' A laugh began to bubble up but Walter nipped in with a question about Herbert's grandchildren – much bragged about – and that quietened him. 'Too many,' he said. 'The little buggers are all down with it.'

'How many?'

'Seven, eight, I don't know. I lost count, didn't I?' There was no stopping him. The laugh roared out on a wind of bad breath; he hit himself and was soothed by it, stopping quickly and looking round to see who might be watching.

'Your wife looking after them, is she?' Walter was against intrusion into another man's private life – although he'd taken it upon himself to oversee Henry's – but he couldn't just stand by. How had Herbert Winter acquired a wife? Walter considered the kind of woman who might wish to spend her life with a man who hit himself. She never came into the shop; he had never seen them together on the street.

'No wife, chum. She's with the angels. July.'

'I'm sorry, Herbert. I didn't know about that.'

'Mind you, she says she's coming back.'

'Is she now?'

214

'Told me yesterday.'

'Where was that, then?'

'Where was what?'

'When she told you. Where was it?'

'In the garden.'

'The garden.'

'Don't you go thinking she's been hiding in the shed!' Another laugh.

Walter looked down at the sawdust and waited. When the laugh was over, he said, 'Are you on your own, then? You and the kids?'

'Mr Speake won't like this.' Herbert got up and ran his hands over his face. 'I've got to get on with the sealing.'

'I could always ask Vi – if you need a hand, like.'

'Have we got more paraffin wax?' The conversation was over.

Walter would ask Vi to look in on them; she might not fancy helping out but she could certainly report back as to the state of the place.

*   *   *

Allen stopped at the bend in the stairs and considered the problem of the coffin. Henry was right, the angle was impossible; Gladys would have to be brought down to the drawing room in a shroud, or a sheet, or whatever they used for these situations. She carried on to Ada's room and found her laying her few possessions on the bare mattress.

'Ada? What are you doing?'

'Leaving this room, ma'am.'

'I'd like you to stay where you are, Ada.'

'I'm so sorry, ma'am, but I don't feel that I can. Not any more.'

'Why?'

'It's not right, ma'am.' Ada clasped her hands in front of her apron and looked down at the floor. The posture was submissive but her chin told the true story: she would have her old room on the upper floor.

'I don't understand. Is it because Gladys died in this bed? We could

215

replace it.' Allen's chest was stretched tight; she had been overwhelmed by this silly piece of news. Was Ada's proximity so important?

'Thank you, ma'am. It's not the bed.'

'It must be the *room*! Of course it is. That's so thoughtless of me, not to have realized. You can't possibly stay in the same room. Why don't we swap? You can have mine – it's almost identical.' She was begging now, her hand on Ada's arm. 'As soon as Gladys is safely downstairs—'

'Downstairs, ma'am?'

'We can't get a coffin up those stairs. Gladys can lie in the drawing room and then we can change over. I'll have this bed and you can help me to bring my clothes through. It'll take no time at all—'

'It's not right, ma'am. I couldn't do it.' Ada looked up. That chin! 'If you don't mind, ma'am, I'd like to take these things up now.'

'And if I order you to stay?'

'I hope you won't, ma'am.'

Allen wanted to hold Ada tightly to her and shout in her ear: *Stop this! Feel what I feel! Stay near me!* She picked up some things from the bed – a Bible, a photograph of Ada's mother in a wooden frame – and said, 'I'll help you, shall I?'

'I can manage, ma'am.'

She was obdurate. Allen laid the frame carefully on top of the Bible and passed them over, contriving to touch Ada's hands as she did so. 'Is Gladys quite ready?'

'Yes, ma'am.'

'Mr Speake should be here within the hour. I'll bring him straight upstairs.' One last pitiful try: 'You'll be cold in the attic room, Ada. You can't have forgotten your first winter.'

'No, ma'am. I haven't. Thank you, ma'am.'

Allen went down to the drawing room and began, absently, to move various items of furniture. To have to live like her peers, with an apparently ill-used and acquiescent servant; how was she to manage this? The proper care of those in one's charge was the indisputable duty of an employer. But if those in one's charge chose to live in uncomfortable circumstances, even when offered better – *particularly* when offered better…

Henry was on time, knocking quietly on the basement door. 'I've got two men with me, Mrs Thompson. We're ready to bring the coffin in. Is there a room prepared for us on the ground floor?'

Their difference of opinion might never have happened! This was the authoritative man – the one she'd seen at work and on the street. The change from his character an hour before was such that she had no difficulty in meeting it without embarrassment. She said, 'I've made space in the drawing room. I'd be grateful if you could make as little noise as possible. Would you all please leave your shoes in the porch?'

'Of course.'

'Thank you.'

'I'll go and open the front door.' The bringing in of the coffin was achieved without mishap. Henry put the trestles along the wall at the far end of the room so that there was free passage for anyone needing to enter. The boy – hardly a man! – was well-behaved and took great care not to knock into anything, even taking the trouble to pick up a speck of sawdust from the carpet. There was some problem with the old man taking off his shoes but he did it, making faces at the boy and testing the hall floor with the point of his foot before stepping on to it. When the coffin was in place, Allen led Henry, Harry and Albert upstairs, turning once with her finger on her lips to remind them of the need for silence.

She had been to Lily's room only once during the day, staying at a good distance from the bed. The conversation had been brief and mostly one-sided. Lily had no wish to be visited by Mr Sucerne and she wasn't ill and therefore didn't need to see a doctor. She would remain in isolation until the house was scoured for Germans and Ada taken prisoner by the police. She was accountable only to God and He would reward her for her vigilance.

The fancy came into Allen's mind that there was grey dust trickling into Lily's body from some internal, unstoppable tap. When the dust reached her mouth, she would die. From the sound of her voice, the time was not far off. And there was absolutely nothing to be done about it. Lily could hardly be carried out squealing and left on the hospital steps; neither could she be force-fed. The choices had boiled down to a single, inevitable end.

While Gladys was being prepared, Ada went down to the kitchen and Allen went to her room. She lay on her bed in the dark, knowing that her hair would come adrift. Henry had found a moment to step outside his role; why were they all tiptoeing about, he'd asked, if her sister was past caring? Her reply, and she knew it to be the truth, was that she abominated Lily's scenes and would go to any lengths to avoid one. The explanation had satisfied him; nothing further was said.

As soon as Allen heard movement in the corridor, she got off the bed and joined the men, following them down the stairs. The body had been wrapped in cloth and some sort of webbing and was being supported from below by Henry and the boy. Albert held from the top, guiding them in a whisper, until they reached the sharp bend and the boy momentarily lost his footing.

The old man shouted, 'Mind out there!'

Henry was so startled that he yelled, 'Be quiet, Albert!'

There was a crash from Lily's room and, as Allen raised her hands to her head, Ada came running up from the basement, banging the door against the wall in her rush to identify the disturbance.

In the silence, Henry glared at Albert, Ada stared at the body, Arthur sucked his bottom lip and Allen clung to her hair. It took her some time to get past Gladys and the men. She found Lily lying on her right side with one arm trapped underneath her and the other dangling down to the floor. The empty jug, the glass and the unused bottles of tonic had been swept off the bedside table.

'What's happening? Who's here?'

'You mustn't worry. I fell downstairs. I'm sorry if I woke you up. I was carrying a—'

'They're everywhere!'

'We're alone.'

'The Germans are all over the house!'

'You're right!' Allen was inspired. 'You're absolutely right! I didn't want to frighten you but I found two Germans under the floorboards in the attic. Ada was hiding in a cupboard and feeding them on scraps. The police are here now and they're taking everyone away!'

*   *   *

Friday, 1 November

Ignoring his wife's protestations, Mr Sucerne put on his hat. 'If they can't get to church, Muriel, the church must go to them. The shepherd', he said, putting on his bicycle clips, 'must save the sheep. And both calls are on my way to the cemetery so there's no time wasted going this way and that.'

'Your mask.'

'I have it here.'

'I've put some chocolate in your pocket.'

He patted his coat. 'So you have. Will you manage without Minnie?'

'I shall have to. There isn't a maid to be had.'

She caressed his face as she always did and watched him as he went down the steps and round the side of the house. A wind was blowing up, pulling the pyracantha away from the wall and flattening the last of the chrysanthemums; the gusts were noisy and unnerving, a hubbub in the trees. She shouted, 'Are you sure you're safe, cycling in this—?' but he appeared again, on foot, before she could finish the sentence.

'My bicycle's gone,' he shouted back.

'Gone?'

'Gone.'

'Did you leave it where you usually leave it?'

'Of course I did.' He looked around the front garden, as if the bicycle might have ridden itself into the flowerbeds.

'Then where's it got to?'

'I don't know. This is too much!'

'Do come inside, Richard. There's no need for us to freeze to death.' Muriel held the door open and stood back, allowing him to pass. 'It's obviously been stolen.'

'It'd take some pluck. To steal it from under my nose.'

'It wasn't under your nose. Anybody could have sneaked in to the garden and wheeled it away.'

'From *me*?'

'Why not?'

'I'm their vicar!'

'It's a bicycle!'

'I'm at the cemetery in an hour. I'll have to find a cab and I shan't have time for visits.' He sat on the stairs and took off his bicycle clips. 'It's too bad, it really is, after everything I've done for them. The police must be told.'

'I don't see how they're going to find it.'

'I shall give them a description in any case.'

'Why don't you see if the Selbournes will let you borrow their motor-car?'

'I saw them go out.'

On his way to the cab-rank, Mr Sucerne called in at the police station. There were two men on duty. They took his details and wrote down everything he said about the bicycle but they held out little hope of finding it – 'Very sorry sir, but we're short on men and if we had a spare chap he'd be too busy with the big burglaries, as you'll appreciate.'

There was one cab waiting and he got in out of the wind with some relief. The journey passed without event until they were within sight of the cemetery when the horse slowed down and came to a stop. Mr Sucerne looked out of the window. They were at the back of a column of hearses and attendant carriages, some twenty or thirty long, edging nose to tail up the road towards the big black gates. Another shorter queue was approaching on the other side of the road and slowing things further as the drivers had to turn right and cut across the column.

He had never before, in all his ecclesiastical life, been late for a service; however inclement the weather, he must walk to the chapel and he must arrive before the deceased. With an exasperated sigh, Mr Sucerne got out of the cab and paid the driver; then, buffeted by the violent wind, he set off as quickly as his legs would allow and tried to pray for the man who had stolen his bicycle.

*   *   *

Since his conversation with Herbert Winter on Thursday, Walter's concern had increased, leading him to ask the man more questions; the replies had been short and oddly phrased. In conversation with the others, Herbert was less and less able to follow a train of thought.

With no coffins to make or finish, they were all otherwise occupied – bearing at funerals or measuring up in the hope of getting wood stocks replenished. Herbert was a big man and, if kept away from public duties, useful to the firm. Even so, he was spending a good part of the day sitting about in the workshop. Whether the convulsive movements of his face and arms were therefore more noticeable or whether his derangement was becoming more pronounced, Walter could not be sure, but at breakfast with Vi on the Friday he made Herbert the main topic of conversation. Vi listened carefully, tutting and shaking her head as the story proceeded.

'Lost two sons,' he said. 'One in Belgium and the other under a train at Etaples. Fell on to the track or got pushed, who knows? There's a daughter in Wales and seven or eight grandchildren who've all got the 'flu. He says one of his daughters-in-law works nights in munitions and the other one's dying of consumption. His wife died a few months ago,' Walter paused for effect, 'but she's talking to him, in the garden.'

'No!'

'That's what he says.'

'So who might be looking after the children?'

'So far as I can make out they're on their own. Then again, he might be making the whole lot up.'

'Why would he do that?'

'Do us a favour, love. Go and have a look-see, would you?'

'Are you asking me to take them on? I couldn't do that, Walter.'

'Just a look? They're not ten minutes from here.'

'And what do I say? Excuse me, but I've come to see if you're real or not.'

'You can say I work with Herbert and you were passing and you heard they weren't well. That'll do, won't it?'

'If they're really there and they're really ill, who's going to let me in?'

'You can look through the window!'

'All right, all right. I'll go this morning. What's Henry got to say?'

Walter raised his eyebrows to imply that Henry didn't know about Herbert, wasn't likely to care about Herbert and was, in general, loafing about with his hands in his pockets. 'We haven't talked,' he said. 'If you know what I mean.'

* * *

In all my life I don't think I've ever come so close to dropping a body as I did that night at Allen's. I don't know whose fault it was – Harry, Albert, I don't know – but that girl was nearly head first down the stairs with us on top of her. The upshot of it was that we made a lot of noise – the very thing we'd been asked not to do – and Allen had to go running off to calm her sister.

While Harry and Albert were getting the deceased settled in her coffin, I took the opportunity of having a quiet word with Ada. We were getting on well enough for me to say what I thought, so I asked her why she'd ever agreed to sleep in that dainty bedroom. She'd have lost her job refusing, she said, and after a bit she'd got to like it: the big bed and the nice curtains.

'Then why go back to your quarters?' I asked her. She didn't know but she needed the change. That's all she had to say on the subject. I liked her. She was very much the sort of woman I might have spent an hour with and it crossed my mind to ask her if we could meet but I thought better of it – her friend's death had upset her and she'd be poor company. I'm surprised that I thought of it at all, given the circumstances, but a man doesn't lose his instincts.

We would have left then, everything being done, but Allen came in. I expected her to say something about the mishap but she didn't; she only wanted to ask me if I could come back that evening. I said I'd do my best but that if I hadn't arrived by ten o'clock then work had got the better of me.

To tell the truth, I felt awkward. You don't get a second chance when you're dealing with the deceased, and whatever mistakes you make, you're stuck with. I could have said that no undertaker should have to consent to a vow of silence, although we do our best to be respectfully quiet, but a job's a job and we'd made a mess of it. I didn't go back to Allen's that night. We had a lot of call-outs and by the time I'd finished I was fit for nothing – not that I slept. Mr Bevens was on my mind, Mr Bevens, Thomas Wey and everything else besides. I didn't even have the heart to listen to the gramophone or play the piano.

There were so many gravediggers falling sick that we'd soon have no graves being opened, even for the dead that we'd managed to get into coffins. Why was the army not releasing men? We'd had forty-odd orders since Sunday and there were no coffins, coffin-sets or wood to be had. Dr Tite was a long way behind with the death certificates – Allen hadn't been able to get one for Gladys and even if she had the registrars were short of staff – and to cap it all, there were still customers wanting the old ways, whatever I said to them about having to make the best of it. More than one had tried to insist on polished oak and I'd even had a woman demanding plumes; she wouldn't believe me when I said they hadn't been used since before the war.

When I came downstairs on the Friday morning, Walter was holding the door open and looking up and down the street. Herbert Winter was late, an unusual thing for him. Had I noticed that he was hitting himself? I said that I'd seen him do it, but that he was a strange man and beyond my understanding. So long as he did what was asked of him, why should I waste time in speculation? There was no sight of him and, after a minute or two more, Walter shut the door and came in. I was at the ledger, filling in some names and figures from the day before and he said how we'd grown accustomed to losing our boys in the war; now they were dying in front of us and young women alongside them. Where would we be without the young when all this was over? That would have been the moment to tell Walter about Thomas Wey but I couldn't bring myself to do it.

I didn't say this to him either, although I can't have been alone in thinking about it, but the closeness of men in the trenches and on the trains and troop ships, how was that working out? Thomas had said to close the ports, which he must have thought the only way to stop the contagion, but what about the places where the men were gathered together, healthy men packed in with the dying and nowhere to jump but over the parapet or down into the sea? Lying awake had given me time to work these things out and I'd begun to consider the chain: the soldiers were reliant on the women in the factories for their food and ammunition. The war therefore would be won or lost according to which side managed to keep the factories going as much as on the quantity of men still able to fight – not that you could have a winner or a loser in a general calamity, but I did believe that an armistice would come all the quicker now. There was a terrible joke to it, the war coming to an end because of a simple thing like influenza.

Although the mortuary had started to take bodies in, many people hated the idea of putting their loved ones in such a place and Walter made the suggestion that we might ask Vasey the carriage-master to let us have part of a stable; I left Walter to deal with the customers and went to enquire. Vasey had thought of it himself and agreed to let me have a small stable in its entirety. We agreed on terms – I would add the extra charge to my bill – and shook hands on it. I keep harping on this, but I couldn't allow the business to go downhill while we still had people walking through the door.

There was some measuring to do at a house in Allen's vicinity. When I'd finished I went to her basement and looked in at the window. Ada was there with her back to me, chopping something up. I knocked on the pane and nearly stopped her heart but she pulled herself together and let me in. That was a cheering moment: the smell of cooking and the warm room. Ada's a particular sort – not for conversation, but good otherwise, I would imagine. After being told that Mrs Bird had decided to eat again and that Allen was washing her, I accepted a cup of tea and settled down to it with a good view of Ada as she finished the chopping. I didn't want to talk and I don't think she did either, but there was a very companionable atmosphere between us. I've never looked for it – in fact, I've gone out of my way to avoid it – but every now and again a touch of homeliness is more than agreeable.

I said no to a second cup of tea – there was too much business to attend to – and got up to leave. I was thanking Ada, with my hand on her shoulder, when Allen came in. I'd heard no footsteps or movement outside the door and it quite took me by surprise. I took my hand away but Allen stared at Ada as if some dreadful thing had landed on her. Ada must have seen that there was a misunderstanding because she went into the scullery and made herself busy clattering pans about.

I said, 'I couldn't come last night and I can't wait any longer today.'

Allen said, 'I hope you've been entertained.'

I chose not to reply to this. Picking up my hat, I went to the door, saying, 'Walter goes home for an hour at eight o'clock. If you want to visit, I'll be upstairs.'

I don't flirt with maids in a house where I've been employed to conduct a funeral and I was angry that Allen should have thought me capable of it. It was up to her: if she wanted to continue our friendship then she could come to me. I had no wish to visit her house again until it was time to take Gladys's coffin to the cemetery.

*   *   *

The more Eric Bevens considered his exchange with the undertaker, the more emphatically he desired to bring the man down. Dr Wey and his theories were no longer a priority; all speculation was running a poor second to the need for mastery over the mutinous working class.

If these mysterious papers were offered up without further entreaty, Eric Bevens knew that he would be disappointed; if the premises were searched and nothing was found – and the man had had ample opportunity to destroy anything that might implicate him – then Speake would escape unpunished. But if a letter was written, a letter on government stationery, accusing Speake of treachery and betrayal...

That would serve the purpose. He pulled a sheet of paper from the rack and began to compose his allegations. The words came easily, fuelled by Henry Speake's sneer. Signing on behalf of the Local Government Board – the office was almost empty, who would find out? – he wrote the address boldly on the envelope then pressed the wet ink so vigorously into the blotter that he might have been trying to push the letter through the table to its destination.

A little calmer now in anticipation of the pleasure to come, he picked up the first of the reports that had been left on his desk that morning: the latest mortality figures. They were still on the increase. Sir Arthur's conference on the 29th of October had brought about no procedural changes; the Board appeared to be unconcerned, confirming his own view that this was merely an exceptionally severe bout of influenza. Even so, the preponderance of young women on the lists was unique in his experience. Young women were currently employed in a way quite unsuited to their capabilities; they were malnourished, like the rest of the population, and exhausted by their labours and the general privations of war. It was therefore not surprising to find them most severely affected by the present epidemic. Pleased with his interpretation of the figures, Eric Bevens dropped the report into his out-tray in the certain assurance that Sir Arthur Newsholme was apprised of, and in absolute control of, the nation's health.

* * *

The tale of the Germans in the attic had been invented to placate Lily in a moment of crisis but to Allen's astonishment, she had accepted every word, nodding and smiling with her eyes shut and her lips tightly closed, like a jolly skull moving up and down on a mechanical device. After cleaning the mess off the floor – a compound of broken glass and Dr Tite's yellow tonic – Allen had re-joined the others, telling Lily that the police might want more information.

They had all been in the drawing room: Henry's two assistants at the side of the coffin and Henry himself standing close to Ada, engrossed in conversation. At Allen's entrance, Ada had broken away and gone directly to the coffin. Henry had signalled to the man and the boy that it was time to leave. He'd been more than usually reserved, guiding them out and not looking back to say goodbye, even though Allen had asked him to return in the evening – an invitation that he'd responded to with a vague gesture and some remark about work.

On her way to bed, Allen had gone in to say goodnight to Lily. She'd been awake and eager to know more about Ada's mortification. Using

Walter as her model for the Germans, Allen had done what she could to flesh things out; the police-inspector, initially faceless, had gradually turned into Henry – an impressive, heroic Henry…

After being reassured that Ada had been dragged from the house in handcuffs, Lily had touched her cracked lips: 'I want beef tea.'

Allen, who'd been walking towards the door, was stopped in her tracks as comically as if she'd been playing musical chairs. Lily might as well have asked for raw beef on the bone. She was hungry. She would live.

Turning slowly back to the bed and forcing herself to look pleased, Allen had said, 'There's no beef in the house but beef will be bought in the morning and tea made of it immediately. Would anything else be acceptable for now?'

Lily, still smug with self-righteousness, had said no, the smile hovering at her mouth.

Rather than miss Henry by not hearing his knock at the door, Allen had spent the evening in the kitchen with a book open and unread on the table in front of her, jumping at every noise and getting up often to look outside. At eleven o'clock, she'd gone to bed. Although Ada was only a floor above her – in yards, probably closer than before – Allen had felt herself to be alone in the house. The silence was no different, neither was the darkness; none the less, she had lain awake with the bedclothes pulled up over her head until her fear got the better of her and she'd had to put on the light, holding her breath and jumping out of bed in a dash.

She woke on the Friday morning at seven, roused by the clanging of the long-case clock – she'd heard every other hour being struck but had fallen asleep just after six, with Edward's pillow in her arms. In the few seconds that it took her to take note of her surroundings, she felt only relief at the coming of the day but the feeling was quickly blighted. Turning on to her side, she drew her knees up and circled her body round the pillow. She could stay in bed but even as she considered it, the idea depressed her. The longer she was prone, the more miserable she would become, and her fear of catching influenza was at its worst when she was idle and aware of all her intermittent headaches and cramps. She straightened out her legs and pushed away the sheets; they were clammy, a reminder of her rotten night. A list was necessary. All things were amenable to lists.

If Lily wanted to eat again then she must be fed from a teaspoon to begin with or risk over-stimulation and probable collapse. Her meals therefore would require the kind of time and attention that one would normally pay to a small child. If she were eating, then she would want to be clean and properly dressed and given the opportunity to use the commode whenever it pleased her. If her madness were only in abeyance, she might yet refuse to accept a new maid, even if one could be found. If she did refuse, then Allen would have to offer up her life in order to save her sister's. The list, so far blank, was begun with the words 'Investigate maid'.

Henry had said that he might be too busy to call back; there was no need to feel uneasy. She would arrange another visit. And she must talk to Ada about the meat coupons; she would go to the butcher's – if she could find one open and bear to wait in the inevitable queue – and then carry on to Henry's. Walter was a problem, but if he was about she could always make some query about Gladys's coffin. She wrote 'Coupons, Beef, Henry' on the next line.

There was no reason to consider the body in the drawing room. It would lie there, out of view, doing whatever bodies did, until Henry could arrange a funeral. Ada might be broken-hearted but she was keeping it to herself and plodding through her duties, her only failing, from Allen's point of view, being her prim, formal behaviour. Again, there was nothing to add to the list, unless she chose to be facetious and write 'Win Ada back'.

Although she was missing Ruth, quite what she was missing she couldn't exactly say. Had that awful father not been so unkind, Allen knew that she would have been expected to visit every day. There was an element of relief in not having to. A letter might be allowed through the cordon – she scribbled '*write to Ruth*' and added '*include small gift*'.

The window began to rattle; the wind was building up. Allen folded a piece of paper and turned out the light so that she could open the curtains and jam the frame. Close to, she could see that the paintwork was beginning to peel. As soon as she was dressed, she went to check on Lily and found her in the same frame of mind as the night before. A change of linen was agreed upon. Lily allowed Allen to wash her and attend to her sores without a struggle and lay helplessly in the chair while the bed was made; she weighed so little that Allen could almost have carried her about the house. Promising Lily that nourishment would be forthcoming by the afternoon, Allen took the dirty washing and went down to the basement, intending to ask Ada about the coupons. She heard a man's voice; it was Henry! She dropped the washing on the laundry floor and pinned a loose strand of hair back into the coil on her head. If she spoke to him now – if Ada went to buy the beef – then she needn't risk facing Walter. They could make an arrangement for the evening, there and then. She opened the kitchen door, pleased to have Henry in the house.

He was standing close to Ada; he was about to embrace her. She saw this as she might have seen a corner of the darkest, most abominable pit.

Unable to speak, she watched as Ada ran into the scullery. Henry asked her to visit at eight o'clock, she heard that, although afterwards, lying on her bed, she could remember nothing else that was said.

Again and again, repeating itself until she thought she would lose her mind, all she could see was Henry's hand raised to Ada's shoulder as he turned her to be kissed.

*   *   *

Charlotte Tite was sitting at her husband's desk, looking at the surgery. She had been in the patient's chair from time to time but otherwise her only interest in the place had been to inspect it. Was the furniture clean? Were the ferns watered? This seat allowed one a panoramic view.

One could scrutinize the approaching patient, taking care to observe the skin, the gait, the breath and the brightness of the eye: the noting of symptoms had its place but, for her, diagnosis would begin from that first glimpse in the doorway. Lionel's chair was high-seated. Her toes were an inch from the floor but in her reverie she was a tall, accomplished doctor with an efficient wife. Although her parents – long dead but eternally active – had refused her an extended education, this imaginary self, this cultivated man, had sailed through medical school to parental applause and peer acclaim…

There was a knock at the main surgery door. Startled, she got up, feeling conspicuous, as if her fantasy had been taking place in a public thoroughfare. There was a second, louder knock and then the sound of a letter dropping on the mat. After giving the caller time to get away, she retrieved the letter and brought it back to the desk. Another new experience this: Lionel's silver letter-opener, pulled from its leather scabbard. Hers, a blunt affair made from bone, was less efficient than her own thumb and she would have dispensed with it altogether had she not thought it vulgar to tear at envelopes. The letter, a dreadful account of a young married couple dying within days of their wedding, was yet another plea for the deaths to be certified. She searched through the drawers in the desk and found that there were thirty-one certificates left. More could be ordered; she would write that afternoon.

Lionel had abandoned himself to the bed. Charlotte said his name twice before he responded, saying, 'What?' without moving an inch from his position.

'I have to talk to you.'

'Why?'

'It's none of my business, Lionel—'

'Yes.'

'— but will you look at these letters? And the messages I've taken on the telephone?' She put the pile down, just below the pillow, so that he could see it if he turned his head to the side. 'Every one of these people is asking for a death certificate. They're all in the most terrible plight. Some of them are having to eat and sleep in the same room as the body.'

'If I go out, I shall drop dead.'

'I'm not asking you to go out. I'm asking you to sign these.'

She held out the certificates; he looked at them.

She carried on. 'You've been so busy these last weeks – have you never been lax with a single patient, never just settled for pneumonia?'

'Charlotte!'

'Please, Lionel. Please sign them. You can't let these people live like animals.'

'I'll be struck off.'

'The war's nearly over. You've retired. Nobody's going to know. Nobody's going to blame you if there's a mistake.'

'Struck off…' He pushed against the mattress. Irritability was restoring him, if only enough to raise himself a few inches from the horizontal. 'Pillows.' She propped him up. 'Read me the letters. Slowly.'

As she read each one he did his best to arrive at a diagnosis and sign the certificate. By the end, he was supporting his wrist with his left hand in order to write at all. She took the pillows away and closed the window; a gale was blowing up and the room was cold.

'Thank you. I do believe you've done the right thing. Shall I bring you up some lunch?'

'Later.'

Back at the desk, with a footstool to support her feet, Charlotte put the certificates into envelopes for the maid to post. Lionel needed an aide and she was the willing volunteer.

*　　*　　*

By the afternoon, when no message had come, Walter decided to investigate Herbert Winter's absence. If Vi had been to the house and found him in a deranged state, she might have got herself boiled up in it and come to harm. There was little point in telling Henry of his intentions. When there was a lull, he went off to reconnoitre.

Herbert lived in a small terrace not far from the railway. The house was poorly built and badly maintained with gaps in the pointing and bare wood showing through the peeling paint. No attempt had been made to deal with the patch of garden, and the wind tore at the browning weeds, pushing them over the fence and into the path at Walter's feet. He knocked several times and looked through the letterbox; a cat was pacing in the hallway. With every gust of wind, the gate banged shut; he tried to close it properly but the catch was hanging loose and there was nothing substantial enough in the garden to hold it firm. Did the neighbours not complain?

Irritated, he walked into the weeds, shielded his eyes and peered in through the window. A dirty curtain, possibly an old sheet, hung across the greater part of the glass but a gap revealed the room; so far as he could see, it was empty. He thumped on the frame, pushing at it with the heels of his hands until he was able to lift it and climb through, cursing at his stiff legs and making a face at the smell. The door was ajar. There was no point breaking in if he wasn't prepared to follow the thing through to the end. If he were challenged, he would say that Herbert's absence that morning had been a cause for worry. Enough to break in through a window? Why not? They were all looking out for each other these days…

The cat was still in the gloomy hall, standing next to a small pile of post that had been pushed, unopened, to the side. Walter called Herbert's name and waited, listening, but the only sound was the banging gate. He needed light, but there was no gas that he could see. Could he find an oil-lamp or a candle? The back room was full of furniture, chair upon chair and cupboard upon table. An assortment of clothes was hanging higgledy-piggledy on the dark wood, as if someone had thrown them in from the doorway. He found a candle in the kitchen. Mould covered the pans and dishes; nothing was clean enough to touch. Walter looked out at the back garden, no more than a scrap-heap, and nerved himself to go upstairs.

One of the rooms was empty. In the other he found a woman and four children, all with their throats cut. He reckoned they'd been dead for no more than a day, laid out as if they were sleeping, with the sheet nicely folded and five pairs of shoes in a row at the bottom of the bed. Herbert was leaning against the wall, in a puddle of blood from his own neck. There was a note on the floor beside him. Walter picked it up: 'Can't do more.' Out in the street, Vi was calling, 'Is anybody there? Are you there, Mr Winter? Are you there?'

*   *   *

At half past seven, after feeding Lily a second bowl of beef tea, sitting her on the commode and tending to her bedsores, Allen went up to her room and lay down in the dark. With Lily below her and Ada above, she felt oppressed, as if the air were being forced from her lungs.

Lily's jovial mood had passed. She was crabby again, drinking the broth but accusing Allen of over-salting it, or deliberately putting too much in the spoon. The possibility of employing a new maid would have to be introduced very gently. And if a new maid *did* come she would have to be a party to the deception from her first minutes in the house. How could a stranger be trusted to hold her tongue? The wind was still beating at the windows; if she wanted to visit Henry, she had better tie on her hat.

He was sitting in front of the ledger with his head in his hands. When he saw her at the door, he stood up and said, 'I'd forgotten.'

Through her mask, she said, 'If you're too busy—'

'No. Now you're here.'

234

'Is Walter in?'

'No. I haven't seen him since this afternoon. Look, I'm going up for half an hour. Have you got time?'

'I have.'

They said no more until they were upstairs. The fire was set but unlit; the room was cold. She put her gloves in her pocket but kept her coat and hat on.

'No fire. Margaret came down with it this afternoon. I've put her in a cab and sent her to her mother's.' He lit the kindling – the last small off-cuts from the workshop – and held his hand out to indicate that she should sit down while he put a few pieces of coal on to the flames.

'I've got some news,' she said. 'When you were shouting on the stairs last night—'

'I've never known Albert do anything so—'

'Please. You mustn't apologize. It was an accident. It could have hap—'

'It shouldn't have happened at all.'

'I had to think of something to explain it away so I told Lily that you were a policeman and that you'd found Germans under the floorboards in the attic.'

'You didn't!' He laughed. His usual expression gave no indication that he could display so much of his mouth; his enthusiasm for the joke was irresistible.

She laughed with him, saying, 'Yes, Germans!'

As the laughter subsided, Allen looked away. She'd meant to be reserved, not to make a joke, but somehow she understood that any mention of his misconduct with Ada would bring the evening to a premature end. He would deny what she'd seen, defend himself against any charges – although he'd been quick enough to accept the blame for the noise on the stairs! – and nothing further would pass between them. That there was a difference between the incident on the stairs and the incident in the kitchen was clear: one was a professional mishap and

235

therefore a loss of face; the other was a deliberate misjudgement, born of whatever feelings had surged up in him on the day. To be caught touching a servant was reprehensible; he had taken advantage of his position in the house. He would know that. He would never admit to it.

'I don't have time to make tea. Can I offer you ginger beer? It's the only thing I've got handy.' He was holding a brown bottle. She refused it and he poured a single glass, setting it in front of the modest fire as he returned to his seat. 'That's the first laugh I've had for weeks,' he said.

She could find no reply. She'd been about to tell him that Lily had risen from the dead but he was dour again, clenching his teeth and working the muscles of his face.

He said, 'I haven't heard from Mr Bevens. There's very little post coming through but I'd have thought a government man could arrange a personal delivery if he wanted. Wouldn't you think so?'

'Very possibly.'

'I'm hoping that's the end of it.'

'I hope so, too. For your sake.'

Should she leave? The pressure was mounting in her throat. If she were free to speak, what would she say? How could you think of kissing Ada in my house? Is this how you behave in other people's houses? Do you always take advantage of your position?

'… and if I tell you that in no time at all, there will be no possibility of burying the dead…'

Allen had missed the beginning of the sentence; he left the end in the air, expecting her to reply.

'Did you know that Ada and Gladys were lovers?' she said. The words flew from her and landed with full effect. She watched his mouth fall open.

'My God!'

Needing to be reassured by her hat and coat, she pulled the one down further and the other more closely around her. She had utterly crossed the line; she was blushing. Even in her marriage, she could never have expressed herself so crudely – and to say such a thing to such a man in such a place!

He shook his head and said, 'My God' again, more quietly this time. If she'd hoped to surprise him into revealing a passion for Ada, his wide-eyed, slack-jawed expression revealed only astonishment. The spectres of Ada and Gladys, entangled and in various stages of undress, now lay on the few feet of carpet between their chairs. Unable to speak, she watched him, expecting a reproach.

He barked out a short laugh. 'Well, you do surprise me. And you let them stay in that room together?'

By accepting her indelicacy without comment, he was reinforcing his apparent opinion of her as neither male nor female. Had she been a man, he would have replied with some coarse joke; had he thought of her as a woman, he would have been outraged. What was she to him? What did it matter? She would go home!

As she sat forward, preparing herself to get up, she looked again at his face. Something unruly had been released; his smile was wolfish. She felt herself to be falling headlong on to a spike. Her sensibilities were jarred, her impressions bombarded with jittery, lustful hunger. She had never been angry with him for stepping out of place. She had been jealous of Ada; she had wanted his hand on her own shoulder!

He was staring at her, waiting for a reply. Too hot now, she undid her coat and laid her hat beside her on the sofa. How could she look into his face? She took a breath. 'From the beginning. I allowed it from the beginning. Do you think I was wrong?'

'It's not my place to say.'

'But do you?'

'She's a maid.' Henry stretched his arms above his head, linking his hands and sighing loudly. 'Shame to waste this coal but I've got to get back downstairs. If I'm passing your way tomorrow, shall I drop in?'

Allen picked up her hat. 'I'm not sure when I'll be there.'

'Shall I knock and see?'

'You can try.'

They were standing close together; there was a tension between them, she was sure of it. Did he wash after picking up bodies? His hands were scarred from the workshop but the nails were well cut and the skin clean. The hair on his chin was coming through grey and black, like his moustache. He needed to shave. He would need to shave twice a day. She averted her eyes and buttoned her coat.

Downstairs, the shop door slammed. Henry walked out of the room, expecting Allen to wait, but she followed, not thinking. As they started to go down, he realized that she was behind him and turned round.

'Go back,' he whispered. 'It's Walter. I'll get him into the workshop.'

'No, you won't.' Walter was at the foot of the stairs. 'You'd better ask your lady friend to leave. I've got some bad news for you.'

*   *   *

Saturday, 2 November

'My feet feel as if they're being stewed up for dinner.' Sarah lay back on Elsie's's sofa and closed her eyes. 'I'm too old for this.'

Elsie picked up the next piece of mending and rattled through the cotton reels in the tin, looking for the right thread. 'Do you want anything to eat, love?'

'No thanks. In a minute, when I've had a rest.'

'How many have you done this morning?'

'Half a dozen. Terrible lot of lice on one of them. And a stillbirth. I've been up since five o'clock.'

'Did you hear about Herbert Winter?'

'I saw Walter. If he hadn't gone looking, they'd still be there now.' Sarah shuddered. 'Finding them like that. And all their little shoes laid out at the foot of the bed.'

'Is that what he did?'

'So Walter says. What would make a man do such a thing?'

'Was it his wife? The woman?'

'No, his daughter-in-law. He'd put her shoes there as well.'

'When you think of it, he was being tidy.'

'Then why did he cut their throats?' Sarah lifted her head and looked up at Elsie's chair. 'And his own?'

'Don't. I can't bear to think of it…'

They fell silent. Then Sarah said, 'He won't be the last. We're being asked too much of.'

'We are, love. You're right.'

'I feel like laying myself out and that's a fact.'

'Have you seen Henry?'

'I have. We had words, you know. On Wednesday.'

'What sort of words?'

'I told him he was letting us all down with his slipshod ways. The workshop, Elsie. It was like a farmyard. And that woman he's carrying on with – do you know what Walter said? He said they were *upstairs*!' Sarah sat up. 'I met her, you know. She asked me to do some laying out – took me to the house and ran off. That was a good dodge, leaving me with a lot of sick children.'

'Perhaps she was upset. Was she upset?'

'Not that she said. She's a cold fish. I can't see it, why he's behaving like a boy. I could understand it better if she were half her age and had a bit of life in her…' Sarah lay down again. 'We should have made him leave, between us.'

'Made who leave?'

'Henry. We could have taken over and done a proper job of running things.'

'And what would he have done with himself?'

'He'd have played the piano. That's all he's good for.' Sarah closed her eyes and fell silent; in a minute she was asleep.

Elsie cut the cotton with her teeth, pushed the needle into the cotton reel, folded the shirt on her lap into a neat rectangle and put it on the finished mending. Then she got up and went to the little kitchen. While the kettle was coming to the boil, she sat at the table with her hands in her lap, waiting; when the tea was in the pot, she stirred the leaves for a minute or more and looked out of the window at the young cabbages lining the flowerbed. In the spring she would plant a pink rose for Jen and Reggie, there at the back where the sun was particularly bright.

*   *   *

Eric Bevens did write to me. The letter was vindictive. He accused me of sequestering papers pertaining to government business and thereby behaving in a treacherous manner; he also wished to inform me that my conduct in the affair had been so unscrupulous as to warrant an investigation and so ungovernable as to constitute sedition and that I should expect further correspondence as soon as the present epidemic had abated.

I read the letter through many times. However much I might fear an inquiry, I was more distressed to see that he had dismissed the situation as a simple epidemic. They had no plan! *I know that it should have been obvious to me by then, what with the delay in getting skilled men out of the army and so on; even so, I'd been imagining that the engine had started up, however slow the wheels. Now I saw it: there was no plan because the only plan worth having would be to bring about an armistice. And why? As Thomas had said, the movement of troops was spreading the disease. Infected men would continue to infect the rest of us. Was there still some chance that the gravity of the situation had been overlooked?*

I took all Thomas Wey's papers and laid them out on the bed. What was there here that Eric Bevens might be stirred by? If he saw the Quaker journal, he might assume that Thomas was a pacifist or a conscientious objector. Would he then assume that Thomas's letter was written in an attempt to stop the war? Irritated with myself for being in a constant state of uncertainty and having no one else to turn to, I decided to put the whole problem to Allen. Between us we would come to a decision and I would act on it without delay.

In our conversation the previous night, she'd been very matter of fact about a strange turn of events, telling me that Ada and Gladys had been lovers! I was speechless. And what's more, she had allowed them to be together in Ada's room, which can't be more than two doors away from her own quarters. How could she have faced Ada that first morning after? What had she heard? I hadn't seen Allen in that light, I must confess, and I've never been spoken to so frankly before by a respectable woman. The effect was rousing and I ended the conversation sooner than I'd meant to. It's not that I felt her to be looming up – that never happens in my own house – but my confusion was such that I needed time alone to recover.

To cap the day, Walter caught us together. He'd been missing for some hours, which I'd put down to Vi being ill, but it turned out that Herbert Winter had murdered his grandchildren and cut his own throat and that Walter had found them all in the same room. He started to tell me the story, even though Allen was behind me and the facts were grim; we were all there, in a line, her at the top and me in between and him at the bottom saying what he'd found. When I could get a word in, I told him to mind out of the way and I showed her out. She said she was sorry, she even looked a bit red in the eye, but I'd have to say I was surprised to find her so composed, as if she'd had years in the trade.

Walter was angry. He said we should have seen it coming when Herbert started to cuff himself. I said there were plenty of men out on the street doing that and worse and should we follow them all to stop them committing murder? His argument – that Herbert was one of ours – made no sense to me. Then he started on Allen, asking me what I was doing with her *in my room. I told him to mind his own business and he said that was exactly what he was doing, minding the business, his and mine, and did I have any idea what people were saying? When I asked him who these people were, he said, 'Anyone who's seen her here.' I* had no memory of a crowd observing us, in or out of the shop, and I told him so. Was I not allowed to have a friend without permission from the neighbours?

By the time we got to Herbert's house, the bodies were washed. The room was a terrible sight, even by the single lamp that had been lit for us to do our work; in fact, the poor light added to the scene, making the children look more asleep than dead. We took the bodies to the mortuary, three at a time, and left them there for the police to carry on with, ending the night with Walter and I reconciled to some degree by the disagreeable nature of the job. I got to bed in the early hours and slept well for a short while, waking with a start to find my heart jumping. There was no hope of getting back to sleep after that so I read the Quaker journal and reminded myself of the poem before getting up to play the piano as loudly as I wished in Margaret's absence.

There were a lot of funerals on Saturday morning and no little organization to get them to the cemetery with one coachman down and the road clogged up with other hearses. While I was outside the chapel I had a talk with James Theobald who runs a firm twice the size of mine; he told me that some men he knew had closed entirely, sending their work elsewhere. There was certainly an abundance of cloth-covered coffins – some of which were ours – as proof of the impossibility of proper finishing. Theobald was managing with over half his staff away; when I asked him where he thought we might be heading he said, 'To my sorrow, I do believe we might never recover.' I was taken aback to hear it said so simply. Was my conviction now a common feeling? On the way back, I asked Walter if he had a view on the subject and he said, 'It'll be worse before it gets better.' In the afternoon I left him in the shop and went out on my own to do the visits, many of which were now spent arranging removal to Vasey's stable. There was a bit of a chord, like quarrelling notes held on with the pedal, that still hung over me from the previous night and I passed Allen's house several times before finding it in me to go down the basement stairs. I looked in at the window first and could see no one, but the door was

opened without my having to knock. Allen said she thought she'd heard a
noise; I believe she was waiting for me.

*   *   *

The church flowers were dying; whoever was responsible for the floral arrangements that week had clearly fallen ill. Mr Sucerne would have to ask his wife to do her best with whatever she could find in the garden. Inspecting further, he found a fine coat of dust on every surface; there was even a dirty handkerchief in the aisle. He bent to pick the thing up and then kicked it under a pew, recoiling at the presence of probable contamination. The church and the vicarage were coupled; housekeeping in one was no different to housekeeping in the other. Until the sexton had recovered from his bout of influenza, Muriel must do the cleaning and polishing.

Mr Sucerne stood at the pulpit and looked out at the pews. With the Sunday school closed and the congregation shrinking away to nothing, she would soon be his only audience.

Was God absenting himself from this pestilence? Mr Sucerne's earlier view, that the just were being caught up in punishment meted out to the unjust, had been modified as each day delivered up more virtuous souls. The scales were out of balance; the good outweighed the wicked. He was asked ten times a day: how does God allow such anguish? His reply – *'Through suffering we come to Jesus Christ. Whosoever liveth and believeth in him shall not die eternally'* – assuaged very few. Alone, he felt himself to be spiritually threatened by the question. Having always held to the view that faith could not be dependent on circumstance, he was shaken to find that his own faith was tottering. How was God able to look down upon a land brought to near ruin by war and yet allow the remaining youth to perish? Suffering in itself no longer satisfied him as a route to eternal life. But what, then? Could one approach God with doubt? Could one challenge God with having

243

botched the job of caring for mankind? Prayer was proving to be no more successful than quack remedies and charms.

By the time he left the pulpit, the afternoon light was fading. Making his way to the back of the church, he saw in the gloom that the hymn books were tidy. Mr Speake would not be playing the organ until he could be released from his own duties; none the less, Mr Sucerne put up the numbers for the hymns and psalms, intending to sing them unaccompanied and alone if need be. The many funerals that morning had been poorly attended; even the undertakers appeared to be short of men. How many parishes were without a priest?

As he was leaving the church, intending to cut through the graveyard to the vicarage, he saw a man digging near the boundary wall. Mr Sucerne changed direction and began to walk towards him, shouting. The man looked up, swore and ran off clutching the spade. Pursuit would have been futile; Mr Sucerne knew his limitations. As he approached, he saw that even at this early interrupted stage the work was incompetent. Earth was scattered in all directions and the sides, no more than a foot deep, were already falling in. Looking about him for explanation, he was rendered immobile.

A body, roughly wrapped, lay on the grass not two feet from the place where he stood, partly concealed by a tombstone. It was a smallish body, probably that of an older child or young woman, and the blanket or sheet that enclosed it was open at one end, revealing two thin legs. Mr Sucerne was no stranger to corpses but he had never found himself alone with one in a graveyard in the dark. Suppressing the urge to cry out for help, he drew a cross in the air above the body and went home to telephone the police.

*   *   *

Allen spent the night revisiting Henry's room and repeating their conversation. The time passed in waves: peaks of anxiety in which she threw off the bedclothes, flaming with whatever thoughts had overwhelmed her, and then dips in which she calmed herself and became a little drowsy. The dips lasted five minutes, no more, and by five o'clock she was wide awake with the light on.

Despite his wolfish appearance, Henry might well have considered her frankness to be an unforgivable violation of good manners. She was a teacher, a well-bred widow in her later-than-middle years and she had dared to give him a crude description of a private matter. At their worst, her fantasies had him closing the shop door in her face, saying that he had no interest in lewd women and that she would do well to recover her modesty. At best, she saw them both by the fire like two fellows at peace with each other, neither intimate nor distant. In the third fantasy, the pinnacle, good and bad became indivisibly muddled. In this, she was in his room and he asked her to his bed.

She dressed for the day as if she expected to see him and then fed Lily her beef tea, washed her and carried her to the commode. Allen's distaste for the latter tasks was undiminished but she said nothing to Lily about employing another maid, having come to no decision about the risk of having her lies exposed. Lily asked for nothing in addition and her demented prattle was tolerable if one shut one's ears to it.

After a barely eaten lunch, Allen established herself in the kitchen, having told Ada to clean the upper floors. There was nothing she wanted to do to pass the time; she left her book upstairs and sat at the table, listening. His step was heavy. As soon as she heard it, she jumped to her feet and waited by the door, opening it on the second she judged him to have raised his hand to the knocker. Had she presumed that he would look different than before? He was in his visiting clothes, unsmiling, the very picture of an undertaker come to measure. While she'd been waiting, she'd practised several possible modes of greeting but at the sight of him she was too discomposed to say more than, 'I heard a noise.'

'I was passing,' he said. 'Are you free for a minute?'

'Yes.'

'May I come in?'

She was blocking the door and peering out. She was guarding herself against him! 'Please,' she said, standing back and gesturing as broadly as if the kitchen had been a stage. They walked to the table and sat at their accustomed seats; his seat, my seat, she thought. His black clothes no longer sucked out the light; they established him in the house like old tree roots.

It would have been simple for her to offer him tea, to describe the change in Lily, to ask after the man who had murdered his children, or any other topic not having a direct bearing on their conversation the night before, but the intensity of her feelings would not allow her to speak until she knew what had brought him back to her.

He said, 'I've had a letter from Mr Bevens. I've brought it to show you.' There was no trace of carnality in his face; he was sober, almost solemn. He had nothing to say about her behaviour! His visit was nothing to do with her at all! Was she disappointed? The spell was cracked. She straightened her skirt and put her forearms on the table. If he wanted to talk about Mr Bevens, she would rejoice in the neutral territory. The image of the two men at peace by the fire came back to her; if he wanted friendship, she would supply it.

'What sort of letter?'

'Vindictive.'

'What do you mean, vindictive?'

He removed an envelope from his pocket and took out the letter. 'See for yourself.'

She looked over it, taking in the sense, and then read it through carefully, raising her head occasionally to glance at him. She said, 'This is very grave. He appears to be accusing you of plotting against the State.'

'Is that how you read it?'

'What else could he mean?'

'I don't know. And I don't think it matters because we're getting to the end and, until we do, I'm necessary. Is Mr Bevens going to take the deceased to the stable or wherever?'

'But what if there isn't an end? Why are you so sure?' None of her fantasies had included this one of his. 'If you're so convinced, then why are we bothering to discuss it?'

'You don't understand.'

'What don't I understand?'

'Why does he describe it as an *epidemic*? It's worldwide! Thomas Wey can't have been the only man to spot this coming. He wrote to them months ago. Why did they do nothing? I'll tell you why they did nothing, because the only thing to do was to call a halt to the war!'

'But you can't stop a war because of influenza!'

'You should have been a politician, Mrs Thompson.'

'But you can't!'

'The soldiers are taking it everywhere. And the war's nearly won. Why don't they stop it now? Today?'

'Because if you're right, it's far too late.'

He let out a long, noisy breath. 'It is. It's far too late. So what shall I do with these?' Reaching into his coat, he took out Thomas Wey's papers and put them in front of her.

At this point a few days before, she would have been exasperated enough to say 'Send them to Mr Bevens and let the matter rest'. But as a friend, should she not make an effort to be reasonable? She picked up Thomas's letter. 'Are you saying this because he does?'

'I know it's the truth.'

'How do you know?'

'Common sense. I read the newspaper. And I'm trying to bury the dead.'

'I think you should send every one of these' – she laid her hand on the pile and pushed it towards him – 'to Mr Bevens with an accompanying note of apology. The work, he must understand, has been very harrowing for you and you were particularly distressed on the day he chose to visit, distressed and exhausted. Within hours of receipt of his letter you happened upon Doctor Wey's papers and although you have, of course, no idea what they might contain, you're very pleased to be able to forward them to the Local Government Board to do with as they see fit. Yours faithfully, et cetera, et cetera. What do you think?'

'I—'

'And you might add that you never met Doctor Wey or indeed saw him until he died outside your shop. *And* you've had nothing to do with anyone of his acquaintance since his death.'

At the start of her recital his fingers had been moving on the tabletop. By the end he was still, watching her speak. He said, 'Do you really think that's the best course of action?'

'I most certainly do.' She was the teacher, bolt upright in the chair. 'You can't go to prison for something so inconsequential. You were wrong to be impertinent but I think he's gone too far in accusing you of treachery! Will you write, then?'

'If you think I should, then I will.'

'I'm pleased to hear it.' Having opened the door to him in a state of speechless agitation, she was now herself again. 'I haven't had much luck getting supplies, but I'm sure I can offer you some tea, if you'd like?'

'I would. I ran out yesterday. And Margaret's got 'flu.'

'How are you managing without her?'

She put on the kettle and took china from the sideboard. Rather than two men, they were talking like two old women. Would he mention rationing? Or the difficulty of cooking poor cuts of stringy meat?

'I'm eating what I can put on a plate with no fuss.'

'If you ever want a meal, you're very welcome here.' The words were genuinely meant – he had no cook after all – but as soon as they were spoken she realized that they were perilous. Her self-possession was dependent on her role as adviser; as soon as she allowed him to reject or ridicule her she was no more confident than a girl. Before he could reply, she said, 'I must tell you: Lily's eating again. Only beef tea, but it's nourishment.'

'I know. Ada said.'

'Did she?'

'It's good news.'

'Possibly. She's very weak. I shall have to give up teaching to look after her.'

'Are you saying that you'd have preferred her to die?' He stood up and took off his coat and hat. 'May I?'

'Of course you may. Hang them on the door. Good heavens, no – I wouldn't have wanted that. But if I'm to nurse her – she's never been well – then I won't be able to leave her for more than a few hours. I feel encumbered.' With his coat off, Henry was very much in the room. 'I suppose you'll say that it doesn't matter one way or the other, if the world's coming to an end.'

He ignored the taunt and stood near the stove with her, leaning on the wall with his left arm. He was too close; she moved a few inches back and tried not to look at his face, shifting her attention between his collar and the top of the stove.

'Why have you put up with it?' he said.

'She's my sister. She's been ill for years. And she's had rather a cheerless life – awful husband, no children. I don't have any children either but I'm with them all day, aren't I? Lily never reads or shows the slightest interest in anything. She just sews. There isn't a piece of house linen that isn't embroidered – I do sometimes think I'd like a plain white sheet! She can't get about, that's the problem – she's very frail. Neurasthenia. It's a weakness of the nerves, you know.'

'I know.'

'Do you? I've no idea what else is wrong with her now – apart from

249

being skin and bone. She's gone mad, I think.' Allen knew that she was babbling; if she stopped talking there might be silence and the space between them, which had already contracted itself into a knot, would disappear completely. She concentrated on the stove, examining a crusty brown mark and scraping it off with her thumbnail. 'Ada used to look after her while I was at work. Now she thinks Ada's gone to prison so it's up to me and I can't ask another maid to continue the deception. I certainly can't dismiss Ada – she's done nothing wrong. The only thing I can do is to stop teaching and become Lily's nurse. And it's not even as if we're devoted to each other. I've had nothing to do with her for years. We didn't even like each other as children. Isn't that silly!' The brown mark had come off but now her nail was dirty. 'Lily's my cross. I shall have to bear her for the rest of her life – or *my* life. Of course, I might catch influenza and die next week.'

'You certainly might!'

Allen lifted her head and saw the bared teeth. He was laughing at her!

'If your sister's as mad as you say, then what does it matter? She could be nursed by anyone.'

'That sounds rather cruel.'

'It's the truth.'

Henry lifted his arm away from the wall and looked at her; she became acutely self-conscious, wanting a mirror in order to see herself – was she old today? Was he passing judgement? If she dared, she could reach out and touch him – but with what extraordinary consequences! An equal force was pulling her from behind, offering a way out of the room altogether – Lily needing to be fed or an imaginary knock at the front door.

'My sisters take care of themselves,' he said, walking back to his chair. 'And as I've never wanted to do it for them, that's just as well. Except for Rose. If you did anything for her you'd be thanked very prettily. Sarah, now – she puts her nose in my business, which she might say is a way of taking care. I'd say it's trespass.'

'What do you mean?'

Allen knew exactly what he meant. Sarah's business, she had made plain, was to separate them. If the subject of their relationship could not be openly dealt with, then might he be trying to introduce it by stealth?

The atmosphere in the kitchen was that of a world entirely reduced; they were in negotiation, creeping up to each other and then scuttling off. He must be aware, as she was, that the outcome – the declaration of reciprocal feelings – could only be successful within this minor territory. Beyond the door there could be no resolution, other than withdrawal, without tremendous harm being done to both sides. If she restrained herself then the whole situation could still be brought under control. But was that what she wanted? Her first weeks of friendship with Edward had been equally provoking but the outcome had been universally blessed. The outcome of her consorting with a tradesman – and an undertaker! – would be universal censure.

She lit a lamp – the electric light was too harsh – and set it as far away from her chair as possible; then she put out the tea and sat down. 'You haven't answered me? How does Sarah trespass?'

'You've met her. You've formed an opinion, I'm sure.' He raised his eyebrows and waited for her to speak.

'She's very capable.'

'Is that all?'

'I can imagine that she might be rather overbearing.'

'She wants to stop us meeting.'

There! It was said! He had jolted them into the truth. Allen put her hand over her mouth and shook her head. 'Does she?' she said, through her fingers.

'So does Walter. I don't listen to them.'

'Really?'

'You don't have any friends, do you?'

'I've never—'

'It doesn't matter. I intend to visit you for as long as possible. And you can visit me when Walter's out.'

'I'd like—'

'I'll write to Mr Bevens this afternoon.' He took his coat and hat from the hook behind the door. 'Thank you for helping me come to a decision.'

Their friendship, Dr Wey's papers, were these the only things he had come to talk about? Allen opened the door to the basement stairwell and said, 'You'll let me know how you get on with the letter, I hope.'

He turned to look at her, nodded once and walked out, putting on his gloves.

Should she have said more? Or less? Neither of them had touched the tea; she emptied the pot before Ada could complain about the waste and put the cups away to conceal the evidence of Henry's visit. Then she sat at the table for a moment before rising abruptly and going to her bedroom. In an hour or so, Lily would have to be fed and washed, then the evening would be hers to do with as she wished. She went to the mirror and tried to see her face in the twilight, drawing as near to the glass as she could over the dressing table. Her hair had broken free of its pins but she looked tolerable – not young but not so faded that she should think of herself as in decay. Turning her back on Edward's pillow, she lay on the bed and stared out of the window until the sky was entirely black.

*　　*　　*

I sent Thomas Wey's papers to Mr Bevens as soon as I got back from Allen's house. The Quaker journal was hardly relevant to him and, after some time spent putting it into the envelope and taking it out again, I have to admit that I kept it for myself, particularly because of the poem. I could have copied it out but I preferred to see it as it was, on the page. The letter was written as Allen had advised, although I added that Mrs White had passed Dr Wey's effects to me and that I had never stolen any article from the deceased. Whether or not I would be prosecuted was, as I've said, not important but I did hope that some small step might be taken, however late, to halt the progression of the influenza. It was fanciful, I know, but as I went to the post box I imagined that Thomas was beside me. I would have taken longer to let go of the envelope but a woman in a mask was standing some feet away and waiting for me to get on with it so I took Thomas's hand and we put it in together, so to speak.

There was nothing I could do in the workshop on Saturday evening. I had several visits to make but otherwise I spent the time alone. With Margaret gone, I had to make my own supper. I ate at the piano, thinking again about my improper conduct with Allen – not that she'd have known it as improper conduct but the wish was so strong that I considered it as tantamount to the deed. I was at a loss to explain the events in her kitchen. After her visit to my room the previous night, I was wary of her, and if the letter from Mr Bevens hadn't arrived I would have avoided her for a day or two more. She'd made no mention of Ada and Gladys this time. In fact, nothing in the least stirring was said, although she was more than usually candid about herself, but my imagination was so active that I was unable to tolerate her company and had to leave in a great rush. Stupidly affected by my feelings, I did insist that we continue to meet but I was hardly on the street before I regretted the impulse. I decided then and there that I would see her when I managed to arrange Gladys's funeral and not before.

My friendship with her up to that point had been without shame. We'd talked freely and neither of us had ever referred to her class or mine, whatever Walter or Sarah might be saying. If a man and a woman find themselves able to speak together then what harm can come of it? But if it turns out, as it clearly had, that one of them has notions not known to the other person then the circumstances change. Walter was right: I was getting ideas above my station. Allen was no different, except for the boldness of her language. The difference had occurred in me. I'd never actually noticed anything particular about her; if pressed I would have reported her as being good-looking but only as I might have described Walter or a *customer. Other than a person's height and their width at the shoulder, I take in very little, but I saw her face properly that Saturday and then found it difficult to dislodge her features from my mind. This emotional disorder was all very new to me; my thoughts about people are rarely coloured by sentiment. I've found that nothing useful comes of it. I did fail with Rose, crying for her when she left, but I've never had reason to correct myself for that. Now here I was on the very edge of indiscretion and with no proper reason for it at all.*

✳   ✳   ✳

Sunday, 3 November

Lily Bird had asked for a lightly boiled egg. No bread, no toast, just an egg, boiled, spooned into a cup and then topped with a little butter. She was quite capable of digesting butter and if she enjoyed it well enough she would expect a small custard to be provided for her lunch the following day. She could feel the strength from the food edging its way into her limbs; every bite was an advance towards her new purpose.

Prayer occupied almost all her waking hours. Even during the humiliation of the morning and evening wash, she had learned to flee her body and apply her mind to her petitions. In these last weeks, alone and ready for death, she had brought about a miracle: the Germans had been found! But the floorboards had contained evil and had been made evil thereby. The house was irresistible to the enemy and would inevitably remain so. The enemy was monstrous but she was its equal; the enemy was unyielding but she was more so.

In an unguarded moment, Allen had admitted that the war persisted. No sooner had the words been spoken than she'd tried to modify them, saying that an armistice was in the air and that peace would probably be declared within the month; such lies! The war was raging, on earth and in heaven. She, Lily Bird, would work another miracle and bring it to a close.

*   *   *

Frimley
Hastings
Hawke's Bay
3 November 1918

Dearest dearest Henry,

This is a terrible letter to be writing to you – I don't know how I can write this down – I wish you were here with me and holding my hand.

Later. I'm writing with stops and starts. I won't say when I stop any more, I'll just keep adding. I want you to be here. Archie got influenza at the camp. There's a lot of 'flu there. They didn't say any more than that. I didn't even know he was ill but they don't tell you, do they? I got the telegram and Peggy was with me when I opened it, which is just as well as I passed out. They've been so kind here and we can stay as long as we want to but I think we'll have to go home to be nearer to Archie and for the funeral.

I haven't told the girls yet, I can't bear to do it. They love their daddy so much. I can't bear this.

I'll write again later when I've decided what to do. Send me love, Henry dear. Send me lots of love. I love you.

Rose xxx

and Flora and Grace xxx

PS I hope you get this letter. Peggy's dad is taking it in to town tomorrow but I don't know how long it's taking to get mail to the boat any more.

*   *   *

I'd told Walter, Albert and Harry not to come in on the Sunday. I said that it was no bother for me to do the measuring up and we could always make a collection on the Monday if a body needed to be moved. The rest of my afternoon, when I wasn't out visiting, was spent answering the door to the bereaved. There was an unusual number of bodies troubled with lice and I had to wash most carefully several times. Then, in the evening, I decided to visit the stables, having promised many more families that we could house the deceased there until the possibility of a funeral came up. We'd taken dozens already and I was becoming concerned about having enough room on the floor, even with the dead packed in quite tightly. I was hoping that Vasey might allow us to spread out a bit into another stable. As I left the shop, I saw that the sky to the east was glowing red. No bombs had been dropped since August so I assumed that a building some-where had caught fire. I walked on. The glow became brighter – a strange thing to have such a light in the dark streets – and then I realized that I was heading directly towards it. As I got closer, a bicycle sped past; the man on it called to me that he was getting the fire brigade but before I could ask him anything, he'd disappeared. I recognized him as one of the stable-hands and then, of course, I understood and ran towards the blaze.

My first thought was for the dead. Would they be cremated without ceremony? The horses were making the most terrible noise and with the men shouting and the crackle of the burning wood and straw, it was impossible to make yourself heard. I ran in, past the men who were trying to control the horses and lead them out. Vasey was at the head of a chain of three or four others, throwing water at the flames. The fire had started in the building where the carriages were stored, which was the next but one to mine. I could see no hope of it staying there but I ran to get water for myself and threw buckets of it on to the adjoining wall in the hope that it might be less easily kindled, trying to avoid the bodies and praying with every bucket that the fire brigade would arrive and save us. The flames were ferocious. Then Vasey found me in the smoke and told me that we were on our own – no one was available to man the fire engines. And there

256

we were, one step nearer to calamity. I don't think I'd really understood until that moment: every single thing we'd come to expect was already failing us.

Vasey's men would be busy with the flames until the fire took over the whole place or was put out. Even knowing that I'd never have the strength, I tried to pull the coffins out of the stable to the pavement and I'd just started when Walter came running in and then other men behind him, some that I knew and some I'd never seen. Nothing was said. We got all the bodies out, before the fire took hold of our stable.

The smoke made it almost impossible to see what was left inside. The bodies in shrouds were already leaking and the general stink was foul, but those men were so plucky you couldn't have stopped them with barbed wire. It turned out that a few of them had dead family housed in the shed. When we'd finished, they tried to help Vasey but there weren't enough buckets and the fire was too strong for the small amount of water.

We ended the night coughing and black-skinned in the street outside; one man was dead from a falling beam and the stable was burnt right out. Poor old Vasey just sat on the ground with his head in his hands. The carriages had gone up west as well so all he had now were his horses.

I was left with a great many deceased. Walter and I were both finding it difficult to talk but he suggested the church hall as a possible place to house them. I couldn't see Sucerne agreeing to that. We had to take the dead stable-hand to the mortuary and I thought it best to take the uncoffined bodies there, too, whatever the bereaved might say. They could always collect them and take them home if they preferred to, out of sentiment. The coffined bodies could be put in a good-sized shed or even an unoccupied hall. I was very disturbed to see them lying out there in the open; it offended me, and again, it was the failing order that caused me the most distress. How could it have come to this? A fire might have happened there at any time but not with a makeshift mortuary inside and no fire brigade. Two of the men volunteered to stay and watch the bodies until we got back; more offered and for all I know they stayed there

257

together. We still had our own cart and Walter said he'd hunt down whatever other transport he could find as soon as it was a decent hour.

There was quite a big crowd outside the gate with nobody too close to anyone else, which made for a strange gathering. A bit unearthly, I thought, with the white masks on most of them. Vi was waiting there for Walter and she told me to go home for clean clothes and then come back to her for breakfast. My coat was ruined and I'd lost the hat I was wearing somewhere in the confusion but it was nowhere near dawn and the streets were quiet so no one saw me walking bareheaded and as filthy as a miner.

I had a bath by Vi's fire and then she made breakfast, most of which Walter and I found impossible to swallow, our throats were so sore. Her sympathy for us and for Vasey was truly meant but I felt her to be a bit withdrawn, not necessarily from the shock, which had made us all quiet. We did talk a little about the events of the night, despite the endless coughing and the pain of speaking above a whisper. The two main things that concerned us were the difficulty of finding a carriage-master when there was such demand and the acquiring of a store for the bodies. There were several tradesmen close by with warehouses and we agreed to call in on them during the day. Vi said, 'You can't put coffins near food,' but I said we were more likely to find other goods being stocked and anyway, we could go round regularly with disinfectant. The weather was cold and we were lucky there; a summer plague would have been truly abominable.

When Walter went off to get himself ready for work, Vi got up to clear the table and then sat down again. I knew she was going to say something of a private nature and she'd been so kind I didn't have the heart to stop her. I don't think she'd have let me in any case.

She started off with something like, 'It's bad then, isn't it, Henry love?' which I took to be an introduction because of the way she was leaning forward.

I said, 'It is.' When I think about it now, I wish I'd left the house, but I stayed, even though I had an idea of what was coming next.

'I haven't seen you for a while,' she said, 'and I've been wanting to have *a word. That Mrs Thompson of yours. It's not helping, you know, having the business talked about the way it is.' Despite the night's misfortunes and the general calamity we were in, she was petty-minded enough to be bothering me about Allen!*

I must have looked at her strangely because she carried on with her voice raised, as if she'd had to shout me down. 'I know you're mad on her, but you've got responsibilities, Henry. I've known you for the best part of your life and I can't stand by and let you make a fool of yourself the way you are. Walter doesn't like to say what he thinks but I do. And I'm thinking that you've gone a bit silly over this. When the 'flu's over and you've got the business back to normal, what do you think you're going to get by way of customers if nobody trusts you to behave yourself?'

Those might not be the exact words she said, but they're certainly what she meant. By the end of it, I was on my feet and Walter had come in. To do him justice, he told her there was a time and a place and to leave me alone for now, but I left them both without a word, not because I couldn't think of anything to say, but because I would have said too much.

*   *   *

Monday, 4 November

'Have you heard about Henry?' Sarah said.

Holding on to the door as if she might fall without it, Nora said, 'No.'

'Can I come in or are we standing on the doorstep?'

Nora stepped back. Her whole demeanour was cheerless; her posture, her expression, her soiled, ill-matching clothes and the lank state of her hair, which was hanging round her face, unwashed and unbrushed. She was still plump but less so, with a grey tint to her skin that made her look as if the dirt had accumulated inside as well as out. She showed no curiosity about Henry and waited for Sarah to lead the way into whichever room she chose.

'Kitchen?' Sarah said, pointing along the hall.

'If you like.'

The kitchen was cold. 'How are you keeping warm? Or cooking?'

Nora pointed at a blanket on a chair then she put it over her shoulders and sat down, folding the ends over her knees. When she was cocooned, she looked at Sarah without interest, as if she were asleep with her eyes open.

'I asked you how you were cooking?'

'I'm not hungry.'

'You've got to eat, you silly woman.'

'I have a bit of bread and jam.'

'Henry, then,' Sarah said, after a pause. 'They've had a fire at Vasey's and lost the lot. Not a carriage left.' She waited for Nora to do what she usually did: to gasp and catch at her throat with both hands, saying 'No!' three or four times and then repeating the news word for word, nodding to accompany herself.

Instead, she said, 'Oh.'

'No carriages. No funerals. They'll never find anything else, not now. Henry's sunk. We'll lose all that business.'

'Yes, I suppose we will.' Sarah might as well have been telling her that she'd put two potatoes in the soup instead of three. 'All that business.' She spoke without emotion, but rather as a child might parrot its parent. The blanket began to slip from her knee. She adjusted it and sat quietly.

Nora always took more words than were necessary to convey a thought even though she rarely had a thought worth conveying. For her to be saying so little, she must be sick at heart. Sarah gave up on the story of the fire and said, 'You're a bit low, are you?'

'I don't know.'

'You're sitting in here too much, that's what's wrong. You should get properly dressed and go out. Have you seen anyone?'

'Not for a bit.'

'Well, you should.'

'I suppose so.' Nora's eyes filled with tears. 'I can't, Sarah. I can't.'

'Why not?'

'I don't know. I can't, that's all.'

'You'll feel better for a bit of company.'

'I don't see the point. What's the point?'

'You've got to think of the family.' Sarah was stern. 'If Henry has to close the business, we'll need to put our heads together.'

'I can't. You do it for me. You'll do it, won't you?'

Sarah lit the stove and used cold water to wash up the few dirty cups and plates. As she left, she picked up a framed photograph from the mantelpiece. 'Here's Samuel for you,' she said. 'You think what he'd say if he knew you were moping about.'

'Samuel.' Nora held the photograph to her face. 'My handsome Sam.'

'Cheer up, Mum. That's what he'd say, isn't it?'

'He would.' Nora started to cry again.

'I'll come back this afternoon with something hot. And stop crying. It's doing you no good.'

*   *   *

Allen had spent most of Sunday looking after Lily. In the intermittent hours, she'd written to Ruth, wasted long minutes with an unopened book in her hand and spent time on her bed, thinking about Henry Speake. Nothing had been resolved; nothing could be resolved! Every time they met, she would be made as helpless as she had been the afternoon before. He thought of her as a friend and an ally in his secret dealings, not as a woman; she might as well wear trousers and smoke a pipe. Did she even like him? If he'd had been of her class, would she have made her feelings clear? And what *were* her feelings? Was desire the driving force or was there some charity, some kindness in her towards him? If he caught influenza, would she be willing to establish herself at the bedside or would she run away? He was older than her, she was sure of it. He carried himself well. He was undoubtedly intelligent. He spoke with authority and with a pleasing voice. But he was a tradesman! And yes, his indecision and self-absorption had irritated her. He had rarely encouraged her to confide in him; she had often felt like the audience in a theatre, personally unknown to the actor but essential to his well-being. And the very fact that she could say none of this to a single living soul without making herself look ridiculous was confirmation that she was absolutely in the wrong. If one loved, one did so openly; there was nothing to be feared about love. Desire, on the other hand, would pass – unless whipped up by revelation. If she touched him, he would – what? Jump away? Be angry? If he sustained her impulse and returned the touch, what would *she* do? The quandary was hers to settle. Henry was inscrutable but even so, she had never seen him look at her with the slightest interest. His ardour, she was sure of it, would terrify her. There *was* no quandary. If he happened to visit before Gladys's funeral, she would behave with impeccable manners; she would restrain every imprudent thought.

On Monday when Allen was in the kitchen making lunch for Lily, Ada came running in from the street with news of the fire: '… And a man died! Nobody came from the fire brigade but Mr Speake was there, they said.'

'Is he all right?'

'I think so, ma'am. Nobody said he wasn't. But it burnt down, they said. Got the horses out anyway.' Ada put down the shopping. Heavy rain had penetrated the basket and made everything damp. 'I hope Mrs Bird won't mind but there's no eggs to be had. But I found most of what you asked for, ma'am.'

'I'm going to see to Mrs Bird now.'

'Ma'am. And shall I open the windows in the drawing room, ma'am? I've sprayed disinfectant again this morning.'

'Yes, do.'

Ada had apologized daily for the inconvenience of having Gladys in the house but Allen had insisted that she stay until the funeral. If Lily mentioned the smell, which was not much worse than the combination of unpleasant odours in her own room, Allen was prepared with a story about blocked drains.

She fed Lily and read her the passage she wanted from St John without taking note of a single word of it. Henry had been in a fire. Her resolution was already faltering. When she thought Lily was asleep she put the book down gently and began to tiptoe to the door.

'I want to be taken to church!'

Allen turned back to the bed, caught out as ever by Lily's capricious timing. Was this a half-dream? A real request?

'Did you hear me?' She was still on her side, but her face was animated. 'Did you *hear* me?' Her voice had gained in power with her appetite. 'I must be taken to church!'

'Why?'

If Lily had been upright and mobile, she might have danced on the spot in agitation. The truth could not be told; she must convince Allen without divulging her true purpose. Looking this way and that, she finally said, 'To thank God for finding the Germans.'

'Can you not thank Him here?'

'No.'

'I could ask Mr Sucerne to come and pray with you.'

'No! Not here. I'll see him in church!'

'Lily, it simply isn't possible. How will I get you there?' She might weigh very little but the prospect of having to carry her to a cab and then into the church and then to do the whole journey in reverse was too tiresome to contemplate.

'You can take me in a cab.' She'd thought it out! 'And I shall want to be left alone.'

'For how long?'

'I shall take my bell and ring it when I've… finished.' She blinked slowly, several times, waiting for Allen to agree.

Knowing that she was certain to end up doing exactly as Lily wanted, Allen tried one last ploy. 'We always prayed by our beds as children, didn't we? And I'm sure that God heard us, every night. Praying in church' – Lily was already opening her mouth to speak – 'is lovely but I really can't believe that God takes more notice of it than he—'

'This evening will do very nicely.'

Where had Allen's new, mutinous spirit disappeared to? Only a few days ago, she'd been prepared to let Lily die. Now she was in a worse position than before and Lily had recognized it. If her willingness to eat had been the first step in Allen's subjugation then this was the second: her presumption that any whim would be complied with. She said, 'I'll do my best.'

'I want to sleep now.' The subject was closed but only in the interim. Allen's afternoon had been mapped out for her. She tried to telephone the vicarage but could get no response from the exchange; she would have to walk down in the rain and see if she could come to some arrangement with Mr Sucerne.

Mrs Sucerne answered the door, stepping back into the hall even though Allen was wearing her mask. Mr Sucerne was visiting and would be back by four. She could see no reason why the church would not be available for private prayer but if Mr Sucerne agreed… he was busy that evening… perhaps the following morning would suit?

Allen agreed to make a preliminary visit, just to confirm that all would be well, said goodbye at the same extravagant distance and then found herself walking towards Henry's shop, even though she'd been quite set on walking home. The door was locked. Although there was no notice to explain the closure, she continued to look for one, walking from one end of the window to the other several times. Should she knock? If there were someone inside, the door would be open. Had Henry been taken ill? Then Walter would be in charge. Unless Walter was ill, too. Perhaps they'd been hurt in the fire, despite Ada's reassurance. It was impossible to think of Henry closing up without an explanation.

There was nothing to be gained by waiting. She would call again the following day – any anxious friend would do no less.

* * *

Although we spent some hours on Monday in search of a new carriage-master, neither Walter nor myself could find anyone able to take us on; at one place we were told that the horses were having to canter to and from the cemetery in order to get through the list! If we wanted to conduct the funerals that were already promised, we would have to use the handbier or shoulder the coffins ourselves, and the cemetery was too far away for such a scheme. Walter said that we should go back to using the local church-yards but there was no time to go about getting permission – and anyway, they were full to bursting. I even suggested the possibility of buying a motor hearse but the cost was far beyond what I could afford.

The mortuary took our shrouded bodies without any of the families opposing it; who would want to live in the company of evident decomposition? So far as the coffined bodies were concerned, we were only able to house three there, no more – not that a coffin was going to be of much value in the weeks ahead. Very few families really wanted their dead brought home again but the mortuary was generally loathed. We would have to get on with finding some temporary accommodation.

I was told about a decent wholesaler, a hardware man, who was low in supplies and had a small space to hire. We spent the best part of that day going backwards and forwards to the warehouse with the handbier in the pouring rain; Walter and I both felt quite ill, with our lungs and throats still burning from the smoke. I'd never imagined that I might get influenza. I was robust and probably too old to die even if I did succumb, but in those days after the fire I kept thinking that my body had been weakened and that my lungs might invite infection. With every bout of coughing, I reviewed myself, even looking at my fingers from time to time to search for signs of blue skin.

Sarah called in at some point, just to make sure that we'd all survived. She spoke to Walter and told him that she'd come back in a day or two. No mention of a helping hand from her or any of them – not that they could have done anything useful. Albert and Harry had both heard about the fire but they turned up for work anyway, not having been told otherwise; I sent Albert home and got Harry to stay and give us a hand with the carting and lifting. It was a long day and made longer by the gloomy atmosphere in which we worked; Harry being the only one of the three of us who was inclined to be lively. I left them both for a few hours in order to visit the families who'd been expecting funerals that day and the day after. Although most of them had heard about the fire and were expecting a postponement I think some were very upset at the news. In many cases, the person I was calling on was too ill to be seen. In one case the last two members of the family had died overnight and I'd had to leave a message with the neighbour for whoever might be arriving to take care of things.

I hadn't needed to say a word to Walter. He understood and his face was grim throughout the day. We would have to cancel all the funerals that had been booked in for the rest of that week and the weeks following, tell the relevant people where the coffins from the stable had been sheltered and refuse any new work that came to us. With no transport, we would have to close the business.

From Walter's point of view, he was thinking that once the influenza had subsided we'd get back to normal; even so, Speake & Son had existed for eighty years or more and had only been shut down for a week in all that time. The shop closing now was a death in itself.

If I'd had more courage as a youth, I'd have taken my chances and gone to America to try my hand with the piano but my quota of spirit fell far short of what I would have needed to oppose the family and make a success of a different life. And here I was with empty days ahead and no interest in filling them with music – that was extraordinary to me and I could only hope that once the shutters were up I'd have a change of heart. I did sit down once or twice but after a few notes I was unable to continue.

266

When we'd done as much as we could, I sent Harry home and Walter and I had a talk in the office: if we cut the list in half and shared the visits, we'd be able to get through it all by the following evening.

'I might offer myself to another firm,' he said. 'You could do the same. You don't want to be here on your own, do you?'

I said I couldn't see me working for another man and he said that with our history we'd be given whatever conditions we pleased. And then when we were ready, we could start the business up again. His eyes were bright and I thought he might be about to cry but he didn't. He just sniffed a bit and said, 'Your dad would have been grieving today.' He left then and I locked the door behind him, thinking that I'd never seen my father grieve for anything in his life, not even my mother.

I'd only written to Rose the week before but this was all too weighty to keep for the next letter and I chose to use the time I had free to tell her the news. I set it down as it had happened: the fire and the consequences. I always wrote as if she were in front of me and I could see that my words had made her cry. To reassure her, I said that I was looking forward to playing the piano and that I might even take the opportunity to give the workshop a good clear-out. I didn't mention the sisters not offering to help – there was no point to it. Rose knew them as well as I did. Being a girl amongst them, I did wonder sometimes if she had a harder time; did they expect her to be one of them? I was always the odd one out. The boy, the musical boy.

And was she well? I asked her as I always did. Even though the question was meaningless, it added to the sense of us being together. I ended the letter as hopefully as I could and then went to bed and slept like a drugged man, my first good sleep for many weeks.

* * *

Lily had responded to the delay in her plans by smiling mysteriously at Allen and saying, 'Of course. Now I have the night to prepare.' Even the lack of eggs and therefore of baked custard had been passed over with a shrug. 'There will be eggs,' Lily had repeated until Allen had found a place to interrupt and ask her what she might want instead. Nothing, she'd replied. She would fast until the rendezvous.

Getting her recumbent body dressed for the morning outing took almost an hour; she was willing to co-operate but had no understanding of the necessary movements. By the time she was in the chair, masked and ready to be wheeled to the waiting cab, both women were dishevelled, although Lily had remained calm throughout, smiling and talking nonsense.

The driver, the only one available for streets around and already suspicious of having to carry an invalid, saw her and said, 'No infectious fares, now, ma'am. You'll swear on oath she's not infectious? Because I'm not going near her, however much you were to pay me.'

'She's not ill at all,' Allen reassured him. 'I told you. Could you put her in the cab?' Lily had been advised that the trip would only take place if the driver did the carrying; the driver had been advised that a good tip was waiting for him at the end of the fare if he took Lily into the church, waited for them both outside and then performed the whole procedure in reverse.

Mr Sucerne, when asked at nine o'clock that morning if the visit would be welcome, had begun by saying that the church was open to all. Then, thinking of his encounter with Lily and her wish to die a martyr, he had been momentarily nonplussed. Allen had explained: she was eating again and wished to pray privately – possibly in gratitude for her renewed health.

'So few parishioners are coming to church,' he'd said. 'Even to the appointed services. Interruptions are most unlikely. The sexton's ill so

I'll be somewhere about if Mrs Bird wishes me to join her in prayer.' Then, to Allen's surprise, he'd held out his hand; unheard of now, to touch without good reason! Intensely conscious of his grip through her glove, she'd said, 'Thank you,' and pulled gently away, glancing at his face. She'd caught him out. His normal kindly, puffy features had been transformed. He was imploring her to leave her hand in place. Startled, she'd thanked him again, more brusquely this time, and walked off, conscious of his eyes at her back.

The masked cab driver, a big man, had clearly had some experience in the lifting and setting down of bodies and was able to make Lily comfortable with the same simplicity of manner that a man shows when he's at ease with dangerous dogs. She was propped between Allen and the wall of the cab with a blanket tucked over her knees and a cushion from the house placed behind her head. To see her out of bed was to understand her frailty; she was very slight and diminished further by her clothes; her coat was too big for her shoulders and her hat too low on her forehead. Every jolt and rattle of the cab lifted her out of position and then jerked her back into it but she spent the journey with her eyes closed, apparently asleep.

When they arrived at the church, the driver took Lily in his arms and carried her down the aisle; she urged him forward, saying, 'Go on, go *on*,' until they were directly in front of the altar. 'Here,' she said. 'On the altar.'

'Mrs Thompson?' Mr Sucerne came through the vestry door and hurried over to Allen. 'Is everything all right?'

'I—'

'The altar!' Lily was wriggling like a child in the driver's arms.

Lifting both hands to Allen as a signal that she should stand away, Mr Sucerne approached the cabman and bent to whisper in Lily's ear. She whispered something in return. Then, in the manner of someone imparting important information, Mr Sucerne took a breath and spoke again, as quietly but with more intent. When he was finished, he took a step back. There was a pause, during which Lily's head began to shake.

'Can I put her down now, please?' The driver went to put her in the first pew but she clung to his neck and said, 'No! *On the altar!*'

'Blimey! I can't put you there!'

'Mrs Bird—' Mr Sucerne pleaded.

Allen put her hand on Lily's sleeve. 'You can't sit on the altar. Sit here' – she pointed at the pew – 'and you'll be able to see the altar quite clearly.'

'Do as you're told, ma'am.' The driver was trying to dislodge Lily's hands without breaking her fingers. 'And let me go!'

'The altar! *Put me on the altar!*'

'Will you get her off me, please?' The cabman was angry now. 'I don't want to hurt her, really I don't.'

Allen and Mr Sucerne did their best to pull her hands away but she clung to the driver like a tree creature in a gale, with her head shaking, shouting as loudly as her thin voice would allow. At the limit of his patience, the driver improvised, fell to his knees and lay down in the aisle, almost crushing her. The surprise loosened her grip and he stood quickly, brushing away the dust and then rubbing his hand across his chin. 'I'll take what you owe me, if you don't mind, and leave it there.'

As Allen was paying him – with a substantial gratuity – Mr Sucerne was kneeling next to Lily on the stone floor.

'Mrs Thompson?' he said. 'I believe your sister may have had an apoplexy.' Her blue-grey face was crooked, one side dragged lower than the other. Her right hand and arm were rigid, the fingers curled in a tight fist. She was still breathing but her eyes were blank.

Allen said, 'Oh—' and stopped, her eyes fixed on Lily's ghastly crooked mouth.

'May I suggest that I ask my neighbour if we could borrow his motor-car?'

'If you think he might agree.'

'I can't think why he would refuse. I'll make Mrs Bird comfortable while I enquire.' He lifted Lily, using more effort than her weight demanded, and took her to the vestry. Allen waited by the open door, not wanting to be too close to Lily's dark, dead-fish eyes. There was a stained-glass window ahead of her; she looked at it steadily, focusing on the blue robes of a seated angel. Mr Sucerne was being very kind... Another man might have been furious, condemning her for bringing Lily in the first place. He was calm, whispering... what was he whispering? And that look of devotion on his face as he'd held her hand that morning! Had she imagined it? Perhaps he was thinking about God – did one look devoted when one thought about God? She'd always seen Mr Sucerne as a decent, if obsequious man, but one could never know what went on in another person's mind and heart. Had his feelings for her suddenly blossomed, or had her feelings for Henry made her more receptive? A heroic figure had emerged from the soft folds of Mr Sucerne's vestments; he was probably using the opportunity to prove himself to her but he had behaved graciously.

He was back within five minutes, waving from the door. 'God is with us this morning,' he said, picking Lily up again and grunting as he shifted her weight across his arms. An old man in a chauffeur's uniform was standing by the gate. He opened the door to the car and Lily was laid flat on the seat and covered with a rug.

Mr Sucerne said, 'Do you know why Mrs Bird wanted to come to church today?'

'To pray. She said it was to pray.'

'She came to put an end to the war.'

'To—'

'She believed that her prayers would bring about a cease-fire.'

'Mr Sucerne, I—'

'I told her that peace had been declared today. I told her it was her triumph.' There was no trace of humour. He was dignified, the shepherd ministering to the sick sheep. Allen was muted in her thanks – to have been effusive would have been to cheapen the deed. In indulging Lily, he had unknowingly followed her example, lying to her as an adult lies to a child. She allowed him to take her hand and to hold it. Then she got into the car and gave the chauffeur her address.

At the house, Allen called Ada and, between them, they got Lily to her room and undressed her; Ada recognized the symptoms at once. Her father had died of an apoplexy, 'only his was on the other side.'

'Will she die?' Allen said.

'Oh no, ma'am. I'm sorry. I didn't mean to frighten you.'

'You're not frightening me.'

'Might go on for ever such a long time, ma'am. It all depends.'

They tidied the bedclothes over Lily's contorted body and stood in silence, looking down at her. Then Ada sighed and said, 'Mr Speake's just called in, ma'am. He says he can't do anything for poor Gladys except take her to the mortuary. He's had to shut the shop.'

So she was nobody in particular! Not even deserving of a note! Despite persistent questioning in the kitchen, Ada could only repeat what she'd been told: Mr Speake was very sorry but they would have to find another undertaker; he'd had to close the business. His expression had been chilly and the only thing to remark on had been the sound of his voice, which was very hoarse.

After reassuring Ada that Gladys would be buried within the week, Allen went to her room and cried into the pillow until she fell into a thick unhealthy sleep. By late afternoon she was lying awake, unable to breathe through a nose still blocked from crying. What was she to do? There were other undertakers near by, she was sure of it. She got up, splashed her face with the icy water on the washstand and went downstairs to Lily, to see if she was still alive. She was.

And here I am, Allen thought. No more the teacher; no more the wife. I'm an ignorant nurse and my horizon is my sister's body. For as long as she lives I will have to wash her and change her bed and brush her hair and put ointment on her sores. Leaving the door open so that she might hear a cry, she spent the evening in her room writing letters to Henry, each more unambiguous than the last, falling asleep on the bed with the pen in her hand and waking in the middle of the night with a stiff neck and paper spread around her skirt.

Disorientated, she got up and put on the electric light but it was harsh and hurt her eyes. There was a lamp on the dressing-table; she lit that instead and then lay back on the bed, rubbing the ache in her neck. Her first waking thought had been of Henry, not a precise memory of him but a kind of amorphous unhappiness that radiated from his name. Now, staring into the shadows, she began to list his slights and her griev-ances as she had in the letters. The purpose of her intended visit had been turned on its head. She no longer felt the slightest concern for his well-being; his curt message had confirmed that he was only interested in his own affairs. If he ever thought of her at all, it was as a receptacle for his delusions.

She was humiliated. Her previous excitement sickened her. And what was she to do with Gladys? How *dare* he leave a body to moulder in her drawing room! At that moment, had she been able to lift and transport the coffin, she would have deposited it on his doorstep with a note saying 'Yours, I believe, with compliments'. She could send Ada out to look for another undertaker; she could go herself. But if Henry was no longer able to bury people, he should be scouring the district for men to take on his unfinished business. And she would tell him so. She would visit him that morning and insist that he shoulder his responsibilities! It was his choice to stand aloof. It was hers to hold him to account.

Allen was invigorated. The room was too small for the spectacular nature of her recovery. She would go for a walk! Despite the hour – a quarter past three – she got off the bed and opened the wardrobe door to get her shoes; by the time she was back on the bed with her foot poised, doubt had sidled up. The streets were dark. Any passing policeman would be certain to question her; how would she explain? She could say she was running to the doctor; there must be women doing that at all hours. And then the policeman might offer to go for her…

But how else was she to occupy the hours till morning? Reluctantly putting back the shoes, she caught sight of a band of brown velvet: the hem of an evening frock that had hung unused since Edward's death. She lifted the hanger from the rail and removed the cotton cover. The frock was still beautiful. She took off her clothes and stepped into it, struggling with the hooks and eyes, and smoothing down the skirt with the flat of her hands, enjoying the odd sensation of the nap against her skin. She went to the mirror, conscious that her carriage had become more graceful. In the poor light she was still a young woman; her waist was as slender, her back as straight. She posed, arching her neck and making what Edward would have called her mirror face. Henry would never see her in this frock. If she lived with Henry, she would never have the opportunity to wear it.

Shivering in the cold, she pulled all her clothes from the wardrobe and the chests of drawers and laid them on the bed, making a dull mountain in the light of the single lamp. She would buy new clothes! When the shops were open again she would buy lovely things, nothing sombre. The room was very cold. Picking a blouse and skirt at random, she put them on over the velvet frock and pinned up her hair. She had work to do and at least four hours to herself before breakfast. Excited by the task, she began to make piles on the floor: to keep, to give to Ada, to give to the poor. By six o'clock, the piles were completed. Allen undressed, hung up the velvet frock and went back to bed to doze for an hour.

＊   ＊   ＊

Wednesday, 6 November

I put the last details into the ledger on Wednesday morning. My entries had lapsed during these weeks; I'd started to form my letters badly, made mistakes here and there, and written jobs up a day or more after the work had been taken on – years of order just swept aside. It upset me more than it should have done. If somebody were to read my ledger, they'd see for themselves how we were unable to keep going so in that respect it was a good record, but for me, it was the last pages of Speake & Son and therefore a part of my testament.

I'd put the ledger away and taken out the accounts when I was interrupted by a banging at the door. There had been constant knocking since I'd sat at the desk, asking me to suggest other firms. In the end I put a piece of card up in the window with all the local and near-local men I could think of, and that seemed to quieten things down. If I'd been equipped for it, I could have been making fifty coffins a week or more – there were more hearses on the road than any other sort of transport. It was ridiculous really, an undertaker being forced to close in the middle of a plague. As I was putting up the card, Mr Bevens came into my mind. What action had he taken over those papers? Was he still intending to report me? I'd forgotten the whole matter in the commotion of the last few days, but I knew that he'd think my misfortune was first rate.

The banging at the door turned out to be Elsie and Sarah. They started off by telling me that Harry had influenza. He'd collapsed that morning and was very poorly. I was sorry – I'd found myself getting fond of Harry – and I said I'd call round there later in the day. Nora was bad, too, not ill but low. I had no intention of visiting her but I didn't say so. My voice was cracked and I was coughing away but neither of them asked me how I was or mentioned the fire. Then Sarah said, 'There's another reason why we're here.'

I suppose I was expecting it. We went into the little office where I see the bereaved; there are three chairs there and we all sat down, me behind the desk and the sisters in front of me in their dark coats and cheap hats: Sarah looking more like my father than I ever did and Elsie doing her best to keep her face harsh. They wanted to know what I intended to do about the money – I pay out a certain amount to them all every month. Rose doesn't get anything, it'd be too complicated and anyway, she's doing well enough, she tells me. When I go, she'll get my share.

'What do you want me to do?' I said. 'The business has to close. Do you want me to pay you out of my own pocket?'

'You've let it go to pieces,' Sarah said, and Elsie came in with, 'You have, you know.' Sarah must have prepared the speech before they came because she didn't pause for breath: there was the shocking state of the workshop, Harry being allowed to attend at funerals, Walter having to run things – who'd been saying that? – Herbert Winter murdering the children because I hadn't thought to look into his mad ways... on and on and on.

'And a funny way you've got of looking after the family,' Sarah finished. 'You don't care what happens to us any more and it's all because of that woman. If you'd been looking after the business properly, you'd have had another carriage-master standing by.'

Elsie volunteered nothing during all this but she'd never had the sense to defy Sarah. Why would she suddenly have a mind of her own?

I told Sarah she was talking nonsense and did she not realize that there were no other available carriage-masters? Or wood? Or coffins? They knew all that, she said, but I'd made things worse by my feckless behaviour. We were shouting by this time and I was about to tell them to leave when there was another knock. I put my head out and saw Allen pressed up against the glass, looking in. When she saw me, she stood away from the window. I thought she was going to walk off but she waited while I unlocked the door and then came in as if we'd never had anything to do with each other. She had to have Gladys buried, she said, and what was I intending to do about it?

*   *   *

When Allen went down to breakfast, she found Ada in the kitchen.

'There are some clothes that might fit you on the floor in my room,' she said. 'Please take them all away. Whatever's of no use to you can be given to the church.'

'Yes, ma'am.'

'And don't worry about Gladys. I shall deal with it.'

'Thank you, ma'am.' Was Ada about to say more? The moment passed.

Lily was still comatose. Allen told Ada to listen out for any disturbance in the bedroom and left the house to visit Henry Speake.

There was no immediate answer to her knock. She looked through the window and, seeing nobody, assumed that Henry was still out making his apologies. There was a notice on the door, listing the names of other undertakers. Should she continue to insist on preferential treatment? Many of the other bereaved families would be in a worse position, living in one room or coping with several dead in a family. The fire left her; doubt replaced it. She was guilty of pride. She would take note of the names and enquire elsewhere. As she made the decision, Henry put his head round the corner of the small office, saw her and came towards the door. He was at his most withdrawn, not meeting her eye as he let her in and then standing with his chin down, waiting for her to speak. In his presence, her sense of injury re-emerged.

'I want Gladys buried,' she said, pulling down her mask. 'What do you intend to do about it?'

'There's been a fire. I've got no transport. I've had to close.'

'I know about the fire. And I'm sorry. But are you expecting me to bury her myself? Can you not make an arrangement on my behalf?'

Sarah came out of the small office. She said, 'The situation being how it is, Mrs Thompson, I'm afraid we can't do any more for you.'

It had never occurred to Allen that she might not be alone with Henry. She was taken off-guard, silenced by Sarah's stocky manliness and the pretty face of the other sister who was poking her head round Sarah's shoulder in order to get a better look.

Henry said, 'Now, Sarah.'

Sarah said, 'I'm sure you understand.' She smiled and opened the door. 'I'm so sorry.'

'Mrs Thompson?' Henry was almost shouting.

The devil came to Allen's aid. 'Henry?' she said. 'Perhaps you'll visit me later? Or shall I come to you?' The silence was reward enough. She waited for him to answer. The sisters looked at them both.

'I'll be there in an hour,' he said.

* * *

Eric Bevens had written to his youngest daughter on the Saturday – not knowing that she was dead – to admonish her yet again for her impulsive, empty-headed marriage. Later that day, on receiving the telegram with the dreadful news, he'd sat for some hours before telling his wife and mother. Effie's elopement, in his wife's opinion, had been entirely as a result of his pig-headedness; her death, so far away from home, would therefore be equally his fault.

The village where Effie's detestable husband had set up house could only be reached by two trains; it had taken a full day for Eric Bevens to get there. According to the maid, the husband was away on some scheme or other, she didn't know in which part of the country. His habit was to write home every few weeks – how dreadful to be getting such intimate details from a servant! – and he would sometimes leave an address where mail could be sent. Effie had had no friends in the village. She'd lived alone, except for the maid, had got sick very suddenly, then turned the colour of ink and died without saying a word. The maid hadn't known what to do until she'd thought to send him the telegram. His letter lay unopened by the bed; unable to sit with the body for more than a minute, he'd picked up the envelope and taken it down to the kitchen, tearing it into small pieces as he went and throwing it into the stove.

The undertaker was apologetic; there would be a delay in procuring a coffin and then a further delay before the burial but he would keep Mr Bevens informed at each stage. He was a mild man, so very much the opposite of Henry Speake that he might have been from a different trade. To think of Speake having anything to do with Effie!

The body could not be left alone in the house. Taking a brief inventory of the few valuables, Eric Bevens left the maid in charge. He dictated some lines to her as a precaution against illiteracy; she was acquainted with enough words to convey the gist of any news about the husband. If a letter arrived from him she was to forward it immediately. The premises were to be guarded at all times, day and night. A reasonable allowance would be made for food and she would be paid in full by him if her master did not return by the date of the funeral.

In an attempt to say his last goodbye to Effie, he went back upstairs and opened the door to her room but the blackened figure in the bed was unapproachable. He had previously removed her wedding ring; it was in his breast pocket. If the husband were to provide an address, he could assure him that the ring was safe and not on the maid's finger. He bowed his head by way of a goodbye and then closed the door. Effie had made her choice.

His wife and mother were both inconsolable, weakened by influenza and intent on condemning him for Effie's death. That she'd married badly was incontrovertible but, they said, had he not driven her away, she would have been properly nursed. If Effie had been at home, he countered, she would have been in the eye of the infection and might have died in any case. It was impossible to maintain a successful argument with two weeping women and he was pleased to return to work on the Wednesday morning.

The papers and letters were piled high. He spent the first hour of the day in discussion with the two remaining clerks, both junior to him; Sir Arthur had not made any specific recommendations but the general advice in newspapers was sound. The Local Government Board was still in authority and would remain so, even if he were the last man left in it to be doing any work. Returning to his desk, he lifted the first letter from the stack in his tray. The handwriting was well executed, the paper of a good weight; the impression made upon him by any thing or person was always, in the first instance, to do with quality. He was a good judge of quality. Effie's husband was third-rate, a felon, and he had told her so. He cut open the envelope and laid the contents on the desk.

Speake! And his secret papers! The letter was grovelling; the man had been brought to his knees. And the papers? Figures... columns of figures... initials? Some gibberish about the world's body...

There was nothing of the slightest interest. Impatient to get on, he dropped everything into the waste-basket and carried on with the rest of the post.

*   *   *

Walking home, Allen kept saying her name to herself, as a teacher might say it to an errant pupil. She'd behaved badly – but then Sarah had been equally rude. The whole display had been about their assumptions; Sarah and Elsie were punishing her for creating a scandal when there was no scandal of any kind. Henry had behaved in an exemplary manner and so had she – whatever fantastical nonsense she had pursued in private.

Would he be angry with her? His sisters were monstrous! She played the scene over and over, becoming more anxious with each repetition. She should keep her distance. She should insist that Gladys be given a funeral and then see him out of the house. But by agreeing to visit her, he had been openly familiar and therefore openly defiant. Why? Was he attempting to alarm his sisters? Or to make recompense for his cavalier message to Ada?

Allen hung up her coat and hat. The smell of death permeated the ground floor and could be detected in every corner of the house. She had taken to keeping her mask on, indoors and out, only taking it off to wash, sleep and eat. The cloth was soaked in eau de cologne – she had given Ada a bottle for the same purpose – but even so, death had lodged

280

in her nose and nothing could overwhelm it. Had Henry ever smelled anything else?

The odour in Lily's room had been slightly improved by the recent regime of daily bathing and the use of the commode. Allen went there now and stood close to her, gazing at the crooked face. There was no change; she was breathing but otherwise one might have thought her dead. Lifting the bedclothes, Allen felt the sheet. It was dry. Thank God!

Two letters waited for her on the hall table. She recognized Miss Carter's hand – precise and high-looped – on the smaller envelope and assumed that she was writing to advise her of the school's continuing closure. Allen opened the letter carelessly, and started to skim it like a circular; but some of the words... she had the sensation of falling slowly into the page.

With her heart drumming, she read the letter aloud:

> ... Miss Bell was a dear friend to you, Mrs Thompson, and a wonderful teacher. I know that we will miss her most terribly in the new term. I pray for us all during these terrible days – my only comfort is knowing that God has our loved ones safely in his charge...

She had not been told. She had not been told that Ruth was dead. She had not been told because she had neglected to find out for herself. How could Ruth be dead? The other letter...

She tore it open and unfolded the thick paper, running her eyes down to the signature and then back to the letter, again and again. It was true.

> I write with a heavy heart to tell you that Ruth passed away on Sunday. She wished me to thank you for your letter and the book of poetry, which, you will appreciate, she was unable to read. We cannot tell you when the funeral will be as the present situation

makes it almost impossible to plan such things. Rest assured that she spoke of you at the end.

Blinded by tears, Allen sat on the stairs with both letters clasped in her hands. It had never occurred to her that Ruth would die; she was invincible. Ruth in the classroom, Ruth here, Ruth on the street, chasing that man and his frightened children, nursing the Dassetts, organizing her, berating her. Ruth was never glib, never treacherous; she was forthright and open-hearted. Had Allen been ill, had she been guarded by a frightened, angry father, Ruth would have persisted, calling every day, calling *twice* a day until she was allowed access to the bedside.

She longed to have Ruth with her, here on the stairs. The difference in their ages – fifteen years – had never been of any consequence. They were like sisters, like *good* sisters. She could hold Ruth's hand; she could kiss her; she could behave like a girl in her company. Allen's mask was wet. She pulled it away and looked for a handkerchief in the pocket of her skirt.

'Ma'am?' Ada was in front of her.

Allen blew her nose. 'Yes?'

'I'm sorry, ma'am. Mr Speake's in the kitchen, ma'am. He says you're expecting him. What should I do?'

'I'll come down now.' The mask was irritating her chin. She untied it with one hand and put it in her pocket with the sodden handkerchief. 'Could you occupy yourself elsewhere for a while?'

'Yes, ma'am.'

'I'm very red about the eyes, aren't I?'

'A little, ma'am.'

Allen touched Ada's cheek. 'I'm sure we'll be able to bury Gladys.'

'Yes, ma'am. Thank you.'

The kitchen was warm. The circle of light cast by the single lamp on the table disguised the room; it had become intimate.

Henry was sitting with his hands spread flat in front of him, lifting each finger in sequence. His coat was on another chair with his hat perched on top of it; he was smartly dressed, as if on a call. As soon as he realized she was at the door, he stood up. 'I hope I'm not inconveniencing you,' he said, after a pause. 'I could come back later?'

'No. No, you must stay.' She gestured to him to resume his seat. The letters were still in her hand; she held them tightly to her and sat opposite him. They surveyed each other. 'Are you angry with me?' she said.

'Not angry. Not at all. You have the habit of surprise.'

'I'm afraid I was rude to your sisters.'

'When you left the shop, they were all for following you with a wooden stick. They think you've ruined us.'

'They think *what*? Why?'

'Because of the talk. And because I've let things slip.'

He was matter-of-fact but the impact of the statement paralysed her and she sat quite still, unable to speak; the unknown had opened its gates and she was bare in a foreign landscape. No skirt, no shoes. As bare as Eve. He had let things slip. He wanted her to know that she was the cause of it. Hot in the face – he made her hot in the face! – she said, 'You've let things slip?'

'I didn't think so. I thought I'd done my best, Mrs Thompson. But since the fire...' His throat must still be sore; his voice was catching slightly, as if a coarse file were being rubbed against it.

'The fire!'

'That finished us. And they think that if I'd been on top of things, I would have had reserves. As if anyone has reserves!'

'You weren't hurt?'

'No. One man died. I was very lucky.' He smiled at her, a rueful smile that showed no teeth. He had tantalized her with small clues and then danced away. She realized that she was trembling.

'Have you been crying?' he said.

'Yes.' She put her hand to her face. 'I have.'

'Because of your sister?'

283

'No.'

Henry lifted his eyebrows in enquiry.

'My friend, Ruth – you met her, didn't you? At the rehearsal—'

'Yes.'

'She died.'

'Ah. I'm sorry.'

His sympathy was genuine and she was made vulnerable by it. Bringing her hand up to the table, she let go of the crumpled letters. 'She didn't like me being friends with you…' Her eyes filled with tears.

For a minute or more, they were silent.

'Nobody likes us being friends,' Henry said at last. He stood up and went to the chair where he had put his coat and hat.

He was going. He was going because of her snivelling self-pity. Frowning, she picked up the letters.

He said, 'About Gladys.'

'Gladys! I—'

'If Mr Sucerne could be persuaded, I could bury her in the grave-yard.'

'Why? Why would you want to do such a thing?'

'It's my trade.' He was touching the hat. His fingers were curling round the brim. His body was bending towards the chair.

She said, 'Why do they think I've ruined you?'

He let go of the hat and sighed, lowering his head until she could only see the place where the hair was thinning.

'Have I ruined you?' she said, more quietly.

'No.' He raised his eyes and stared at her. 'No, you haven't.'

She was Eve again, standing naked in the garden. She was frightened! He was walking towards her. What if he touched her? She should run away! She had provoked him – she had pressed him to answer her and his answer was…

Henry put his hands on her shoulders and looked down into her face. His breath was surprisingly sweet.

* * *

Frimley

Hastings

Hawke's Bay

7 November 1918

Dear Mr Speake,

I have to write to you with some very sad news. I am sorry to have to tell you this but Rose became ill within half a day of getting the telegram about Archie and she passed away this morning. Flora and Grace are here in my safekeeping. They are loved by me and by my own children and I will take them for good if it relieves you of any worry about their futures. I should have sent you a telegram, I know, but believed you to prefer a letter as it would not be so heartless a means of telling you, even though it will be some time before you get this.

My father was an undertaker and he and I will see to it that Rose has a good funeral. (Archie is being buried by the army.) I know that she missed you alone of all the things she left behind. This Spanish 'flu is very cruel. If there is one comfort it is that she died quickly. I was with her at the end to help her passing.

I send you my most sincere condolences and hope that you will feel able to write to your nieces here. They love what they know of their Uncle Henry.

Yours sincerely,

Peggy McKenzie

* * *

Allen's impudence in the shop had caused Sarah and Elsie to round on me like dogs; you'd have thought I'd engineered her entrance, the way they carried on. Why hadn't I shown her the door? Who did she think she was, expecting special treatment? I was not to visit her! I'd never seen Elsie so ready to condemn. They followed me out of the shop, telling me what to do and what not to do, and I think they would have followed me right into her kitchen if I hadn't turned round and told them that it was my life, whatever I chose to do with it. I've told them that before but I've never been able to add, 'whatever there is left of it.' There must have been something in my face because they stopped where they were and stared at me; if they had a reply, I didn't hear it.

I spent the rest of the walk trying to think of a way to bury Gladys's body and as I passed the church, I was blessed with the solution. Why not put her in the graveyard? The ground was full; there had been no interments there for many years, but there were one or two spots where I could dig a decent hole and not knock into any other graves. It would have to be done at dawn or dusk because we wouldn't want to start a fashion but with a bit of encouragement – he obviously held Allen in some regard – I thought that Sucerne might just allow me to conduct one last funeral.

Certain events occurred in Allen's kitchen and they can't be explained. My arousal some days before, her standing up to my sisters, the closing of the shop, the death of her friend – these things and not these things; I really can't be sure what overtook me. I was moved to a new understanding and then I behaved in a way I could never have imagined, not if you'd put me to torture. We were able to speak about it but nothing was resolved. How could it be?

When we parted, I went directly to the vicarage. Mr Sucerne's wife told me that I might find him in the church and he was there, sitting by himself in the choir stalls. There was an air of dejection about him which I assumed to be related to poor attendance – in its own way, his business was closing down as much as any other. He asked me about the fire and commiserated with me about the outcome. At the cemetery on Monday, he had officiated at twenty-nine funerals. How many more if mine had been added to the list! After a few more exchanges during which he spoke of 'these innumerable small catastrophes', I asked him, too bluntly as it turned out, whether he might allow me to conduct a single burial in the churchyard. He answered me by saying no repeatedly until I interrupted him with, 'Mrs Thompson would be very grateful.' I might as well have cast down Aaron's rod at his feet, he was so taken aback by the sound of her name.

'Has her sister died?' he said.

I said no, her sister was still alive, and then I told him about Gladys. Not the absolute truth but a portion of it: the coffin in Allen's drawing room and Ada's fear that Gladys would be dispatched to the horrors of the mortuary and how kind Allen – Mrs Thompson – had been throughout. From his candid look of admiration, I realized that he was relenting. I also realized that he was besotted with her.

'And how would you go about this burial?' he asked me.

My plan was this: the hole to be dug overnight by me, the service to be conducted before dawn and the turf replaced as if nothing had disturbed it. I had a site in mind, I told him, at the very back of the graveyard, invisible to any passer-by out walking in the dark. He wanted to know how I might transport the coffin. That had caused me some anxiety but I assured him that a discreet man could be found to help me. Anyone seeing us on the road would assume that we were on our way to the mortuary. And would I be strong enough to dig a grave? I said I had no intention of going further than four feet, possibly three – with a coffin measuring not much more than a foot, that would be an ample depth for the present circumstance.

He took no further time to think. 'You may tell Mrs Thompson,' he said, 'that I shall be honoured to serve her in any way possible.'

I went straight back to Allen's and found Ada in the kitchen, ironing. She fetched Allen and I told them both what I intended to do, making as little of it as possible. They wanted to attend and no protestations on my part would prevent them; all I could do was to warn them to wear good boots in case of mud. Ada's presence acted as a restraint but Allen saw me to the door and touched my hand in parting, which set my nerves on edge for some hours after.

My first task was to find a man to help with the carrying. I decided to go home for something to eat – I'd had nothing since a poor breakfast – and then go through my book until I came across some reliable bearers. If one was sick or dead, I'd have to try another. I was upstairs making a plate of bits and pieces when I heard Walter calling me from the shop. He'd come in to tell me that he'd been offered employment by James Theobald and that they were very keen to have me, too. I suppose I'd been toying with the idea since Walter had first suggested it, if only to stop me sitting about waiting for the end, but the stifling nature of working for another man – I couldn't do it. I offered Walter some food but he took one look at my plate and refused it, which is what I'd have done in his place. He accepted tea, though, without milk because there wasn't any, and we sat in the cold office to drink it. I'd left my book out ready on the desk and he asked me who I was trying to get hold of. On any other day, I might have lied but the truth just fell out of me – well, not the whole truth but a bit more of it than I'd told Sucerne.

He was angry to start with, telling me that I had no right to make one dead person more important than any other and that I couldn't ask a bearer because they'd be bound to talk – 'The churchyard'll end up as busy as Brighton beach.' And then he said, 'I'll be here at three o'clock. You'll need a hand with the digging.'

So there it was. When he'd gone I wrote to Allen, asking her to visit me in a day or two; then I sat down to play the song I'd written from the poem. After believing that the piano would be put to better use stripped down and made up as a coffin, it was a great comfort to me to want to play again and I would have carried on if I hadn't had to find some warm clothes and go downstairs to wait for Walter.

It took us just under two hours to get the grave right, then we went back to wash and change and make what we could of some beer and old cake. Vi hadn't liked Walter going out in the middle of the night but he'd told her some story about an extra job for Theobald and she'd swallowed it. She was relieved to have him working, and so was I.

We didn't see a single soul; the streets were deserted. I expected Allen and Ada to have changed their minds but they were ready in their coats, both looking very pale. The coffin went on to the bier without any difficulty; to stop the noise of the wood sliding along, I'd put down some blankets and, as a compliment to Albert's sealing, there wasn't a mark left on them. We left the house at a quarter to six as planned, with Ada carrying a lantern to guide us. She'd picked some chrysanthemums for Gladys but I told her to wait until we were by the grave before she put them on the lid; they might have fallen off if we'd stumbled in the churchyard. We arrived at exactly six o'clock. Mr Sucerne was waiting for us. He shook hands with Allen and then, to his credit, he offered his hand to Ada and she took it, not knowing how to refuse. Then, with Walter walking backwards and all of us guided by Ada's lantern, we walked to the graveside, arriving without mishap.

The service went without a fault, although my father would have been outraged by it, with us talking in whispers for fear of attracting attention and the owl hooting and the lack of proper form. Ada held the lantern by the prayer book so that Mr Sucerne might read without hesitation; the coffin went down nicely and the sides of the grave stayed put despite there being no lining. When it was time to throw the earth on, Ada led us and we all followed her, even Walter.

Walter and I filled in and replaced the turf as best we could – I intended to return at daybreak and finish the job in better light. Then we trooped back to the gate and I got a chance to approach Allen without being observed. Mr Sucerne was close by but I only had to touch her arm and she opened her hand in readiness for mine. I slipped the note I'd written between her fingers and joined Walter and Ada. The goodbyes were formal: Allen thanked Mr Sucerne, Ada said nothing, and Walter and I stood aside and waited, as at any other funeral, except that we were badly dressed, dirty and our backs ached with lifting.

Not wanting Allen and Ada to walk by themselves, I left the cart next to the church in order to accompany them to their house. Nothing was said. When we reached the door, Allen read my note and held it to her mouth for a moment, then she told Ada to give me the lantern and they went inside.

The cart was heavy and my journey home was slow; dawn was just breaking as I reached the shop. Too tired to do more than climb the stairs to bed, I left the earth under my nails and got under the blankets with most of my clothes on. There was no reason to get up; the shop was closed. I could lie there for as long as I pleased. Gladys's funeral had been my last. As I went to sleep, I thought that if every one of the newly bereaved were to hold a lantern to the sky, the man in the moon would think the world to be on fire.

I

I am in deep woods,
　　Between the two twilights.
Whatever I am and may be,
Write it down to the Light in me;
I am I, and it is my deed;
For I know that the paths are dark
　　Between the two twilights.

I have made my choice to proceed
By the Light I have within;
And the issue rests with me,
Who might sleep in a chrysalis,
In the fold of a simple prayer,
　　Between the two twilights.

Having nought but the Light in me,
Which I take for my soul in arms,
Resolved to go unto the wells
For water, rejecting spells,
And mouthings of magic for charms,
And the cup that does not flow.

　　I am in deep woods
　　Between the two twilights:
Over valley and hill
I hear the woodland wave,
Like the voice of Time, as slow,
The voice of Life, as grave,
The voice of Death, as still.

II

The stars are with the voyager wherever he may sail,
The moon is constant to her time, the sun will never fail,
But follow, follow round the world, the green earth and the sea,
So Love is with the lover's heart wherever he may be.

Sir George Newman
Untitled, published in the *Friends' Quarterly Examiner*
September 1918

Historical Note

The influenza pandemic came to an end in May 1919. Mortality statistics can never be certain; many deaths were attributed to other causes or simply unrecorded but in the United Kingdom the registered figure was nearly 230,000 and in America approximately 675,000. The global figure is unknown but thought to be between 50 and 100 million. Although anyone was susceptible to the virus, the dead were predominantly young men and women aged between twenty and forty-five: a unique feature of this particular virus.

Although the first official cremation in England took place at Woking Crematorium on 26 March 1885, burial was to remain the preferred choice until the 1960s. American professors of embalming visited London in 1900 to instruct undertakers in basic arterial embalming techniques but as the cost was high and the body had to be attended to at home, very few families made use of the practice. In the 1950s, when the funeral director was beginning to play an active role in the care and housing of the dead, embalming became more widespread. Handbiers would have been used to transport coffins from the house to the churchyard, especially in rural areas, until the interwar years.

Acknowledgments

Acknowledgements

There are many living people that I'd like to thank but I must start by mentioning Sir George Newman, whose eloquent official report, written in 1920, was my introduction to the full scope and horror of the pandemic. An extraordinary man, he worked tirelessly in many areas of social reform and became Chief Medical Officer when the Ministry of Health was first created in 1919. He was also a Quaker and an accomplished, prolific contributor to the *Friends' Quarterly Examiner*.

From our very first meeting, Dr Brian Parsons, funeral historian, has been most helpful and generous, answering my countless telephone calls with good humour and erudition. His contribution to the book is greatly appreciated. My profound thanks are also due to Dr Aslan Mordecai for his microscopic and telescopic wisdom; to David Lurie for patiently answering my many questions; to Gillon Aitken for his expertise, enthusiasm and encouragement; and to Laura Barber for her editorial grace and perceptive eye. I'm also indebted to Rachel Leyshon and Sarah Barlow for their care with the manuscript.

Bunny France, Keith Leverton, Andrew Crowley, Susan Denny and John Garside, funeral directors, have all given freely of their time and expert advice, as have Sharon Messenger and the Wellcome Trust, Dr David Tyrell, Dr Robert Brown and Andrea Tanner. To the many archivists, particularly Graham Dalling, who've delved deep, thank you. Bet Balcombe, Sue Bancroft, Helen Bauckham, Eunice Defries, Simon and Andrea Defries, Hussein Eshref, Lee Humber, Yurek Idzik, Ena Norris, Dr Estelle Pollock, Javier Romano, Flora D. Smith, Jonathan Sutcliffe, Anne-Line Sutcliffe and Bea Taber have all helped in their various and wonderful ways.

Mike Reinstein has been so involved with the telling of this story that it could never have been written without him. I thank him with all my heart.

Reina James
Sussex, 2006

For news about current and forthcoming titles
from Portobello Books and for a sense of purpose
visit the website **www.portobellobooks.com**

encouraging voices,
supporting writers,
challenging readers

Portobello
BOOKS